Madhulika Liddle is a novelist and award-winning short story writer. She is best-known as the author of the Muzaffar Jang series, about a seventeenth-century Mughal detective, though she also writes other fiction in different genres and across themes, ranging from black humour to romance. She was the first Indian to win the Commonwealth Broadcasting Association's Short Story Competition in 2003, and the first Indian to be long-listed for the Sunday Times EFG Short Story Competition in 2016.

Madhulika is also writing a series of four novels, *The Delhi Quartet*, which will span eight hundred years of Delhi's history. The first of the novels, *The Garden of Heaven*, was published in 2022.

In addition, Madhulika blogs about classic cinema, travel, food and history, at www.madhulikaliddle.com

Kannan Iyer is a feature film writer-director. He co-wrote the Sanjay Dutt starrer, *Daud*, and directed a supernatural thriller, *Ek Thi Daayan*, starring Emraan Hashmi, Konkona Sen Sharma, Huma Qureshi and Kalki Koechlin. He is presently directing *Aye Watan Mere Watan*, which he has also co-written.

ALSO BY MADHULIKA LIDDLE

The Muzaffar Jang Series

The Englishman's Cameo
The Eighth Guest & Other Muzaffar Jang Mysteries
Engraved in Stone
Crimson City

The Delhi Quartet Series

The Garden of Heaven

Short Stories

My Lawfully Wedded Husband & Other Stories
Woman to Woman: Stories

FILMS BY KANNAN IYER

Daud (1997) (as co-writer)
Ek Thi Daayan (2013)
Aye Watan Mere Watan (Forthcoming)

the Pledge

ADVENTURES TO SADA

Madhulika Liddle
Kannan Iyer

SPEAKING TIGER

SPEAKING TIGER BOOKS LLP
125A, Ground Floor, Shahpur Jat, near Asiad Village,
New Delhi 110049

First published by Speaking Tiger Books 2023

ISBN: 978-93-5447-412-5
eISBN: 978-93-5447-416-3

10 9 8 7 6 5 4 3 2 1

Typeset in Garamond Premier Pro by SÜRYA, New Delhi
Printed at Chaman Enterprises, New Delhi

CONTENTS

Inspired by a story by film producer Amit Bolakani

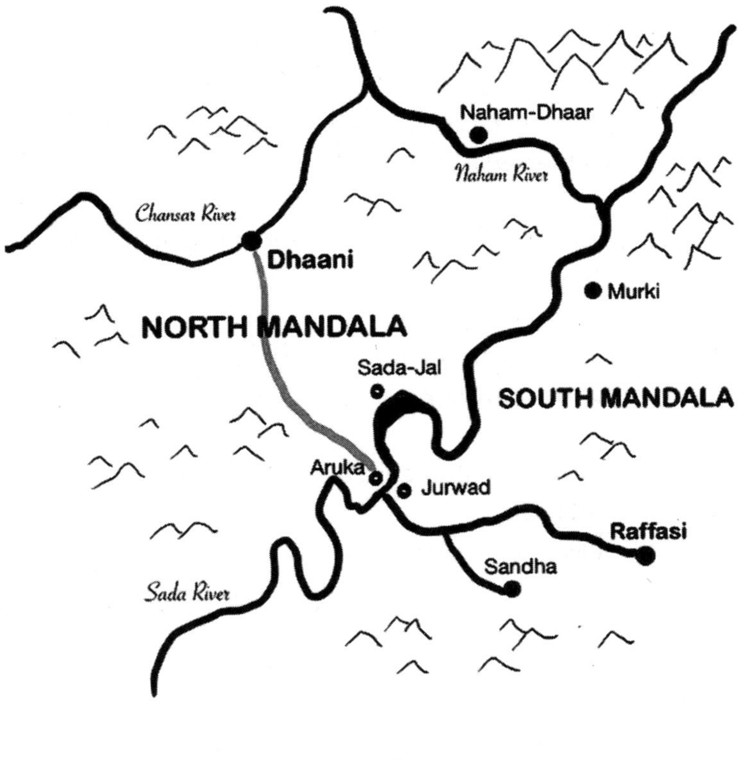
Naham-Dhaar
Naham River
Chansar River
Dhaani
Murki
NORTH MANDALA
Sada-Jal
SOUTH MANDALA
Aruka
Jurwad
Raffasi
Sandha
Sada River

Timeline

0EM	Year of Emergence of Mandala (EM), the lake submerging Mandala is drained; Mandala is established
1200EM	Vandaav the Tyrannical comes to power and begins his reign of terror in the Mandalan Empire
1236EM	Death of Vandaav
5000EM	Tanit Mahabeyan ascends the throne of Mandala
5025EM	25th anniversary of the coronation of Tanit Mahabeyan
5270EM	General Umur Tut Naash gains control over Mandala
5283EM	Death of Umur Tut Naash
5441EM	Dhanjog Mahabeyan is crowned Emperor of Mandala
5444EM	Sarjaand, religious leader of the Terrisans, begins a campaign for a separate Terrisan land
5447EM	Raibhu is born in Raffasi, to Jaadum the Magician and his wife Asi
5448EM	Jaadum and Asi join a campaign to oust the weak-willed, useless Emperor Dhanjog Mahabeyan
5455EM	Jaadum, Asi and Raibhu meet the orphaned Afhash

5456EM	Under Sarjaand, the Terrisans break away to form the Southern Mandalan Empire. Sarjaand is crowned first Emperor of South Mandala, with its capital at Raffasi
5460EM	Dhanjog Mahabeyan dies. His son Gunjog Mahabeyan comes to power as Emperor of North Mandala, its capital at Dhaani
5475EM	Jaadum tells Afhash to fetch Raibhu from Dhaani; the adventure starts

Glossary

Aaboneer: A religion that venerates the Water Spirit.

Bhaagi: A pigeon. Messenger bhaagis or carrier pigeons are used on both sides of the border to transmit messages quickly.

Calmroot: A herb found in the two Empires. Its root, pounded and infused in water, is supposed to have soothing properties, calming both mind and body.

Celestial View-Glass: An instrument made from a shard of a very rare, highly transparent mineral formed when a fireball crashes into a particular type of rock. View-glasses serve to make distant objects appear close and clear, and are extremely expensive due to their rarity.

Dreamflower: A flowering plant found in the two Empires, its dried blossoms being used to brew a stimulating infusion.

Ekdut: A long-distance vehicle, pulled by a team of six or four horses and consisting of two boxes or compartments, one behind the other. Ekduts connect the main towns and cities of North Mandala, with the horses being changed at regular intervals along the way.

Elder: A term of respect for an elder person. When addressing an individual, the word 'My Elder' is used; when referring to the individual, 'The Elder' is used.

Golbol: Found in the high mountains of the Southern Empire, these are large balls of a very light, fibrous material that grows on massive trees. The golbols are believed by the Mandalans to have air-purifying properties.

Humur: A hard, unyielding metal. It is used predominantly for making weaponry and ammunition.

Jijit: Mystic.

Lahargam: A herb with small, pungent leaves, widely used in Mandalan cooking

Mahabhaagi: A rare bird of prey. The feathers of its breast and stomach are blue, grey and white, allowing the bird to be invisible against a daytime sky, while its upper feathers are deep green, camouflaging the bird when it roosts in trees.

Manodium: A soft, malleable honey-coloured metal, used for making decorative items.

Nabhang: A religion that venerates the Sky Spirit.

Rishya: A majestic four-legged creature with a single horn, an ungulate mammal that is found in the forests of Mandala. Tamed by the Mandalans primarily as a mount for its royalty and aristocracy.

Sada stones: Deep red precious stones mined from the Sada River Valley. These are highly prized because of their healing properties; simply keeping these stones in one's vicinity is believed to keep one healthy.

Tanka: The coin of the realm in the Empire. A tanka is in the shape of a double helix. Different denominations are designed in different colours and sizes.

Terrisan: A religion revolving around the worship of the Land Spirit.

Vaanik: A long-distance vehicle used in South Mandala. Unlike the two-compartment ekdut of the North, this has a single compartment, with a narrow slit near the top of the walls to let in air and light.

Yang-Pra: A small ruminant mammal, bred for its heavy pale pink wool and for its meat; common across the two Empires.

Zansal: A common and popular metal in the two Empires. It is a bright blue in colour, and is put to various uses.

Prologue

Dhaani, Capital of the Mandalan Empire
Year 5025 of the Emergence of Mandala

'Your Majesty, my Emperor, my liege.' The Prime Minister bows low, his gaze resting on the sun metal sandals of the bearded man he addresses. The assembly that stands behind the Prime Minister bows in unison. The Emperor Tanit Mahabeyan, from his seat on his throne of polished stone, with veins of moon metal running through it, smiles benevolently as he looks at the people gathered in his court.

'May I be the first to congratulate you on the twenty-fifth anniversary of your accession to the throne of Mandala?' says the Prime Minister. He pauses for effect, then adds, in a deeply sonorous voice, as if reciting a poem. 'Blessed was Mandala the day you became Emperor, my liege,' he says. 'Blessed are its fields, blessed its mines. Blessed its people who call you Emperor, blessed more than when the jijits helped our land emerge from the deep seas—'

He is cut off by the Emperor. 'No, Prime Minister,' he says brusquely. 'No. It is blasphemous to compare me to the mystics. They were incomparable, and what they did for Mandala cannot be matched by anyone else, ever.'

The Prime Minister's smile has slipped briefly at this

admonition, but he regains his composure soon enough. He smiles again in a benign way and says, 'If further proof was needed, there it is, of Your Majesty's goodness and selflessness. You are great, indeed, my Lord!' The crowd behind echoes this last sentence, and the strains of it waft out through the windows and into the street outside. The sound travels faintly to the adjacent hill, atop which a man sits. He is a broad-shouldered, muscular man, middle-aged and battle-scarred, with a deep scar across one cheek. He sits on a flat boulder, the very picture of patience, listening and watching. Beside him, on the rock, lies a flattish package wrapped in rough sacking. The man's eyes are piercing, his gaze riveted on the gates of the palace.

The skies are overcast; fresh snow threatens. But in the streets of Dhaani, there is a mix of jubilation and quiet emotion. After the courtiers have dispersed from their audience with the Emperor, a solemn procession sets out from the palace. It is a large procession, with many horses, all uniformly white, a few horse-carriages, and many people on foot, but there is no fanfare and pomp. They move down the main road of Dhaani, the Emperor's Way, its entire length paved with dazzling white lunarstone. At the head of the procession rides the Emperor himself, his robes regal and the beautiful golden-maned rishya he is mounted on as tall and proud as the Emperor it bears, its single horn gleaming like a well-polished sword.

The procession makes its way to the magnificent Terrisan Sanctuary, whose vast grounds stretch for more than two miles on each side. With its solid stone walls thick and seeming to hug the land, its façade decorated with clay and minerals of different colours, the very look of the Sanctuary is a reminder that the Terrisan people who worship the Land Spirit venerate it in all its forms: as clay, as rock, as mineral. Beyond the massive mica-plated gates of the Sanctuary lies the Sacred Ground, a huge field grown over with short shrubs and grasses. At this height, on the plain, an oblivious onlooker would see nothing extraordinary about this field. But to the scarred man who watches from atop the hill, the Sacred Ground shows itself from the perspective that has given it its name. At precise intervals, the vegetation of the field is punctuated by perfectly circular patches of bare ground.

'The footprints of the Land Spirit! Hail to thee, Land Spirit!' A group of people, all clad in robes that echo the colours of the land—tan and brown, ochre and deep red and black—move forward to the front from amidst Tanit Mahabeyan's entourage. In unison, they fall prostrate, their foreheads pressed to the ground, their hands lifted, palms up, in supplication. By the time they rise up, the Terrisan priests have emerged from within the Sanctuary building. Along with the Emperor's Terrisan group, the priests lead the Emperor into the Sanctuary, the rest of the procession following silently in. While the devotees hum a low, wordless tune, the Emperor, guided by the Terrisan priests, offers prayers and lays handfuls of many-hued sand at the stone altar of the Sanctuary.

The priests of the Terrisan Sanctuary bless the Emperor, marking his forehead with a paste of yellow clay. 'Thanks be to the Land Spirit,' they intone. 'Live long and prosper, O Emperor.'

Then, still solemn, the group emerges back on to the Emperor's Way and takes the road to the river at the point where it enters the hills surrounding Dhaani. The Aaboneer Temple, its façade glittering under miniature waterfalls that cascade down its outer walls, stands on the riverbank just opposite a spot where the water seems to flow uphill. From the procession, a small group comes forward, its members all clad in long, shimmering robes of silvery grey. Without uttering a word, they link hands and move forward, down the bank and into the water, wading through it till they reach the point where the river defies gravity and begins to flow up rather than down. All of these people are obviously deeply moved by what they are experiencing; they are weeping now. As one, they kneel, submerging to let their tears mingle with the water.

Then they emerge, dripping, out of the river and make their way up to where the Emperor stands. They are the ones who lead Tanit Mahabeyan and the rest of the procession onto the long pier jutting out from the Temple over the river. Here stand the high priestess of the Aaboneer and the other priests of the Temple. As they guide the Emperor in presenting votive offerings and thanksgiving to the Water Spirit, the Aaboneer devotees bring out moon metal flutes, each a yard long, from within their robes. Together, they begin playing, but no sound audible to the human ear emerges. They sway, their lips and fingers move, their eyelids flutter shut, but there is silence. The only thing that moves is the water in the pool that acts as an altar at the end of the pier: it shimmers and eddies, forming concentric circles, waves that move endlessly, round and round... all with the same rhythm that makes the Aaboneer devotees sway.

Just as the Emperor is turning to go back down the pier to the riverbank, a loud sound, between a whoosh and a whistle, fills the air. Instinctively, everybody looks up. From the nearby hill, the man who has been watching the Emperor and his procession also looks up as a ball of fire, about a yard across, comes flying out of the clear blue sky. Down below, there is consternation and dread, dismay and fear: a collective gasp goes up from the crowd surrounding the Emperor. Some of the more nervous panic and try to run; others, perhaps of a more spiritual bent of mind, begin an ululation. But the ball of fire is too swift: barely has the first note of the ululation been uttered than the meteor has hit the river, causing a loud splash and a sizzle. The steam from the impact of the fireball causes a mist over the river, and the water bubbles violently.

'The spirits themselves rain gifts and benedictions down on Your Majesty,' says a sycophantic courtier in an oily, wheedling voice.

Tanit Mahabeyan turns to the man, his gaze level. 'Surely,' he says, in a quiet voice that reaches only the man, 'it would be tactful to not imply that the Sky Spirit was smiling down on me while I'm here at the Aaboneer Temple.' The man blanches, and the Emperor smiles. His eyes twinkle as he bends closer to the man's ear and whispers, 'Besides which, we don't know yet if this fireball bears any precious metals, or is just fire and ashes.' He turns and strides briskly away, calling out to the Prime Minister, 'Send the divers to examine the riverbed once it's safe to do so. See what this one contains.' The Prime Minister bows, and further orders are passed down the chain of command.

The third and last place of worship the Emperor leads his group to is that of the Nabhang, further along the Emperor's Way. This requires a long climb up the tallest of the hills ringing the city of Dhaani, but there is not one complaint from the crowd that follows the Emperor. Young and old, frail and hale, all of them quietly and devoutly climb the long staircase that leads up to the Nabhang Shrine, the more infirm being helped along by the others. Perhaps what they see up above them, hovering eternally in the sky above the Shrine, drives them onward. It is a cloud, shaped like a giant bird with its wings spread. But this cloud is ethereal in its beauty, the whiteness at its centre giving way to wide swathes of pink, yellow and greenish-blue around its edges.

Right at the top, where the tall slim spires of the Nabhang Shrine are tinted with the iridescence of the cloud, the Emperor is met by the priests of the Nabhang Shrine. Already, from among the procession, the Nabhang devotees have come forward, all dressed in the colours of the sky they worship: the azure of a clear summer sky, the midnight blue, studded with glittering chips of moon metal, of the night sky; the fleecy white of clouds and the dull, looming grey of storm clouds. All of them have their faces tilted up to the sky, and as they line up in front of the Sky Altar, its shining surface of sun metal reflecting the many-coloured cloud above, they start singing. Their voices are high, their notes drifting up into the sky and melding with the wind, which adds its own note to theirs.

An offering is burnt, the smoke rising up from the embers into the sky, and Tanit Mahabeyan murmurs words of gratitude. The spirits of Land, Water and Sky have smiled on him.

Once back on the Emperor's Way, the mood of the procession changes; there is now unadulterated celebration, and the people of the city have come out into the streets to join in the festivities. The streets have been cleaned and washed; the white stone of the Emperor's Way sparkles, and bunting, tinsel, and flowers decorate windows and balconies, even the few horse-drawn carriages that stand outside some of the grander homes. People are laughing and singing, playing music; excited children are running around, trying to keep up with the procession. Tanit Mahabeyan smiles and laughs and waves at his subjects. Several of them, perhaps bolder than the rest, come right up to him, extending their hands, greeting him: 'May you live long and prosper, Your Majesty! Blessed be this day when you became our Emperor!' To each of them, Tanit Mahabeyan gives a special smile and a personal word of greeting and gratitude. Behind him, several courtiers who are part of the procession are scattering tankas for the populace to gather. The people scramble to pick these up, small double helixes in varying colours and sizes, all of denominations high enough to purchase a meal or a suit of clothing. There is much jubilation and excitement; the Emperor's largesse is appreciated by his subjects.

Among the throng stands the man with the scarred face. The sack is slung over his shoulder; it is moth-eaten, has patches of dirt and mould in places, and seems to contain something flattish and rectangular in shape. The man looks on as Tanit Mahabeyan heads towards his palace, his entourage following behind him. On the man's face is an expression almost sinister in its fierceness. He exudes strength and purpose, but to what use he will put these is impossible to tell. The ferocity in his stance, the ominous scars that mark him: these suggest a man with whom it would not be wise to pick a quarrel.

Behind the man, four other men watch him. They are dispersed through the crowd, far apart from each other but closing in swiftly, all four making a beeline for their quarry.

Back in the palace, the birthday celebrations continue. In a private chamber, surrounded by his most senior courtiers,

Tanit Mahabeyan is weighed against sun metal, moon metal, manodium, humur, zansal and other precious metals, grain, and other items, all of which are then taken away to be distributed among the poor. Musicians and poets play and sing and recite the Emperor's praises, and to each of them he gives tokens of his pleasure, in the form of little bags of tankas.

And then come those bearing gifts for Tanit Mahabeyan. This is a very motley crowd indeed; it begins with the wealthy and distinguished emissaries from distant lands, bringing fine and rare gifts. One dignitary offers a small box full of precious sada stones, glistening a deep blood red. 'To safeguard the health of Your Majesty,' he says.

Another, a woman from the southern lands, ushers in a couple of men carrying a large, glass-topped chest. Looking down at the lid of the chest, Tanit Mahabeyan can see four light-as-air fluffy white orbs, golbols, each a hand-span across, floating under the glass. 'Purifying orbs?' he asks the woman, his voice hushed with awe. 'I have only ever heard of these, never seen one, not in all these years.'

'The trees on which these grow are to be found only high up in the mountains of the south,' the woman agrees. 'My master bids me offer these to you by way of felicitation. Each of these golbols can purify the air in a hall this size for a year. Release them wherever you wish, Your Majesty.' She bows, and the Emperor, smiling and murmuring words of gratitude, indicates to his attendants to have the chest placed on the side.

There are other ambassadors from further away. One has brought a pair of beautifully matched silver grey rishyas, which he shows Tanit Mahabeyan through one of the windows of the audience chamber, as the rishyas stand in the courtyard below.

Below too, but unseen because it's out in the street, a small battle erupts. With the rest of the crowd disappearing into the palace to participate in the celebrations of the Emperor's coronation anniversary, the streets have been left almost bare. The four men use this opportunity to lunge forward and assault the scar-faced man. From the start, it's obvious that what they want is to grab the ragged sack he holds; it is equally obvious that the man will do anything he can to safeguard it.

The four attackers are vicious, and highly skilled in martial arts. They come at him with daggers drawn, one also holding a long flexible strip of yang-pra hide which he uses both as a whip, and as a lethal garrote. Their quarry seems hopelessly outnumbered, but he fights back. It's a close call; the garrote slips round his neck, the sack is pulled from his almost nerveless fingers—but he claws his way back up from near-unconsciousness and throws off the assailant who's trying to throttle him. Kicks, punches, swipes with daggers: the air sizzles and hums with the sound of pitched battle, but nobody is here to see it. Everybody is inside the palace, rejoicing.

In the hall where he is holding court, Tanit Mahabeyan looks benignly on as his poorer subjects come forward with their gifts. The very fact that they offer up simple things like a sack of grain or a hand-embroidered scarf for their Emperor shows the confidence they have in his affection for them. And the Emperor shows that he is worthy of their confidence; Tanit Mahabeyan receives every single gift as if it were the most precious thing he has ever received; the gratitude and the emotion he displays are heartfelt.

Right at the end, when everybody else has offered their gifts and been given something in return by Tanit Mahabeyan, there steps forward the man who had been in the street a short while back, fighting for his life and for the safety of the ragged sack he had been holding. Between the street and the hall of audience, he has wrapped his package in a piece of beautiful old brocade, embroidered in fine threads of zansal. The flat rectangular shape of the object he carries is discernible through its fine covering, and momentarily, as he moves forward, a corner of the brocade slips to show the sacking underneath. The man pulls it into place and rubs away, with an absent-minded gesture, a smear of blood from the back of his hand. There is more blood on him, more signs of the fight he has been in, but the euphoria in the hall is such that nobody pays any attention.

Tanit Mahabeyan's eyes narrow in curiosity as the man, still kneeling, hands the gift to the courtier who is in charge of receiving each gift and presenting it before Tanit Mahabeyan.

Tanit Mahabeyan accepts the gift and is about to undo the knot that ties the brocade wrapping when the man says, 'Your Majesty, not here in court, please. It is something meant only for your eyes. And I would beg to be with you when you open it.'

The Emperor is taken aback, but he is also curious, as well as suspicious. 'Why?' he asks. 'Why would you want to be there? And that too if only I am to see it?' On either side of the Emperor, his guards have stiffened, their hands moving to the scabbards at their belts.

'Because this is a secret that is meant for your eyes only, Your Majesty,' the man says patiently. 'I bring as proof of my good intentions, these words from your teacher, the Venerable Dayadhan Jijit. He knows me.' From his pocket he withdraws a folded piece of thin parchment and holds it out. It is accepted by the courtier in attendance and passed to Tanit Mahabeyan,

who opens it, reads it, and remarks, half to himself, 'Yes, these are the Venerable Jijit's words.' He looks up. 'Very well. You may accompany me.'

Later, the Emperor walks into his private chambers, the brocade-wrapped gift in his arms. The man who had given it follows close behind, and the Emperor's chamberlain shuts the doors behind them. Soldiers stand on guard outside the chamber, ready to enter if required.

The Emperor leads the way to a wide window overlooking the river and the city of Dhaani. 'Shall I open it now?' he asks the man, who inclines his head to express his agreement.

The Emperor seats himself on the mattress beside the window and places the package in front of him. The man, at a gesture from the Emperor, seats himself opposite Tanit Mahabeyan. Now impatient and eager to see what is inside the package, Tanit Mahabeyan fumbles to open the knot of the brocade wrapping. It eventually opens, and he draws the brocade aside—to find that the package is wrapped in another layer of wrapping, and this could not be worse. It is sacking, moth-eaten and splashed here and there with dirt, with mould growing in one corner and some vile black gunk stuck to one side. Tanit Mahabeyan recoils, repulsed by the thing, disgusted and at the same time taken aback.

'What is this?' he demands. 'What further horrors lie buried inside this?'

'Your Majesty,' says the man quietly, 'there are things on this planet and in the heavens above that we know nothing about. And sometimes, when we come face to face with them, they wear disguises. Much is not as is it seems, Your Majesty.'

Chapter One

Central Prison, Sandha
Southern Mandalan Empire
Late summer, Year 5475 of the Emergence of Mandala

'And—voila!' The magician, with a flourish of a garish purple satin handkerchief, revealed a red egg in his hand. There was enthusiastic applause from the crowd watching. The magician had started off a little shakily; the men, all of them convicts—and a handful of guards—were intimidating. There were thieves here, murderers, rapists, criminals of all kinds, and several of them looked the part: broad, muscular, viciously scarred. Others, though more innocuous to look at, compensated for what they lacked in looks by their behaviour: hoots, catcalls, snide remarks. But there were many, too, who had set aside their worries and become children for the duration of this treat.

Right at the forefront were two men, as different as chalk and cheese. Afhash and the man everybody knew as Wartak the Elder.

Afhash, in his mid-twenties, had the pleasant, cheerful face of one who knew how to laugh through all that life sent his way. He cheered the loudest, no matter how clumsy the magician was, and when the man asked for a volunteer to assist in an act, Afhash was always the first to jump up, eager to be part of the proceedings.

Now, as the magician pulled out three bowls from his sack and placed them on the table, Afhash's eyes brightened. He looked up at Wartak the Elder, who was seated on the only chair in the courtyard. Everybody else sat cross-legged on the flagstones of the courtyard or stood: this man, perhaps because he was older than most of them—in his mid-fifties, though he looked older—or perhaps because he was so frail, all skin and bones and tired eyes, had been given a chair.

He exchanged a smile with Afhash. 'You like this trick, don't you, Wartak My Elder?' said Afhash, affectionately. The older man nodded, and they turned back to watch the magician, anticipation written all over their faces. Above them, a fluffy golbol hovered, white as the newly fallen snow, lighter than a feather, floating gently about the courtyard.

~

Later, when the magician had finished his performance, Afhash came to him. The magician looked anxious; Afhash nodded and said, 'Good, good. It was good entertainment. Wartak the Elder enjoyed it.' The magician looked past Afhash towards the older man, who was now sitting with his eyes closed, looking exhausted. As Afhash carefully counted out the money in red and blue tankas and gave it to the magician, the magician remarked, 'He's not looking well.'

'He isn't,' Afhash said brusquely. He glanced back at his old friend with concern in his eyes. Then, with a brief nod to the magician and a murmured 'Thank you', he hurried back to Wartak. A prison guard, deputed to ensure that the magician did not go wandering around—or, worse still, help someone escape—urged the man to gather up his things and get going. The magician, satisfied with the payment he had received, nodded. He had already collected all the odds and ends he had used, and now slung the sack over his shoulder. 'Afhash is very devoted to the old man?' he asked.

The guard, escorting him out of the courtyard and through the dim stone-walled corridors, shrugged, non-committal. 'I suppose so. He paid most of the money for your performance, but Wartak the Elder also contributed some out of his savings. As a sort of farewell party for Afhash; he's being released tomorrow.' He glanced briefly towards where Afhash was helping Wartak to his feet, the older man moving painfully. 'Wartak also paid for that golbol,' he said, tilting his chin towards the purifying orb that still circled the courtyard. 'Just for Afhash, as a gift.'

The magician looked impressed. 'I had wondered who would spend so many tankas as to purchase a golbol. The old man must have saved up a lot, eh?'

But the guard did not care to satisfy the magician's curiosity. As it was, they had reached the yard that surrounded the prison buildings. Down a narrow path, lined with precisely arranged blocks of bluestone, the magician and the guard walked. On one side was a little plot that had been turned into a makeshift garden, with a few flowers blooming under a small tree. Beyond that was an area fenced off with barbed black metal wire. The magician's eyes widened as he glanced towards it: he saw one memorial stone after another.

~

Afhash was accompanying Wartak the Elder back from the courtyard. He offered help, a shoulder to lean on, an arm to support—but the older man was adamant. 'I'm not dead yet, Afhash,' he said. 'When I am, you can lend a shoulder and be a pall-bearer, yes?'

'Don't talk like that,' Afhash said gruffly. 'You have many years to go before your body will be taken to the Terrisan Sanctuary and entered into the embrace of the Land Spirit.' He patted the older man's shoulder. 'You're barely in your fifties, you have many years to live.'

They had reached the barred door of the cell the two men shared. Afhash unbolted the door and waited patiently while Wartak, lifting each foot with obvious difficulty, stepped in. He closed the door and helped Wartak to the narrow wooden bed that sat at the far end of the cell. Wartak collapsed onto the thin mattress with a deep, shuddering sigh of mingled pain and relief. 'Shall I get you some water?' Afhash asked. 'Or some calmroot infusion? I might be able to wheedle some out of the kitchen staff.'

Wartak the Elder shook his head, too spent to even speak.

'Then lie down,' said Afhash, 'and I'll press your legs for you.'

A few minutes passed, with Afhash massaging Wartak's feet and legs, until finally the older man opened his eyes. 'Thank you,' he said softly.

'Thank you for what? For pressing your legs? Would you thank Raibhu for pressing your legs? Really, anybody would think I really was a stranger, and you really were Wartak the Elder and not Jaadum the Elder.'

The man who had once been Jaadum and was now known as Wartak smiled with affection in his eyes. 'You are right,' he said, patting Afhash's shoulder. 'You are a son to me too, just as Raibhu is.'

'Glad you remembered,' Afhash said with a teasing grin. 'Thanking me, indeed! But if that's the way it is, thank you for the golbol. At least my memories of my last day in this prison won't be of the stench and the close air of this place.' He shook his head. 'You needn't have done it, My Elder. You would have done better to save your tankas.'

'For what, child?' Wartak said, his hand resting briefly on the younger man's head. 'For you, for Raibhu, I would give away all my life's savings.' He looked pensive, and his eyes grew intent, watchful. 'You remember Raibhu. I thought you had forgotten.'

Afhash grinned. 'Forgotten! Forgotten those weeks, the only time in my life I had a family? I don't think I'll ever forget.'

~

Twenty years earlier: Year 5455 of the Emergence of Mandala

Against a backdrop of the snowcapped peaks flanking the Sada River, a village fair is in progress. The air hums with excitement and joy, as children and adults crowd around the attractions: a storyteller, a small village dance-and-theatre group; sellers of trinkets, wooden toys, utensils and more; hawkers selling various foods—and, the biggest attraction of all, a magician. A brightly coloured but obviously amateur sign announces his prowess: 'Mandala's greatest magician! The fantastic, the famous, the one and only Jaadum!' A long line of eager would-be spectators jostles outside, impatient to enter the little tent where Jaadum is performing.

To the sound of thunderous applause, Jaadum completes yet another act. This is a very different Jaadum from the tired and ill Wartak of Sandha Prison in the year 5475. This Jaadum is in his mid-thirties, a lithe, powerful man with the build of an athlete. His performances sizzle with his physicality: he leaps and jumps, he is flamboyant and self-confident. And he is immensely likeable, a showman all the way.

There are oohs and aahs from the audience, but the most vociferous praise comes from a boy sitting in the front row. He is thin and shabbily dressed, but the enthusiasm in his bright eyes and the wide grin on his face are proof enough of his admiration for Jaadum's talent and skill. Just behind him sits an elderly man with a long white beard; he smiles benevolently at the boy now and then, obviously amused as well as charmed by the child's sincere, uninhibited enthusiasm.

Jaadum reaches the last act of his performance. 'And now,' he says, 'a simple little performance, but one I especially love.' He gestures to the side, and his wife Asi, beautiful and smiling, comes forward holding a tray. On it are three bowls, which Jaadum places on a small table. 'I need a helper now,' he says to the audience. He glances affectionately towards Asi and smiles. 'I could ask my wife to help, of course, but that would not do, would it? You might think it was cheating—' he is drowned out by laughter. Before he can finish, the boy in the front row has leaped up and is jumping about excitedly. 'May I help, please? Please!'

Jaadum looks amused, but he nods and says yes. Then, when he realizes the boy is too short to climb up onto the stage unassisted, he jumps down, lifts the boy up, and then jumps back up onto the stage, in one fluid sequence of movements. The boy watches, regarding Jaadum with something very like hero-worship in his eyes.

Jaadum slips quickly into his routine, telling the boy—and the audience—what he's going to do. He lines up the bowls, all upside down. He brings out a large shiny bead from his pocket and shows it to the boy, even letting him hold it briefly. He then does his most famous sleight of hand: after placing the bead under one of the bowls, he switches the bowls around, juggling them very quickly, back and forth, back and forth. Forward, sideways—and finally, when he stops, he asks the boy: under which bowl is the bead? The boy thinks it over, and tentatively points towards one bowl. 'Are you sure?' Jaadum asks, his eyes twinkling. Behind the boy, the audience starts yelling: 'No, it's not that, it's not that! The other one!'

Jaadum grins. 'Well?' he asks the boy. The boy, now even more unsure, points to the other bowl. Then, because he's so uncertain, to the third.

Jaadum's grin widens. 'This one?' The boy nods in affirmation, and Jaadum gestures. 'Aabra ka daabra, khushi paane ka mashwara,' he intones, his voice swelling as he speaks. Abracadabra, some advice to gain happiness. The crowd in front breaks into cheers, and some of them start chanting along with him; they've obviously seen this act often enough to have memorized Jaadum's ditty. 'Dhoondne niklo toh mile nahin,' Jaadum says as he upturns the bowl the boy had indicated. If you set out to find it, it eludes you. The bowl is revealed to be empty, and Jaadum turns it upside down again, going on to upturn the other two bowls. 'Khushi dafn pyaar mein yaara.' Happiness is buried in love, my friend!

He makes a startled face, eyes wide in mock surprise, as if shocked that the bead has disappeared. Then, with a flourish, and with a loud, joyous yell of 'Aabra ka daabra!' Jaadum again upturns the first bowl, the one the boy had chosen, revealing that the bead is under it after all. The audience breaks into wild cheering, and the boy grins sheepishly at them as Jaadum puts his arm around the boy's shoulders and bows to the crowd.

As Jaadum turns to go backstage, the boy turns and follows him too. 'What? Won't your parents worry about you?' Jaadum asks. The boy shakes his head, and says he doesn't have parents. He's an orphan.

Meanwhile, Asi has come forward, and by her side is a young boy, about the same age as the boy who's tagging along behind Jaadum. The contrast between the two boys is visible: the one beside Asi is healthy and fresh-faced, tall and sturdy, while the boy beside Jaadum is thin, undersized and dirty. 'This is my son, Raibhu,' says Jaadum. 'He's eight years old. And that's my wife, Asi.' He turns to the boy at his side and asks who he is. 'Afhash,' says the boy, looking up confidently. 'And I am eight years old too.'

'And a very clever eight-year-old, too,' says a voice behind them. It is the white-bearded old man who had been sitting next to Afhash. He pats the boy on the head and smiles at Jaadum. 'You were brilliant as always, Jaadum,' he says, even as he dips his head in salutation to Asi. 'Asi-Gari, how are you, my lady?'

'I am well, Mehjaan My Elder,' Asi replies, bowing as she does so. Raibhu follows her example.

'I am glad you liked the show, My Elder,' Jaadum says. 'Dare we hope that you will come again? It is always such a pleasure to see you.'

The man's wrinkled face breaks into a broad grin. 'I will not just be here again, I may even accompany you part of the way on your tour. I need to go to Sandha and Raffasi later this month.'

'Excellent!' Jaadum puts an arm around the old man's shoulders. 'It will be a relief to have one friendly face in the audience.'

Mehjaan bursts out laughing. 'As if you should need any more! You must know by now how well-loved you are, Jaadum.'

The next day, Jaadum is putting up another show. Asi is there, along with Raibhu, both of them helping behind the scenes before the performance is to start, when Afhash peeks in backstage. 'May I come and help?' he asks shyly. He is so obviously eager to be part of the show that Jaadum agrees. 'I won't be able to pay you very much, though,' he tells Afhash in a mock serious tone. Afhash, on the other hand, replies perfectly seriously that he doesn't want money. His voice respectful, he says that he only wants to watch Jaadum the Elder do his magic. And, please—he adds, very hesitantly—could Jaadum the Elder teach him some magic tricks, please? He is good with his hands, Afhash adds hurriedly. He will learn with all due diligence; Jaadum the Elder will be proud of him.

Jaadum, touched by his sincerity, and perhaps pitying the child, agrees.

At the next performance, Afhash is there, alongside Asi and Raibhu, rushing about, obeying instructions, helping carry this on to the stage, tidying up here, putting that prop away—on his face is an expression of immense self-satisfaction. Asi's gentle smile as she thanks the boy for running an errand for her, or the approving look of Jaadum as Afhash conscientiously cleans up, make Afhash's chest visibly swell with pride. In the audience, sitting right in front, is Mehjaan; he smiles, his eyes crinkling in affectionate pride, as Afhash joins Jaadum, Asi and Raibhu in the performance.

After the show, Mehjaan comes backstage, bringing with him some snacks wrapped up in a piece of clean linen. 'Come, come,' he tells Raibhu. 'Let's sit down and eat together, shall we?' As they draw up stools and push a wooden crate into place to act as a table, Afhash slips away. He's barely out of the tent when he is stopped by a hand on his shoulder. He turns around to see it's Raibhu. Behind him, watching, are Jaadum, Asi, and Mehjaan.

'Where are you going?' Raibhu asks.

'It's lunchtime,' Afhash mumbles, after some hesitation.

'So? Why are you leaving lunch behind? Don't you want to eat with us?'

Afhash looks beyond Raibhu, to the others. Asi nods, her face full of kindness. 'We would like you to eat with us,' she says.

She leads him inside, and sits Afhash down. On the makeshift table is a modest but adequate selection of food, all of it echoing the customs of Mandala: in inverted pyramid-shaped bowls are cooked grain, lentils, and a stew of pyramid-shaped meatballs. On a large triangular platter are triangular flatbreads. Yellow-and-green-striped salad leaves, torn into rough triangles, sit in a triangular wire basket. The snacks Mehjaan has brought, pyramid-shaped fritters and patties, sit alongside the flatbreads.

'May the Land, the Sky and the Water bless our meal,'

says Asi, her hands moving to form a triangle in the air above the food. Mehjaan, Jaadum and Raibhu bow their heads, and Afhash, watching them, follows suit.

'Eat,' Asi says, smiling at Afhash. 'Eat well and grow big.'

From then on, Afhash is with them, all the time. Between performances, when Jaadum practices and also teaches both Raibhu and Afhash. During performances, when he helps. And in the brief moments of respite that they get: he plays with Raibhu, he gazes wonderingly at the books Raibhu reads (when Raibhu tries to teach Afhash how to read, Afhash shakes his head vigorously). He lets Asi clean him up and mend his ragged clothes. He hangs on every word that Jaadum says. Every now and then, Mehjaan too joins them, and treats Afhash just as he treats Raibhu: like a much-loved grandson. He takes the two boys off with him now and then, treating them to sweets and juice from the food stalls around the fairground, taking them to watch some of the other entertainers, and giving them a few tankas to indulge in some games. Raibhu and Afhash are delighted to be pampered, and Mehjaan basks in their company, happy and free.

Afhash is part of the family when they go, on the last day, around the fairground. At one end is a small space that's been appropriated by an illustrator of portraits. For a few tankas, he makes quick sketches in inks and coloured chalks: swift but faithful depictions of the people who sit for him. Jaadum, Asi, and the two boys watch as a family which has just had its portrait made crowds around the finished drawing, gushing over it and admiring the illustrator's skill as the father fishes out tankas from his pocket.

'What do you think?' Jaadum says. 'Shall we get portraits done of ourselves too?'

And so they do. Jaadum, Asi, Raibhu—and Afhash, proud as he can be to be standing with them.

'You take it,' Asi says gently, pushing the completed illustration into Afhash's hands. 'When we are no longer together, it will remind you that we are there, whenever you need us.' A cloud passes over Afhash's face; he is distressed by the thought of being separated from these three people, to whom he has drawn so close in these few days.

But before Afhash can say anything, there is a sudden shout. Someone else too begins screaming, a few children start wailing, and a loud shuddering rumble fills the air. Jaadum and Asi, along with the boys, instinctively look up into the sky to see a fireball go whooshing past. Somewhere, out of sight, it collides with the ground, so hard that the tremors can be felt even where they stand.

'Thanks be to the Sky Spirit,' Asi whispers, 'which directed the fireball away from us.' Her expression suddenly changes, to one of nervousness; she looks around, but the only person who appears to have overheard her words is her husband. Jaadum gives Asi a quick look of understanding, and his fingers curl about hers. 'Thanks be to the Land Spirit,' the two of them say in unison. Others around them are voicing the sentiment in other words too, all thanking the Land Spirit.

'This is our last performance in this village,' Jaadum tells Afhash later, as they're preparing for the show. 'We will be going on.' There is regret in his expression and in his tone.

Afhash looks on, unperturbed.

'We will leave this village tomorrow,' Jaadum says, looking a little wary now. 'We will miss you.'

Afhash shakes his head. 'No. Please, My Elder. Don't leave me behind. Let me come with you.'

'This is your home, Afhash,' Jaadum points out. 'How can you leave and come away with us?'

'Home is where one finds love and belonging,' Afhash says quietly. His eyes have filled with tears; he lowers his head, trying to stop the tears, but they come spilling out, dripping down his cheeks. 'Please don't shake me off,' he adds, in a voice nearly inaudible. Jaadum bends down to hug the boy, and Afhash wraps his arms as far as they will go around the man. He cries, tears of relief coursing down his face. Beyond Jaadum's shoulder, Afhash sees Asi and Raibhu standing, looking on with twin expressions of joy. Raibhu's grin widens and he gives Afhash a triumphant thumbs-up gesture.

~

'You haven't mentioned Raibhu even once in all the years I've been here,' Afhash remarked. 'Whenever I've asked you about him, you've always evaded the question.'

Jaadum shook his head. 'I wanted to keep him away from this—' he gestured, his hand indicating the squalor and darkness of the prison. 'He would be heartbroken if he knew his father had landed up here.'

'Why should he be heartbroken?' Afhash countered. 'My Elder, you hadn't done anything wrong. Instead, *you* were wronged. If it hadn't been for all those people—' but he doesn't get a chance to complete the sentence; Jaadum cuts him off midway.

'It's all right,' Jaadum says. 'Water under the bridge. It's too late now, anyway.' Afhash opens his mouth to protest, but Jaadum holds up a hand, dissuading him. 'No, listen to me. You will be released tomorrow, and I want you to do something for me. Go and fetch Raibhu. He is in Dhaani'—Jaadum reaches into his pocket, and pulls out a small slip of paper on which an address is written—'here. I don't know how you will get across the border and into the Northern Empire, but you are resourceful enough. Go and get him, as soon as you can.' He sees the bafflement in Afhash's face, and slowly wags his head. 'I may wish for a long life, Afhash, and you may tell me that I have many years to live, but I can feel death creeping over me. I won't last long, my child. I am dying, I know it.'

'My Elder, don't say that—'

'I wish I didn't have to, but it's true. Fetch me my son, Afhash. Bring him here so that I can see him once before I die. I had hoped I would be able to meet him after being released, a respectable man.' He shakes his head. 'That was a pipe dream. If Raibhu must meet me here in prison, so be it.'

~

Afhash's nose wrinkled as he stepped from the broad main street into the snaking alley known as Alchemists' Street. Not that there was any sign naming this length of smelly, dirty road; but it was not needed. The scorched patches on the shopfronts, the clouds of evil-smelling multicoloured smoke emitting from the chimneys, and the very look of the sewage running in the open drain—its depths changing colours, now sada stone-red, now zansal-blue, with flashes of green and yellow; its surface covered in a shifting film of mist that took on odd shapes, circles and spirals and wavering columns—was proof enough of the sort of work that went on in this area.

Afhash moved forward, narrowly escaping a sudden puff of bright yellow smoke which burst out of a torn pipe that protruded into the street. Just a few steps ahead, and there was his destination: a small, ragged-looking shop with a tarnished square of fake sun metal hanging on the shop front. Afhash looked about, puzzled; there was no sign of any door. 'Kimanchi!' he called, and waited a few moments before repeating the name. 'Kimanchi! Open up!' When nothing happened, he banged on the wooden panels of the shop, but except for a few puffs of dust, there was nothing. Afhash heaved a sigh of impatience, and was just turning away when there was a scrape and a crash, and the section of wood paneling on which the square of fake sun metal hung, swung away. A thin little man, his hands stained a bright purple and wisps of smoke coming out of his wild hair, stood there, blinking in the sunlight.

'Don't you know?' he said irritably. 'Use the doorbell.' He placed his palm on the square of fake sun metal and pressed hard, at which a strident screech sounded in the depths of the shop behind him.

'Ah.' Afhash looked impressed. 'No, I didn't know, Kimanchi. Surely you haven't forgotten? They'd clapped me in prison.'

'What? Afhash—goodness me, may the Land Spirit bless you! It's you. Escaped, eh?'

'No,' said Afhash, with dignity. 'My sentence was over. I've come here to buy something from you.'

'Yes, yes.' Kimanchi hustled Afhash inside the shop. 'Come on in, come on in. What is it you want, eh? I have something you will like, I think. See—' he bustled away into the gloomy depths of his small, dingy shop with its rows of jars full of dried herbs, insects, minerals and more.

He stopped briefly to stir something bubbling away in a pot-bellied cauldron, and peered into a large vial that contained a bright orange liquid. Then, having scrabbled about in a drawer, he pulled out a little dagger. 'Look, this. I thought of you when I made this. You don't even need to put it to someone's pocket in order to cut it; just get it in the line of sight, like this.' He held it up, shutting one eye as he did so, and squinted at Afhash. 'And see, I pull it across like this, nowhere close to you, and—'

There was a loud tearing sound, and a sack that hung from a hook halfway across the room ripped open, spilling its contents, dozens of dead beetles, on the floor. Kimanchi flung the dagger down and scuttled off to clear up the mess.

'Very clever indeed,' Afhash said, his tone dry but his eyes laughing. 'Oh, very clever, Kimanchi! So, if one wants to pick a pocket, one should aim at another pocket a few yards away?'

Kimanchi, red-faced, shoved the last of the dead beetles into a large box he had found. 'It's work in progress,' he growled. 'You'll see when it's done.'

Afhash shook his head. 'Thanks but no thanks, Kimanchi. I'm a reformed man now, no more thievery for me. I've promised myself that.'

Kimanchi's face fell, but he shrugged. 'Ah, well. All the better, I suppose. What do you want, then?'

'Fire crackers,' said Afhash. 'The noisier, the better. And several lengths of good rope.'

'Getting married or what?' Kimanchi said a few minutes later, as he placed the last of the fire crackers in a bag. There were three large bags, each stuffed to the brim with fire crackers.

Afhash grinned as he handed over the money. 'Not me. Some friends.' He picked up the bags. 'Give me a good heavy sack, will you, Kimanchi? Thank you.'

At the far end of Alchemists' Street, where all the refuse of the street piled up and the stench was bad enough to deter anybody else from straying there, Afhash found a secluded spot inside the ruins of a shop that had exploded long ago. Within its soot-stained walls, Afhash sat down and went to work, quickly tying the fire crackers onto the ropes at intervals. When one coil of rope was ready, he put it into the sack Kimanchi had given him and started on the next coil.

~

The sun was setting by the time Afhash got off the vaanik, the long-distance transport vehicle in which he had taken a lift. The six horses that pulled the vehicle were tired by now, their heaving flanks turned crimson by the flying red dust that coated the Terrisan Highway from Raffasi to Jurwad. Afhash hitched the sack—his only luggage—onto his shoulder, and trudged along the road, his shoes and the hems of his leggings acquiring a coat of red dust as he walked.

Beyond the Sada River on his right stretched the Northern Mandalan Empire. Back when Afhash had been a child, it was all simply one Mandalan Empire, one Mandala; but then one faction among the Terrisans, led by the fanatic Sarjaand, had grown powerful and begun demanding a separate nation, a nation exclusively for the Terrisans. A land where their rights would come first and where the Land Spirit would rule. Sarjaand preached the purity of the Terrisans, their superiority over Aaboneer and Nabhang. He clamoured for a land where Terrisans could live unfettered and free, unrestrained by considerations that had no place in the faith he professed. He had had enough of the easygoing attitude of the Empire, with its unrestrained tolerance of Aaboneer and Nabhang and others who worshipped spirits as diverse as those of trees and glaciers.

Eighteen years ago, that split had happened. The Terrisans had broken away, and taken for themselves a swathe of land on the southern one-third of the Empire. The North had remained a mishmash of religions and ethnicities: Nabhang and Aaboneer, and the many Terrisans who had refused to go south, because the north had always been their home.

Eighteen years, but nobody had forgotten, and nobody had forgiven. Sarjaand was dissatisfied at the relatively small tract of land he had been able to wrest from the North. He had wanted more land, more resources, and more people to join his cause; that he had got a fraction of these was, for him, unforgivable.

For Emperor Dhanjog Mahabeyan, who had ruled the North, the slight—that so many millions had not wanted to be among his subjects any longer—had rankled. He had not had the strength of character to counter Sarjaand, and he had never been able to do anything more than rave and rant. His son and successor, Gunjog Mahabeyan, was a better Emperor, with a better sense of justice, a deeper feeling for his people, and a more powerful character. But the fractured realm he had inherited needed too much in the way of repairs and nurturing to leave time for Gunjog to think of attempting to reunite the two empires. For the time being, at least, North and South looked on each other across the Sada's waters, with suspicion and hatred. They had alert sentries on either side, constant patrols and scouts on the lookout. To slip across over the Sada and into the Northern Empire was no easy task.

But Afhash was prepared.

On a promontory looking out over the river was a Southern Mandala Imperial Force outpost. Off to the left, at the foot of the mountain was a small village. Between the village and the outpost was dense forest. Afhash moved off into the forest, and once he was safely out of sight, he reached into his sack, pulled out one coil of rope crackers and stretched it out, going as deep into the forest as the length of the rope permitted. The other coil he left in the sack, which he hitched onto his shoulder.

Once that was done, Afhash turned and made for the village. He did not go all the way to the village; halfway there, he saw a boy of about twelve years of age, with a small herd of woolly yang-pra, their thick fleeces a froth of pale pink. Just as Afhash stepped out from the trees and headed towards the boy, a shadow passed above him. Brief, soundless, swift. Afhash turned to look up. The boy, who had noticed the shadow too, glanced up as well, into a cloudless blue sky. Afhash and the boy wore identical expressions of mystification: there was nothing there, not a sound, not a bird, nothing that could have caused the shadow—

Suddenly, the stillness of the woods was shattered by the panicked scream of a frightened animal. There was a flash of deep green, and then, as the two humans stood, staring, a small rabbit rose up in the air, limp and lifeless, as if dragged along by a ghost.

'It's a mahabhaagi,' Afhash whispered.

The bird of prey was glimpsed only briefly as it flapped its widespread wings, deep green on the upper surfaces and pale blue, grey and white on the underside. A few moments, no more, as it lifted its prey and flew to a nearby tree, bringing its wings together as soon as it had alighted on a branch. Its folded wings camouflaged the bird completely, letting it blend into the green of the tree canopy. The rabbit could still be seen, an indistinct patch of beige fur, seeming to hang by itself from the branch.

Afhash let out a long breath. 'I'd only heard of these things,' he murmured. 'I thought mahabhaagis had died out.'

The yang-pra herder shook his head, his eyes alight with excitement. 'They're alive, the Elders in our village talk of them. But this is the first time I've seen one too. Wait till I tell them—'

His words seem to break the spell Afhash had fallen under. With a sudden jolt, he said. 'What you have to tell is something else! Quick, enough time's been wasted! Quick, I need help!' The boy stared, puzzled, even as his yang-pra skittered about nervously, unsettled by Afhash's excited outburst.

The words came pouring out of Afhash: to the boy, this looked like a man in an odd panic, a far cry from the one who had stared up at the mahabhaagi with such unhurried wonder. A man both fearful as well as excited. He gripped the boy's arm, and hissed, 'You have to help! If you love your land—do as I say! There are some men trying to get across the river from the Northern Empire!' He panted, hanging on to the boy's arm. 'I am heading off to try and stop them, but go to the Imperial Force outpost'—he pointed in the direction where he had seen the post—'and alert them. Tell them there are intruders in the forest, they need to attack! Okay? Go!' He did not wait to see if the boy obeyed, but raced off through the trees.

Only when he was out of sight of the boy did he stop and slink back to check. As he had expected, his urgency had communicated itself to the boy: he had abandoned his herd of yang-pra and was running, heading for the outpost, a good five minutes away even if the boy was a good runner. Afhash, as he watched, tied the sack around his shoulders, where it would stay clear of the water.

When the sack was secure, he turned and quickly cut across the forest to where he had laid out his rope fire cracker. He sat down on his haunches and quickly reached into the deep, capacious pocket of his tunic, to retrieve the tinderbox he carried in it. He had not even pulled it out when a shadow fell across the ground in front of him.

Afhash looked up, surprised.

A man stood there, regarding him with eyes full of suspicion. A man who wore the uniform of the Southern Mandala Army. A soldier.

Chapter Two

'Who are you?' said the soldier. 'And what are you doing?'

Afhash glanced in dismay at the rope of fire crackers stretched out on the grassy ground before him. He could not afford to let this man delay him; but knocking him out was not going to be easy. He was almost certainly carrying a weapon of some sort, perhaps a dagger or a slingshot tucked away in the belt under his tunic. And even if he wasn't armed, the man's lean, muscular build was enough to convince Afhash that if it came to a face-off between the two of them, only a very sudden and violent attack from Afhash, easily the smaller and weaker of the two, would have any chance of success. He had to catch the man unawares. Or he had to send him off on a wild goose chase. Or something.

But Afhash had grown up on the streets, and the streets of Mandala had been a good training ground. He knew how to think fast, and he knew how to act equally fast.

'I am a magician,' he said, rising easily to his feet. 'And more. A herbal physician for one, an alchemist for another. What you see here,' he remarked, gesturing at the rope of fire crackers, 'is an experiment. The herbs you see growing here, when subjected to the smoke and sparks from these, should end up having their healing qualities enhanced tenfold.'

The soldier did not look convinced. Afhash decided to step it up a notch. 'Look here,' he said, bending down and ripping up a double handful of leaves from a wild plant that grew nearby. 'I won't use the fire crackers, because that would set the whole thing off, and I don't want to waste it.' He took out his tinderbox and handed the herbs into the hands of the startled soldier. 'Even mere fire and smoke can have some effect,' Afhash added, striking the flint as he sat down. 'Will you please sit down, too,' he told the soldier. 'I can't make fire standing up, you know.'

The soldier was perhaps too dazed by how he had been so summarily diverted; maybe, he guessed, it was the way of those obsessed with whatever scientific experiments they were doing. Afhash projected the air of the obsessed, the absent-minded, with a zeal and fervour he had seen often in Kimanchi. Whatever it was, it carried the soldier along. Wordlessly, and with a certain amount of curiosity, he knelt down beside Afhash, still holding the herbs in his hand. Afhash had positioned the flint in such a way that the sparks flew on to a clump of dried grass just below. The dry grass ignited, catching fire readily; and as soon as the first flame leapt up, Afhash grabbed the herbs from the soldier and threw them onto the flame. Smoke billowed up, and in that moment, taking advantage of the soldier's distraction, Afhash swung out at him with the tinderbox. It hit the soldier hard on the temple, felling him with a single blow.

Afhash did not wait to check whether the man was alive or dead; he grabbed a handful of the burning grass and threw it over the string of fire crackers. He waited only the few moments it took to convince him that the rope was indeed burning. Then he raced off towards the river, making sure his path did not cross that which any Imperial Force soldiers, moving from the outpost to the forest, might follow. He reached the river, using the shelter offered by bushes and boulders, just as the first bang sounded from the direction of the forest.

Afhash grinned to himself. 'Somebody's getting married,' he whispered smugly. He quickly rolled up his leggings, pulled off his shoes and put them into his sack before he stepped into the water. Far off, a stream of figures had emerged from the outpost. They ran towards the trees, their shouts and cries carrying on the breeze as Afhash quickly made his way across the water. More bangs sounded, and then came the assault of the weaponry that had been unleashed by the soldiers at the outpost. Arrows tipped with humur went whizzing past; a series of loud thumps revealed the action of a massive missile discharger, spewing cylinders of stone. A musical click-click-click announced a cascade of deathly spine-studded spheres, raining havoc down on whoever happened to come in their way.

Afhash reached the opposite bank, but stayed low in the water, peering about to gauge the situation. But it was as he had guessed it would be: the discharging of the weapons, the suspicious noises and the shouting had convinced the Northern Empire soldiers patrolling their side of the border that something was up on the southern side of the Sada. Their focus was on the opposite bank of the river, not their own.

Afhash waded out and made his way into the forest fringing the river. He was in the Northern Mandalan Empire.

~

Dhaani, Northern Mandalan Empire
The next day

The headquarters of the Northern Mandala Imperial Justice Force was an imposing edifice, its façade stark white and punctuated by tall windows that stretched all along the length of the double-storeyed building and reflected the white stones of the Emperor's Way beside which the building was situated. At its four corners stood four short turrets, each flying the flag of the Northern Mandalan Empire: three hands, one ochre, one pale grey and one blue, entwined together to hold high a torch. The three faiths of the Northern Mandalan Empire. Terrisan, Aaboneer and Nabhang, holding aloft a reminder of light and hope.

Inside the office, things were rather gloomy. A meeting was in progress, and at the head of the long stone table sat the senior commander of the Imperial Justice Force. On his fitted black tunic were the insignia of his rank: the sun metal arcs at his shoulders, the tiny bell of justice which hung from a chain around his neck along with an equally tiny sword, symbolizing the power of justice. The men facing him wore the same tunics, the same bell-and-sword emblem, but their epaulettes were simple squares of punched zansal. Looking kindly down on them, on the wall opposite, was a portrait of the Emperor Gunjog Mahabeyan, resplendent in his gold-edged tunic and leggings, his cloak of mahabhaagi feathers glinting as if it were real and not a painting. The emperor of North Mandala was a gentle man, a just and good man, and it showed in the expression on his face.

In front of the commander, on the smooth polished

surface of the table, was spread a map of Northern Mandala. The senior commander traced a finger along the lines marking the southern fringes of the land. 'Here,' he said. 'Here, at Garghat.' His finger moved to the north. 'Vandhara,' and then to the west. 'And Bistin.' He pursed his lips, chewing on his moustache as he did so. 'We have informal reports of infiltration from all of these points. The Imperial Army still insists that they cannot be certain it's the Southern Empire's spies, but considering the way they've been behaving since the spring, I think it highly probable.'

He glanced at the men around him, his gaze wandering across until it stopped at a broad-shouldered, handsome man in his late twenties.

'Raibhu,' said the senior commander. 'I read your report of the tour of inspection in the Sada-Jal Reservoir area. You don't seem to have noticed anything untoward.'

Raibhu nodded. 'Yes, sir,' he said. 'The reservoir is old, of course, and it's been many years since any repair work was carried out on its walls. The water is still, but not too deep,' he explained to the other officers, who seemed to not be completely aware of the problem. 'Which is why we were worried that it might be a relatively easy path to cross the river into Northern Mandala.' He turned back to the commander. 'But the area is too remote, and looked utterly devoid of human population on that side of the river. And on this side, there's a nearby village, where they're quite vigilant. Plus we have our soldiers patrolling the riverbank. I don't think we need fear an incursion across the reservoir.'

The commander nodded. 'The patrolling will have to be intensified all along the bank of the Sada. I've just received information that there has been some disturbance along the border. What it is, whether someone crossed over, or whether it was a false alarm, we don't know yet, but still. I'll be sending out orders for heightened security.'

He turned back to Raibhu. 'Your informer Bhasrath was due back today, wasn't he, from his trip across the border?' he asked. 'Did he get anything?'

'I'll only know when I've met him, sir. He's waiting for me.' Raibhu paused. 'I doubt if he could have got anything important; he usually manages to convey urgency pretty well. Nothing of that sort this time.'

'Anyhow,' said the senior commander, 'better to meet him as soon as you can. Let's just finish this up, then you can leave. Report to me when you're back.' He pursed his lips, letting his anxiety show. 'I'll have to send a report to His Majesty. If this information is correct, it may well be the last straw. His Majesty will make sure we give as good as we get. If that self-styled Emperor Sarjaand is looking for a fight, he'll get it.'

~

The rendezvous was an old shack in a narrow lane below the Nabhang Shrine. Raibhu, his fitted black uniform exchanged for the flared tunic of a civilian, glanced up briefly at the Shrine at the top of the hill. Above it still hovered the iridescent cloud that had been here since time immemorial, but its colours had dulled and shrunk over the years. The pink and blue and gold were now mere wisps against the more general whiteness of the cloud.

Raibhu hurried on, glancing swiftly up and down the lane

to make sure he was unobserved. At the crumbling boundary wall of the shack he was heading for, he paused briefly and looked around, before vaulting over the wall. Landing neatly on his haunches Raibhu straightened up, his hand at his belt, ready to pull out the dagger he carried. He moved quickly, swift and sure on his feet, as alert as a panther on the prowl.

He approached the shack at an angle, keeping to the shadows, ready to take on any unexpected company. As it was, with Raibhu lay the element of surprise: when he stepped into the shack from the back, the man peering out of the window and watching the gate whirled around, his face ashen. 'Raibhu!' he gasped. 'You nearly made my heart stop!'

'Which makes me wonder if we're doing the right thing sending you on these expeditions,' Raibhu said dryly. 'If you can't guard your own back, what can you do?' He pulled a fold of his loose tunic over the loop in his belt where his dagger was concealed. 'Anyway, tell me what you discovered.'

It did not take long for Bhasrath to give his report. It was a disappointing one, as Raibhu had suspected it would be. 'There are unverified reports coming in from Bistin, not too far from where you crossed over,' Raibhu remarked. 'Did you see anything? Any signs of the Southerners entering our country?'

Bhasrath looked a little sheepish. 'I was too busy keeping under cover while crossing over to see if anybody was crossing over the other way,' he mumbled.

Raibhu heaved a sigh of exasperation. 'Then I take it you didn't end up getting to Raffasi, did you?'

'Raffasi? How on earth could I have got till Raffasi, with the way things were? A few leagues past the river, and that was it. It would have been suicidal—'

'All right, all right.' Raibhu shook his head, disappointed. 'I had been hoping this time you would have managed to make it there, but I suppose it's too much to expect, given the situation.'

The informer was looking on, curiosity in his eyes. 'Tell me, Raibhu,' he said, 'why do you so desperately want me to get to Raffasi, and to that house? What is there in that house? It must be something very important, right? After all, I've been going back and forth for the past two years, and every time you ask about Raffasi.'

Raibhu shook his head. 'It's nothing,' he said. His voice was weary; he looked disheartened. 'Nothing to do with work, at any rate. That's why I've never insisted you go all the way to Raffasi.' He paused, glanced outside—it was all quiet, a boring sleepy Dhaani afternoon—and then turned to Bhasrath. 'All right, get along. Contact me when you have something to report.'

~

It was a large old house, built in the traditional old Mandalan style, with a tiled sloping roof, rows of miniature fruit trees on the window sills, and long strips of multicoloured soils decorating the façade. The garden outside had a wall slightly higher and more formidable than of similar houses in the neighbourhood, but that was all that indicated that Raibhu's house was the dwelling of an officer of the Imperial Justice Force. The garden was bursting with flowers; there were shady trees along the wall, and the view from the upper storey, of the mountains and hills and the river, was panoramic.

Raibhu had not bothered to change out of the clothes he

had worn to meet the informer; he stood at the front window of his home, looking out, still dressed in the same flared tunic and leggings he had worn to the rendezvous. He watched as the sun set, briefly restoring the colours of the iridescent cloud above the Nabhang Shrine, but a sadness lurked deep in his eyes. Confusion and misery seemed to have made their home deep in this man, even though he hid it well when he was with others.

When the vivid colours of the sunset had given way to darkness and the Lesser Moon had appeared above the horizon, Raibhu stepped away from the window. This room, the central and largest chamber of the house, was decorated in the Northern Mandalan style too. At the very centre of it was a skylight that, on clear days such as this, usually remained open, allowing in fresh air and a breeze that touched the many threads of moon metal that stretched across the space and hung down from it. Some of these threads were finer than spider silk, some were as thick as a finger: and between them, they treated the wind in different ways, coaxing from it a music that was unique and ever-changing. Below the skylight, the threads hung down into a shallow pool of clear water that reverberated with the music, its surface dimpled and dotted in constantly changing patterns that moved in time to the music of the winds.

Nabhang, Aaboneer and Terrisan all came together in Northern Mandala.

Raibhu stood for a few moments, looking down at the pool, watching the water dance its never-ending ballet. Then he turned away, moving about the room, going to the rows of thick, polished zansal rods that lined the wall, holding within clips hundreds of books. More than the silverwood chairs, more than the elegant vases holding dried flowers, more even than the exquisite painting of a Mandalan forest, this was the heart of the room. Its owner's library. In a dozen different languages, its books ranged from treatises on philosophy and art to scientific works, plays, and novels.

Raibhu moved slowly along one rod, reading the titles, occasionally stopping at a book to pull it out of its restraining clips and examine it, as if he was trying to decide what to read next.

On the zansal rods, at random intervals, were odds and ends, bric-a-brac and mementoes. A small figurine made of silver-powdered terracotta, an intricate spiral horn fossil from an ancient rishya. A trio of portraits. Raibhu paused at these paintings, gazing at them. The first one was of a teenager, his face recognizably that of a younger Raibhu. The second was of him again, this time with two old people: an old man and an old woman, both seated and smiling brightly while the boy stood behind them, his hands stretched across the shoulders of the older people in a hug.

It was the third painting, though, that Raibhu gently touched, in what was almost a caress. It was an old painting, now faded, of another family. Handsome father, beautiful mother, a young son standing in front, his toothy grin wide. The image radiated joy and love. Raibhu's eyes softened as he picked up the painting and looked fondly at it before replacing it.

He wandered on, still looking at the books, and then picked one out: *The Teachings of the Venerable Dayadhan Jijit*, a well-worn old book. Raibhu went up the stairs to an upper chamber, where he settled down on a comfortable chair and opened the book.

He had barely turned over a few pages when there was a knocking at the front door. Raibhu sat up, instantly alert. Putting the book aside, he rose to his feet and left the room, hurrying downstairs—but instead of going all the way down to the front door, he paused at the landing, from where a strategically placed window offered a good view of the doorstep. Raibhu frowned; a man of about his own age was standing there. Hawk-faced, lean, and dressed in shabby, ill-fitting clothes. Even as he watched, the man raised his hand and knocked again.

The book still in his hand, Raibhu paused only to collect his dagger from the shelf where he had placed it; then, weapon in hand, he opened the door so suddenly that the visitor nearly fell in. For a moment, there was confusion; the newcomer stumbled and grabbed at his surprised host. Raibhu, wary and prepared for an attack, dodged briskly, and the visitor recovered his balance all on his own. But even as he did so, he whirled around and said, 'Raibhu! You're Raibhu, aren't you? You bastard, you always were good at slipping away and leaving others in the lurch!'

Raibhu, grip steady on his dagger, stared, steely-eyed. 'Who are you?' he asked, unflinching: the man, still half-bent, had instinctively raised his arms to show that he was unarmed. From that half-crouch, he looked up into Raibhu's face. He had gone pale. 'I—surely you recognize me?' he blurted out. Then: 'You moron! Raibhu!' he added, his fear turning to anger as he got to his feet, though prudently he still kept his arms raised. 'How dare you forget me! And to think we were so close at the age of eight—'

'*Afhash*!'

The flurry of expressions on Raibhu's face made it difficult to tell exactly what he was feeling. Disbelief, bafflement, extreme joy, curiosity—all of them brimming up in the form of helpless exulting, in hugging Afhash, asking a dozen questions all at the same time. And then stepping back, holding the other man at arm's length, to look at him again. 'Ah, how good it is to see you,' he smiled. 'I thought I'd never see you again.'

~

Year 5455 of the Emergence of Mandala, later that year

A magic show, but this time, it's on a big stage, in a big town. Jaadum, dressed in a blue embroidered tunic and leggings, with a matching turban, bows to the applauding audience. 'Thank you, thank you,' he murmurs. 'And now, let me present to you my son. So far you have seen him only beside me in some of my acts. Someday, this boy,' he places his hands on little Raibhu's shoulders, 'will be my successor, and I hope you will give him as much warmth as you give to me.' He smiles, bows again, and says, 'For now—our next act!'

For this act, Raibhu stands in the centre of the stage, while Jaadum surrounds him with odds and ends—an outsize vase of papier mâché, a large bouquet of paper flowers, a cardboard cutout depicting a range of mountains—all of them brought on to the stage one by one by Asi and Afhash. 'These,' says Jaadum, as he arranges them around Raibhu, 'are what will come to you as accolades! But,' he looks at the audience with a grin and a wink, 'I am a poor magician who can afford nothing better than paper and cardboard. You will do better, won't you?' There is laughter, even as the audience waits expectantly to see what happens next. Jaadum adds some more paper flowers, and then Afhash brings him a box.

'What is this?' Jaadum says dramatically, peering inside. 'Fire crackers? Oh, yes! Yes, of course. A hero must be felicitated with crackers!' He quickly places them around the array of objects. By now Afhash has also brought him a burning candle. 'Good, good!' Jaadum says with exaggerated satisfaction. 'Come, my son! Get a taste of the fame and the celebration that you will see!'

He bends down and sets off one of the fireworks—it's a miniature volcano, spewing showers of bright red, gold and orange sparks. Quickly, Jaadum lights up all the other miniature volcanos set around Raibhu and the boy is obscured by the sparks and smoke. Suddenly, there is a mini explosion, followed by a ball of fire. All the items ranged around Raibhu are inflammable, and they catch fire quickly. He seems to be engulfed in flames. They can't go beyond a certain point, because Jaadum is doing this act on a large stone-paved platform placed on the stage. But Jaadum screams, cries, jumps about and tries to extinguish the fire. Asi runs out onto the stage, holding a bucket of water, which Jaadum pours onto the fire. Soon, the fire—raging fiercely but briefly—has died down. Jaadum, wailing and calling for Raibhu, cries that his son is dead, dead because of his own stupidity...

He moves into the smouldering, wet pile of blackened things and finds something: a charred skeleton. Jaadum cries even more loudly, mourning his boy.

'But at least I should pay my son a tribute of some sort,'

Jaadum announces tearfully to the audience, who by now are looking confused—and also excited, because they can sense that this, though it appears tragic, is part of an act.

Jaadum raises his arms and claps his hands dramatically. A red curtain falls from the ceiling, shielding the charred area where Raibhu had been standing. 'What is this I have done?' Jaadum wails in frustration. 'Now I can't even see where you had stood last! Oh, I am losing my skill!' He claps again, and the curtain rises again—and this time we see Raibhu standing behind it, whole and healthy and smiling. Jaadum makes a big show of embracing him, exulting over his son. To loud cheers and thunderous clapping from the crowd, Jaadum and Raibhu bow to the audience. Mehjaan, who has come here for this performance, stands up, clapping louder than anyone else.

Later, Jaadum and Raibhu come backstage, where they are met by a jubilant Asi and Afhash. Mehjaan joins them too, just as Asi, hugging her husband and son, says, 'That went really well! It's so good, I think you can easily make it part of the show. As long as you don't let my child harm himself,' she adds, her tone mock admonitory. Raibhu gives her an embarrassed look. 'I'm not a child, Mother!' he protests. 'And I was very careful. I did just as Father had instructed. Not even a hair is singed, see?' Afhash, watching them, looks longingly at the affection between mother and son. Jaadum notices his expression and pulls Afhash into a group hug along with Asi and Raibhu. Mehjaan looks on, his eyes moist.

'Jaadum My Elder?' They are startled by the sudden sharp whisper from the door. They move apart, and Jaadum says, 'You?' He looks surprised, and alert too. Asi steps up beside her husband as he moves forward to stand face to face with the newcomer.

'I have a message for you,' the man says. He pulls out a letter—a brief note—and hands it to Jaadum, who opens it and quickly reads it. When he's finished, he hands it to Asi and says, 'There's a protest planned in Dhaani, against Emperor Dhanjog Mahabeyan. They're saying his spinelessness and ineffectiveness cannot be tolerated any more, it will destroy Mandala if it isn't stopped.' He glances at Mehjaan. 'Have you heard any news of this?' Jaadum asks. Mehjaan nods, but says nothing; he glances towards the two boys.

Asi looks thoughtful. 'Yes. As it is, that fanatic, Sarjaand, is clamouring for a separate land where only the Terrisans will live. If he has his way, Mandala will be split into two.'

Jaadum nods. 'Precisely. And our Emperor only says pretty things about not letting Sarjaand have his way. He doesn't do a thing. His son Gunjog will be a far better ruler.' He folds the letter, a pensive expression on his face as he does so. 'We need to go and join the fight again, Asi,' he says softly. 'We've been away from it these past few months; it's time we returned.'

Asi looks towards the two boys, Afhash and Raibhu, who are standing together, looking wide-eyed at the adults. Raibhu has an inkling of what this is all about; Afhash is looking utterly lost. Jaadum nods to the messenger and tells him to wait outside. Once the man is gone, he goes to Afhash, and kneels in front of him so that he is looking Afhash in the face. 'My child,' Jaadum says gently, holding Afhash by the shoulders, 'Asi, I and Raibhu have to leave for Dhaani, right now.'

Afhash has realized that they are going to leave him behind; his eyes are full of hurt and sorrow as he mumbles, 'Take me with you.'

The pain in Afhash's face is mirrored in Jaadum's eyes. 'No,' he says. 'We cannot. It is too dangerous.'

'But Raibhu is going with you.'

'Only till Dhaani. When we reach Dhaani, Raibhu will go and stay with his grandparents. He will not be with us.'

'But—' Another protest is rising to Afhash's lips when he is interrupted by Mehjaan, who places a hand on the boy's shoulder.

'Afhash,' Mehjaan says. 'Will you stay here with me? Until Raibhu and his family return from Dhaani, will you keep me company, please? I get so lonely, I would be very happy to have someone beside me.'

Jaadum looks up at the old man, his eyes full of gratitude. Afhash looks a little taken aback, but finally nods and says in a gruff little voice, 'But I will work. I will do whatever work you will give me. I won't take charity.'

'Of course you won't,' Mehjaan agrees. 'I expected nothing else from you.' He smiles and putting an arm around Afhash's thin shoulders, draws him close. 'You see, we will be very happy. And we will wait together for Raibhu to return. Yes? When you have someone to wait along with you, the waiting doesn't seem so long.'

Later that evening, Afhash stands by the side of the road, beside Mehjaan. Jaadum, Asi and Raibhu are there, with their bags and rolls of luggage. This is where ekduts stop to collect passengers and let them off: there are seats here, and clean water, and a row of stables where grooms maintain fresh horses to replace worn-out ones. Jaadum and his family are all too tense and fidgety to sit down, and when the thundering clip-clop and rattling wheels of the approaching ekdut announce its arrival, Jaadum bends down to hug Afhash and reassure him again. Afhash does not reciprocate, though when Asi and Raibhu hug him, he hugs them back, a little awkwardly.

The ekdut arrives. The family gets in, and finds seats. Raibhu gets a seat at a window close to where Afhash is standing. He waves to Afhash as the ekdut leaves. He keeps waving, as the ekdut moves on, and Afhash, with Mehjaan holding his hand, waves back with his free hand. He is a small, diminutive figure, but there is a certain sturdiness about him, as if he will not let life grind him down.

~

'Who would have thought that was the last time I would see Asi the Elder,' Afhash said glumly. 'Or that I wouldn't see you or Jaadum the Elder for so many years.'

'Or that Mandala itself would split into two within a matter of months,' Raibhu added, his tone sombre. 'Father and Mother fought so hard to try to stop that, but it was all in vain.' His face clouded over at the memories of those turbulent days. 'You know,' he added, 'when we returned to Raffasi a few months later, it was because Mother and Father felt certain that Mandala's unity was in no danger any more. But it was all an illusion.'

'You returned to Raffasi a few months later? But—no, of course you wouldn't have met me. I was no longer there; Mehjaan the Elder had died, and I was—'

'Tell me later,' Raibhu said, taking Afhash by the arm and leading him upstairs into the room he had been sitting in. 'Make yourself comfortable,' he said. 'Sit. I'll get calmroot infusion; you look like you need it. Have you eaten, or should I get you something to eat too?'

'Forget about all of that,' Afhash said. His expression had turned pensive, and Raibhu, taken aback by the sudden change in Afhash's mood, lifted an eyebrow by way of query. 'I came here to fetch you back,' Afhash added, laying a hand on Raibhu's sleeve. 'To Sandha, to meet Jaadum the Elder.'

Raibhu stared, his eyes unbelieving. 'Father?' he whispered. 'Father is alive? *Father is alive*?!'

'He's been in prison in Sandha,' Afhash said. 'These past eighteen years.'

Raibhu shook his head, still finding it hard to absorb the news. 'And here I thought he was dead, I thought he had died long ago.' A frown pulled his eyebrows together. 'Why couldn't he have at least let me know? He knew where I was, it wouldn't have hurt to send a letter.' There was resentment in his tone, pain at what he thought of as a betrayal.

'I'm sure he had his reasons,' Afhash said. 'You can ask him yourself. You have to come, Raibhu. He's dying, and he wants to meet you.'

'Dying? But Father was always as strong as a horse—and he would be in his fifties, not even that old yet. What happened, did he get hurt? Why is he in prison? Eighteen years in prison? What did he do?'

Afhash lifted a hand. 'Slow, slow. You'll find out. Just come on now, we can't waste any more time.'

Raibhu nodded. 'Yes, you're right. Wait, I will need to give a message to the senior commander, to let him know I'm going on leave.'

He moved across the room to the small desk next to the book-rods, and sat down, pulling out a clean page from a rectangular page-case made of gleaming zansal. From the shallow groove in the side of the page-case he withdrew a slim tube pen and pressed its point into the inkwell to draw up a tubeful of black ink.

'We can drop this off at headquarters when we leave,' he said, beginning to write.

Afhash nodded absently; he was too busy going about the room, gazing at everything with admiring eyes, gently touching the more unusual items of furniture and décor. He examined the zansal threads hanging from the skylight with interest, he dipped a hand into the pool below, and watched as the water swirled about his fingers and then went back to dancing in tune with the Aeolian music.

'This is all so different from Southern Mandala,' he murmured, more to himself than to Raibhu. 'There's no trace of Aaboneer or Nabhang back there, not even in the old houses. All Terrisan.'

He rose to his feet. As he did so, he noticed his own shoes. 'Damn!' he muttered. 'All that red dust!' He searched about inside his pocket, pulled out a handkerchief and quickly wiped his shoes. 'The southern part of what used to be the Grand Highway has now been covered in red dust,' he said, though Raibhu was concentrating on his letter. 'It gets everywhere. You can't travel that road for a furlong without it getting onto your clothes and your shoes.'

He replaced the handkerchief, satisfied himself that all was well, and resumed his perambulations around the room, finally ending up at the desk where Raibhu sat, and where he had put down the book of the Venerable Dayadhan Jijit's teachings. Afhash picked up the book, just as Raibhu, his missive written, looked up.

'Sit, Afhash,' he said, as he stood up and folded the letter. 'I'll be back, let me just pack some clothes for myself.'

It took Raibhu no more than five minutes to go upstairs to his private chamber, to pull out a travelling sack, and fill it with a few changes of clothing. 'Come on,' he told Afhash once he was back in the main room. 'Let's go.' He paused to pick up the letter, and hurried to the door, where Afhash was already waiting for him. It was only when Raibhu had locked the front door and they had reached the gate of the house that Afhash said, 'Damn! I've brought your book along.'

'We'll waste time going back in,' Raibhu muttered, and taking the book from Afhash, shoved it into the travelling sack. 'Come. Headquarters isn't far. Once I've given the letter and talked to the officer on duty, we'll go.'

'I came through Aruka after crossing the river,' Afhash said. 'Let's go back the same way. It's tried and tested.'

Raibhu nodded. 'Whatever you say,' he said, as he shut the gate behind him and hurried down the lane with Afhash in tow. Above them, the Lesser Moon was high enough to be seen, blood-red and perfectly circular, above the trees. Its bigger counterpart, the Greater Moon, would rise perhaps an hour or so from now, and once that was high in the sky, its silvery light would flood the land. Even when, as now, the Greater Moon was only still a sliver.

Afhash looked up at the sky as if reading Raibhu's mind. 'These moons,' he grumbled. 'So much light. If we could wait just another week, the Lesser Moon would be as thin as the Greater Moon is now.' He shook his head. 'Of course, by then, the Greater Moon would be that much bigger. Damn!'

Raibhu nodded absently. 'But we have no option,' he said. 'Come on, Afhash. We have to get across the river, no matter what.'

~

When Raibhu emerged from the headquarters of the Northern Mandala Imperial Justice Force, Afhash was hopping about impatiently. 'Look at the time!' he grumbled, pointing to the Lesser Moon, now high in the sky, with the Greater Moon already beginning to peep over the horizon. 'It's so late; we'll not even be able to get to Aruka at this rate—'

Raibhu was already racing up the lane and towards the main road, where they could see a horse-carriage for hire standing, its horses gleaming silver in the gloom of the night. 'Come on!' he yelled, over his shoulder.

The road connecting Dhaani to Aruka was the Grand Highway, once a road that linked the two biggest cities of Mandala: Dhaani, its capital, in the north; and Raffasi, in the south. Paved with azure-tinted bluestone, the Grand Highway had been slashed in half eighteen years earlier, when, under the leadership of the fanatical Terrisan Sarjaand, Southern Mandala had been created. Sarjaand, who had crowned himself Emperor of the newly formed South Mandala, had immediately adopted a policy of dissociating his fledging empire from even the memories of the united Mandalan Empire. The road from Raffasi to Jurwad, on the northern border of Southern Mandala, still remained, but its blue paving had been obliterated and replaced with red.

From Dhaani to Aruka, though, the Grand Highway still stretched, in the blue it had been since the time of Tanit Mahabeyan.

They got to the stop for the ekduts just as an ekdut bound for Aruka was leaving, and it required much shouting and sprinting to make it aboard. The ekdut had few passengers, and all of them were clustered in the front box of the vehicle, just behind the driver. The second box, in contrast, was empty. Raibhu immediately headed for it, and once he and Afhash were settled in, he said, 'Now. Tell me what this is all about. How Father landed up in prison, how you landed up there too. Everything.'

'I suppose I had better begin with how I met The Elder again,' Afhash says. 'Two years ago.'

~

Year 5473 of the Emergence of Mandala

Night in Sandha. The streets are deserted, and there is only very sparse illumination from the sporadic street lights, flaming torches held in sconces atop stone columns at street corners. Clouds are scudding across the sky, hiding the Lesser Moon completely and obscuring much of the Greater Moon. There is a chill in the air. A large, grand mansion stands on a slight rise, its very location and size a good indication of the wealth and stature of its owner. A window creaks open on the upper floor, and slowly, cautiously, a face looks out and about. It is Afhash. He makes sure there is nobody about, before using the branch of a tree near the window to shin down. A bulging and heavy sack that is slung from his shoulder hinders his progress a bit, but he still makes good time. He reaches the ground undetected, and sets off down a narrow lane.

Ahead of him, he sees a wash of light: a lone street lamp is throwing a pool of yellow light across a strip of ground. In the light, Afhash sees a man walking along carefully, trying to keep to the shadows but not really succeeding. As he moves along in front of Afhash—unaware that he is being followed by the thief—Afhash notices a large bulge in the man's tunic pocket. Afhash's eyes light up: there is an acquisitive gleam in them as he moves forward.

He times the moment precisely: a well-executed stumble, a sharp cry of dismay, and he grabs at the man, ostensibly in an effort to steady himself. Simultaneously, his other hand goes to the man's tunic pocket. Just as he takes out its contents—a package wrapped in an embroidered cloth—Afhash also looks into the man's face.

~

In a gust of dust and flying gravel, the ekdut had come to a halt. Afhash broke off; there was too much of a din outside for him to be able to continue the conversation. The horses were being changed, the exhausted ones being unharnessed and fresh ones from the roadside stable being hitched; there was much neighing and whinnying and stamping of hooves. At the same time, there were passengers alighting, and new passengers climbing aboard. A wave of noise—loud laughter, many people talking excitedly, a baby crying, a man shouting—hit them. A huge crowd, all dressed to the nines, their tunics embroidered with zansal thread and sequins of manodium, their thick cloaks lined with fine yang-pra wool, dyed a deep orange. They had bundles with them, and large sacks. A group of villagers off to a wedding or something. They filled the ekdut, occupying every vacant seat in the front box. A few of them spilled over into the second box as well, cheerfully oblivious of being intrusive.

Afhash glared at them. Raibhu whispered, 'Tell me later.' The longing to know more was there in every line of his face, but there was no help for it.

Only long after, when the chattering, happy crowd had disembarked further down the highway, did Afhash get a chance to get back to his story.

~

Afhash looks into the face of the man. It is Jaadum. A much older Jaadum than that of Afhash's childhood, of course, but also a shabby and somewhat bedraggled Jaadum. He looks at Afhash with no recognition, and Afhash bursts out excitedly: 'Jaadum My Elder! It's me—Afhash! Do you remember me? Afhash. How are Asi My Elder and Raibhu? Where—'

'Stop! Stop, spy! Stop, or I'll shoot!' There is a sudden shout from the far end of the lane, and Afhash and Jaadum instinctively turn away, even as the thump of boots, the sharp hoot of a whistle, and angry shouts pierce the night.

Jaadum runs, and Afhash, not keen on being caught with the loot, runs too. They don't get far; they've barely gone a few yards when their pursuers arrive on the scene. This time they give no warning: the Southern Mandala Law Officer already has his slingshot out; he pulls its flexible leather thong back, the humur-tipped projectile in it targeted at Afhash. Just at that moment, Jaadum looks over his shoulder—and shows a glimpse of the speed and strength of his prime. In one swift movement, he swings himself around, pushing Afhash behind him and placing his own body between Afhash and the law officer. The humur-tipped projectiles slam into Jaadum, one after the other, and he collapses, bleeding profusely, as a shocked Afhash tries to get a grip on what's happening. They are there, huddled in a heap, Afhash's hands and clothes already reddening with Jaadum's blood, when Jaadum whispers frantically to Afhash:

'Call me Wartak, all right? Remember: Wartak. They know me as Wartak, not Jaadum. And never ever say I'm a magician!'

Afhash barely has the time to promise he will do as Jaadum says, before the law officers arrive and clap humur handcuffs on both of them.

~

'That was two years ago,' Afhash said gloomily. 'If it hadn't been for me, perhaps Jaadum the Elder would have been able to escape, finally. He'd been trying to get out of that hell-hole for sixteen years before I bumped into him that night. Sixteen years, imagine.' He shook his head, an expression of mingled bafflement and regret on his face. 'And if it hadn't been for me that night, he wouldn't have been so badly hurt. The law office's sawbones at the prison worked hard on getting out all those humur projectiles that had hit him, but one was buried too deep; in any case, the sawbones said it was unlikely to do any harm.'

'Humur can leak toxins into the blood,' Raibhu remarked.

Afhash looked at him with respect. 'You do read a lot, don't you?'

'And I'm a law officer, too. I know weapons. Go on.'

'Well, as you say, humur leaks toxins. That's what happened with the Elder. A few months back, he started having a lot of pain, nausea, dizziness. The physicians poked about and said that the humur in that projectile was poisoning him. They can't do anything about it.' He grunted, a sound of deep disgust and anguish, combined with guilt. 'It's all because of me. If it hadn't been for me, he wouldn't have got hurt.'

'There's no point bashing yourself over something you

could not have helped,' Raibhu said quietly. 'And I'm pretty sure Father did not blame you for any of it.'

'He didn't,' Afhash agreed. 'But I still feel bad about it.'

There was a long silence. 'Anyway,' Raibhu said. 'Tell me the rest of it. Why is Father in jail? Why did the law officers think he was a spy?'

Afhash rubbed his chin. 'The Elder told me he was arrested eighteen years ago at Jurwad, on the bank of the Sada. He had crossed over from Northern Mandala into Southern'—he broke off, his eyebrows drawing together in puzzlement—'But I never asked him: what was he doing in the North? You said you and your parents had returned to Raffasi even before Southern Mandala was formed.'

Raibhu shook his head in an irritated way, impatient with the interruption. 'A few months after Southern Mandala was formed, Father had to take me across the border to Dhaani. I'll explain later; just go on, please, with what you were saying.'

Afhash was not pleased to have his curiosity brushed aside so summarily, but he complied. 'Well, as I said, he was crossing the border from North into South, and a bunch of Jurwadi warriors in the area pounced on him, accusing him of being a Northern spy. They must have seen him coming across the border, I suppose. And tempers were so high in those days, when Mandala had just split in two. Everybody was suspicious of strangers.' He shook his head, his face reflecting some of the despair Jaadum might have felt then and in the years since. 'Jaadum the Elder was horribly unlucky. The law officers arrested him without evidence, and flung him into prison. Again on no evidence, just suspicion.'

'But—it's been eighteen years! How can he have been in prison for so long?'

Afhash shrugged. 'That's the way things work in the South. Who cares about a suspected Northern spy? They repeatedly tortured him, trying to get him to confess, but they couldn't get anything out of him.'

'Because there was nothing to get out of him,' Raibhu said bitterly.

'True. But they were convinced there was. The Elder went through a succession of prison-keepers, each worse than the other. He has some hair-raising stories to tell, you know. Only someone as strong as him, in body and mind, could have borne it. If I had been in his place, I would have cracked and told them whatever they wanted to hear, even if it was all fiction.'

The ekdut rattled on. Aruka, the last town on the highway in Northern Mandala, was still a way off. Some of the other passengers had alighted at various stops along the way, and now there were just a few people left.

'You said he was trying to escape when you bumped into him,' Raibhu said, after a while. 'Knowing Father, I'd have thought he would have tried to escape long before, not just two years back.'

Afhash nodded. 'He did. He told me he made several attempts. Not just to escape, but to get out of prison any way he could. He bribed prison-keepers with however many tankas he could earn. He made appeals for his release, insisting on his innocence and pointing to the lack of evidence for his imprisonment.'

'Nothing helped?'

'Nothing. They didn't listen to him. When he tried to approach other inmates, asking them to carry a letter for him, or to deliver a message—nobody would agree. They probably thought they would get into trouble too.'

'Messages and letters? Whom was he writing to?'

Afhash shook his head. 'I don't know. I asked him, but he wouldn't say. And he never wrote any letters to send through the permitted means. He was too jittery for that, too scared that a letter would get intercepted.'

A gloomy silence descended on the pair of them. Raibhu, lost in his own thoughts, stared out of the blurry glass of the window, looking at the peaks looming dark and high into the midnight blue of a starlit sky. Afhash, fidgeting about, hooked a finger in his belt and withdrew from it a slingshot which was hidden away under the flap of his tunic. He fiddled with it, testing the strength of the flexible strip of leather, tightening the knots that bound it to the two branches of the forked piece of humur that formed the weapon. Raibhu glanced at him, then back again, out of the window.

Above them, the six stars of the Brihan Punj, the most visible constellation in the sky above Mandala, twinkled brightly.

~

Many millennia ago, just before the Emergence of Mandala

In a clear midnight blue sky, the six stars of the Brihan Punj twinkle. Far below, on Mandala, the constellation is reflected in the vast waters of a lake that covers a huge stretch of land.

In the light of the two moons, one can only see a vague impression of faraway peaks protruding here and there above the water.

On one of these mountaintops, a small group of people meet. They are all gaunt, tired-looking men and women, thin and half-starved.

'We cannot go on like this much longer,' one of them says. 'There is too little to eat for our children, and if we do not move away, we will all die here, in the midst of all this water.'

'But how can we leave?' another speaks up. 'This is where our forefathers lived, this is our land. We cannot go.' The man looks out, across the never-ending sea that surrounds them. 'In any case, where would we go?' he adds, plaintively. 'We are imprisoned here, by the water, and by the demons.'

They sit in silence, their despair surrounding them, sinking them even deeper in the gloom.

'Look,' one of the older women whispers. She points at a distant peak, from which a little star seems to gleam: it is a fire, lit atop the mountain, burning steadily, but so far that it can be seen only as a tiny twinkling spot of light. 'Do you think we could go to him?'

It is said that the saviour of this flooded land and its people was the sage, Mahamandalam Jijit. Mahamandalam not only drained all the water away from the land, freeing it for the people, he also got rid of demons that were plaguing the inhabitants of the land. In their gratitude to Mahamandalam Jijit, the people named their land after him: Mandala.

But that old legend leaves some questions unanswered, or even unasked. Did Mahamandalam Jijit, powerful as he was, accomplish all of this on his own? Was he not helped by some others, as powerful as or even more powerful than him? And—most importantly—where did all the water go?

~

Aruka, modest in size but big in importance, stretched along the northern bank of the Sada. The last stop of the ekduts traversing the Grand Highway from Dhaani to the border with Southern Mandala, this town guarded an especially vulnerable section of the Sada. At Aruka were none of the high mountains, the steep cliffs and rugged boulders that hindered passage across the border elsewhere. Here the Sada flowed relatively unchecked, its currents smooth and gentle, its banks clear. This was where a hostile army, or its spies, might cross over without difficulty; this was where the mutual suspicion between North and South was at its peak.

The ekdut pulled into Aruka with only six people other than Raibhu and Afhash. The others, local villagers by the looks of them, hurried off, probably heading for warm homes and waiting families. Raibhu and Afhash alighted from the ekdut and when they were out of earshot of the other passengers, Raibhu said, 'Which way now?'

Afhash did not answer him immediately; he was looking around, eyes searching for a secluded space. On one side of the road, next to the designated stop for the ekduts, were a handful of shops. Across the road, beyond a belt of trees and some fields, ran the Sada, its course marking the border between Northern Mandala and Southern. Afhash looked up and down the road, and finally pointed to a little grove of trees some distance further.

'There,' he said, moving towards the trees. 'Let's go there.' When they had reached the trees and Afhash had satisfied himself that they were in no danger of being either seen or overheard, he put down his sack and pulled out the rope with the crackers strung on it. 'This is what we're going to do,' he said.

'Are you sure this will work?' Raibhu asked sceptically, as they made their way back to the road. 'It all looks somewhat shaky to me. Too dependent on others,' he added, by way of explanation.

Afhash laughed. 'You'll see. It worked like a dream when I came over. Why shouldn't it work this time too?' He gave Raibhu a reassuring pat on the shoulder. 'Let's first go and see where the nearest outpost is.'

It did not take them long to find it: it was a regional outpost of the Imperial Justice Force, about five hundred yards from the place where the ekdut had stopped. But that was not all they found. This outpost was right on the bank of the Sada River, and the river seemed to have become the focus of a lot of activity. On the opposite bank, in Southern Mandala, huge stonefires had been lit at intervals of perhaps two furlongs. They blazed, flames leaping bright and yellow from a heap of golden, shining fire-stones, illuminating the bank and the river as clearly as if it were daylight. It wasn't even as if the stonefires were confined to this stretch near Aruka; both upstream and down, as far as the eye could see, the stonefires lit up the night.

Raibhu was usually sedate and calm, even in a crisis; this time, he could not stop the curse which rose to his lips. 'Damn it,' he spat out. 'Damn, damn!'

'It's lit up like the Main Square in Raffasi on Festival Day,' Afhash said gloomily. 'How are we ever going to get across that unseen?'

Chapter Three

On the Northern Mandala side of the river, there were no stonefires, but there were flaming torches, held aloft by soldiers who patrolled the riverbank. They walked, each covering a stretch of perhaps a furlong before he turned and went back the same way.

'This wasn't around when you came by, was it?' asked Raibhu.

Afhash shook his head.

'You must have triggered it,' Raibhu said. 'The commander did say there had been a disturbance along the border. They feared an incursion, which is why all this has happened.' He stared out at the stonefires and the patrolling soldiers, his mind working.

'There probably aren't too many soldiers patrolling on the southern side,' Afhash observed. 'We don't have that many soldiers in our army.'

Raibhu nodded. 'That's why they're compensating with the stonefires. The stonefires are pretty effective,' he added, in a bitter voice. 'They'd be able to see a moth fluttering over the river in that light.'

They crept back, away from the riverbank. Raibhu was still deep in thought.

'I doubt if the stonefires would extend all the way along the border,' Afhash said, after they had been walking a couple of minutes. 'It would take too many fire-stones, and someone would need to keep the fires going, too. Perhaps if we went north? To where the Naham rises? The mountains there are so high, so inaccessible, that I'm pretty sure there wouldn't be any stonefires around—'

Raibhu was already shaking his head, and now he interrupted before Afhash could complete the sentence. 'No, that would take up too much time. We wouldn't get there before daybreak, and trying to cross in broad daylight would be too dangerous, even in a place like that. Besides,' he added, 'have you seen the Sada in that region, just before it joins the Naham? It's a torrent, a series of really dangerous rapids. We'd get swept away before we knew what was happening.' He shook his head. 'No, Afhash, if we're taking the risk of crossing the river, I'd rather do it in a place where there's a ford of some sort, or the water's still—' he broke off, his eyes widening in sudden realization.

'What?—' Afhash began to say, but Raibhu was already tugging at his arm, hurrying him towards the main settlement.

'Don't talk,' Raibhu said, almost dragging his friend along. 'Hurry! Come along, we need to find horses, and some good strong rope! By the Spirits, will this place even have shops open at this hour?' He was running now, and Afhash, bewildered, raced after him.

'What?' Afhash panted, running alongside Raibhu, trying to understand what was happening.

'I'll tell you,' Raibhu assured him, 'later. Come on, now—

ah, here, this might be where we can find some rope.' They had reached the row of small shops that stood on the main street of Aruka. It had few shops, and not much variety in the way of things to be bought. The very basics were available, and often those too were moth-eaten and old.

'Rope,' said Raibhu, half to himself as he looked around, his eyes scanning the shops.

'I've got rope,' Afhash said, 'you've seen it. It won't take much to remove the fire crackers from it.'

Raibhu shook his head. 'No, that rope is too flimsy. I need something much thicker, more sturdy. Here, this shop. He will have it, I think, among those baskets and mats he's selling.'

Five minutes later, they were hurrying down the street, heading for the stables pointed out by the shopkeeper in response to Raibhu's question. Raibhu had a very large, thick coil of rope hanging on his shoulder; Afhash had another, an identical one, on his shoulder. The rope was heavy, and by the time they reached the stable, he was sweating and breathing hard. The stable was a long wooden shed divided into stalls with ropes, the interior smelling of hay and horse manure. Several pitch torches, stuck into sconces along the walls, lit up the stable, illuminating some eight or nine horses, all the traditional Northern Mandala whites. They were not the fine, glossy-coated mounts Raibhu was used to, but neither were they ill-fed and scrawny. They would do.

'We need horses till the village of Sada-Jal,' Raibhu said to the groom who emerged from behind one of the stalls, a steaming bucket in one hand, a piece of dirty sacking in the other. 'How many tankas for two horses? And is there any place we can leave them in Sada-Jal, from where you can have them collected?'

~

'Sada-Jal?' said Afhash, as they rode into the night. The last twinkling lamps of Aruka fell behind them, but the two moons, both now high in the sky, bathed the landscape with enough light to make the broad blue-paved surface of the Grand Highway glitter bright as zansal. 'Why are we going to Sada-Jal?'

'I went to Sada-Jal a few days back,' Raibhu replied. 'I think we'll be able to cross over there, let's see. It's not too far, less than an hour from Aruka. Let's at least try at Sada-Jal before thinking of other options. If we can cross there, we will not need to travel far to the north.'

Afhash looked as if he wanted to ask more questions, but Raibhu was too intent on getting them to Sada-Jal as soon as possible. Afhash settled himself into his saddle and concentrated on riding; unlike Raibhu, he could not afford a horse of his own, and the handful of times he had been on one were not enough to have made him a horseman of any standard. It required all his focus to make sure he stayed in the saddle and the horse obeyed him.

When they drew rein, it was at the village that took its name from the Sada-Jal Reservoir. Sada-Jal village was not as large as Aruka, but it seemed less sleepy. There were surprising signs, too, of a modernity and an air of busy commerce that were at odds with its size and its remoteness.

Raibhu looked up at the sky, where the Lesser Moon had already reached its zenith, while the Greater Moon was still rising. He glanced at the cluster of shops that lay ahead of them, on the fringe of Sada-Jal village.

'It's too early to attempt anything just now,' he murmured. 'Let's go and eat something, then we can find the stable and return these horses.'

'This village isn't anything like what I'd expected,' Afhash remarked as they rode on, towards the shops. 'It's busy, it has the air of a big town rather than a village.'

'That's because of the reservoir,' Raibhu said. 'The Sada-Jal Reservoir was built two hundred years ago by one of the emperors to stock fish and game, you see, and he and his courtiers would come here for shooting and hunting. Later, even when the hunting stopped, this remained a popular picnic spot.' They had reached the row of shops, and Raibhu dismounted. Afhash followed suit, somewhat painfully; his lack of familiarity with horse-riding meant that even this ride, of barely an hour, had left him stiff and sore.

'In autumn, the reservoir and the mountains are very beautiful,' Raibhu continued, even as he examined the row of shops for one where they could eat something. 'The slopes around are covered with gold and orange and red: it's spectacular. The well-heeled come in droves from Dhaani, for picnics. That's why this village is so important: it caters to the tourists.'

He stopped. 'This looks like a likely place. Should we eat?'

He indicated a restaurant, the entire front of it taken up by a low counter which functioned as a combined larder and workbench. On it sat two huge purple pumpkins, baskets full of white bean pods and an assortment of leaves, ranging from the tiny fingernail-sized pungent herb known as lahargam, to the large, yellow-and-green-striped leaves that were used in salads. There were other odds and ends, jars of ground spices and sacks of grain, as well as a large glass urn containing the vibrant orange oil which was used to cook most of the food.

Beyond the workbench was a single rectangular fire-pit, its depths crowded with glowing golden fire-stones. The fire-pit was crisscrossed by heavy humur rods that hung above it, and from which were suspended an array of cauldrons and vertically rotating spits. Above one end of the fire-pit was a thick slab of stone, which was being used to bake triangular flatbreads. One cook manned this end, pressing out dough and slapping it onto the hot stone, while the pots and skewers across the rest of the pit were overseen by two others. These cooks, dressed in leather aprons, stirred cauldrons, rotated spits, and ladled out bowlfuls of simmering stew to the lone waiter on duty. He was a skinny boy, lavishly pimpled and knock-kneed, bustling about urgently, at the beck and call of the cooks as well as the handful of patrons who were eating there. They sat on scattered bits of rough furniture, mostly three-legged stools and a couple of old benches.

Raibhu tethered their horses at a post beside the restaurant, and managed to wheedle a rough, heavy bench out of the waiter, who went off to fetch their food from the fire-pit. As soon as he was gone, Raibhu moved the bench to a more secluded spot a few yards further away. 'Nobody will be able to eavesdrop here,' he said, 'without us seeing them first.'

Afhash nodded. He was staring enviously at the fire-pit. 'Even in such a remote place as this, they've got fire-stones fuelling their fire!' he said. 'They must make a lot of money, to be able to afford a fire-pit.'

Raibhu was matter-of-fact in his response. 'They get good business when tourists visit. And for them, fire-stones make more sense than wood, anyway. Wood will burn up and need to be replaced within a couple of hours. Fire-stones keep going for hours on end; they do half their cooking through the night, over the dampened embers of the fire-stones.'

'Anyway, while we're waiting, tell me about yourself,' Raibhu said, settling down on the bench with his travelling sack on his crossed legs. 'How did you end up a thief? Not that I should be surprised—' He broke off, cuffed sharply by an indignant Afhash.

Afhash's indignation was not in earnest, and blew over quickly. 'What else was there for me to do,' he finally said, in a resigned voice. 'Mehjaan the Elder died, just a couple of months after all of you left. He had gone to Raffasi for some work, and when he was coming back, the ekdut he was travelling in toppled over. It tipped into a deep ravine; nobody survived. After that, what could I do? There were his things, and some money, but I didn't want to touch those. They weren't mine.' He shook his head, as if remembering those long-ago days of being lonely and adrift. 'Jaadum the Elder had given me some tankas when you left for Dhaani. But after a while the tankas started running out, and there was no sign of any of you. What could I do but go back to the only way I knew to stay alive?'

~

Year 5456 of the Emergence of Mandala

It is a sunny day in Raffasi's main market. The high street is lined by luxurious emporia, their façades pearl grey and turquoise, their star-shaped windows and tall doors accented with lines of zansal. This is where the wealthy of Southern Mandala go to buy their silverwood furniture, their jewels and brocades, their sada stones and golbols. Horse-carriages stand on the street outside, and attendants rush in and out of shops, ferrying piles of goods from shops to carriages. The tunics of these wealthy people are heavy with precious stones and embroidery; the men's turbans are double the size of their heads, and the women's necklaces hang to their waists.

On the other side, behind the stylishness of the emporia, is a market of a different sort. This is cramped and smelly, the shops no more than rough stalls made of wood. Here are sold the items used by the poorer of Raffasi's population: wooden and terracotta utensils, everyday cloth, baskets, fruit, vegetables, grain. This is barebones, no-frills trade. Shopkeepers call out to passersby, encouraging them to try their wares; others haggle with buyers. Shop assistants scurry about, hauling loads into shops, rushing up and down the lanes with handcarts loaded with bulging sacks. There are beggars and itinerant entertainers, a few idle loungers drinking infusions of dreamflower and calmroot outside a stall. The drowsiness of a summer day mingles with the bustle and liveliness of a busy marketplace.

Suddenly, the calm is shattered by an angry shout. 'Thief! Thief! Stop that child—he's picked my pocket!'

Afhash, a small and dirty figure, comes racing down the lane, weaving swiftly in and out between the crowds. He's so intent on shaking off the pursuit that he doesn't look where he's going, and almost stumbles to the ground when an arm whips out from a narrow alley. A hand grabs his arm. Afhash, eyes wide and terrified, stares up...

...and stumbles back, as he's thrown to the ground. This ground is not the cobbled stone of the Raffasi bazaar; it is the shale and dust of the upper reaches of the mountains flanking the Sada Valley. Around Afhash stand other children, very much like him: small, thin, dirty, and scared. Beyond them, keeping guard, stand a few men, hard-bitten and muscular, several of them wearing projectile-hurling slingshots in addition to their daggers.

'Take care,' says a voice, low and menacing. 'Take care you do nothing I will disapprove of.' The man pauses, and a stubby finger reaches out to tilt little Afhash's head up. 'Hmm.' The man says. 'I think you have nobody here to care for you, yes? All alone, poor child.' The words may be gentle, but the tone is at odds with the words. The man's hand slips around Afhash's shoulders, clamping him to the man's body. 'Come, then, child. I will help you. Yes? And you will help me. Help all of us.'

~

'They were mining sada stones in the Sada Valley,' Afhash said, 'and orphaned children, or children who had run away, or been kidnapped—we were the miners.'

They were interrupted by the arrival of the waiter, who brought their food and drink. Triangular flatbreads on a triangular plate; a pyramid-shaped fried dough encasing vegetables; a large bowl in the shape of an inverted pyramid, filled with purple pumpkin chopped into wedges and cooked with meat. A quick trip back to the counter, and the waiter brought two conical tumblers full of calmroot infusion.

Having put everything on the bench, the waiter traced a triangle in the air above the rough wood of it and recited the customary intonation. 'May the Land, the Sky and the Water bless your meal.' Afhash and Raibhu dipped their heads, readying to eat; but the waiter was in no hurry to leave. He was a curious lad, and eager to chat. He wanted to know where they had come from. Big city gentlemen—he looked fawningly at Raibhu—usually came in the autumn, not in summertime, when the Sada-Jal Reservoir was hardly worth seeing. Would they be staying? There was a small travellers' inn that was still open, though the others, owned by outsiders, were shut for the season. He did not seem to realize that he was interrupting, or that the two men wanted to be on their own.

'I was under the impression Northern Mandala wasn't terribly crowded,' Afhash grumbled once the waiter had gone. 'I'll tell you, Raibhu, but let's eat, please. It's been more than a day since I ate.'

Raibhu ate slowly, hardly paying attention to what he was eating: it was as if it made no difference to him. He could see, however, that Afhash was ravenous, so he waited until the other man had finished eating. Then, as they were sipping their calmroot infusion, he said, 'I take it you managed to escape from the sada stone mines.'

'I did. It was horrible. Every other day someone died, or was killed.'

~

A hand, its fingers long and elegant, with a beautiful ring on one finger. The ring is studded with a blood-red sada stone, in the depths of which throbs a pulse that echoes the heartbeat of the wearer. This sada stone pulsates gently at its heart; its wearer is relaxed and calm as he fiddles with the ring, the fingers weaving in and out. Beyond, a boy goes sprawling in the dust. A man, sweaty and dusty, places a booted foot on the child's back and says, 'This is the one who tried to run away, Master.'

The ring is rotated around the finger, slowly, playfully. Then: 'So we must show him how much we love little children, shouldn't we?' says that suave voice, macabre humour dripping from its tone. 'Let's help him. If he wants to leave this place, help him do so. Send him on his way.' The finger lifts, then sweeps to one side, in a cutting gesture. The man bends his head in acquiescence. He pulls his dagger from his belt, and before the boy can even grasp what is happening, the man has bent down to slit his throat. A bloodcurdling shriek rings out, echoing through the mountains.

~

'We barely got anything to eat, and we were beaten regularly,' Afhash said, the memories of those long-ago days clouding his face. 'You slipped and fell, you were beaten. You took too long, you were beaten. You didn't find enough sada stones in one day, you were beaten. Can you imagine what it was like?'

Raibhu reached across and placed a hand on Afhash's knee. 'How long were you there?' he asked gently.

'Two years. It felt like a lifetime.' Afhash sighed.

'I'm sorry,' Raibhu said. 'I truly am, Afhash. We were already back in Raffasi by then, Mother, Father and I. We had gone to Mehjaan the Elder's home as soon as we returned, but of course, he was dead; and nobody knew where you had gone... we searched. So many places. The bazaars, the riverside, even the infirmaries and the Terrisan Sanctuary; but we couldn't find you anywhere. I wish we had not given up looking.' He shook his head, his lips pursed into a thin line of regret.

Afhash smiled at him, a weak smile but sincere. 'I was not as badly off as the others,' he said. 'I was wilier than them, possibly more hardened too. They hadn't grown up on the streets; I had that advantage over them. And I was smaller than most of them.'

~

A noise like prolonged thunder, growing louder by the moment, fills the air as a cloud of dust rises. Terrified screams pierce the rumble, and then there is silence. Through the haze of dust, the dark mouth of a cave becomes visible. The darkness is deep, and inside it echo whimpers, screams, the sound of someone scrabbling among the stones. Little Afhash's face, covered with dust and streaked with blood, comes into view as he pushes his way out from behind a boulder: it has been his shelter in the recent rock fall. He wriggles out and looks about, but there is nothing to be seen except the dead bodies of a couple of other children.

Afhash moves, crouched over, towards the right, where there is the semblance of a path. With some effort, he manages to shift some rocks aside: beyond, far beyond, he can see a pinprick of light. His eyes narrow as he focuses. Behind him, from the mouth of the cave, come the sounds of approaching men. Hammers thud against rock, and boulders roll away. A man shouts, 'They can't be too far now.'

Afhash plunges into the narrow neck of space he sees in front of him. He wriggles along, heading for the light.

~

Raibhu drew in a long, deep breath. 'That must have been harrowing,' he said.

Afhash nodded. 'It was, and half the skin was scraped off me by the time I managed to get out. But I didn't care. I came upon a string of wagons carrying sand to Raffasi, and stowed away in them. After that, I shuttled between Raffasi, Sandha and the nearby towns, not staying more than a few months anywhere. I was so terrified of being caught again.' He washed his hands from the stone trough nearby. 'And I made sure to keep a low profile. The first time I dared to try my hand at something beyond picking pockets was when I met Jaadum the Elder again.'

He wiped his hands briskly on his tunic and stood up, stretching. 'It's pretty late, there aren't too many people around now. What do you think? Should we go?' The waiter had again surfaced, looking with puppy-dog eyes at Raibhu and asking anxiously whether the food had been to his liking. Raibhu assured him that yes, the food had been good; and then he asked the boy, 'Where is the stable, do you know? We are supposed to leave these horses there.'

The stable was not far, the boy said. It could be seen, there: he pointed towards it, standing beside the larger, more streamlined building on which the shining zansal emblem of the Northern Mandala Army, three crossed swords forming a triangle, could be seen glinting in the moonlight. 'There, Master,' he said, 'right next to the Army outpost.'

Raibhu bit his lip and exchanged a quick glance with Afhash. They did not need to say what was in both their minds; two strangers, at a time of the year when Sada-Jal village was not inundated with visitors, had already attracted the curiosity of the waiter. To go near the Army outpost might invite greater attention, even outright suspicion. They could not run that risk.

'Will you do us a favour,' said Raibhu, reaching into his tunic pocket for a tanka. 'While my friend and I have a look at the inn, will you go and hand over our horses at the stable? Thank you.'

The waiter was eager to please, and the tanka had been that extra incentive he had needed. He pocketed the tanka and hurried away towards the two horses.

'Come on,' Raibhu said to Afhash. 'Let's go.' He led the way, heading for the fringe of the forest that lay beyond the fields abutting the road and the shops. Most of the shops had shut by now, and except for a few lamps at the restaurant, a shop selling infusions, and a small coal depot, there were no more lights. The huts that formed the village spread out further along, well behind them. All that lay ahead was the forest, and the river, the Sada-Jal Reservoir.

At the edge of the restaurant, the waiter had begun to untie the two horses from the post. He liked horses; he patted and cooed to the animals as he untied their ropes. A few yards away, the cooks were shutting shop, cleaning their counters, wiping up their tools, lowering a large cauldron of lentils into the fire pit to cook in the embers through the night. A shower of sparks flew up into the air, suddenly illuminating the side of one of the horses. In that momentary brightness, the waiter noticed something. He stared, his mouth open; then he moved across and pulled out one of the flaming torches from a post beside the counter.

He held it an angle beside the horse and peered at the stirrup that hung down the horse's flank. Where the rider's shoe sole had rested, dried mud had been left on the stirrup. Red mud.

'Spies!' the waiter shrieked, his suspicions confirmed. 'Spies! They were spies from the South!'

~

Raibhu and Afhash were well inside the shadow of the trees, but they heard the panicked screaming of the waiter. For a moment, the two of them froze, and looked back simultaneously before taking to their heels. 'Damn it!' Afhash swore. 'How did he guess?!'

Raibhu did not answer; he was busy weaving his way in and out of the trees, racing for the Sada-Jal Reservoir.

And there it was. From between the trees that stood along its bank, they saw the water gleaming in the moonlight, still and reflective as a mirror. On the far bank, the Southern Mandalan stonefires still burned bright; on this bank, Raibhu and Afhash could see a Northern soldier walking in measured steps along the bank, patrolling the riverside.

A hand on Afhash's sleeve, Raibhu drew his friend away, indicating a tall tree nearby. He whispered something in Afhash's ear, and while Afhash sat down and quickly undid the two coils of rope both men had been carrying, Raibhu rummaged about in the undergrowth. It took him a few minutes of searching to find something that suited his purpose. It was a forked stick, the end of a branch. Raibhu pulled out his dagger and quickly cut away the end of the stick, leaving a piece about five inches long.

'Afhash, give me your slingshot,' he said. Already, they could hear shouts as the alarm was raised. The waiter had run off to the outpost to summon the soldiers, and they had begun searching the woods. Afhash had finished opening out the rope; he handed it to Raibhu and looked back in the direction of the village. Their pursuers were still far, but it was only a matter of a few minutes before they would catch up with their quarry.

'Raibhu,' Afhash said, 'you do what you need to. Give me a moment, I'll try and distract them.' Saying that, he got to his feet, pulling out the rope of fire crackers that he had been carrying in his travelling sack.

'Afhash—' Raibhu began to say, though his hands did not stop moving, as he knotted the end of the thick rope around the forked stick and began climbing the tree with the slingshot in his belt, and the forked stick with its trailing rope slung over his shoulder. He had already put a firm knot tying together the two lengths of rope they had bought; their combined length was now enough to stretch several times beyond the height of the tree.

'I'll be back!' Afhash replied, racing off into the night, away from the tree.

Raibhu was more than halfway up the tree when the distant shouts and sounds of pursuit were interrupted by the first of a series of sharp bangs. It was in the opposite direction to the Sada-Jal Reservoir: Afhash must have run very close by the village, and gone further on, leading the soldiers on a wild goose chase. Well away from Raibhu.

Raibhu went on climbing, stopping briefly at the stoutest branches along the way, wrapping the rope around them once or twice. By the time he reached the top of the tree, he had used up about a quarter of the rope thus, but at least it was now firmly anchored around the tree. From his vantage point, Raibhu looked out at the still waters of the Sada-Jal Reservoir, the stonefires of Southern Mandala bright beyond it. Reflected in the waters of the reservoir on the near side were dead trees, many of them very old. The reservoir had not been repaired for years, and the wall of stones across the river was broken in places: not enough to allow the water through, but no longer very sturdy either.

Raibhu's gaze settled on one particular dead tree that stood right at the edge of the reservoir, its shadow falling across the moonlit surface of the reservoir wall. It was a massive old tree, its roots exposed where they clung to the reservoir wall, clamping down like fingers amidst the stones.

The shouts had faded away, the pursuers distracted by the fire crackers that Afhash had exploded. Hopefully he would be headed back, hopefully he was safe and well.

Raibhu lifted the slingshot with the forked stick pressed against the leather. He had made a heavy knot at the stick end of the rope, to make it easier to control the end of the rope, to make it go where he wanted it to. Barely stopping to take aim, he let fly at the dead tree he had pinpointed. The stick flew, pulling the rope behind it. Just as the stick touched the dead tree, Raibhu tugged sharply at the rope, altering its trajectory. The rope swung around the tree, tightening around it.

As soon as he was certain it was as tight as he needed

it to be, Raibhu shinned down the tree, pulling the rope behind him as he went down. He was still descending the trunk when he heard the soft swish of someone running through the trees from the direction of the village. Raibhu paused for a moment, his free hand going to his dagger, but it was only Afhash.

Raibhu did not even bother to get to the ground before he grabbed the rope where it hung beside the tree trunk. Afhash arrived at the foot of the tree, panting, and Raibhu snapped out an order: 'Quick! Grab the rope and pull as hard as you can!' He swung himself down from the tree, and together the two men leaned in, pulling with all their might. Their strength, combined with the leverage provided by the sturdy tree, the rope wrapped around its limbs at strategic places, took effect within a matter of moments.

The dead tree at which Raibhu had aimed may have been once a giant, but it was a hollow giant now, its wood fragile and brittle, its trunk bulky but without a tenth of the strength it might have had a hundred or two hundred years ago. A loud creak filled the air, then a harsh shrieking, a ripping sound as if the ghost of the dead tree was wailing into the night. 'Left, left!' gasped Raibhu. 'Lean to the left! Yes!' With the sweat pouring down their faces, the tendons standing out along their necks, they strained.

With an increasing shudder, the great tree began to shiver and tremble, and then, with a loud tearing sound that could surely be heard all the way to the village and beyond, it came down with a mighty crash and a splintering and a splash, falling across the reservoir wall as it did so. The tree may not have been as sturdy as it once was, but it was still massive, and its roots, clinging to the stones of the wall, had made their way deep into every nook and cranny along the portion around the tree. Those roots now clawed out stones, and the weight of the tree did the remaining work. The wall crumbled away, its stones crashing and splashing, the water rushing forward, suddenly freed.

The weight of the water was enough to complete what the tree had begun; with a gurgle that grew instantly into a thunderous whoosh, the water of the reservoir broke free of its now ruined wall. The Sada breached its banks.

Raibhu and Afhash had run upstream, upriver of the now erstwhile Sada-Jal Reservoir, as soon as the tree had collapsed. Crouching low, they made their way through the reeds fringing the riverbank. Downriver, as the water surged over the banks and spilled onto the land, the blazing stonefires went out, some toppled right over and submerged so suddenly that all that was left of them was great clouds of steam hanging in the moonlit night; others, a little further away from the rush of the water, flickered, their flames wavering until every crack in each fire-stone filled with enough water for the stone to finally stop burning.

In the dark, shouts rang out on both sides of the river: Northerners and Southerners, the soldiers and perhaps the civil populace, too, at least of Sada-Jal village, were out in full force along the riverfront. They were all of them clustered around where the reservoir had been; on the Northern side, some already beginning to wade into the water, trying to repair the breach, put stones back together while the water swirled and rushed all about them. On the Southern bank, there was less activity; there were fewer people there, perhaps only the soldiers deputed along this stretch. Some of them held aloft torches in a weak attempt to replicate what the stonefires had done to illuminate the riverbank, but it was useless.

And further upstream, clear of the people thronging the riverbank, well away from even a chance glance in that area, Raibhu and Afhash crossed the Sada.

~

A couple of hours later, several furlongs downstream from Aruka, they finally crawled out of the river, on the southern side of the border. Night had settled in, and it was quiet.

They were both soaked through, and Afhash was shivering loud enough for his teeth to chatter. 'Damn that stupid waiter!' he grumbled. 'I wonder what alerted him? How did he guess I was from the South?'

Raibhu shrugged. 'Are you keen on crossing the river again and going back to ask him?' He grinned. 'Let it be; we'll never know. Let us go on and find a place to shelter. I don't know how far we are from Sandha, but I'm certain we'll need to take an ekdut or something to get there.'

Afhash nodded. 'First we need to get to the road,' he added. 'And, vaanik; not ekdut. In the South, they're called vaaniks. There won't be any running at this hour of the night. We could rest a while.'

They moved on, further away from the riverbank and further away, too, from the danger of being anywhere close to the border. This part of Southern Mandala was sparsely populated, and the forests across the river from Sada-Jal meant that, other than the soldiers deployed in the area, there were not even any villages nearby. If Raibhu and Afhash kept low and got away from the vicinity of the river quickly, they could hope to go undetected.

They were soon far enough for even the sound of the river to have melted into the silence of the night.

'That was a stroke of genius, using the water to put out the stonefires,' Afhash remarked as they moved through the forest, looking for a clearing where they could rest for a while. 'Those stonefires were huge, weren't they? I'm surprised the Army here hit upon that idea. I wouldn't have thought they'd have had the sense for something like that.'

'They don't have as many soldiers as we do in the North,' Raibhu replied. 'And by lighting up the border where it's most vulnerable, those stonefires help do the work of several soldiers. Besides, the stonefires don't need to be fed at regular intervals through the night. Once they've been ignited, they keep burning for hours.'

'And why doesn't your lot follow the example? Those stonefires are bloody effective.'

Raibhu could not suppress a laugh. 'Since when have you heard of either of our lands following the example of the other? If the South says nay, the North *will* say yea. And vice-versa, even if all logic says otherwise.' He pushed aside a branch. 'Look at that,' he said, stepping forward. 'What do you think of that clearing, eh? Shall we camp here for a while?'

Afhash looked over his shoulder. 'Looks good to me,' he said. 'Come along, then. We can let our clothes dry while we rest. And, you can tell me what you've been doing these past eighteen years. I told you everything, but you haven't said a word.'

~

'You've been with Father these past couple of years,' Raibhu said, 'How come he didn't tell you what happened?'

Afhash used a long twig to poke at the fire they had lit. It was a small fire, but necessary, because that was the only way they could hope to get their tunics—at least—dry. 'Jaadum the Elder has never told me anything about you,' he replied. 'I've asked several times, both about you and about Asi the Elder, but he has always evaded it. He tells me she died, and that you went away. Where, he doesn't say. And why, too, he doesn't say. All he says is it hurts too much to remember.'

Raibhu had been busy rigging up a rough trellis of fallen branches; with Afhash's help, he now draped their damp tunics across this and moved it closer to the fire. Afhash chatted on as they worked. 'Jaadum the Elder is very cagey,' he said. 'Suspicious of pretty much everybody around. The prison-keepers, of course. They were a nasty lot, all except this last one. But the Elder even thinks most of the other prisoners are somehow part of a huge conspiracy.'

'Conspiracy?' Raibhu said. 'What sort of conspiracy?'

'I don't know. But he seems terrified of being discovered. That's why he calls himself Wartak, and he told them, when he was first arrested, that he sold trinkets for a living. Not that he was Jaadum the magician.' Afhash shook his head, as if putting the thought aside. 'Let that be. Tell me about yourself, everything.'

'It's a long story,' Raibhu said, as he looked up at the stars. 'And I have no idea what it all means.'

~

Year 5457 of the Emergence of Mandala, a few months after the formation of Southern Mandala

Night in Raffasi. A two-storeyed wooden house, its balcony overlooking a large garden, stands in a secluded lane abutting the woods beyond. There are no other buildings in the vicinity; above, the two moons shine down onto the house and the trees surrounding it.

Inside a room at the back of the house, little Raibhu, about ten years old, is sitting at a table and reading a book. As he turns a page, he stiffens: he's heard a sound outside. It's followed immediately by other sounds: the hoofbeats of approaching horses; many horses, far more than there should be in any one place for any legitimate purpose. Raibhu looks worried and quickly blows out the flame of the lamp beside him, which is the only light in the room. He goes to the window and looks out. A couple of hundred yards from the house, he can see a large group of horsemen approaching: there are at least thirty of them, and a third or so carry flaming torches held high above their heads. There is something distinctly ominous about the approaching group, and as they draw closer, the sounds of the horses, the men, the fire they carry, fill the air.

Raibhu withdraws from the window, and looks about, searching for an escape route. He hurries to the door of the room, and goes towards the rooms facing the back of the house. There are windows here, overlooking the trees behind the house.

Raibhu is just reaching up to open one of the windows, when a shadow rises beyond it, a hand balled up into a fist, wrapped in cloth...there is a muffled crunch as the fist breaks the glass. Raibhu has reeled back at the first sign of the intruder, but when he sees who climbs in, he hurries forward, relieved. 'Father!'

The bright light of the two moons has silhouetted Jaadum all this while, and only when he turns towards his son does Raibhu notice that something is wrong: one sleeve of Jaadum's tunic has been torn off, and there's a deep gash in one pant leg, through which his bloodied leg can be seen. There are more bloodstains, some of them vicious and frightening, on other parts of his clothing as well as his hands.

Raibhu is stunned; in the same moment, he realizes something else, too: Jaadum is alone. 'Father,' he whispers. 'Where is Mother? Is she downstairs?'

Jaadum, his face strained and blood-streaked, hugs his son close. 'Your Mother,' he whispers, 'is dead. She was killed.'

'No! No, Mother can't be dead—' Raibhu stares up into his father's face. Jaadum nods, and holds Raibhu even closer. Raibhu sobs, burying his face in Jaadum's shoulder. His father does not allow him much time to mourn. 'Raibhu,' he says, soon after, 'We have to get out of here.' To the sounds of the horses and men outside has been added another sound: a loud banging, as the men at the forefront attack the gate of the house and try to break it down. Even as Jaadum talks, there is a sharp screech and then a loud crash as the gate finally collapses.

Raibhu puts aside his grief for his mother and moves towards the broken window through which Jaadum had entered. 'This way, Father,' he says. 'If we go down now, we can escape through the back.'

But Jaadum stops him. 'No, Raibhu,' he says. 'Not right now. We need to do something first.'

'Father! We don't have time, they've already come in—!' Panic is now beginning to seep into Raibhu's face and his tone.

'Yes, but we have to do something else, it's important.' Jaadum pulls Raibhu away from the window. 'Listen to me, son. I know what I'm doing. Come with me.'

Raibhu looks unconvinced, but he obediently follows Jaadum to a small room at one end of this upper floor. Tucked away at the back of the house, overlooking the trees behind the house, this is some sort of storage space, an attic or junkyard or both: it is full of odds and ends, bric-a-brac that spills out of chests and shelves and sacks on the floor. Jaadum rummages about among the items and pulls out a fake skeleton, which is soot-stained, and several old bedsheets. From another shelf he gets down various props and costumes, including a wig and makeup. These he puts into a sack, while he hands the bedsheets to Raibhu. 'Make knots,' he instructs his son. 'You'll need to climb down these.' While Raibhu is knotting the sheets, Jaadum goes to the room next door and gets two sturdy pieces of wood from the fireplace. He tears up one of the sheets into rags, and wrapping the rags around the ends of the wood, he fashions two torches. From the fireplace, he also picks up more bits of wood, and ties them up in a bundle along with some of the rags. He nods at Raibhu: they're ready. The show must begin. 'Take the sack with you,' Jaadum instructs Raibhu. 'They're our disguises, don't leave them behind.'

Out in the garden, the group of men is jolted out of their wait by the sound of a door opening. On the upper balcony facing the garden, Jaadum emerges, holding a flaming torch in each hand. 'You were waiting for me,' he calls out defiantly. 'Here I am!' Of the men, several run into the house. Their booted feet can be heard pounding up the stairs, even as Jaadum continues. 'You murdered my wife, but don't think you'll get away with it! I will avenge her!' The men who had entered the house burst out on to the balcony from the staircase that goes up the house from the front.

'You will not get the better of me!' Jaadum shouts. The men swarm in on him from either side, and he lashes out at them with the torches.

Behind Jaadum, in the dark room that abuts the balcony, Raibhu watches as the curtains at the windows separating the room from the balcony billow. One of the torches Jaadum is holding comes in contact with a curtain, and it catches fire. Raibhu moves forward, crouching as he lights a candle and holds it to a bundle of rags, beneath which is a pile of twigs and bits of wood salvaged from the fireplace. When the rag has caught fire, he holds it near the flaming curtain, on the inside. The fire quickly spreads, feeding off the rag and the wood, and simultaneously the curtains, the furnishings, and the woodwork. Outside, Jaadum battles his attackers. Inside, Raibhu stands well back from the inferno and screams. His cries are audible even above the increasing roar of the flames.

After a few moments, Raibhu backs away towards the window at the back of the room. From this window hang the knotted bedsheets: Raibhu goes down them swiftly, with the sack slung over his shoulder. Once he reaches the ground, he retrieves a tinderbox from his pocket. Even though so young, he's already an expert at quickly teasing a spark from the tinder. As soon as there's a tiny spurt of flame, he holds it to the end of the sheet. Once it's caught fire, he tosses the sheet up expertly back into the room.

Raibhu darts away to the side, crouching in the shelter offered by a high hedge. From here, he can see some of the remaining men who are still standing on the lawn, looking up at the bright orange and gold of the flames above. The only man who does not look up at the balcony is the one standing well back from the others. He is tall, and there is something brooding about the way he has his head lowered. Even as Raibhu watches, a portion of the balcony collapses and the shower of sparks illuminates the scene vividly for a moment. Raibhu sees that the lone man wears something on the side of his head that glitters momentarily in the light.

Within moments, the rest of the balcony has also collapsed. There is mayhem, and Jaadum, taking advantage of it, slips away, using a water pipe to climb down because the stairs are aflame. He meets up with Raibhu and the two of them climb quickly over the wall. Amid the sounds of the roaring fire, there can be heard screams of pain and shouts from the men who are rushing about, trying to find Jaadum and their companions amidst the inferno.

'Come on,' Jaadum says to Raibhu, taking the sack from him. They run, making their way through the trees and staying away from the road. Only when they're far away from the house and Jaadum is certain they aren't being followed yet, do they stop, beside a stream. From the sack, Jaadum pulls out the disguises for both of them. While Raibhu changes into the clothes brought for him—he is now disguised as a girl, his hair concealed beneath an embroidered scarf, his tunic a more flowing one, his shoes and pants delicate—Jaadum

cleans himself up with water from the stream. As he's washing off the blood, tying up the wound on his leg, and putting on clean clothes, Raibhu pelts him with questions. 'Were those the Emperor's men, Father? And why did we not just run away right then? It would have been so much easier.'

Jaadum pauses, thinking before he answers. He ignores Raibhu's first question, though. 'These are the people who killed your mother,' he says. 'They won't stop at anything; they will kill you too, if they think you're still alive.' He pulls out a fake beard and moustache from the sack, along with glue which he uses to affix them. 'The house is likely to burn down. If not to the ground, at least enough to destroy the top storey. They may find the skeleton, and will hopefully assume it's you. That means you have to stay hidden. Until I can solve this problem, you must live as if you were dead.'

Raibhu, tying a scarf around his head, looks up. 'How will I do that, Father? And why do you say I must live as if I were dead? What about you? Won't you live with me?'

Jaadum shakes his head. 'No, I can't. I have to sneak you across the border and to your grandparents in Dhaani. You'll be safe there. But I must come back here. I have to.'

Chapter Four

Raibhu stopped abruptly. Afhash looked up as his friend stood up. 'What happened?'

'Dawn is coming,' Raibhu said, pointing to the east. 'Can't you see the greyness over that side? If we want to get to Sandha as soon as we can, we should get to the highway and catch the first vaanik to Sandha.'

Afhash scowled. 'But you were telling me about what happened—'

'Yes, and I will. But let's get moving, now. Our tunics are more or less dry.' He pulled them off the contraption he had rigged up the previous night and tossed Afhash's to him. 'Put it on, and let's go.'

Once he had pulled on his tunic, Afhash looked about him. 'Let's see where we are,' he murmured, half to himself. 'Once we find the river, it should not be difficult to find the highway too, because the road runs parallel to the river most of the way.'

It did not take them long to find the river, but from there to head due west took time, and it was not even as if the highway was right beside the Sada. They had to climb part of the way up a mountain to get to the road, but by the time they hauled themselves up onto the road, the sun had risen.

It was still very early in the morning. 'I'm hungry,' Afhash complained. He looked about. 'There doesn't even seem to be a small village where we could get breakfast.' He huffed in annoyance. 'Oh, well. Let's sit down here'—he indicated a boulder on the side of the road—'and you can tell me what happened then.'

~

They have an uneventful vaanik journey from Raffasi to the border along the Sada River, and a distraught Raibhu keeps asking Jaadum, 'What happened, Father? How did Mother die? Who killed her?' His father puts an arm around Raibhu and tries to comfort him.

'I can't tell you right now,' Jaadum tells Raibhu. 'But I will go back, once you're safe in Dhaani. I will make sure that your mother is avenged.' He lifts the boy's tear-streaked face to look up into his own, and whispers, 'Raibhu, you have to remember: your mother will want you to stay safe, all right? She gave her life trying to protect me, and you—and whatever is good in this world of ours. She died for a good cause. You and I, whether we're together or apart, must make sure that her sacrifice doesn't go in vain. Do you understand, son?'

Raibhu nods, not understanding what lies beneath his father's words, but recognizing the sentiment behind them.

At the Sada, they disembark from the vaanik and Jaadum, obviously familiar with the wilderness, quickly takes his son deep into the forests cloaking the banks of the river. Sovereignty in Southern Mandala is so new a concept that the new nation is still in a boisterous, exuberant mood; the exhilaration has not dulled yet and security systems are not in place. There are few soldiers along the borders apart from at the towns and villages, and it is not difficult for them to ford the river a little upstream. They make their way to a small trading post on the northern bank of the river, and are able to get onto an ekdut bound for the capital, Dhaani.

At Dhaani, they alight from the ekdut at the point where the Grand Highway meets the Emperor's Way, the white and the blue of the two roads meeting at an intersection marked by a tall stone column. The column rises high into the sky, its surface a mosaic of different coloured stones, and with fountains playing all round the base of the column. This is the centre of the capital; around it flows the populace of the city: horse-carriages and horses, ekduts and pedestrians, people coming and going, transporting goods, walking in the gardens, entering the nearby Terrisan Sanctuary.

Jaadum is alert to the point of being almost jittery: he keeps looking about him, wary and nervous, until they have moved past the hustle and bustle of the column and away from it, towards the Aaboneer Temple beside the Chansar River that flows through Dhaani. It is only when they are walking down the narrow lanes of the riverside area that Jaadum is finally able to relax. 'I'm taking you to a friend of mine,' he tells Raibhu. 'Not to your grandparents right now.'

The friend lives in a small, nondescript house in a sleepy neighbourhood. He opens the door to Jaadum's knocking, and Raibhu looks up into the sharp-nosed, grey-eyed face of a man of about fifty.

'You have forgotten me,' Jaadum says, when the man looks blankly, though kindly, at him. He glances around to make sure nobody is watching them, not in the street and not from the

shuttered houses opposite. Then, hunching forward, he detaches his false beard and moustache. The man's eyes light up with sudden recognition, but before he can say anything, Jaadum says, 'Four years ago, I was being chased down this lane by a group of the Emperor's soldiers. You came to my rescue then. You didn't just fight them off and save me, you even brought me into your house and looked after me until I was well enough to leave.' The man is smiling already, his eyes crinkling up at the corners and his face radiating a warm friendliness. When Jaadum finishes, he wordlessly embraces Jaadum. As he draws away from Jaadum, there is a glimpse of a tattoo on his wrist: a representation of the Brihan Punj, its six stars in their shape of a bud halfway to blossoming.

'Come in,' he says. 'And this is—?' he glances towards Raibhu.

'My son,' Jaadum says, once the door is shut. 'Though he is made up to look like a girl right now,' he adds, with a brief grin. 'Raibhu. I want you to keep Raibhu here till I can come and get him back. Or until someone else can.' He sighs, and the strain and weariness of the past few hours show clearly on his face. 'My wife has been killed. The men who killed her will be after me. I think I've managed to convince them that Raibhu is dead, but I cannot take chances. He must lie low.'

'You did the right thing by bringing him here,' the man says. 'He will be safe with me. For as long as is needed.'

'Only until it's safe,' Jaadum replies. 'I brought Raibhu here instead of to my parents' home because my enemies might be able to track down my parents, and from there to discover Raibhu would be easy for them.'

Shortly after, just as he's leaving, Jaadum hugs Raibhu tight.

They are alone; Jaadum's friend has left them by themselves so that father and son may have a private moment. 'Raibhu,' Jaadum says, cupping his son's face in his hands, staring into his face as if trying to imprint Raibhu's features in his mind. 'Raibhu, remember what I told you? We have to make sure your mother's sacrifice does not go in vain. I am going out to avenge her death, but who knows whether I will be successful or not? And who knows whether your destiny is like mine too?' Raibhu, puzzled, stares up into his father's face.

'I don't understand, Father,' he says. 'Why do you say Mother sacrificed her life? For what? Who killed her? They were the same men who attacked our house, isn't it?' He is young, but perceptive enough to see the look in Jaadum's eyes, the unspoken acceptance of the truth. 'Who are they? Are they the Emperor's men? Are they out to get us because of all the work we've been doing to pull him down?'

He stops, out of breath and agitated. Jaadum pats his shoulder. 'I can't tell you, my child,' he says patiently. 'For you to even know the identities of those men—especially of their leader—would be dangerous. It is best for you to be here, to lie low.' His fingers tighten on Raibhu's shoulder.

'Train to be a warrior,' Jaadum says. 'You already know some of the skills I have been teaching you, these past couple of years. Practice hard, and keep at it.' His voice is choked by emotion. 'I don't know when I'll see you next,' he says softly, 'but do not forget what I said. Yes?'

Raibhu nods, his eyes big with fear and distress.

'I will go to your grandparents' home now, before I leave for Raffasi,' Jaadum adds. 'Those bad men are very cunning, and they may well have their spies across the border here in

Northern Mandala as well. If that's the case, it is likely that they will find out where your grandparents live. They may come and enquire about you, or keep an eye on the house to check if you're there.'

'But you said they would be fooled by the skeleton?'

Jaadum nods. 'I am hoping they were. But I also fear that they are very canny. Even if they are convinced that you are dead, they will still be looking for me, and they might go to your grandfather's home in search of me.' He smooths back Raibhu's hair from his forehead in an affectionate, caressing gesture. 'I will tell your grandfather that he is to come and fetch you only when he is absolutely sure that there is nobody around anymore, keeping an eye out for you. It might take weeks, but don't worry. Grandfather will come for you—or I will.'

~

'That was the last time I saw Father,' Raibhu said. 'He must have been arrested on his way back to Raffasi.'

'But you became a warrior,' Afhash said. 'An officer of the law, at any rate.'

Raibhu nodded. 'I continued practicing all the martial arts Father had taught me. I pushed myself as much as I could; that was what helped me get into the justice office—and I wanted to join, too, so that I could try and get at the truth. Father hadn't told me right out that those men weren't Emperor Dhanjog Mahabeyan's. I thought they might have been; after all, it was a known fact that Father and Mother had been part of the anti-royal protests for a long time.' He sighed. 'I thought, if I got into the justice office, I might be able to search out old records from eighteen years back.

Perhaps find something about Mother and Father. Some clue about what happened that night.'

'Jaadum the Elder would have told you,' Afhash said, 'if he thought they were the Emperor's men. Wouldn't he?'

Raibhu shrugged. 'He might have had his reasons. But,' he continued with a sigh, 'I haven't found anything. I looked hard, through all the records, but there was nothing. Since then, I have been in touch with someone who crosses the border every now and then. I've been hoping he can make it to Raffasi and visit whatever remains of our old home there. Perhaps some of it was left unburnt.' His gaze met Afhash's: there was a well of pity in Afhash's eyes.

'I know,' Raibhu murmured. 'A house that was mostly burnt eighteen years ago would have long vanished. And even if it's not been razed to the ground, the wind and the rain would have reduced it to nothing by now. Still.'

Afhash was silent for a few moments. Then he got up, patted Raibhu on the shoulder, and said, 'Come, let's go and meet Jaadum the Elder before it's too late. Here comes the vaanik.' He regarded the approaching vehicle, drawn by its team of chestnut horses, with a critical eye. Unlike the two-compartment vehicle that was the ekdut in Northern Mandala, this one had a single compartment, boxy and with a narrow slit along the top of each wall instead of proper windows.

'Your Northern ekduts are far more comfortable,' Afhash said, as the contraption drew to a stop near them. 'But what's to be done? We Southerners cannot possibly have anything that resembles something Northern, can we! It wouldn't do.' He grinned. 'Come on. Welcome to Southern Mandala.'

~

They dozed in the vaanik, both exhausted from the long trek and the sleepless night that had followed. Besides, the very meagre daylight that entered the vehicle through the narrow slit at the top meant that the inside of the vaanik was gloomy and dim even when the sun shone brightly outside. It was conducive to dozing off.

When they woke up, with a sudden start, it was because the vaanik had come to a halt: there was a military barricade ahead, a few branches and rocks piled up to block the road. One of the passengers opened the door to peer out, and they heard the conversation that ensued between the driver of the vaanik, and the officer of the Southern Mandalan Army.

'A messenger bhaagi flew in from Jurwad a little while back,' the officer was saying. 'The patrols at the border reported some disturbances along the frontier last night. Someone may have crossed over.' He was already moving towards the body of the vaanik, his voice growing louder as he approached. Afhash and Raibhu exchanged a glance; Afhash was looking panicky, but Raibhu motioned to him to stay calm.

The officer peered into the vaanik, looking around at the passengers seated inside. A quick glance, and he turned back, summoning one of his men. As the two of them climbed into the vaanik, over his shoulder, the officer called to the driver, 'Get started. We have to be in Sandha by noon.'

The inside of the vaanik was claustrophobic, even without its full complement of passengers. As the horses set off again, pulling the vaanik along, the two soldiers settled down and began scrutinizing their fellow passengers. They turned from one passenger to another, peering into faces, asking questions.

Where are you from, where are you going. The officer finally turned to Afhash and Raibhu, who were sitting at one end of the seat opposite him. 'Where are you from?' he asked.

Afhash told him they were from Sandha, and heading back there. 'Where had you gone?' the officer asked.

'Just for a day's visit to the riverside,' Raibhu answered.

'Where?' The officer was getting irritated now; it was obvious he did not like their reluctance to volunteer information.

'Mahshira,' Afhash butted in.

'But you didn't get in at Mahshira,' the man sitting in the seat beside them piped up. 'You got on at some place which wasn't even a stop for the vaanik. And it wasn't anywhere near Mahshira. I remember.'

The officer looked narrowly at Raibhu and Afhash, now suspicious.

'We *had* been to Mahshira,' Afhash said patiently, while directing a look of pure hatred at the man beside them. 'We left there this morning, but we hitched a ride on a cart which was passing by. The cart wasn't going all the way, so we got off where we had to.'

The officer gave them both one last, searching look; then he sat back in his seat, folded his arms across his chest, and closed his eyes. Beside him, the other soldier stared into space.

But only for a brief while; within five minutes, the officer had opened his eyes again and was looking about him. This time, he was in no hurry; his gaze rested long on each of the passengers. He took his time scrutinizing each one of them, subjecting them to his gimlet-like stare. The gaze was about to move off from Raibhu when the officer's eyes narrowed. He sat up, then leaned forward and touched Raibhu on the arm.

'What's this?' he murmured to himself. He had not merely touched the woollen sleeve of Raibhu's tunic, he had picked something off it. He held it out, the thing barely visible in the meagre light entering the vaanik. Before Raibhu could even see what it was, the officer had supplied the answer. 'That's horsehair,' he said, addressing his colleague, holding out the small clump of hair to show him. 'From a white horse.' He glanced pointedly at Raibhu, and said, loud enough for everybody in the cramped confines of the vaanik to hear, 'We only have chestnut horses in Southern Mandala. The white horses are in Northern Mandala.' He paused to let that sink in, before he sat back and looked at his colleague. 'What do you think, eh?' he said, in a stage whisper. 'How would a man in Southern Mandala have got white horsehair on his clothes?' He did not look at Raibhu, yet it was obvious that every word, every syllable was meant for Raibhu's ears. There was open menace in the man's voice.

'Something deeply suspicious about it all,' the officer said, as he folded his arms and sat back, closing his eyes as he did so. His colleague, his hand on his dagger, stared belligerently at Raibhu, as if daring him to speak up and account for the horsehair on his tunic. Raibhu did not fear that stare as much as he did the cold, menacing air of the officer, who had not put even a single question to him.

'We—' Afhash began to say, but Raibhu squeezed his arm, silencing him. To provide an explanation when none had been explicitly demanded would be playing into the hands of the officer. Catching Afhash's eye, he shook his head. It would be safest to play along with the officer; only when he asked, would he be given an answer.

Afhash looked into Raibhu's face, his eyes full of helplessness and frustration. Raibhu shook his head. It would be a tense and stressful ride in the vaanik, but there was no help for it.

~

They were on the outskirts of Sandha town when the vaanik came to a halt. To Raibhu's surprise, even this early in the morning, the road was jam-packed with people: men, women and children milled all about the road and on either side of it, raising clouds of red dust as they moved about, filling the air with laughter and shouts and conversation.

'It's a fair,' Afhash said when the passenger nearest the door of the vaanik opened it. He glanced towards Raibhu, silently urging his friend on to make a dash for it. The tension of sitting cooped up in the vaanik all this while with the two suspicious soldiers breathing down their necks had shattered Afhash's usual calm. He was a bundle of nerves, and if Raibhu had not reached out and placed a steadying hand on Afhash's arm, Afhash may well have bolted.

The two soldiers were the first to alight, followed by the other passengers. When Raibhu and Afhash finally got down, cramped and sore and stiff, it was to find that the two soldiers were still there, standing still and watching them. Around them the other passengers of the vaanik alighted hurriedly and raced off, eager to be out of sight of the soldiers. Some people, waiting beside the road for the vaanik, moved forward to climb into the vehicle.

Beyond them, the fairground thrummed and throbbed with life. Even here on the road, outside the grounds, the music, the laughter, and the voices of happy people visiting the fair could be heard. Through the large gateway, decorated with flowers, Raibhu and Afhash caught glimpses of the fair. It was small but busy, stall after stall crowded with trinkets of manodium and coloured stones, woven baskets and mats, lengths of cloth, wooden and earthen toys, and more. Hawkers here and there had set up smaller stalls, selling food: spherical dumplings bobbing about in hot soup; circular pancakes, fried fresh; bright green citrus fruits and yellow melons.

On one side, a small troupe of entertainers had gathered an admiring audience: the performers had placed a huge, sturdy hemispherical drum on the ground, its drumhead measuring two yards across, and on this drumhead two lithe young women danced, jumping and pirouetting, swirling and tapping with their feet. Their movements were graceful, a very pleasing dance: but the ingenious way in which that dancing also produced music to accompany the dance was what drew enthusiastic applause from the onlookers. A little beyond, a professional storyteller was talking, his voice rising with excitement as he told a tale of adventure and intrigue. Still further, a wrestling match was in progress, the two wrestlers cheered on eagerly by a small but devoted group.

The smells, the sounds, and the sights were all of busy, bustling, happy people. Many hundreds of people, amongst whom it might not be too difficult to lose oneself.

But to try and break loose at this moment would be foolhardy. Raibhu glanced involuntarily towards the officer, and found the man regarding him with a sardonic smile. He had drawn his dagger and was fiddling with it, making it obvious that he was itching to use it.

'I wouldn't advise it,' he said drily. 'I can throw a dagger accurately at a hundred paces. You wouldn't even make it to the gate.'

Raibhu drew in a deep breath.

'Now,' said the officer. 'Now that we have more space around us and less chance of injuring a bystander if you should do something foolish...now let me ask you: how is it that you have horsehair from a Northern horse on your clothes?

'And,' he added, 'don't dare try to tell me you've been hugging your grandmother. I have grown up amongst horses, I can spot horsehair a furlong away.'

'It is from a Northern horse,' Raibhu said quietly. 'A relative of mine smuggled one across the border to try and cross-breed it with a chestnut.'

The officer was not convinced; the stony look he gave Raibhu was proof of his scepticism.

'I am actually from Raffasi,' Raibhu said. 'Our house was the one at the western edge of the town, between the canal and the old Nabhang Shrine.' That was true, at any rate, and if he were asked further questions, he thought he would be able to answer them, though of course there was always the chance that things had changed a lot in Raffasi over the past eighteen years. 'My friend,' he indicated Afhash, 'now lives in Sandha, and I live high up in the mountains, near the border.'

'And do what?'

There was one innocuous answer to that, which he could

support with a demonstration if it came to that. 'I am a magician.'

'A magician! Why would you leave the city and go off into the mountains?'

Raibhu had to think fast, and he said the first thing that came into his mind. 'To be with my wife,' he said. 'She belongs to the borderlands. It's her brother,' he added, 'who wants to try cross-breeding the white horses with ours. He stole a colt—'

But the officer waved a hand at him. 'I don't have time for your stories. They sound made-up to me, anyway.' His eyes narrowed. 'I have my eye on you,' he said frankly. 'There is something fishy about you, and I don't for a moment buy your claim that you're a magician or anything.'

'I'm not lying, Master,' Raibhu said. 'I am a magician, really.'

'Really?' The officer's mouth twisted. 'Show us some magic, then.' He tilted his chin towards the fairground, where so many performers were vying for the attention of the constantly shifting crowds.

Before Raibhu could react, Afhash had grabbed his arm. 'Yes!' he said, nodding frantically at the officer. 'Yes, of course, we can show you what we can do!' He pulled Raibhu along, through the gateway and into the fairground, heading for an empty space next to a bunch of food stalls.

Within moments, Afhash had commandeered an empty crate and a flimsy rag to cover it. While Raibhu was busy setting up his improvised show, Afhash got up onto a small wooden stool he had borrowed from a nearby hawker of sweets. 'Come along! Come on over, come over here!' he called out. 'Come and see the finest magic ever! Just a tanka, and you will have a treat like never before!'

To give the still-sceptical passersby some incentive, Afhash pulled out a tanka from his pocket and proceeded to show them how proficient he was at making it dance to his tune. 'And see!' he said excitedly, 'see how it goes up my fingers, pulled by my mind, no more—' with a disappointing thud, the tanka fell to the ground. Afhash, heedless of the sniggers of those spectators who had stopped to watch, bent down and picked up the tanka again. Again, he tried to weave magic with it, and again it fell ignominiously to the ground.

'No magician after all,' said a voice, loud and clear. It was the officer, and when Afhash looked up, there was the man, standing right in front, looking on with contemptuous eyes.

'He isn't the magician, Master. I am.' Raibhu stepped forward. He looked around at the small, much-diminished knot of people who still stood there.

'Allow me to show you something,' he said, to no one in particular.

With a flourish, he plucked the tanka out of Afhash's hands, and from his own pocket drew out a string. A flick of his wrist, and the tanka was enveloped completely in the string, which had wrapped itself neatly in a spiral down the length of the tanka. Another quick flick, and the string flew out in an arc, the tanka whirling on its end.

Within moments, Raibhu had drawn a substantial crowd. It started with a few curious bystanders, many of them children, and soon, attracted by their enthusiastic applause, others drew near too. Raibhu borrowed a handkerchief and a cap from one bystander to perform one act; he bought a bunch of flowers from a vendor nearby for another. His sleight of hand, his clever tricks, even the very panache with which he performed each trick, won him one round of applause after another. Raibhu's final act, the Aabra ka daabra one, which he improvised with the help of three borrowed caps and a small green citrus fruit, was the biggest hit.

'You're pretty damn good,' Afhash said, when the crowd had dispersed. 'We've collected sufficient tankas to not have to work for a few days.'

'I wasn't looking for tankas,' Raibhu remarked. 'I was just trying to convince those soldiers I was a harmless magician.' He looked about; the soldiers were hanging about on the fringes of the crowd, looking at the two friends, but for once not menacingly. Even as Raibhu watched, the officer gave him a pointed look, combined with a somewhat sardonic smile, as if to say, *I'm letting you go this once, but...*

The impromptu act seemed to have paid off.

'Well, all's well that ends well, I suppose,' Afhash said philosophically. 'But horse smuggling!' he added as the two of them made their way out of the fairground and towards the road. 'What possessed you to say that? I was surprised he didn't grab you by the throat right then—'

'Shh. That was inside information. I know there have been horses smuggled across the border for years now. Your chestnuts may look beautiful, but they are prone to a slew of diseases, so your border guards turn a blind eye when Northern stock is smuggled South to improve the horses here.'

Afhash was looking suitably astonished. 'And the North? Don't they try to stop it?'

'Why would they? It flatters them, that their horses are better than the South's. And they get good money for it.' He shook his head, seeing a crowd of people drawing close, gathering around the dancers. 'I guessed that if that soldier was so very keen on horses, he would know.'

'You're a lucky bastard, you know that?' Afhash said admiringly. 'That was pure luck, that you knew just the thing to say.'

'Come on,' Raibhu added. 'Let's get to the prison. I want to meet Father.'

~

Barely had he spoken the words when the hubbub of the fairground was pierced by a woman's scream. Raibhu and Afhash turned, even as the scream turned into loud wailing, punctuated by more screams. Off to one side, a small group of men had thrown a man down on the ground and were kicking him, while a woman, held back by two other men, screamed. 'We didn't do anything!' she wailed between sobs. 'Please let us go! Oh, please! Please don't hit him—*no*!'

Raibhu stepped forward, ready to come to the man's rescue, but Afhash stopped him with a hand on his sleeve. 'No! You don't want to draw attention to yourself.'

In any case, the two soldiers had hurried forward to see what was happening. As the crowd watched, the men let go of the woman and stopped their brutal thrashing of the man. The woman immediately ran to him, sobbing and begging others to help her take him away. One man from the crowd came forward a little hesitantly, and that too after increasingly desperate appeals from the woman. As the trio moved away, the injured man almost being dragged along by the woman and her reluctant helper, the soldiers turned to the men who had been beating the man.

Raibhu heard snatches of the conversation as he and Afhash moved away.

'Really, Master,' said one of the men to the officer, laughing as he did so. 'Did you think it was our fault? The Mighty Naash's cadres are the very epitome of good behaviour, didn't you know that?' His comrades hooted loudly at that, and the soldiers joined in too. 'Those two were trying to steal from us,' another man said. A third added, 'The woman was there to distract us, the man was the pickpocket.'

'Since you caught them before they could steal your tankas,' said the officer, grinning broadly, 'you can treat us to a meal, eh?' They were all laughing as they turned away, moving off together towards a large food stall.

'The Mighty Naash?' asked Raibhu, as he and Afhash hurried towards the road. 'I saw you look very uncomfortable when that man mentioned the name. Who is he?'

Afhash shook his head vigorously, as if trying to shake off a thought. He shuddered. 'I don't even want to remember him.' Then, perhaps realizing that Raibhu deserved his confidence, he added, 'He's a feudal warlord in this area. He was already very powerful back then, when we were children. He was the one who owned those sada stone mines I told you about, where I was held captive.'

Raibhu stared. 'Naash? But—but what you described was outright criminal. Do you mean nobody's caught him yet? Or nobody's caught on to him yet? After all, his men seem to be out and about, proud of being Naash's men—'

Afhash grimaced. 'He isn't just any warlord. He rules the Sada Valley now; they say he is so powerful, even Emperor Sarjaand fears him. The politicians, the Army, the law officers, the Terrisan priests: everybody's in his pocket. He bribes, he threatens, perhaps he also blackmails people. Whatever methods he uses, they seem to be very effective in having everybody look the other way.' He looked about him. 'Let's go, Raibhu. Let's hurry up and go to Jaadum the Elder.'

~

The guard at the gate of the Sandha Central Prison looked narrowly at Afhash when he arrived outside the gate with Raibhu. 'I had hoped we wouldn't see you back,' he remarked. 'But since you haven't arrived with a law officer leading you, it's all right, I suppose.'

Afhash winked at Raibhu, but only said to the guard, 'I'm here with my friend to meet Wartak the Elder. How is he?'

The guard's face suddenly went stiff. He was silent for a moment, and looked undecided. 'You better go in and speak to the Chief Prison-Keeper,' he said, when he opened the gate. He signalled to a second guard who was inside the little guard post beside the gate. The man emerged after a minute or so, to escort the two visitors to the Chief Prison-Keeper's office, a small mud-brick room that sat between the gate and the main prison buildings.

'Wartak the Elder? And—and you are his son?' the prison-keeper said, rising to his feet behind the stone-topped table at which he sat. Beyond him, visible through one of the windows, stretched the outer yard of the compound. Just at the edge could be seen a glimpse of the prison's own sacred ground, with its many rows of memorial stones.

The prison-keeper looked from Afhash to Raibhu, and then back again. 'I am so sorry,' he said, his voice low and full of sincerity. 'Wartak the Elder passed away yesterday morning.'

Raibhu stared, his face ravaged, his eyes full of denial. 'No,' he whispered. 'No, it can't be.'

Afhash moved forward hurriedly, putting an arm about Raibhu's shoulders, murmuring words of consolation. Raibhu shook his head, denying again what he had heard, what his mind refused to accept. 'I hadn't seen him for eighteen years,' he said. 'Eighteen years! Most of my life—and now, just when I discovered that he was alive?' The denial burgeoned into grief and spilled over, choking his throat and filling his eyes with tears. 'I had longed to meet Father for so long, Afhash,' he whispered. 'So long. And now I will never ever see him again.' He turned away, burying his head in his arms as he pressed himself to the wall.

~

'May the Land Spirit bless the soul of my father,' Raibhu said softly. 'May the Land Spirit hold him in its embrace forever after, may the Land Spirit keep him safe.' He bent his forehead a little further to the ground on which he knelt, his arms raised in supplication, his eyes closed. Behind him, Afhash stood silent, his expression one of shock as well as grief.

A few moments of quiet, and then Raibhu touched the ground with the tips of his fingers. Gently, pressing the tips into the dust where his father's body lay buried, he left his imprint there, as a reminder that even if he had not been there when Jaadum was interred, he had come here and grieved. He pressed his dusty fingertips to his forehead and temples, symbolically imprinting the memory of his father on his mind. It was not needed, for Raibhu would never forget his father.

'Where are his things?' Raibhu asked, when he reached the prison-keeper, who was standing and waiting for them at the entrance to the sacred ground. His voice caught in his throat; the shock of discovering that the father he had been so looking forward to seeing again was dead and buried had hit deep. 'I am a relative of his. If there's anything he left behind, I could collect it.'

The prison-keeper nodded. 'Yes. There are a few things. Most of them are of no consequence, though there is the urn which contains the mud from the place his wife was interred—you would know about that, Afhash?'

Afhash nodded. In response to Raibhu's look of enquiry, he explained. 'Wartak the Elder always kept it with him. He had had it at the time he was arrested, too, and he valued it more than his life, I think. Never let it out of his sight.'

'That's the one,' the prison-keeper said. 'He's left that, and there's a letter for you. Wait here, I'll go and get them.'

~

The prison-keeper was sensitive enough to realize that Wartak the Elder's young relative would probably want some privacy, so he allowed Raibhu and Afhash the use of his own office. 'Nobody will disturb you here,' he said, ushering them in and then leaving them to themselves.

On the table, Raibhu put down the threadbare old

satchel which the prison-keeper had handed over to him. It contained some odds and ends—worn-out clothing, a little bowl, a finely carved wooden comb—besides the urn. The urn was a beautiful one, an old brass vessel which was engraved on the outside with geometric designs. It had been wrapped in an embroidered scarf, its pattern an intricate one of billowing clouds, blue skies, and stray orange and golden rays of sun shining down on land tinged a hundred shades of grey and brown and ochre. A meeting of Nabhang and Terrisan, if one recognized the symbolism of the design. It was a frayed old scarf, worn threadbare and with its colours faded, but it made Raibhu's eyes fill with pain.

'I remember this,' he whispered, touching the scarf. 'It was my mother's.' He was silent for a moment, and then, just as silently, he reached out a hand for the letter, which the prison-keeper had handed over to Afhash.

Raibhu opened the letter. From within its folds fell out another piece of paper, which he put aside while he read the letter. The first half page of the letter brought tears to Raibhu's eyes, but after that, Afhash saw his friend's expression change dramatically. As he read, Raibhu's eyebrows drew together in a puzzled frown. The frown grew more and more pronounced, until with a perplexed 'What?!' Raibhu turned the letter over.

'What is it?' Afhash asked. 'Tell me, what's wrong?'

Raibhu motioned to him to keep quiet, indicating the open window that looked out onto the open yard outside.

'Nothing,' he said out aloud. 'It's just that Wartak the Elder seems to have become overly sentimental. He says he wants me to collect a handful of mud from where he has been interred, which I am to immerse in the Sada. Let's ask the Chief Prison-Keeper if I can take the mud from beside the memorial stone, and we can leave after that.'

~

'What is it, Raibhu?' Afhash asked, as soon as they were out of the prison and out of earshot of the guards standing at the gate. The prison-keeper had produced a battered old tin and given it to Raibhu to keep the mud he had collected from beside Jaadum's memorial stone in the sacred ground. The tin now sat in Raibhu's pocket while he carried the scarf-wrapped urn in his hands.

'Let's find a place to sit,' Raibhu answered. 'It's all very confusing, this letter of Father's.' He spotted a small and scrubby garden, deserted except for a beggar asleep under a tree. 'Come on, let's go in there. That space next to the pond is secluded, and nobody will be able to eavesdrop on us without us noticing.'

Afhash grunted. 'You're getting to be as paranoid as Jaadum the Elder was, seeing eavesdroppers and conspirators everywhere.' He followed Raibhu tamely enough, though, and sat down on the patch of grass on the bank of the pond. 'Tell me, then. Read out the letter.'

'The first paragraph isn't unexpected,' Raibhu said, opening the letter. 'Mostly about how much he wanted to see me once. How much he loved me'—he broke off. After taking a deep breath, he continued, 'And there's more about that stuff about destiny. Do you remember, I told you that when he left me in Dhaani, he said something about my destiny perhaps requiring me to train to be a warrior?'

Afhash nodded.

'He's written about that. He says—wait, let me read it to you—yes, here it is. *"It is our destiny, not just mine, and not just yours. Ours. I am leaving this world without having been able to fulfill that destiny. You must do it then, Raibhu. On you rests the responsibility."* And then, there's this: *"To fulfill what life has in store for you, remember to dig deep. The truth will only emerge when you keep at it, working relentlessly to unearth it, because what is on the surface may be very different from what lies underneath. No matter how difficult it may be, keep trying. Treasures await those who persevere."*'

'That's pretty profound,' Afhash commented. He was looking a little taken aback.

Raibhu nodded in agreement. 'It's also rather uncharacteristic of Father. Unless he changed a lot—Father was never so philosophical when I knew him.'

'He hadn't changed,' Afhash said. 'Unless he suddenly decided he had to spout philosophy in his last letter to you.'

Raibhu shrugged. 'He gets even more obscure in the next paragraph. Listen to this. *"Do you still remember any of the magic you learnt as a child? Do you remember what the basis of all magic is? It is illusion. It is as so many of our jijits have said: the world is illusion. Everything is illusion. What appears as something may not be that at all. Scratch the surface, and the good may be discovered to be evil personified. The strong may be weak, and the truth may emerge as a lie after all. Look at humur: so powerful, so durable, so seemingly impermeable—but it has its weaknesses, and it may be overcome by the most fragile of elements. Bring it in contact with water, and it will rust. Bring it near a magnet, and it will become hopelessly weak."*'

'The Land Spirit save us all,' Afhash breathed. 'What on earth was he thinking of? This rambling tone is not the Elder at all. Are you sure that's his handwriting?'

'It's been ages since I saw his writing. But the first few lines are him, all right: they sound like him. And these lines are all in the same writing...I wonder what he was trying to say. Oh, and there's this, too. *"Do not let these words of mine make you negate humur. Humur may hold the answer to your questions. The bearer of news may bring not just news, but knowledge that will help you in your quest. Listen to the bearer of news, look carefully to humur."* I can't make head or tail of this. It sounds like complete gibberish.'

Afhash shook his head, as befuddled as Raibhu. 'I cannot understand anything of what he was trying to say. But what else? And what's on that other sheet of paper?'

Raibhu turned the letter over. 'This is more to the point. More like Father. He says that I should take the urn containing the mud from where Mother was interred'—he touched the urn, wrapped in its scarf—'and a handful of mud from the sacred ground at the prison, where he himself was interred, and take them to a place on the banks of the Sada. There I have to combine the mud from both sites together, and immerse it in the river. At the point indicated on the map; that's where they first met.'

He glanced at the letter again, re-reading the last few lines. 'He says it's to keep a promise they had made to each other when they fell in love. They promised they would be together all their lives, and after their deaths, the mud from where they were each interred would be mixed together and allowed to mingle with the waters of the river beside which they met.'

'That's very romantic. I always did think your parents were very deeply attached to each other.'

Raibhu nodded. 'They were. I am sometimes surprised by how they managed to spare so much love for me. I would have thought two people who loved each other so much would not have had space in their hearts to love anybody else.' He took out the small container in which he had put the fistful of mud from the sacred ground at the prison. Placing it on top of the urn, he added, 'But I suppose when your heart is so full of love, that love expands to embrace others too.'

'You're pretty profound too,' Afhash remarked, half-jokingly. 'Where along the Sada do we have to immerse the mud?'

'"We?"' Raibhu raised a quizzical eyebrow. 'Do you mean to say you want to come with me too?'

'What a question to ask! Of course I do. They may have been your parents, but to me too they were the closest to parents I ever had. Now tell me where we need to go.'

Raibhu unfolded the second sheet of paper and spread it out on his lap. 'Here,' he said. 'It's quite far from here. See,' he pointed to the meandering line that marked the river, 'there's the river. And this is Sandha.'

Afhash looked lost.

'What's wrong?' Raibhu asked, when his friend did not say anything.

Afhash blinked, cleared his throat, and finally mumbled, 'I can't read maps. This doesn't make any sense to me. You'll have to tell me all of it. How far is the place from Sandha?'

Raibhu nodded. 'Of course. See, here is Sandha. And

this'—he indicated a spot on the map—'this is Murki. Murki seems to be the nearest place to the spot. Though even that's not too close.' He examined the map carefully. 'This is odd,' he said to himself after a moment. 'Father's written that Aabra ka daabra rhyme over here. Look, these large words.'

Afhash frowned. 'Why? Why would he write that here?'

Raibhu shrugged. He turned to the last page of the letter, and pointed out some words at the very end of the missive. 'He's written the rhyme here too. He prefaces it by saying that I should remember that the bead may be under any of the bowls. *"If you do not find it under the first one, look under the second. And the third. If need be, go back to the first. But keep searching; do not give up."*' He paused. 'There's something more here. Father says that the route is difficult and through very bad terrain. He writes that I will not be able to do it on my own, and I should go to a friend of his. Shervaan, who lives in Murki. Shervaan will be able to guide us to the place by the river.' He glanced again at the map. 'Perhaps that's why he marked Murki on the map.'

'Shervaan?' Afhash sat up, suddenly alert. 'But Shervaan, in Murki—why, that's the address to which Jaadum the Elder asked me to deliver a letter, the day I left prison!'

'Are you sure?'

'Yes. He gave me the letter when I went to say goodbye to him. He said I should take it at once to the message relayers and employ one of them to carry it. Pay the relayer extra too, to make sure he delivers it as fast as possible. And, of course, there were the usual precautions: nobody must see me taking the letter from the prison, nobody must see me going to the message relayers.' He paused. 'The Elder must have let his friend know that you would be coming to meet him.'

'Yes.' Raibhu folded the letter and the map and replaced them in their envelope. He sat, staring into space and silent, for so long that Afhash grew restive.

He finally moved to sit next to Raibhu and draped an arm across his shoulders. 'I can't say I know how you feel,' he said, a little awkwardly. 'I've never had parents, or anybody I could feel so deeply about. But if there ever was anybody—it would be Jaadum the Elder. I miss him, too. I wish you could have met him again. I wish he had lived long enough for the two of you to see each other.'

Raibhu gave a wan smile. 'Thank you,' he murmured. 'I was just wondering what I should do now. I have been trying for so long to find out what happened to Mother, who killed her—and just when I had thought I would find out from Father, I come up against another dead end.' He heaved a sigh. 'I keep thinking that if there's a chance of discovering any clue as to who killed her, it might be at our old house in Raffasi. Or possibly among some of Father's old associates, the people with whom he worked, organizing the resistance to the Emperor back then. Maybe they will know.'

'You want to go to Raffasi? But—you're an alien here, Raibhu. You had a narrow escape with that officer just a few hours back! The Land Spirit be thanked, he didn't ask you for your identity tag, otherwise you would have been sunk.'

Raibhu frowned. 'Identity tag? Is there something like that here?'

As answer, Afhash fished about in his pocket and drew out a slim bar of wood, which fitted easily into his palm. On it was inscribed his name, his place of residence—Sandha—and a number. 'This,' Afhash said. 'All adults are supposed to carry this. If the officers of the Army or the law officers ask you for it and you can't produce one...' his voice trailed off and he shook his head mournfully. 'You'll be in for the same fate as Jaadum the Elder. That will certainly be one shared destiny!'

Raibhu chuckled despite his grief. 'If one doesn't arouse suspicion in the first place, that may not happen. I was careless the first time; I should have noticed that horsehair on my sleeve. But I'm going to be careful now onwards. Hopefully, nobody would even suspect I'm a Northerner. And if I go to Raffasi, and quickly finish whatever searching or questioning I need to do, I can be out of Southern Mandala and back in Dhaani before the week is over. Without anybody being any the wiser.'

Afhash shook his head, sceptical. 'You don't know this area any more. You've spent most of your life outside. What will you remember? You'll do something stupid and get yourself into trouble. No, I'll come with you. That way, I'll make sure you stay safe.' He put up a hand in a gesture to stall the objection rising to Raibhu's lips. 'No, that's not up for discussion. I'm coming with you, first to this place by the river to immerse the mud, and then to Raffasi.'

'No.' Raibhu was firm, his tone uncompromising. 'I have some idea, even if it's eighteen years old, of what that area is like, and it's not hospitable. It could be dangerous. I'm trained to handle danger, I can do it on my own.' He saw the hurt in Afhash's eyes, and tried to make amends. 'I don't want anything to happen to you, don't you understand that? I appreciate your concern, but perhaps you should also see that I am concerned—'

'Nonsense!' Afhash spat the word out, his eyes blazing. 'I don't know about concern or anything else, you are my friend and I'd be a pretty shitty friend to let you go into the wilderness all by yourself. Or even with only one of the Elder's decrepit friends to help you along. No, whether you like it or not, I'm coming with you.' His agitation had made the words come out in a torrent, each word running into the one before. He paused to draw breath before adding, 'No arguments. We will first go to Murki and meet this Shervaan. Then he'll take us to the place in the map. Once we've immersed the mud, we'll say goodbye to Shervaan and go to Raffasi. Right?'

Raibhu was silent for a moment or two. Then he nodded. 'Right.'

'Good. Let us go then, shall we?' Afhash stood up, and dusted down his clothes. 'Murki is a long way from here—I think at least twelve hours, if not more. We could start off right now, see if we can get a vaanik going at least part of the way north.'

They set off towards the stop for the vaaniks, two young men heading into the unknown.

~

Somewhere, at some point in time

The same stretch of land, with the tall peaks of Mandala soaring up into a bright blue sky, the river flowing in the distance. It is daytime, in the morning of a sunny day. Two figures walk along the bank of the river, so far away that one can only see them as human beings. Perhaps they are men, but they may be women.

Perhaps they are old, but they could be young or middle-aged. They are too far away for anything to be said about them. Two figures walking slowly, leisurely, on the bank of the river.

A low hum suddenly appears in the still air of the mountainscape, which was earlier just dominated by birdsong and the sound of the river. The hum grows rapidly, building into a thudding, and fills the air.

The two figures come racing into view, drawing ever closer. They are men, both middle-aged, and their clothing is not the standard flared tunic-and-leggings of Mandala. Instead, they wear thigh-length coats over fitted shirts and baggy trousers. With wide, fear-filled eyes, they stare at a point in the mountains, and when their worst fears seem to have been confirmed, they turn and run towards the nearest settlement...

Which is not Sandha. Not an urban settlement, not a town. Or at least, not a town as we know it. This settlement has houses of sunbaked brick, plastered with river mud and embellished with carved wooden balconies, wooden frames and wooden beams. There are no ekduts or vaaniks here, no white-paved, blue-paved, or red dust roads. No gleaming zansal inlays decorate the doorframes of the houses, and the few horses that can be seen in the streets are all a deep, unrelieved, glossy black.

Fields spread around the periphery of the settlement, and through these fields the two men come running, shouting in terror-stricken voices: 'Run for your lives! Run, run!'

In the heart of the settlement stands a temple: a temple unlike any in modern Mandala. This is an Aaboneer Temple, dedicated to the Water Spirit in a way no temple, not even the now-decrepit one in Dhaani, has ever been. This temple stands on an artificial island in the middle of a lake: the approach to the island is over a path along which fountains play constantly. The temple building itself is shrouded in tall fountains, and the curtain of water around it is so tall and so dense that the crystal pavilions that comprise the temple look as if they were made of water.

The two men run into the precincts of the temple, pulling the gate shut behind them before they race for the lake and the temple building beyond. The noise behind them has coalesced into more definite sounds: the clamour of weapons, neighing and galloping horses, people screaming in fear and soldiers bellowing angrily. There is blood and dust, flying limbs and the debris of broken houses. Inside the temple, a high priestess sits at the head of a small group of acolytes and laypeople, most of them sobbing with fear and cowering. The sounds from outside, of ravage and plunder, penetrate into the temple and most of the people inside are close to panic.

The high priestess remains impassive, so serene through it all that the others regard her with anxious eyes. 'There is nothing we can do except wait it out,' she says, with resignation. 'We have no armies to fight back, we have never known anything like this.' As she is talking, a loud, rhythmic thudding begins at the gate: the attacking soldiers have brought battering rams to bear on the main gate. It is just a matter of moments before the blue-painted wooden gate, never built to withstand an assault such as this, splinters and bursts open. The terror-stricken people inside the temple scramble out; in their panic, some of them leap into the lake and strike out, swimming blindly towards the shore, away from the approaching attackers. Inside, somebody starts shouting in a panic: 'Shore up the temple doors! Don't let anyone enter the temple!' The people press, in a mass, against the inside of the crystal doors of the temple building.

The old high priestess watches them stoically and whispers, 'That will not help. As long as the one door is open, it will not matter how many other doors you try to close.'

The temple door flies open. Hordes of soldiers stream in, their swords dripping blood, and set about hacking at the crowd. While a group of soldiers attack the crystal altar placed in the inner sanctum, another lops off the head of the high priestess.

Chapter Five

'Stopping, stopping! Everybody off!' called the driver of the vaanik, as his horses finally pulled the vehicle to a halt. The man swung off his seat outside the vaanik and made his way around the outside, slapping hard on the body of the vehicle before he flung the door open. By then, all the passengers who had drifted off to sleep were awake, stretching and blinking and beginning to reach for possessions that had lost their moorings in the course of the bumpy ride. Among those who stirred and stretched was Afhash, who had been deeply asleep. Raibhu, sitting next to him, was awake, though from the dark smudges under his eyes and the tired look on his face, it was obvious that he was as much in need of sleep as his friend was.

'Didn't you sleep?' Afhash asked, as they alighted from the vaanik. He glanced about: they were at a nondescript hamlet, a tiny settlement of a few very basic shops. The greater altitude of this place compared to Sandha was apparent in the cleanness of the air, and the clearness of the night sky. The black velvet of the sky was studded with a million stars, of which those of the Brihan Punj shone among the brightest.

'I wasn't able to sleep,' Raibhu admitted. 'There was too much going through my mind.'

Afhash patted his shoulder. 'Anyway, come on. There isn't going to be a vaanik to Murki till the morning, so whether we like it or not, we're stuck here for the night. Let's see if we can get some calmroot infusion somewhere around here.'

One of the shops, the only one open at that hour, turned out to be one that served simple snacks and drinks: little circles of fried pastry, small spheres of dried fruit and sugar, and balls of rice mixed with spices and herbs. There was a single small fire-pit over which hung a cauldron of hot water, and beyond it, neatly arranged on a stone shelf, were large glass jars full of the ginger-like rhizomes of calmroot, the dried yellow flowers of dreamflower, and mixed dried leaves. Beside these were neat piles of spherical earthen tumblers, waiting to be filled with infusions.

There was no place to sit, but the boulders by the side of the road made adequate, if somewhat uncomfortable, seats. They sat with their fingers wrapped about tumblers of calmroot infusion, sipping the hot, fragrant brew. 'I thought you had concentrated all your energies on being a law officer,' Afhash said, blowing at the infusion before taking a sip. 'But from what I saw at that fair, you're as skilled a magician as Jaadum the Elder was. How come you didn't become a magician? You'd have done well.'

Raibhu shook his head. 'Father wanted me to be a warrior. That was what I had to do.' He hesitated. 'And,' he added after a while, 'every time I perform magic, it reminds me of Father—and that hurts. Doing a trick here or there is all right; I can deal with it. But if I had to earn a living from magic, performing all the tricks Father taught me, day in and day out, I wouldn't be able to bear it.'

'Not even now? Not even when you know what happened to the Elder? Don't you think it might be a way of paying tribute to the father who taught you all the magic you know?'

Raibhu frowned, taken aback by the comment. His gaze grew pensive and when he finally spoke, there was a note of uncertainty in his voice. 'I hadn't thought of that,' he confessed. 'Yes. I suppose that makes a difference....' His voice trailed off.

'Excellent!' Afhash drank down the last of the infusion in his tumbler in a big gulp and clapped Raibhu so hard on the back, Raibhu nearly lost his balance and fell off the rock he was seated on. 'That was just what I was hoping you'd say. See,' he said, huddling closer to Raibhu and dropping his voice to a conspiratorial whisper, 'why don't you teach me some magic, eh? You saw what a fool I made of myself today at that fair; I really don't remember anything of what Jaadum the Elder taught me when I was a child...but if you teach me, it would help me earn an honest living. I wouldn't have to do all these things that a law officer's friend should be ashamed of doing.' He made a mock-embarrassed expression which made him look so comical that Raibhu could not help but burst out laughing.

'You seem to have got on pretty well without feeling any pangs of conscience all this while,' Raibhu teased.

'I did! I felt really ashamed. But what could I do? There was no way out. But now, if I go back and take to picking pockets all over again, every time I peer into a stolen wallet, I will see your face looking out at me and wagging a finger, telling me I shouldn't do that.' He waited, then added in a more serious tone, 'Please, Raibhu. I mean it. Teach me some magic tricks so I can at least try living a decent life.'

There was a sudden sincerity and gravitas in his voice, which made Raibhu agree. 'All right,' he said. He finished drinking the infusion, and stood up to return the tumblers to the shop. 'Get out a tanka,' he told Afhash over his shoulder. 'I'll teach you the tanka trick first. It'll help get your fingers used to the dexterity that most magic tricks need.'

~

Dawn came to the mountaintop earlier than it did to the towns down in the valley. Raibhu blinked and squirmed, trying to find a comfortable position, but it was no use. He had used his travelling sack as a pillow, but sleeping all hunched up, with the hard rock for a seat, had left him cramped and aching. He stretched to work the knots out of his muscles, and glanced across to where Afhash had lain down the previous night.

To his surprise, Afhash was awake. Awake, and trying to twirl a tanka through his fingers. Even as Raibhu watched, the tanka slipped from Afhash's hand and fell.

Afhash cursed. 'This is what happens when you try doing magic when you're sleepy,' he muttered. He picked up the tanka and pocketed it. Rubbing his eyes, he glanced around and noticed a small rivulet a little way beyond the shops. 'Oh, good,' he said, half to himself. 'I'm going to go wash up. We don't want to turn up at Shervaan's doorstep looking all dirty and unkempt, do we?' He strode off, and Raibhu joined him.

Afhash had just straightened up from washing his face and hands in the cold water of the little brook when Raibhu rolled up the sleeves of his tunic and the shirt underneath it, right up to the elbow. Just below the elbow of his right arm was a vivid crescent-shaped scar, the scar tissue a pale shiny pink, and the skin around it puckered.

Afhash winced. 'That looks painful,' he said. 'How did it happen, Raibhu? I don't remember you having that when I met you and your parents.'

Raibhu wiped the droplets of water off his arms with a handkerchief pulled from his pocket. 'No, I didn't have this back then. I got it—oh, close to two years later, I think.'

The vaanik had drawn up by then, its horses still fresh and strong. They got in, two of just a handful of people: it was too early in the day for many people to be travelling. Raibhu and Afhash settled in and even before the vaanik had set off again, Afhash had pulled out his tanka and begun practicing the trick Raibhu had taught him. The tanka kept falling and rolling about all over the vaanik, getting under the feet of fellow passengers, getting lost, being replaced by another tanka. Afhash cursed, apologized, and went back to trying to perfect the trick. Raibhu sat, staring into space. Outside, beyond the cramped, dark interior of the vaanik, the Sada Valley spread out in all its glory. The sapphire blue river, its waters clear as the sky above. On either side, towering above the river, the slopes of the mountains of the Mandala Ranges, dense with fir and pine, the fresh, clean fragrance of them so powerful that it even managed to enter through the thin slit near the ceiling of the vaanik.

Raibhu was jolted out of his reverie by a sound resembling thunder, a sound growing louder with every passing moment: a sound that Raibhu immediately recognized. The odd design of the vaanik made it impossible to see what was outside, but the sound had drawn the attention of others in the vaanik too, and the man nearest the door was reaching for it even as the vaanik slowed. By the time the vaanik came to a halt, the door had been opened and they could see what was making the noise. Ahead of them, in a long line, trundled the massive carts that the Mandalan armies on both sides of the border used to transport material. Drawn by specially bred oxen, their shaggy shoulders two yards across and their hooves the size of dinner plates, these carts were built of the durable and strong humurwood, further reinforced by humur. Their wheels stood taller than the average man, and when even a single of these carts moved along a road, its trundling could be heard loud and clear at least a furlong away.

This was not one cart, but many. There was no way the vaanik could proceed, with the carts blocking the road for as far up the mountain as they could see.

'We'll wait here,' called out the vaanik's driver, swinging down from his seat and beginning to unharness his horses. 'Get off, everyone.'

Raibhu looked with interest, and worry, at the carts that went past, coming up a road that joined the one they had been travelling on, and moving up, towards the north. The men who drove them were soldiers; the men who sat in them, holding on to the sides of the carts, were soldiers. The huge shapes, shrouded by rough canvas and sacking, that were carried in the carts, were obviously weapons: massive catapults from which stone balls and flaming spheres of pitch and tar could be hurled. There were battering rams there, he knew, and grappling hooks that could be used to tear down enemy defenses.

The Southern Mandalans were moving north with all the preparations for war.

'What's the matter? Why the glum look?' Afhash said, looking up from his tanka. It promptly fell from his hand, but he grabbed it before it could fall to the ground.

Raibhu shook his head. 'Nothing,' he said, but not before Afhash, his gaze following Raibhu's, had seen what Raibhu was looking at.

He grinned. 'Aha. It looks like our Emperor Sarjaand is trying to add to his territories, eh? And your North Mandalan loyalties are coming into play, eh?' he said. 'Gathering some intelligence to take back when you're done?' He had spoken in a whisper, but despite that, Raibhu turned on him with blazing eyes.

'Are you out of your mind?!' Raibhu said in a fierce whisper. 'Do you want me thrown into prison or what?' He need not have bothered to say anything; even before Raibhu had opened his mouth, Afhash had realized the faux pas he had made. He winced, and frantically motioned Raibhu to be quiet.

'I'm sorry,' he whispered, his voice so low that it was barely audible. 'I didn't mean it, you know. *You know!* I wouldn't want you to get into trouble.' Raibhu had relaxed a bit, but the anger had still not completely dissolved from his expression. 'Raibhu,' Afhash pleaded, the tanka forgotten for the moment. 'Listen. What's a border between friends, eh? It's Mandala on that side, and it's a Mandala on this side. It doesn't matter. Not to me. I don't care. All I care about is you, okay? That's all.'

Raibhu was quiet for a while, and Afhash kept watching him with concern. The vaanik's other passengers had made themselves comfortable, some sitting on the roadside rocks, others lying down under a spreading tree further away. The horses, untethered, were grazing, glad of the relief. The driver was chatting with one of the passengers, watching his horses as he nibbled at some nuts he had been offered.

Beyond them, on the road, the carts went by. Raibhu watched, while Afhash continued to twirl the tanka, with increasing success.

~

Shervaan's address was vague. A man near where the vaanik had stopped in Murki peered at the address written in Jaadum's letter and shook his head. 'This is near the village,' he said, indicating a place further uphill. 'But it's not in the village. You'll have to get to the village and then ask around.'

It was already late afternoon. Raibhu and Afhash were tired and dirty, their clothes crumpled and their faces grimy from the long journey to Murki. Afhash looked longingly towards a nearby shop selling fruit juices, flower teas and calmroot infusion, but Raibhu hustled him on. 'Let's not waste any more time,' he said.

The path the man had indicated led up a mountainside, its slopes covered with pine and cedar trees, the clearings in between carpeted with wildflowers. In one of these clearings, a large one that spread out across a flat space, stood the ruins of an old Nabhang Shrine. It was made of bluestone, of its tall spires only one now standing intact. Raibhu and Afhash's path took them across the front of the ruined shrine, and they glanced towards it as they walked past.

'Oh, look,' said Afhash, stopping in mid-stride. 'What's that carved above that arch? It looks like a mahabhaagi. Is it? And did I tell you, I saw a mahabhaagi the other day—actually saw one, with my own eyes—'

'Yes, yes. But let's go, please? We don't have time, Afhash.'

'But the mahabhaagi—'

'Yes, I heard, you saw one.' Raibhu tugged at his friend's sleeve, and Afhash fell into step beside him.

'No, not that,' Afhash said. 'Why the mahabhaagi on the shrine, was what I was wondering. I haven't seen any Nabhang shrines, they pretty much destroyed all of the ones in the bigger towns, you know, when Sarjaand claimed the South for the Terrisans—but I never heard that they had mahabhaagis carved on them. What's the Sky Spirit got to do with mahabhaagis?'

'The Sky Spirit worshipped at Murki does,' replied Raibhu. 'Or did, I should say, given that the shrine has fallen into disuse.' They turned a corner around a tall lone cedar that immediately hid the ruined shrine from their sight. Up ahead stretched a clear path, ascending the mountain towards the houses further uphill. It was easy to see that the climb would take at least a few minutes, so Raibhu began to speak.

'The legend goes that a woman named Murka found an injured mahabhaagi in the yard of her home here,' Raibhu said. 'Its wing was broken, so Murka bound it up and tended to the bird. Soon, all the villagers came to her doorstep, telling her to get rid of the bird. It's a predator, they said. It will attack our yang-pras, it will maul our children. Murka refused. She said that it was a bird, and unlike humans, birds and animals kill only when they need to, not because of malice. She would make sure that the mahabhaagi would not need to kill; she would supply it all the food it would need while it healed.

'So every day, Murka would go out, to catch rodents and frogs and other small creatures to feed the mahabhaagi. Every day, she would clean its broken wing and dress it again. She would feed it and look after it and admire it as it sat there on the perch Murka had made for it in the yard. The other villagers resented it, but Murka fought them off.

'Then one day, while coming back from her foraging, Murka slipped and fell and broke her leg. She somehow got back to her hut, but after that, because of the broken leg, she could not go out. The few things she had managed to bring back that day were soon eaten up by the mahabhaagi, and whatever eggs or milk Murka had at home were soon gone as well. The grain and the vegetables the mahabhaagi would not touch; it was a raptor, after all, and Murka was at her wits' end. Finally, she decided that since she had promised, she should continue to feed the mahabhaagi any which way she could. She fetched a dagger and sat herself down in the yard in front of the mahabhaagi. "I will give you my left arm," Murka said, and drew up her sleeve.'

Afhash made a face. 'Ugh. Where did you hear this horrible story?'

Raibhu smiled. 'It's legend. It's fairly well-known.' He continued. 'Just as Murka was about to cut her arm, there was a howling wind, and leaves began flying all around. When it cleared, the mahabhaagi was gone, and in its place stood a tall pillar of luminous cloud, from which the Sky Spirit spoke to Murka. It thanked her for her bravery and her perseverance, and it promised to bless her forever more.'

'With a shrine?'

'The legend does not say what; all it says is that Murka

lived very happily the rest of her life. But that's why this village was named after her, and that's why the shrine to the Sky Spirit here was carved with the image of the mahabhaagi, because that was the shape in which the Sky Spirit showed itself to Murka.'

Afhash nodded. 'Hmm. Interesting. Somewhat gruesome, if you ask me, but interesting.'

'It used to be highly respected till about fifty years back,' Raibhu volunteered. 'There was a particular sect of the Nabhang that revered all birds, as being messengers and friends of the Sky Spirit. To them, Murki was the epicentre of their worship; they would make annual pilgrimages here, and hold special worship in which birds were feted.'

'All gone now, of course,' Afhash said. 'Now that Southern Mandala is for Terrisans alone. Of course,' he conceded, 'there are a few Nabhang people here and there, but they're so few, nobody even bothers about them.'

A few minutes later, they had reached the woods above the shrine. The path narrowed as it entered the forest, and after a while, it emerged into a large meadow that opened out onto tableland on the mountainside. Ahead of them was a cluster of huts, with terraced fields of grain on one side, and a few scattered fruit trees here and there.

The only person they could see around was a small boy, about six years old. He had a long thin twig in his hand and was busy whipping off the heads of wildflowers with it, racing up and down the edges of the fields, arm held out and twig poised like a sword. Raibhu called out to him, and he stopped, looking at them with curiosity.

The boy began shaking his head even before Raibhu had

finished asking the question. 'Shervaan the Elder died,' he said. 'There's only Inosa now. Do you want to meet Inosa?' A sudden spark of suspicion appeared in his eyes, and he looked at the two visitors with dawning dislike. 'You're not here to court Inosa, are you? She doesn't want to marry anyone, she's already said that plenty of times. Though I'm different,' he preened, sticking out his little chest and smacking it with a small hand. 'Inosa promised she'll marry me when I grow up.'

'You're welcome to her,' Raibhu said, amused. 'We're not here to court Inosa. Who is she, though?'

'I don't know,' the child confessed. 'I think Shervaan the Elder's daughter. She couldn't have been his wife, no, him being so old and she so young? But she used to stay with him, and now that he's dead, she still lives in his house.'

Raibhu exchanged a glance with Afhash. 'What do you think? Should we go meet her? If Shervaan died, then this Inosa might have received Father's letter. Perhaps she could advise us.'

'If she's your average village woman,' said Afhash, 'she probably doesn't even know how to read. But let's go meet her anyway.'

So they went along with the little boy, who skipped merrily on ahead of them. It did not take them long to reach a small but sturdy wooden hut that sat by itself near the edge of the forest. The boy ran up to the front door and pounded on it, calling for Inosa. There was no response, and he raced off towards the wood nearby, calling back to the two men he had guided, 'Wait! I'll get her!'

~

Two people were walking down a forest path, a man and a woman. The man, who was perhaps thirty years old, or a couple of years younger, was stocky and built like a bull. His face was not a memorable one, neither strikingly handsome nor ugly: plain would have been the best word to describe him, but what struck one about his face was a goodness and innocence that seemed to radiate from him. This, one would think, was a good man. Good and kind and humane. He was wearing, above brown leggings, a double-breasted tunic, one side beige and the other side dark brown, with brass buttons all down the side: the uniform of the Southern Mandala Justice Force. The uniform suited him well; seemed to lend credence to his image as a law-abiding person—if one assumed, of course, that the officers of the justice force were really law-abiding.

The woman who walked beside the law officer was in her early twenties, and in her case, it would be forgivable if an onlooker forgot to even wonder about her character, she was so beautiful. Her beauty, moreover, was not the vapid, milquetoast beauty of the average mythical princess, waiting for her prince to arrive to rescue her: this girl, by the energy she exuded, her flashing eyes and her quick movements, made her way through life on her own terms. Her clothes were clean but not fine: a plain and simple tunic worn over baggy pants, with a scarf thrown about her shoulders and over her head. Rough clothes, a little worn, and unadorned with embroidery or any other feminine patterns. She wore no jewellery, not even earrings. A no-nonsense woman.

Right now, she was busy berating her companion. 'How many times do I have to tell you, Xindaar?' she said, as she hefted her load of firewood, which she was carrying back from the forest. 'Umur Naash was the one who tortured Shervaan the Elder so much that he died. I saw it with my own eyes. Every single blow. You know that window in my hut which overlooks the forest? At the back? We used to peek in through that when Grandfather and Shervaan the Elder would be chatting and they told us to play outside? That window. I was looking in through that, and I saw it all. Umur Naash and his men.' Despite the resolute, determined look of her face, she shivered as if someone had stepped on her grave. 'He is a monster, and I don't understand why you cannot arrest him.'

She glared at Xindaar, who shrugged his shoulders helplessly.

'There's nothing I can do, Inosa,' he said. 'I've told you. It's only your evidence, and that too no evidence. Your word against his. What chance do you think you'd have? He's one of the most powerful and richest men in all of the Sada Valley, and you're nobody. They'll laugh you out of court.'

Inosa shook her head obstinately. 'I refuse to accept that I am the only one who has witnessed him committing murder. There have to be others. It's just that he's bought off people.'

'Oh, come *on*.' Xindaar groaned. 'You are paranoid, Inosa. Just because you think—'

'I am not paranoid!' Inosa snapped back at him. 'It's you who's not making enough of an effort! If you searched enough, if you asked enough people, and if you weren't so scared...' Her voice trailed away; through the trees, she could hear a shrill, childish voice calling her name. A few moments later, the little boy who lived next door to her had burst through the trees.

'Inosa, Inosa!' he panted, disregarding Xindaar's incensed, 'Inosa *the Elder* to you, brat.' He also deftly dodged a playful cuff Xindaar directed at him. 'Inosa, two men have come to meet you.'

Inosa looked immediately suspicious. 'Who?'

The boy shook his head, indicating ignorance. 'I don't know. They were asking for Shervaan the Elder, but when I told him that he was dead and you were the only one around, they agreed to meet you.'

Inosa hesitated for a moment; the expression on her face was hard to read. It was as if she was curious to meet whoever had come, but was also wary.

'I'll come along with you,' Xindaar said. 'Who knows who these fellows are?'

'I think I can guess,' Inosa replied. She adjusted her bundle of firewood so that it was firmly on her back, leaving her easy access to the dagger that was stuck in her belt. She gave the dagger a quick pat, as if reassuring herself that it was close at hand; then she nodded. 'Come along.'

~

Raibhu was pacing about in front of the hut and Afhash had seated himself on a nearby boulder. Both heads turned simultaneously when the boy's high-pitched voice was heard saying, 'There they are, in front of your house.'

Inosa came down the path towards her home. Xindaar was a few steps behind; the boy had run off, his errand completed. Raibhu had stopped almost in mid-stride, his eyes wide as he stared at Inosa. Beside him Afhash muttered a curse, a small and muffled sound of disbelief. Inosa glowered at him, then looked past him to Raibhu.

'Yes?' she said. 'I was told you came to meet Shervaan the Elder.'

Raibhu had regained his composure. 'And we were told that he had died. But my friend here,' he indicated Afhash, who looked flustered and blushed vividly, 'my friend had sent a letter through the relayers, addressed to Shervaan the Elder some days back.'

Inosa turned to look at Afhash. There was so much impatience in her expression that he tried desperately to make himself look solemn, and succeeded only in ending up looking ridiculously pained.

'What did you write to Shervaan the Elder about?' she asked Afhash brusquely.

'Me? I didn't write to him. I only employed the relayer to carry the letter. Someone I knew, a friend, he wrote it.'

Raibhu butted in. 'A man named Jaadum, my father.' He noticed the sudden flash of recognition in Inosa's eyes, but it was gone in an instant. 'He might have written to Shervaan the Elder asking for help. Afhash and I—I am Raibhu—we have to go to a spot beside the Sada, and my father thought Shervaan the Elder may be able to help us get there.'

Inosa stood still, fingering her dagger as she looked from one visitor to another. 'Wait here,' she said after a moment's consideration. She went to the door of the hut, unlocked it and went in, depositing the load of firewood just inside the door. When she came back out, she was carrying a letter in her hand. She opened it and handed it to Raibhu, pointing to the last paragraph. 'Read that,' she said.

"Ask the man who comes to you to show you the gift little Inosa gave him, many years ago in the clearing in the woods beyond Murki."

Raibhu looked up, puzzled.

'Well?' Inosa said. She was standing, legs spread and arms folded across her chest, the very picture of authority. A strong-willed woman, on her own territory and very confident of herself. 'You are here, and I am Inosa. Show me this gift I gave you.'

Even as she spoke, a small smile of realization had appeared on Raibhu's lips. 'Ah,' he said quietly.

~

Year 5456 of the Emergence of Mandala

In the mountains, a few hours' walk outside of Murki. These are dense woods, so dark that the light does not penetrate to the forest floor even at noon. There are no villages so far in the woods, nothing but the beasts of land and air.

But right now, human sounds drift on the air. A low murmur of voices, the rhythmic thwacks of someone hitting a hefty stick against something sturdy: a tree trunk perhaps. A soft cry of triumph, a sudden cheer in a childish voice.

In a clearing in the woods, a temporary camp has been set up. The remains of a small fire show that these people have been here for at least a night already, and will perhaps spend more days and nights here still. Their blankets, neatly folded, are draped over a couple of travelling sacks that sit against a pile of firewood.

And, in the centre of the field, are the two people who have lent the flavour of their personalities to these woods for now. They go through a routine of calisthenics, twisting and turning, leaping and bending. A man and a boy of about nine or ten years of age: Raibhu, with Jaadum. Jaadum leads, Raibhu follows, imitating his father well. Even as they go through their moves, three other people emerge from the woods and into the clearing: two elderly men, both muscular and big-built, and a little girl, about six years old. She is wearing a tunic and baggy pants, like any other girl, but with that, she wears sturdy little boots rather than delicate shoes or slippers. The taller of the men holds the girl's hand; from his shoulder hangs a sack which bulges with whatever is inside it.

'This is Inosa,' the old man says, introducing the little girl. Jaadum smiles at her, pats her on the head, and says, 'I have heard about you from your Grandfather, Inosa. He's very proud of you.' Little Inosa greets Jaadum shyly, but glares at Raibhu. Her grandfather teases her, 'Why, Inosa? Don't you want to make friends with Raibhu? He's not much older than you.'

Inosa shakes her head vehemently but doesn't say anything.

'Oh, well,' her grandfather says, removing the sack from his shoulder. 'Jaadum, let's get started, shall we? We don't have much time left now. Just a few weeks, and then you should take over. Come, Shervaan,' he says to his friend. 'Let's start.' He puts down the sack, along with his turban and his shoes, under a tree at the fringes of the clearing. Shervaan follows suit. The three men then move into what is obviously a familiar and often-practiced routine for them. These are not the relatively gentle, no-contact martial arts moves that Jaadum practiced with Raibhu: this is in earnest. Inosa's grandfather and Shervaan attack Jaadum, and Jaadum fights back skillfully. The trio is a whirl of flying legs, arms, and sticks. Dust flies, their cries ring out in the silence.

'Why are you clinging to that sack?' Raibhu says. He's

wandered over to where Inosa is sitting on the grass. She's wrapped her arms around the sack her grandfather had placed on the ground. She looks up at Raibhu belligerently. 'None of your business,' she says.

'Why the anger?' Raibhu asks, curious as well as a little annoyed at her bratty behaviour.

Inosa glares at him. Then, seeing he's not going to back off, she pats the sack and says, 'This is going to be your father's. After him, I suppose you will get it. It should have been mine, I am my grandfather's child.' Tears of anger and frustration brim up in her eyes.

Raibhu is hardly looking at her; he's more intrigued by the sack. 'I've seen your grandfather bringing this along every day when he comes to meet Father here,' he remarks. 'What's inside it?'

Inosa is immediately on the defensive. 'Nothing you should be concerned about!' she snaps back, and hugs the sack even tighter. This only makes Raibhu more curious. He reaches out to touch the sack, and Inosa retaliates. From inside her boot, she whips out a dagger, and before Raibhu can react, she's slashed out at him. Raibhu dodges it, but it still catches him on the arm, opening a crescent-shaped gash that begins spewing blood, covering both Raibhu and Inosa within moments.

~

Raibhu rolled up his sleeve till his elbow, revealing the scar Afhash had seen before. He extended his arm to Inosa, showing her the scar. 'There you go,' he said. 'Satisfied? It's not gone in all these years. The physician Father took me to in Murki that day said it would stay with me for life.'

Inosa looked a little shamefaced, but she nodded. 'All right,' she said. As Raibhu rolled down his sleeve again, Inosa turned to Xindaar. 'It's all right,' she said. 'I can handle this. Go on.'

Xindaar frowned. 'Go on? What do you mean, go on? Are you sure?' He looked past her, towards Raibhu and Afhash. 'Let me wait until these two have gone their way.'

Inosa shook her head. 'No. It's—it's all right.' She smiled reassuringly, though if Xindaar had looked more closely, he would have noticed that there was anxiety in her eyes. He was distracted, however, by the two strangers who had come to meet Inosa. 'Go, Xindaar,' she repeated. 'I will be fine, really. I know this man.'

Xindaar still looked wary, but when Inosa waved him away again, this time a little impatiently, he nodded and left.

'All right,' Inosa said, turning back to Raibhu. 'So you are Jaadum the Elder's son. So what?'

Raibhu grinned, suddenly amused by her attitude. 'You haven't changed a bit, have you?' He said, disregarding her question. 'Still so belligerent. What's the matter? It's not as if I have that sack you were so possessive about.' Even as he spoke, a thought seemed to occur to him, a flickering memory of something he had perhaps seen in the long-distant past, but he blinked, brushing it away.

Inosa looked annoyed, but also embarrassed, like a child caught out doing something wrong. She chose not to react to his comment, however. 'Answer the question,' she said. 'And if you want something, tell me. I don't have a lot of time to hang around chatting with you.'

Raibhu sighed. 'Father left a letter for me, saying he

wanted me to travel to a place somewhere near the Sada. It was the place where he and Mother first met, and they had vowed to each other that when they were both dead, the mud from their sites of interment would be mixed together and immersed in the river at that spot.'

He had been watching Inosa with some trepidation, fearing scorn, but she merely nodded. 'Where is this place?' was all she asked.

'I have a map.'

'Show it to me.'

When she had examined the map carefully, she said, 'This is deep in the wilds. Your Father was right; you won't be able to get there without help.' Her eyebrows drew together as she read the letters inscribed on the map. 'What's this Aabra ka daabra thing?' she asked.

'Father was a magician, you know. This was his favourite trick. Perhaps he just wanted to mention it one last time.'

'I'm going to be a magician, too,' Afhash piped up. He had pulled out a tanka from his pocket as soon as Inosa had mentioned the inscription, and now he proceeded to twirl it about his fingers, only to drop it after a few seconds. He bent, red-faced, to pick it up.

Inosa, one eyebrow raised, turned to Raibhu. 'I will take you,' she said. 'On one condition: this clown doesn't come along.'

Afhash sprang up, but before he could say anything, Raibhu lifted a hand in a gesture to silence him. 'Afhash comes with me,' he said. 'He's my friend. But how will you take us? Do you know this area?'

Inosa looked unconvinced about Afhash; she cast a

sceptical glance at him, but replied to Raibhu's question. 'Of course I know the area. I was brought up here. You'd seen my grandfather, hadn't you? And Shervaan the Elder too? They brought me up ever since I was about five years old, and they made sure I was capable of looking after myself.' She tilted her head up, a self-confident and somewhat triumphant smile on her face. 'Ask anybody in Murki, and they'll tell you you couldn't find a better guide to take you into the wilderness.'

'That may be, but I'—Raibhu looked briefly tongue-tied, before he overcame his embarrassment and continued—'I feel awkward about taking a woman with us into the wild. What if something should go wrong?'

'What will go wrong? The two of you won't be able to suppress your lust?' she snapped back, suddenly angry. 'If that happens, believe me, you'll regret it.'

'That wasn't what I meant,' Raibhu retorted angrily. 'Let it be,' he added. 'I will find someone else to take us. Goodbye. Come along, Afhash.'

He had already turned away, so he did not notice the sudden change in Inosa's expression. She looked startled, and then flustered, as if this reaction was not what she had expected, or even desired.

'No, wait!' she called out. She moved forward quickly and caught him by the sleeve. 'That's not what I meant,' she said.

He turned, and Inosa took a deep breath. 'I did not mean that I didn't trust you.' She looked towards Afhash, who had also stood up. 'Or you,' she added. 'I wouldn't have offered to be your guide if I didn't think I would be safe around the two of you. But why do you hesitate? Do you think I don't know my way around?'

Raibhu did not answer immediately. 'How can I tell?' he said. 'It's not as if it's written on your face.'

'It's because I'm a woman, isn't it,' Inosa said bitterly. 'You think a woman is only good to stay at home and do all the housework.' She shook her head. 'I'm not that woman, I'll have you know. I was taught very early on to fend for myself. I can defend myself'—she gestured towards his arm, on which she had left that scar—'and I can track, run, hunt, as well as the best. If you're worrying about me not being able to do it, you're mistaken.'

Raibhu glanced at Afhash, who was nodding his head vigorously, his eyes gleaming in anticipation. Raibhu sighed, resigned to Afhash's obvious infatuation with Inosa. 'All right,' he said to Inosa. 'But, won't you have to ask your family?'

Inosa shook her head. 'I don't have anybody. Grandfather died eighteen years ago, and then Shervaan the Elder brought me up. But Shervaan the Elder also died a few years back, and since then I've been on my own.'

~

Around the corner of Inosa's hut, at the point where the path leading to the village below went past a clump of young trees, Xindaar stood. He was pressed hard against the wall of the hut, his eyes narrowed and his every sense alert. From beyond, he could hear faintly the conversation between Inosa and Raibhu. When the sound of Inosa shutting the door came to his ears, Xindaar relaxed and stood back. There was an expression of perplexity on his face.

'So she's going,' he murmured to himself. 'What can she be thinking of, the idiot!'

He stood for a moment longer, looking indecisive; then he nodded to himself, and crept away, taking a path through the trees so that he emerged closer to the village without coming in view of the two men standing in front of Inosa's home.

~

'What the hell is the matter with you?' Afhash hissed at Raibhu as soon as Inosa was gone. 'Such a beauty wants to guide us to the place, and you're hemming and hawing about it! She nearly lost her temper and gave up on us!'

'On the contrary,' said Raibhu, 'she seemed very anxious to guide us. Didn't you see, she stopped me when I began to leave. Why is she so eager to accompany us? I mean, come on: you're a lone woman, and two strangers turn up at your doorstep, asking, not for you, but for someone else, who's now dead. Would you be so eager to guide them into the forest?'

Afhash looked flummoxed. 'Perhaps she doesn't think of you as a stranger. After all, she recognized that scar—what was that about? She was the one who gave it to you? When?'

'Long back. I think a few months before Mother was killed and Father took me to Dhaani. I only met Inosa that one time, and she was a little hellcat even then.'

'Don't call her that! She's a little strong-willed, but she's so beautiful, too.' Afhash gave a dreamy smile. 'Oh, it will be a pleasure to be able to look at her for a few days, at least.'

'Pleasure, my foot! I can't understand why she's so intent on going with us.'

Afhash wagged a finger at Raibhu. 'Tell the law officer

in you to shut up. You're too, too suspicious. Come on, it's possible she thinks of you as a childhood acquaintance—maybe she even feels sorry for having hurt you so badly. And she thinks that since her grandfather was a good friend of Jaadum the Elder's, she too should be generous. Maybe she's just friendly, eh, Raibhu? Don't be so suspicious, please. It's not good. There is no crime here, no mystery. It's all clear and clean and wonderful.' He squinted up into the sunlight, at the blue sky above, and sniffed appreciatively at the pine-scented air. 'It's a beautiful day, Raibhu. A beautiful world. Put your suspicions aside for the time being.'

~

Inosa emerged after a few minutes. Her arms were laden with old clothes: tunics, leggings, turbans. 'Here,' she said, dumping the lot in Raibhu's arms. 'The two of you, change into these. You can go there'—she pointed to a small and rickety shed that stood to one side of the hut—'to change. When you've finished, you can give me your own clothes, and I'll leave them in my home. You can collect them on your way back.'

'Wait,' Raibhu said, before Inosa could go back inside. 'Why do we need to change? What's wrong with our clothes?'

'There's nothing wrong with them,' Inosa said patiently. 'It's just that they mark you out as outsiders. You, especially. You look too much the city slicker. Your friend could probably pass off as a local, but not you.'

'Why would we need to pass off as locals? It's not as if we're on some clandestine mission. It's perfectly innocuous; we're just going to fulfil the dying wishes of my parents.'

'That may be, but people in these parts are suspicious of outsiders. Especially of townspeople. And surely you know how the situation is between Northern and Southern Mandala? I don't know how it is in big cities like Raffasi or Sandha, but here, so much closer to the border, it's very tense. Strangers are looked upon with suspicion. You might be taken for a Northern spy if you don't fit in.'

Before Raibhu could raise any more objections, Inosa had gone back into her home, shutting the door behind her.

'The Land Spirit preserve us,' Afhash murmured, beginning to sift through the pile of clothes in Raibhu's arms. 'How old are these? They must have been her grandfather's, or Shervaan's. So shabby!'

'I'll go change,' Raibhu said.

~

By the time Inosa re-emerged from the hut, both Raibhu and Afhash had changed into the clothes she had brought them. The sleeves of their tunics were too long, the hems of the leggings were frayed, and the collars of both shirts and tunics were greasy. The garments hung on both men, shapeless and worn out. Raibhu took it in his stride, but Afhash was distressed.

'Seriously,' he said. 'How on earth is one to make an impression on a pretty girl in clothes like this?'

Raibhu raised an eyebrow. 'Pretty girl?' He chuckled. 'Inosa, you mean?'

'Is that even a question to ask!' Afhash said indignantly. 'Of course, Inosa. By the Land Spirit, Raibhu. She's *beautiful*.' There was awe in his voice and in his eyes. 'I know, I know.

Since she's an old friend of yours, you take her for granted. But just look at her, what a woman! She's so lovely, I can't keep my eyes off her.'

Raibhu laughed. 'You're really infatuated, aren't you? And no, she's not an old friend. I only met her that one time, and I don't have pleasant memories of it.' He pulled at a loose thread hanging from the end of his sleeve. 'I only hope she really is able to get us there and back without any trouble. That's all.'

Inosa emerged just then, and both men stared at her. She had changed into a man's clothing: a tunic and loose pants, with a turban on her head under which she had tucked up her hair. She looked like a somewhat effeminate young man in this new garb. Slung from both shoulders were two heavy travelling sacks, and she held a third sack, also bulging, in one hand. 'Stop staring,' she said brusquely, 'and come and take these.'

'What's in these?' Raibhu said, as he and Afhash took the two sacks she handed them.

'Food and blankets and other things we need to survive in the woods,' Inosa said. She had put down the third sack, and now Raibhu noticed that from the open mouth of it something was sticking up: a large bow and a quiver full of arrows. Inosa pulled the bow and quiver out and slung them over her shoulder. 'Do you have a weapon of some sort?' she asked, looking first at Raibhu and then at Afhash.

Afhash pulled out a small but serviceable dagger, but Raibhu shook his head. 'No,' he said. 'But why do we need weapons? Surely there are no bandits around here?'

'There are always criminals of all sorts,' Inosa said. 'And

anyway, even if we don't encounter any thieves or cutthroats, we need to be prepared for wild animals. There are bears, wolves, panthers.' She was checking her travelling sack, moving things around to make them fit better. 'Though they don't usually attack people, there's no knowing. If a female animal is with her cubs, she could attack.' She retrieved a large dagger from somewhere deep inside her sack. 'Here,' she said, holding it out to Raibhu. 'You can use this. Do you know how to use a dagger?'

Raibhu nodded. 'I do.'

'Okay.' She hoisted her travelling sack onto her shoulders and looked at both of them. 'Let's go, then.'

~

Xindaar glanced back over his shoulder to check that the two junior law officers following him were right behind. They were, hunched over and looking as alert as their superior. Catching his eye, both of them tried to look even more alert than they already were; Xindaar nodded, and gestured to one to move to the left, while the other he sent to the right. He moved forward, in a direction that brought him approximately in line with the front door of Inosa's hut. As soon as he was in sight of her hut, he dropped to his haunches and scuttled back into the shelter of the bushes and saplings through which he had come. His two men joined him almost immediately. 'They've just left,' Xindaar whispered. 'Come on, we'll follow.'

Soft-footed and silent, the three law officers crept through the fringe of trees bordering the dirt track as it descended the mountain.

~

A gaunt man, his eyes bleary and red-rimmed from lack of sleep, his chin blue-grey with stubble, watched from the narrow gap between two wooden planks that made up part of the wall of a shed. The shed, dilapidated and half-rotten, was long abandoned and stood on a little rise just above Inosa's home. It offered a good view of her hut and its surroundings, as well as the path that led away on either side.

The man watched as Inosa, Raibhu and Afhash, all laden with their travelling sacks, went down the path and disappeared out of view around the mountainside. He was about to turn away when he saw a movement and stopped. He leaned forward again, eyes narrowed and intent, and looked down again. There, parallel to the path and screened from it by a thick stand of dreamflower bushes, was some movement.

The man twisted about a bit, and from a heavy sheath-like leather pouch carefully drew out a somewhat strange-looking object. It was a roughly triangular piece of what looked like thick glass, set in a frame of dark humurwood. The frame had sturdy handles on either side, and a strap of thick leather that could be looped around the user's neck if he chose not to put it back in the protective sheath. Thin strips of highly tensile zansal wire corded with silk were twisted into the frame on all three sides of the triangle, and between these strips was held a thin ring of zansal, about an inch and a half across.

Carefully the man held the celestial view-glass up, and as carefully moved the ring of zansal to where he wanted it, in a place from where he could get a good view of what he was looking at. Immediately, it all sprang into clear, close view.

The man watched intently for a minute or so, before he put down the celestial view-glass and stood up.

While Xindaar and his men followed Inosa and her companions downhill, the man who had been watching hurried uphill from the ramshackle shed, making his way into the forest. A minute or two, and he had passed through a narrow crevasse formed by a rock which had collapsed on another: from even close quarters, it looked as if the resultant crack would accommodate nothing bigger than a cat, but it was deceptive. The man slipped through, and went a little further into a secluded space, a cross between a large cave and a rock overhang.

He made his way to the far end, where there was a wooden contraption: a dovecote, about five feet long and three feet wide, divided horizontally into two sections. In both, pecking around among the birdseed on the floor, were green-winged pigeons and blue-winged ones, all messenger bhaagis. The man sat down on a rock nearby, and took out a small pad of paper from a pocket. From another pocket, he drew out a length of dark charcoal wrapped in a screw of paper. Carefully, speaking the words as if to make sure he wrote them correctly, he spelled out his message on the paper. 'Master,' he murmured, writing slowly and painstakingly, like one not used to writing. 'Two men had come to meet the woman. All three of them have gone off together. All are carrying heavy travelling sacks, they have probably gone on a longish journey.' He paused, wondering what else to write. 'I could not hear what was said. The woman's law officer friend is also following her,' he added, 'with two of his men.'

That done, he read through the message he had just written, to ensure that it was correct. It was then quickly folded up, placed in a small leather pouch, and tied securely to the leg of a messenger bhaagi the man pulled out from the dovecote. He took it to the edge of the hideout, and climbing up onto one of the rocks, flung the bird into the skies. Its strong wings immediately caught the air currents, and the bhaagi went, swift and sure, flying to the south. The man watched it until it was out of sight; then he climbed down from the rock and left the hiding place, running on soft feet back towards the way he had seen Inosa going with her two companions. He had been gone no more than ten minutes; when he looked, he could just about see the three figures walking up the mountain opposite, heading north.

'Towards the Wildlands,' the man murmured to himself. Then he headed back into the hiding place and having retrieved a thin, green-and-brown patterned blanket from behind the dovecote, he wrapped himself in it and settled down, back against a rock wall, to wait.

The shadows were lengthening when another bhaagi, blue-winged, came flapping in. The man, dozing now, came instantly awake. Barely had the bird alighted when he caught it up, cooing to it and removing the small leather pouch it wore on its leg. Gently caressing the bird with one hand, the man read aloud the missive he held in the other. 'Follow them. Send others to follow them too, and take along messenger bhaagis to keep me informed.'

The man hurried to put the newly-arrived messenger bhaagi into its cage. He got out another of the green-winged pigeons, and to this bird's leg, he tied a simple message.

Following the woman and two men, heading for the Wildlands. Master orders for you to follow too. Carry messenger bhaagis along.

He let the bird go, and then, wrapping the blanket more securely around him—the evenings were cold in the mountains, even in summer—he set off towards the Wildlands that shrouded the Upper Ranges around the Sada Valley.

Chapter Six

Inosa was leading the way, carrying as heavy a load as either Raibhu or Afhash. She strode along, chin up and shoulders straight, certain of where she was going. Raibhu, a step behind her—the path was too narrow for two people to walk abreast—was quiet, but Afhash grumbled and groused. 'I don't believe you've put food and blankets in this sack,' he complained. 'Unless up here in the mountains you people eat rocks. It's so bloody heavy!' He harrumphed angrily as he tried to shift the load.

Inosa stopped. Turning around to look at him, she made a face of exaggerated sweetness. 'Why don't we do one thing,' she said. 'Give me your travelling sack. I can easily carry that as well as mine. And perhaps your friend,' she glanced towards Raibhu, who was looking on, amused, 'can pick you up and carry you, piggyback?' She waited long enough to see the look of embarrassment on Afhash's face, and the vehement shaking of his head, before she set off again.

'Why do you go around with this character?' she asked Raibhu, a few steps further along. She did not bother to lower her voice, and Afhash flushed when he heard what she had said.

Raibhu turned momentarily to glance at Afhash before he answered Inosa's question. 'Because he's my friend,' he said, with an affectionate grin in Afhash's direction. 'He's my brother from another mother.'

'We shared a mother for a month,' Afhash added.

Inosa looked puzzled, but before she could ask why they said that, they had reached the ruined Nabhang Shrine at Murki. Raibhu stopped and with a mumbled 'Just a minute, I'll be back,' he put down his travelling sack and ran towards the ruined old shrine. Close to the stone doorway of the shrine, he veered off to one side, where some colourful wildflowers were growing. He gathered up a little bunch, and raced back with them to the threshold of the shrine. There he stopped and stretched his arms up towards the arched doorway above which the carved mahabhaagi had been immortalized, frozen in stone. Raibhu uttered a few quick words under his breath, before bending his head down and simultaneously flinging the flowers up towards the sky. Even as they fluttered down in a miniature shower of multicoloured petals, he turned away and hurried back to where Inosa and Afhash, both with their sacks still on their backs, stood watching him. Raibhu lifted up his travelling sack and began walking again.

'What was that for?' Afhash asked.

'That was for Mother,' Raibhu said. 'Mother was Nabhang by birth.' He saw the astonished look on Afhash's face, and explained. 'It's true. She was born Nabhang, but when she met Father and they decided to get married, she made the decision to move her faith from the Sky Spirit to the Land Spirit. Father didn't want her to give up her beliefs, but for him, she was even willing to do that.'

'Oh. I didn't know that. Somehow Asi the Elder never struck me as being different.'

Raibhu grinned. 'Why, what did you expect? Even if she'd stayed Nabhang, it's not as if she would be any different, would she? Perhaps, like most of the Nabhang people, she would not have eaten any birds or their eggs, and of course she would have gone to the Nabhang Shrine to worship, but that would have been all. It would not have changed who she was.'

'Of course not. And I didn't mean it that way. The Elder your Mother was a wonderful person.' Afhash added in an aside to Inosa, 'Did you ever meet her?'

For a moment, a shadow seemed to flit across Inosa's face, as if she was reminded of some unhappy memory. But she merely shook her head, and said nothing.

Instead, as they moved on, she asked a question of her own, addressed to Raibhu. 'What happened to your father?' she said. 'In his letter to Shervaan the Elder, he said that he was in the prison at Sandha. Why was he in prison? How did he die?'

Raibhu hesitated. When he replied, he only said, 'He died of an old wound, from a humur projectile that had stayed embedded in his body. He had been arrested on suspicion of being a spy. I don't know much—'

'If you want to know about Jaadum the Elder, I am the one you should be asking,' Afhash interrupted, eagerly coming forward. 'I was with him for a couple of years in prison, you know. I knew him very well. This man here,' he clapped Raibhu on the shoulder, 'didn't even know where his father was these past eighteen years.'

Inosa looked up at Raibhu, her eyes wide. 'Is that true? Your father was arrested eighteen years ago?' She saw him nod. 'I'm sorry,' she added, her voice surprisingly soft. 'Where were you when he was arrested? And your mother: was she—was she alive then?'

Raibhu looked a little bewildered by Inosa's question. 'Why are you asking about my mother? You never met her.'

'I was just wondering, that's all. Where you were, whether you were alone.' Inosa was flustered, and it showed.

'Father took me to safety. Mother had already died. She was killed, by whom, I don't know, and Father never got around to telling me. He did say he was going back to avenge her death, but in the process he was taken captive and ended up in prison.' Raibhu heaved a sigh. 'I don't know who was responsible for Mother's death. Whom I should track down, whom I should haul before the law—or to whom I need to be a law unto myself, if that's how it's going to be.'

Inosa nodded slowly. She did not say anything but she looked thoughtful. The three of them walked on in silence, the two men concentrating on the rough, steep path, and Inosa lost in her own thoughts.

~

'The two of you haven't done much walking in the mountains, have you?' Inosa said. 'Especially you, Afhash? That's your name, right?' He grinned beatifically at her, grateful that she remembered his name. 'You, at least, are fit,' she said to Raibhu as she lowered her travelling sack onto a soft patch of grass. They had arrived at a mountain pasture with pine trees on one side and a splendid view of the Sada River far below on the other side. Inosa, having noted that there was a small stream running along one edge of the pasture, had declared that this was where they would stop for a break.

From her travelling sack, she took out a chipped earthenware tumbler and handed it to Raibhu, along with an equally shabby pot. She rummaged about a bit more, and took out a tinderbox and some flints. 'Do you know how to make a fire? You do? Good. Make one, then. Fill water in this pot and get it boiling. I put some dried calmroot in that travelling sack of yours; brew some.' She pulled out a large scarf from her tunic pocket and fashioned a pouch-like sack from it, which she tied around her waist. 'I'll be back. If you need to pee, don't do it in the stream.' And, with that, she strode off through the grass.

'This—! This woman! How brazen can she be!' Raibhu, dumbfounded and red with embarrassment, spluttered while Afhash doubled up with laughter. Inosa, nonchalant, had already vanished.

Afhash, guffawing, picked up a fallen branch and handed it to Raibhu. 'Here. For your fire. Don't put it out,' he added, wiggling his eyebrows suggestively. When Raibhu swiped at him in retaliation, Afhash ducked expertly, laughing. 'Come on, Raibhu!' he hooted. 'This is how village girls are. They may not have the demureness of your city girls, but they're the best. And Inosa is the best of the best. What a woman, eh?'

Raibhu, still glowering, said nothing.

By the time Inosa returned, the men had got a small fire going. Afhash had wandered off to the fringes of the pasture, looking for twigs and dried wood that could be used to feed the fire; Raibhu had filled the pot with water and put it on to boil while he searched through his travelling sack for the dried calmroot.

Inosa had returned with her scarf-pouch bulging with the results of her foraging. She lowered the scarf onto the ground and opened it, revealing an assortment of wild mushrooms, herbs, nuts, berries and more. She sorted through them quickly, putting the berries and nuts on one side, the mushrooms, herbs and leaves on the other.

'I hadn't realized Shervaan the Elder was your grandfather's friend,' Raibhu said. He poked at the fire with a stick. 'When Father mentioned him in the letter, I didn't know that the old gentleman who used to accompany your grandfather was Shervaan the Elder.' He put the stick aside and peered at the water, which had now begun to boil. Opening a rough cotton bag full of dried calmroot, he lowered a handful of the twisty brown roots into the hot water; immediately, a cloud of steam erupted from the pot and hung over it for a few moments. When it had cleared away, Raibhu continued. 'And of course, I didn't even make the connection with your grandfather. Father had never told me his name, neither his nor Shervaan the Elder's.' He closed the pouch, drawing the string around it shut. 'What happened to them? To Shervaan the Elder and your grandfather?'

'I told you. Grandfather died eighteen years ago, Shervaan the Elder a few years back.' Inosa opened her travelling sack and rummaged around in it, finally drawing out a small wooden box full of salt.

'Yes, I know. But how? Both of them looked strong enough to live many more years.'

'You can never tell,' Inosa said evasively. 'After all, Jaadum the Elder died, didn't he? And he was much younger than either of them. I think that calmroot infusion can be taken off and poured now,' she said, changing the topic. 'I need the pot to cook these things.'

Afhash had returned by then, a bundle of twigs under his arm. Inosa, having added a little more water to the pot, had thrown in all the mushrooms, herbs and leaves, along with a pinch of salt. She sat back and indicated to Afhash to add some kindling to the fire. 'That'll be ready soon,' she said. 'We'd better eat something hot while we can. The higher we go, the scarcer the food will get.'

Afhash sat back comfortably and pulled out a tanka from his pocket. 'I may as well practice while we wait,' he said, to no one in particular. 'Every little bit of practice counts.' Barely had the words left his mouth than the tanka tumbled to the ground. With a muffled curse, Afhash gathered it up and began trying to twist his fingers about it.

Inosa reached for her travelling sack and searched through it, finally drawing forth three pieces of homemade flatbread. They were made of some rough brownish flour, and were a far cry from the silken, soft white flatbreads to be found in the markets. This was obviously something someone—a someone, too, who perhaps did not have much skill as a cook—had hurriedly made on a domestic hearth.

'They aren't great,' Inosa said, handing one each to her two companions, 'but it's better than nothing.' She cocked an eyebrow at Afhash, who had dropped the bread back into her palm as if it had burnt him. 'What's the matter? Don't you want to eat?'

Afhash indicated the bread. 'That's—who made that?'

Inosa looked bewildered. 'I did, who else? Why, what happened?'

'They're triangular,' Afhash said, his voice filled with dread. Beside him, Raibhu, realizing what Afhash was indicating, made a sound of exasperation. But Inosa, unaware, still continued to regard Afhash with puzzlement.

'I don't understand,' she admitted. 'Perhaps I'm very stupid,' she added drily, 'so maybe it would be kind of you to enlighten me.'

Afhash steadied his voice and explained. 'Triangular food is Northern. In the South, here, we eat circular food. Or spherical, something that evokes the Land. Not three religions, but one.'

Inosa had gone white, the veins standing out on her temple. Without saying a word, she reached for the dagger at her belt. Afhash scrambled away with a squeak of horror, but Inosa was not even looking at him. With quick, deft strokes of her dagger, she cut away the corners of the flatbread he had returned to her. A few more strokes, and she had neatened its edges, forming it into a clean, tidy circle.

She slammed the dagger back into its sheath at her belt and flung the flatbread into Afhash's lap. 'There you are,' she said. 'Happy now? It's a circle.' Then, with a snort that indicated that the topic was closed for discussion, she turned back to the stew she had been cooking. Wrapping her thick scarf around her fingers, she pulled the pan off the fire to put it on the ground. 'Here you go,' she said. 'Dig in.' When there was no response, she looked up from breaking the bread which she held.

'What?' she said, looking at Raibhu and Afhash, both of them sitting with their bits of bread in their hands, looking at a loss for words. 'Why aren't you two eating?'

'How?' Raibhu mumbled. 'Straight from the pot?'

Inosa chuckled, more amused than irritated. 'You two are a class apart. What, you've just walked out from a palace, or what? Of course, straight from the pot. Do you see plates and spoons around here?' She did not wait to hear a response, but dived straight in, fishing up the steaming soup with bits of bread.

Raibhu and Afhash watched, Afhash looking on with something close to awe, while the expression on Raibhu's face was rather more inscrutable.

~

The sun was dipping towards the horizon. Sunset was probably still an hour away, though for Raibhu and Afhash, both unused to living in the mountains, it was hard to tell, since they had no way of saying exactly how high above the horizon the sun was.

'We'll walk on a bit more,' Inosa said. 'We still have enough light for that, and it would be a waste of time to stop now.'

In the still light of the waning day, the silence broken mostly by the sounds of birds flying home, the three of them moved on. Gradually, they became aware of other sounds intruding on the sounds of nature. Somewhere, in the direction of the river, the muted sound of one of those large war-carts could be heard, trundling along on its gigantic humur-lined wheels. On the breeze came other, less intrusive sounds: the thump of booted feet, the shouting of commands. Raibhu, immediately alert, stopped briefly at a high point on the path and peered down, craning his neck to try and see where the sounds emanated from.

'You Northerner,' Afhash said, coming up behind him and giving him a quick nudge. 'Stop your spying. If you get caught—' He broke off, realizing too late that they were not alone.

It had been said sotto voce, but Raibhu had winced and whirled around, his expression a mixture of exasperation, anger, and anguish. Afhash held up his hands, pleading guilty. 'Sorry,' he mouthed, looking beyond Raibhu to Inosa, who was further up the path. Raibhu turned to look too, but Inosa, it seemed, was oblivious of Afhash's remark. Raibhu and Afhash exchanged a look, Afhash suitably contrite, quickly touching his earlobes in a mute gesture of repentance. Raibhu shook his head in annoyance, but his anger had already half dissipated: he was swiftly realizing how completely impetuous and impulsive Afhash was. How he spoke without thinking, how he lived in the moment. How he could not really be held responsible for his off-the-cuff remarks, unless one also blamed him for being immature and guileless.

With a sigh and a resigned grin, Raibhu turned and set off in Inosa's wake. Afhash fell into step behind them.

~

The sounds of the Southern Mandalan Army hard at work in the vicinity accompanied them all the way for the next few minutes as the path climbed, but they saw nothing except the mountains and the trees, the rocks and the blue sky.

Until suddenly, descending the path, they found themselves in the middle of a large herd of fluffy pink yang-pra. Inosa muttered something under her breath, and turning to Raibhu—who had come up to her by then—said, 'We'll have to wait. We have to cross that bridge, and these yang-pra will take their own time getting across.' She indicated a rickety-looking rope bridge which spanned a chasm before them. The bridge was narrow, and it swayed frighteningly. It was obvious that two people, or even two yang-pra, could not cross it simultaneously. And this herd of yang-pra was large enough that if one yang-pra at a time made its way across, it would take probably close to an hour for all of them to get across.

'Is there no other way across?' Raibhu asked.

Inosa shook her head. She slipped off her travelling sack. 'We have to wait, whether you like it or not.'

This, it seemed, was a place where others too had had to wait for their turn: a fallen log had been dragged here and positioned to act as a bench. From one of the roots of the tree trunk hung a piece of wood, scooped and polished into a smooth dipper, for anybody who wanted a sip of water without risking the chance of toppling into the stream which the bridge spanned. Inosa helped herself to a sip of water, then broke off a low-hanging branch from a tree nearby. She took it with her to the log, seated herself, and began whittling at it.

Afhash, smiling ingratiatingly, inched closer to her and finally seated himself on the other end of the log. 'What are you making?' he asked. Raibhu, who had walked on till the end of the bridge, did not pay any attention to the two of them. The river of yang-pra ebbed and flowed around him, a seething, constantly moving mass of heavy bobbing fleeces. The older shepherd, a teenager, had crossed the bridge in advance of the yang-pra and was on the other side. On the side where Raibhu waited, a younger boy, helped by two yang-pra herding dogs, was in charge. The dogs, weaving expertly about, hustling the yang-pra along, nudging them towards the bridge while keeping them away from the edge of the cliff, were doing most of the work. Raibhu watched, a small smile on his lips.

'I'm making a walking stick,' Inosa replied to Afhash. 'Or something to drive away wolves, if we encounter any. Or something to hang a travelling sack from, if I get too tired of it hanging off my shoulders. Or a digging tool.' With a few practiced strokes of the dagger she carried in her belt, she had shaped one end of the branch into a point, and now she began on smoothing it out, sharpening it.

Afhash was a little dazed by Inosa's blunt, matter-of-fact way of speaking, but he rallied around. 'You're very independent,' he said awkwardly.

Inosa shrugged, but she did not say anything.

After a few seconds, though, she looked up from her work. 'Don't you have anything better to do than to sit here and stare at me? It's irritating.'

Afhash flushed. 'I—I can practice my magic.' He fumbled about in his pocket, and withdrew the tanka he had been using to practice with. Inosa, spotting it, heaved a sigh of resignation. Afhash shot her a grin and went into his routine, only to have the tanka fall from his hands and go rolling down the smooth incline of the path. He plunged after it and caught it just before it disappeared under the hooves of the yang-pra milling about near the entrance to the bridge.

Far above them, the sunlight glinted off something shiny. Xindaar, a celestial view-glass in his hand, was watching them. He had focused the view-glass on Inosa, but seeing Afhash move, his view-glass had followed Afhash. He now trained the view-glass on Raibhu. At this range, nothing could be heard of what the people below at the rope bridge said. Xindaar had to be content with watching them.

A rough parapet, consisting of a single block of stone, had been placed at this point, and Raibhu had seated himself on it. Afhash, straightening up, heard his friend tell the little shepherd, 'Come here. I can see something behind your ear.'

Raibhu's smile had a warmth to it that reassured the child. He came forward, curious. Raibhu leaned towards him, and let his fingertips travel quickly down the boy's hairline and behind his ear.

'Oh, look what I found!' he said, his eyes wide and his mouth an O of astonishment. He held out a shiny tanka, its spiraling curves gleaming bright. The boy grinned, impressed with what he realized was a neat sleight of hand.

'Here, take it,' Raibhu said, handing the boy the coin, but he backed away, shaking his head. 'No. Mother and Father say I should never take money I haven't earned. It's wrong to take other people's money.'

'It's not anyone else's money, since it came out of your hair,' said Raibhu, with a twinkle in his eye. 'But if you insist, I will have you earn it. All right?'

The boy nodded, his grey eyes wide, his cheeks apple-red in the glow of the setting sun.

'Good. Now, I am feeling really sleepy and tired. But my friends there'—Raibhu gestured towards Inosa, who was still sitting on the log, but watching Raibhu and the boy with interest—and then towards Afhash, standing a little closer—'my friends are relying on me to let them know when it is time for us to cross the bridge after your yang-pra have gone.' He tapped the boy's forehead gently. 'You understand my predicament, my friend? I need to sleep, I must sleep. But I must keep watch too. Can you do that for me? You don't need to sit beside me, or anything of the sort; but you must stay very alert, and as soon as the last of your yang-pra have crossed over, you must come and wake me up. Will you do that? If you will, the tanka is yours.'

The boy nodded.

'Remember, it is a big responsibility, yes? You cannot wake me up before the yang-pra have all gone across, because then I will lose out on my sleep. And you cannot delay after your yang-pra have gone, because then that will mean our getting late. I'm depending upon you.'

'Yes.'

If the little boy had not been quite as conscientious, he might have sneaked a peek at his temporary employer. He, however, now decided to devote himself so thoroughly to keeping an eye on his yang-pra and making sure they didn't linger and loiter, that he missed seeing the small but affectionate smile on Raibhu's face as he sat on the stone, eyelids narrowed to pretend that he was asleep.

The little boy did not see, but Inosa noticed. Her eyes softened as she watched Raibhu, and Afhash, looking at her, followed her gaze. 'He's a good man,' he said quietly.

Inosa said nothing, but she looked a little embarrassed.

When the last of the yang-pra had gone, its hooves clattering and its fleece wobbling, over the bridge, the little boy nudged Raibhu to wake him up. Raibhu thanked him, commended him on a job well done, and handed over the tanka. 'You let your parents know you earned this, all right?' he said, ruffling the child's hair. 'It wasn't a gift.' The boy nodded eagerly, and raced off after the herd of yang-pra.

~

A hundred feet or so above the rope bridge, and on a ridge overlooking it, a man, a folded green-and-brown blanket draped over one shoulder, had his celestial view-glass trained on Raibhu, Inosa and Afhash as they crossed the bridge one at a time. The man was the same one who had been keeping an eye on Inosa's home, and who had sent off a messenger bhaagi to report her departure. He lowered the view-glass, his eyebrows pulling together into a puzzled frown as he did so. 'A magician?' he murmured to himself. 'And a good one. What's he doing here?'

~

'You're much better at magic than your friend is,' Inosa remarked. They had crossed the bridge a while back, and were now ascending the mountain. Inosa slowed her pace and was walking only a step ahead of Raibhu. Afhash still lagged behind a bit.

'Afhash's learning,' Raibhu replied, with a fleeting grin directed over his shoulder at his friend.

Inosa did not comment, but from the wry smile on her

lips, it was obvious she did not think highly of Afhash's chances of ever mastering the art. 'Your father was a very good magician, wasn't he?' she asked Raibhu. 'I remember Grandfather and Shervaan the Elder praising him, though I never got to see him perform.'

Raibhu nodded. 'He was brilliant.'

'And you have inherited his talent. Are you a magician by profession too?' She saw him shake his head, and added, 'Then what do you do for a living?'

Raibhu hesitated for a few moments, as if wondering what to say. Then, coming to a decision, he said. 'I'm a law officer.'

To his surprise, Inosa looked taken aback. Almost instantly, her astonishment changed to something rather like suspicion. 'A law officer?' she said. 'But then how is it that you didn't know where your father was all these years? Especially if he was in prison? As a law officer, you'd have come to know of him being in prison very quickly, wouldn't you?'

Raibhu shook his head. 'He was masquerading as a seller of trinkets, named Wartak. An assumed name. How could I have known? And I had no reason to believe that Father had been arrested.'

The faintly defiant air Raibhu assumed would have put most people off questioning him anymore, but Inosa was not so easily deterred. 'If I were looking for someone,' she murmured, half to herself, 'I would search everywhere. And I have done that, you know. Shervaan the Elder and I spent years—' she stopped and changed the topic. 'Which of the offices of the law are you posted at? Are you here, in the Sada Valley? Or further—'

'I am getting sick and tired of being left out of the conversation,' Afhash interrupted, pushing his way to the front. He gently nudged Raibhu aside. 'My friend, give me a chance to have a chat with our guide. If Inosa wants to know about Jaadum the Elder, I'm the one she should be talking to, not you.'

He turned to Inosa with a winning smile, but Inosa just lifted an eyebrow eloquently and said, 'We'd better get going, or we won't be able to find a decent place to set up camp for the night.' She looked Afhash in the eye. 'And you. Let me warn you. I don't like people sucking up to me, or treating me as if I'm some sort of doll. I am not that type. Understand?'

Afhash looked chastened, but he also bristled. 'I'm not sucking up to you,' he said indignantly. 'And I don't think you're a doll. You're'—he took a deep breath—'you're a brave and strong woman. I admire you.' He flushed, suddenly embarrassed by what he had said, the way he had bared his heart. 'Come on,' he said, turning to Raibhu. 'Let's go.' And he hurried off down the track, only to come up short: he had come to a fork in the track and he did not know which way to go.

Inosa, walking up with Raibhu beside her, did not say anything, but there was a twinkle in her eye. 'This way,' she said quietly. 'Right, towards the river.'

~

Somewhere, at some point in time

A tanka is held up briefly between a thumb and a forefinger. It catches the sunlight and glints. It turns, still gleaming, and the hand that holds it moves down, to stop in front of the excited, rosy-cheeked and chubby face of a little girl. She is standing beside her mother, holding the woman's hand, and she looks up shyly as the man who's holding the tanka now holds it out to her. 'I found it in your hair,' says the man with an affectionate smile, as he presses the tanka into her small hand. 'It is yours then, yes?' He gently places his hand on her head, wordlessly blessing the child before he goes on. His companion, a man of about the same age—they are both in their thirties or so—smiles as they continue their ascent of the path.

These two stand out from the rest of the crowd. They are wearing the flared tunics and leggings of Mandalans, whereas everybody around them is dressed in something or the other that invokes the Water Spirit: a flowing silver scarf, a pale blue turban with its end hanging loose. A long grey stole, a flowing dress with many layers of azure, white, and silver. There are even, here and there, the long silvery-grey robes of a more dedicated devotee, perhaps even an acolyte. Most of these people, too, have facial features that set them apart from the two outsiders. They have slim, slanting eyes and high cheekbones, while the two outsiders have large eyes and aquiline noses. This is Inosa's grandfather, long before Inosa was even thought of, and by his side is his faithful friend, Shervaan.

They are on a mountain path, snaking its way up through rugged, windswept terrain, just beyond the wide expanse of the Naham River. The only vegetation around consists of sparse tussocks of grass, some low-growing shrubs, and huge bushes of blue-flowering roses. But if there is little vegetation here, it does not imply a colourless, lifeless landscape: on the contrary. All along the side of the path runs a rivulet, its rippling song a constant accompaniment to the wind. Beside the rivulet, a low railing of finely carved grey stone meanders its way, and from this hang down fine wires of zansal that droop into the water of the rivulet. Every now and then, one of the devotees stops and kneels, touches the water with their fingertips, whispers a prayer, and then, having pulled out a finely coiled zansal thread from inside a pouch, a pocket or a satchel, proceeds to knot it around the railing, murmuring prayers all the time.

Ahead, the rivulet widens, and this is where the gate of the Aaboneer Temple has been built. A crystal gate, its archway scalloped and shaped like waves. Beyond this lies the Temple, sitting in the midst of a pool formed by the icy waters of the rivulet at its source. The source lies just beyond, where the Temple straddles a bridge of rock: a glacier, its pristine whiteness stretching far up into the mountains, beyond sight.

A throng of happy, excited people mills about the precincts of the Aaboneer Temple. Some, having removed their outer garments, have descended into the cold water of the pool and are praying. A couple of others sit on the bank of the pool, carefully plaiting together zansal wires, which they lower into the pool, chanting prayers as they do so. At one end of the pool, a waterside altar has been erected, at which stand two junior priests, clad in long flowing robes and playing yard-long silver flutes.

This is the Naham-Dhaar Aaboneer Temple, and it is hosting the annual Naham-Dhaar Temple Festival. Thousands of devout Aaboneer from across Mandala have converged on the Temple to participate in the two-day long celebrations. The fragrance of incense and flowers floating in the pool perfumes the air. The playing of the yard-long silver flutes and the high voices of devotional singers subdues the conversations, the laughter, and the muted cries of children. Even as the two outsiders step into the courtyard in front of the Temple, from inside the Temple there emerges a large group of priests, heading towards the centre of the courtyard to perform the ritual dances that are an integral part of the festivities. They are dressed in shimmering robes of silver-grey, white and the palest of blue, and each of them wears a mask made out of beaten zansal or humur. Humur, black and forbidding, for those depicting demons, finely painted with bulging eyes, red-lipped mouths, and sharp fangs. Blue zansal masks for those who will play the forces of good: their eyes heavy-lidded and benign, their mouths smiling, long silver hair flowing down to their waists from the crown of the masks.

For a moment, Inosa's grandfather stares, mesmerized, into the face of a masked Aaboneer ritual dancer, his eyes wide in awe and wonder as he stares at the mask. A whirl, a sudden breeze stirred up by the swirling of the dancer's voluminous robes—and the dancer has gone on.

Grandfather turns to look at Shervaan. 'That was it, wasn't it Shervaan?' he asks, his voice a little breathless. 'You recognized it, didn't you?'

Shervaan nods; he is too awestruck to speak.

His friend looks back at the dancers, and at the eager crowd beyond. His gaze wanders up the mountain, to the dazzling white of the glacier, before he looks again at the main building of the Temple. 'I think we've come to the right place,' he says. 'Perhaps we will find the answer here.'

~

The sun had set and the light was dying fast. The three of them were very close to the river, the path having brought them to the edge of the mountain. On the evening air floated the sounds of nature winding down for the day—but to that had now been added other sounds, the sounds of humanity getting ready for something. The thunderous lowing of the huge oxen that pulled the war-carts, the rumbling of the wheels of the carts. The occasional strident shout, the rhythmic thudding of booted feet moving in unison.

And then, piercing the air, a sharp scream, followed by a loud splash. There were more screams, half-choked off, intermittent.

'Someone's fallen into the river!' Even as he said it, Raibhu had thrown off his travelling sack and was racing towards the edge of the cliff, just beyond. He reached the edge, and looked around: just a few feet further on, the slope was less precipitous, and was all scree. He sprinted towards it and scrambled down, going sideways to minimize his chances of a fall. He stumbled and slipped even then, but picked himself up and kept going.

Behind him, Afhash and Inosa too had begun running, Inosa pausing only briefly to pick up Raibhu's travelling sack before setting off again. By the time she and Afhash had reached the bottom of the slope, Raibhu had already plunged into the water.

The riverbed sloped here a bit, the water racing over rocks as it went down a slight gradient. The current was strong, and the presence of the rocks made it dangerous. Raibhu fought the current, battling it with every ounce of his strength as he made his way to the man who was being carried away by the river. Inosa and Afhash raced along on the bank, looking for a place that would allow them to enter the water without risking breaking their necks in the process. Before they could join Raibhu, though, he saw them and shouted out, 'No! Don't come in!'

It was obvious why he had said that: he had managed to get a grip on the person he had gone in to rescue. And, at the same time, he had found a large piece of driftwood—a substantial part of a tree trunk that had stuck between several rocks—and had anchored himself and the other man to it.

For a few moments, they all stopped, caught in limbo and unable to think, unable to move. The current was strong and Raibhu, bogged down by the weight of the unconscious man he was holding onto, would not be able to go much further without running the risk of losing his grip on the man. 'I'll go in,' Afhash said, dropping his travelling sack onto the sand of the riverbank.

'Wait,' Inosa said. She quickly pulled off her travelling sack, opened it and rummaged about, bringing out a loop of sturdy rope. She opened it and handed one end to Afhash—'Tie it around your waist, really securely,' she instructed—and looked around swiftly, her eyes searching for something to anchor the rope to.

'You're not coming in!' Afhash said, horror-struck. 'It's too dangerous!'

'I'm not coming in,' Inosa agreed. 'Because someone has to stay ashore too. But we need something stronger than me to anchor the rope.' She had already found a tree that stood close to the water's edge, and was looping the rope around its trunk. 'Go!' she shouted to Afhash. He waded into the river, and was almost immediately swept off his feet by the current, but he managed to stay on course.

It was a hard fight against the current, but by combining their strength, and helped by the rope, Raibhu and Afhash were able to haul out the man. He was still unconscious when they carried him up out of the water and deposited him on the sand. He was wearing a uniform, a double-breasted tunic in grey and brown, with bronze buttons down the front: Raibhu had rescued a soldier of the Southern Mandalan Army. Afhash whispered urgently to Raibhu, 'He's alive, let's go. You can't be caught.' But Raibhu wasn't listening; he was too busy attending to the man, turning his head to the side and pumping his chest. It took a few moments of rhythmic pumping, before the man suddenly gave a gurgling, choking gasp and brought up a lot of water.

'Your hand is bleeding,' Inosa remarked as Raibhu drew away and Afhash attended to the man, helping him sit up, rubbing his back vigorously and patting him. Raibhu glanced down at his hand, looking a little bewildered, as if he had not even noticed the blood flowing from it. 'I must have scraped it on a sharp stone,' he murmured.

They were interrupted by the sound of running feet, muffled somewhat by the sand of the riverbank. A bunch of soldiers were approaching, an officer at the forefront. Their expressions ranged from worry to curiosity, to outright relief. The bedraggled and wet soldier, still coughing and gasping for air, tried to stand up when he saw the officer, but he was waved away. 'Take him,' the officer called over his shoulder to the men following him. He moved forward towards Raibhu, Inosa and Afhash while his men went to their comrade and hoisted him up to take him back to the camp.

'That was very brave of you,' the officer said, patting Raibhu on the shoulder. He was a man in his late thirties, powerfully built and good-looking in a severe sort of way: he gave the impression that he could be a strict disciplinarian when it was required of him, but he could also be genial and friendly, as he was now being. 'And very prompt, too. You outstripped us even though we were much closer to start off with. Well done.'

He glanced down at Raibhu's bleeding hand. Raibhu had taken out his handkerchief, but it was sodden and not much use. The officer, seeing his plight, took out his own handkerchief and offered it. 'Come back to our camp,' he said. 'It's right round that bend in the river'—he pointed upstream—'and we'll attend to your hand.'

'I'm fine,' Raibhu said, tying the handkerchief around his hand with Afhash's help. 'Thank you. For this,' he indicated the handkerchief, 'and for the offer. But we need to go on.'

'Nonsense. Where will you go at this hour? It'll be dark in half an hour's time, you won't be able to go anywhere. Come and stay at the camp, there is also space there for people who have done us a favour.'

Raibhu smiled. 'That you should think we have done you a favour—that is enough for us. Your goodwill is all we would want.' He could see that the officer was not going to be so easily deflected from his somewhat obstinate desire to be hospitable. 'Really, Master. All of you do so much for the country. It is a small thing if we can do something to repay that.'

Afhash snorted, and when the officer whirled around to look at him, changed the snort into a cough. 'I—I just wanted to point out, we are awaited at the next village,' Afhash said hurriedly. 'My uncle will be looking out for us,' he added.

'We had better leave,' Inosa agreed from where she was untying the rope around the tree trunk. She deliberately pitched her voice low to make it sound like a teenaged boy's, a voice that was somewhere between the soprano of a child's and the deeper tenor of a man's. 'It will be dark soon.' The officer glanced towards her, as if he had not noticed her before, but he glanced away again, dismissing her as of no consequence.

But even if he had dismissed Inosa, it seemed he had not dismissed her words. 'Oh, well,' he said, shrugging. 'If you must be on your way, you must. Are you sure you don't want anything to take along? Food? Medicines? No? Very well, then. May the Land Spirit protect you and guide you.'

And, just as abruptly as he had appeared on the scene, the officer disappeared. One minute he was there, urging them on to stay at the camp; the next moment, he was striding off across the sand, heading towards where the camp was located upstream.

'Come on,' Inosa said, looping the rope over her shoulder. 'It is going to be dark very soon, and I would not like to be out on a trail when darkness falls. It can be dangerous.'

~

'I thought you were an intelligent fellow,' Afhash said softly. He had been carrying Raibhu's travelling sack in addition to his own, despite Raibhu's protests, and now that Inosa had picked a spot for them to rest, he put down both the sacks.

'Here was your chance to be one enemy less, and what do you do?'

Inosa had put down her travelling sack and retrieved from it an earthen pot. With it, she had gone a few yards away, to where a narrow brook flowed between the rocks. The gurgling of the water, the birdsong and the chirping of crickets in the undergrowth filled the air.

'So be it,' Raibhu said. 'I didn't see an enemy. All I saw was a man in mortal danger.' He looked down at the now bloody cloth wound around his hand. 'My conscience would not allow me to let him die, Afhash.'

Before Afhash could react to that, Inosa was back, bringing with her the earthen pot, now brimming with water. 'Take off your wet clothes,' she said to Raibhu as she set the pot down. She glanced over her shoulder at Afhash. 'And you, go collect some wood like you did earlier today. We need to build a fire. Don't take all day about it, all right?' She sat down on her haunches and opened her travelling sack again. As she rummaged about in it, she looked up again at Raibhu. He had pulled off his wet tunic and was standing with it in his hand. The handkerchief wrapped around it was red through and through.

'Why haven't you taken off your clothes?' Inosa snapped. 'Stop being so prudish, please! I'm not going to assault you.' She went back to the task of searching her travelling sack, muttering audibly as she did so: 'What misconceptions people have about themselves!'

Raibhu contented himself with removing the shirt and undershirt he was wearing under the tunic, but refused to take off anything else. Inosa noticed, and though a small and mischievous smile hovered about her lips briefly, she did not say anything as she set about attending to his hand. Raibhu was embarrassed about being bare-chested, but Inosa did not even seem to notice. She poured out some water from her leather water bottle onto a clean rag and gently but efficiently cleaned out his wound. Dabbing at his hand, examining it minutely, she murmured, 'It's only a scrape, not a cut, thank goodness for that. You don't need it stitched up.' She wiped it one last time, and discarding the rag, retrieved a small leather pouch she had taken from her travelling sack. Inside it was a coarse, dull green powder which she shook into her cupped palm.

'What's that?' Raibhu asked, his voice brimming with suspicion.

'It's the dried stem of calmroot,' Inosa said. 'Everybody knows the roots make a good infusion, but we, up in the mountains, know that the stem has healing properties.' One-handed, she closed the pouch, before lifting the bottle and pouring out a tiny amount of water into her palm. As she used her fingertips to work the green powder into a paste, she asked, 'Why were you so reluctant to stop at the Army camp?'

'It would have been a waste of time,' Raibhu replied. 'I don't want to spend days on end trekking through the woods.'

Inosa gently rubbed the paste onto the wound. 'That was not the reason you refused,' she countered. 'I saw you and Afhash look at each other. The two of you were worried, not impatient.'

Raibhu did not say anything while she bandaged his hand.

When, work done, she looked up into his face questioningly, as if wordlessly repeating her query, he sighed. 'I am North Mandalan,' he said softly.

Inosa's eyes widened. 'You said you were a law officer,' she muttered. Then, as if realizing what that implied, she added, 'A Northern law officer. Ah.' She sat back on her heels, her eyes narrowing as they scrutinized his face. Raibhu had to struggle to not look away, Inosa's gaze was so unrelenting in its intensity.

'So that's why, even though you are a law officer, you couldn't find out about your father being in prison.' The next moment, she frowned. 'And you were planning to keep this hidden from me?' There was accusation in her voice, a hurt that made Raibhu flinch. He looked away, saw his travelling sack lying nearby, and went to it to dig out dry clothing. Inosa continued to speak, her anger rising with every word she uttered.

'You don't trust me an inch, do you?' She fumed. 'You only decided to have me along as a guide because I insisted, and because you were in too much of a hurry to go looking for an alternative!'

Raibhu had found a fresh shirt and undershirt in his travelling sack. He tugged at them, pulling clumsily because of the bandage on his hand. Inosa strode across to him, snatched the travelling sack from him, and pulled out the clothes, shoving them at him. Then, as if suddenly awkward at his shirtless state, she whirled around and stood with her back to him, still ranting and raving. 'You haven't changed much, have you! Even back then, when we first met in that clearing in the woods, you didn't think anybody was quite as good as you, did you? Oh, yes. Why trust Inosa, eh? Inosa is a villager, Inosa is a stupid woman—'

'I never said anything of the sort!' Raibhu retorted. 'And I never thought anything of the sort. Calm down and at least listen to what I have to say!' He had thrown on the clothes, somewhat untidily, and was trying to spread out the wet clothes across a couple of bushes.

'Why should I listen?' Inosa snapped back. 'Why should you bother to explain anything to me?' She blinked frantically, and took a deep breath to steady herself.

'Well, I'll explain it, whether you listen or not,' Raibhu said. 'No, please don't interrupt. Listen. Afhash brought me news of Father in Dhaani. I hadn't met or seen Father—I didn't even know where he was—for the past eighteen years. That was when he left me in Dhaani, and that was when he was arrested here, in Southern Mandala, when he was crossing the border again to get back. They thought he was a North Mandala spy.' Inosa was quiet now, listening attentively, and Raibhu slowed down, choosing his words carefully. 'Father was dying. I had no choice; I wanted to meet him, not just to say goodbye to him, but to find out what had happened to Mother.'

Afhash had stepped into the small clearing where they had set up camp. He looked quizzically at the two of them, and gauging the seriousness of the conversation he had barged in upon, remained silent. He put down the load of twigs and driftwood he had found and crouched down, piling them up preparatory to lighting a fire. His attention, however, was all on Inosa and Raibhu rather than on what he was doing.

'Father died before I even reached Sandha,' Raibhu said.

'So I'm back at the beginning, I still don't know who killed Mother.' He was staring into space, his gaze on some invisible long-ago memory; had he been looking at Inosa, he would have seen the momentary look of something like guilt that seemed to pass over her face.

'But you see, don't you,' Raibhu added, 'why the fewer people who know who I am, the better it is? Father was arrested on suspicion of being a spy, and he died in prison with that charge still against him. If anybody finds out I'm Northern, I would be immediately arrested. Or killed straightaway without even being arrested.'

'I wouldn't do something like that,' Inosa said. 'You really think I'd betray you to the cops, or the Army?' She was still annoyed and sullen, but not as much as earlier.

'No, I didn't think that,' Raibhu said, before adding, 'it's just that the fewer people who know I'm Northern, the better. Afhash anyway knows; I would have liked it to remain at just him.' He sighed. 'Please, Inosa. Don't get so angry at something that wasn't meant to cast aspersions on you. Believe me, it wasn't that way. Can we rest a while, now? Eat something? There must be something to eat in the travelling sacks, right?'

For a brief moment, Inosa looked as if she was going to argue, but she seemed to change her mind and nodded a little reluctantly. She glanced towards where Afhash was struggling to build a fire, and shooed him away. 'Check your travelling sack,' she said. 'There's some dried fruit in that. And some bread. Triangular, the only way I know how to make it. If you can't trim it yourself into a shape that suits your idea of what food should look like, give it to me.' Afhash had the grace to look sheepish at that, but Inosa had already turned away.

She was busy arranging the dried twigs, grass and leaves, and even as Raibhu watched, she got out her tinderbox and flints. A few strikes, some expert positioning of the kindling, and she had managed to coax a few sparks from the flints. It took a little more time, a little nurturing, some shielding of the tiny flame, a judicious touching of it to the driest of the bits of wood and grass, and the flame caught. Inosa poked and prodded at it, teasing it along, feeding it until it had grown strong enough to keep going on its own.

'It's doesn't matter to me whether you're Northern or Southern or what,' Inosa said suddenly. She had been quiet so long that both Raibhu and Afhash had assumed she had forgotten the topic; her return to it took them both by surprise. Inosa did not appear to notice their astonishment; she simply went on talking.

'After all, eighteen years ago, you lived here too, in the Sada Valley. You belong here as much as we do. And even if you didn't, what difference does it make?' She reached for the pot Afhash had unearthed, and which he had filled with water from the water bottle he had been carrying. Placing the pot on the fire, Inosa reached into her travelling sack for dried calmroot. 'We are all Mandalans, all said and done,' she continued. 'Whether we eat circular food or triangular'—she glanced at a red-faced Afhash with a sly smile—'it doesn't matter. Whether you are legally a Northerner or a Southerner, it doesn't matter. What matters is that we are all Mandalans. Nationality is a matter of politics, the essence of Mandala is a matter of the heart.'

'Uff,' Afhash said, quickly shuffling along into place next to Inosa. 'Here you are chatting away with this dull dog, Raibhu, and completely neglecting me! I'm the one with the heart, Inosa. I'm all heart, don't you see that?' He gave her a big goofy grin and waggled his eyebrows suggestively, making Inosa burst out laughing despite herself.

'Oh, go away!' she said. 'Go and practice your tanka-twirling or whatever!'

~

The Army camp on the bank of the Sada was a large one, with sixteen war-carts lined up along one side parallel to the river, and the space between these carts and the river taken up by tents, pitched in neat rows. At one end were the stables for the oxen that pulled the war-carts, and for the horses. These were big-boned chestnuts with the occasional splash of white, like a star on the forehead or socks, or even some of the hairs in the mane. Southern Mandala horses, but with those telltale signs of the clandestine efforts to infuse more durability and strength by cross-breeding them with the Northern white horses that were periodically smuggled across the border.

At the other end of the camp was the small open tent that acted as the office of the man who had recently met Raibhu, Inosa and Afhash and invited them to the camp. He now sat behind a makeshift desk crafted from a tree stump, looking through a sheaf of papers in front of him. The sun was about to set, the last few rays that lingered in the sky were just sufficient for the officer to see what was written. But even this meagre light was suddenly blocked out by someone who came and stood in front of him.

The officer's irritation at being disturbed turned to puzzlement as he took in the law office uniform of the newcomer.

'Yes?' he asked as Inosa's old friend Xindaar stepped into the tent. The law officer was looking a little dusty and dishevelled, but he came to attention and saluted the Army officer. Behind him, hovering in the patch of ground outside the tent, was the officer's servant, looking apprehensive.

'I am Xindaar, from Murki, Master,' Xindaar introduced himself. 'I—I saw your man being rescued from the river.'

'And?' The officer was growing impatient again; he had a lot of work to do, and each moment was precious.

'I saw you talk to the people who rescued him, Master,' Xindaar said hurriedly. 'Did they say who they were, Master? And where did they go?'

'What's the matter, Xindaar?' The officer was looking suspicious now. 'What have they done? Why are you trailing them?'

'No, Master. Not trailing them—or at least not because of anything they've done. They're clean. I happen to know one of them, from Murki. I was just curious, wondering why they were headed out into the woods.'

The officer did not look convinced, but work was beckoning and he was in a mood to end the conversation. 'They mentioned having to go on to some village nearby where they were awaited. I didn't ask more. And I didn't see where they went. Is that all?' he asked, as Xindaar, looking indecisive, shifted his weight from one foot to the other.

'Yes, Master,' Xindaar said, his expression one of disappointment. 'Thank you, Master. My apologies for having disturbed you, Master.' He bowed, hands held forward in the Mandalan gesture of greeting. The officer, automatically reciprocating the gesture, reached his hands forward and clasped Xindaar's hands. For a moment, as he looked down at the officer's hand, Xindaar froze. His reaction made the officer glance down too.

On the inside of Xindaar's wrist was a distinctive tattoo. A small replica of the constellation known as the Brihan Punj, its six stars arranged in the form of a flower bud.

The officer, a small smile making his lips curve up at the corners, tilted his own wrist up to look at its inside, to see the tattoo that mirrored Xindaar's.

The two men exchanged a look that could have meant anything. It could have been utterly harmless, it could have been conspiratorial. It could have meant nothing more than an acknowledgement of kinship.

Chapter Seven

Inosa, Raibhu and Afhash had settled in comfortably. They had eaten their frugal meal, had drunk their calmroot infusion, and were now engrossed in whatever interested each one of them. Afhash was busy practicing his tanka trick, and though his fingers had not become any more adept at the trick than they had been the previous day, he persevered doggedly. Inosa had picked up the branch which she had been honing while they waited at the rope bridge; she had been carrying it all along, and now sat down to whittle it.

Raibhu, after sitting for a while staring into the fire, suddenly recalled something. He went to his travelling sack, and retrieved from it the smaller pack he had carried from Dhaani. From inside that, he pulled out the book he had been reading when Afhash had arrived, the book he had flung into the bag in his hurry. *The Teachings of the Venerable Dayadhan Jijit*.

With a smile of anticipation, Raibhu opened the book.

He had been reading for a while when Inosa remarked, 'That looks like an absorbing book. Or at least you seem to enjoy it.'

Raibhu looked up. He had been so deep in the book that he was startled by her voice.

'It's not so much enjoyment as introspection,' he said. 'It's making me think.' Inosa looked interested, as if waiting to hear more, so Raibhu continued. 'It's a collection of sayings by the ancient philosopher Dayadhan Jijit, who was the teacher to the Emperor Tanit Mahabeyan. His wisdom is very—well, thought-provoking, I suppose.'

Inosa gave a somewhat ambiguous smile, but did not say anything.

Raibhu pursed his lips, looking through the book, turning a page. His eyes lit up as he found what he was looking for. 'This, for instance.' He cleared his throat and read out a sentence. 'Listen: "When you stand with the oppressor, the two of you stand alone. When you stand with the oppressed, the Spirits stand with you." Is that not sound philosophy?'

Inosa nodded approvingly. 'True.' She turned back to her work, and Raibhu was about to return to his book when she spoke up. 'And how about this: "Beware of reaching for power and glory, for this power will one day be gone, this glory will fade. Dust will cover all, the water will wash it away, the winds will sweep it to a distant land. All that endures is humanity and kindness; even the Spirits uphold those." Is that not sound too?'

Afhash had let the tanka fall from his fingers as he listened to Inosa. He clapped enthusiastically now. 'Wah, wah! Superb! Excellent, Inosa, really excellent!' He turned to Raibhu, his eyes shining. 'What do you think of that, eh? Inosa is as good a philosopher as that Daya—whatever—of yours! And a far better poet, too!'

Inosa was smiling, and Raibhu grinned too. 'Inosa is just quoting,' he said. 'Those are the words of Vidyanjika Jijita, am I right?' he asked, turning to Inosa.

Inosa nodded, a ghost of a smile on her face. 'The ancient poetess and mystic of the Sada Valley. Here, few of us revere Dayadhan Jijit like the rest of Mandala does, but Vidyanjika Jijita holds a very special place in our hearts.'

'I have only a very fleeting acquaintance with her verses,' Raibhu admitted. Then, in an apologetic tone, he added, 'Forgive me for presuming you did not know of Dayadhan Jijit. That was pompous of me.'

Inosa brushed away his apology with a wave of her hand. 'My grandfather was a scholar of sorts, and Shervaan the Elder made sure he continued the education Grandfather had begun. If it hadn't been for them, I suppose I would have remained as illiterate and ignorant as the average village woman.'

'I don't think so,' Raibhu said softly, half to himself. 'I don't think anybody could ever equate you with the average village woman.' He turned back to his book, and Inosa, after looking at him with astonished eyes for a few moments, turned her attention back to the stick she was whittling.

Afhash looked a little disconcerted. Perhaps if his mind could have been read by the two people who shared that campfire with him, they would have seen how suddenly out of place he felt. Inosa, whom he had thought of as a simple, if strong-willed and independent village girl—one very much of his own class—had, in one fell swoop, proved that she was not all she appeared. He had known she was educated; that was apparent by the fact that she had read Jaadum's letter without any difficulty. But that she wasn't merely literate, but learned—that was disconcerting. For a moment, he seemed to grapple with the idea, and then, with a snort of disgust, tossed the tanka into the air, grabbed it and placed it in his pocket.

'What's the matter?' Raibhu asked. He had been watching Afhash even as Inosa spoke, and Afhash's growing frustration had had its effect on him too. Although his tone was bland, there was concern in his eyes.

'Oh, who cares! You two can sit around and discuss philosophy deep into the night! Don't mind me, I'm just an illiterate thief—'

'What on earth is the matter with you?' Inosa retorted. 'Who said anything about you being an illiterate whatever? Why should that make any difference?'

'Just the way being Northern or Southern makes no difference?' Afhash said, bitterly. 'Yes, go on, both of you. Don't bother about me. I'll just sit here and learn all I can from listening to the two of you, high and mighty educated people.'

Inosa looked furious enough to get up and bash Afhash, but Raibhu intervened. His voice was calm and collected, even sympathetic. 'I was lucky enough to have a family who brought me up and looked after me,' he said. 'Even when Mother was dead and Father had vanished, I had my grandparents. If they had not been there, I don't think I would have studied beyond the little I had learnt.' He paused. 'My having been lucky in life in no way makes me better than you. If I had been in your place, having gone through the experiences you've had to endure—I don't think I would have survived. Life teaches much more than books can, Afhash. You, of all people, should know that.'

His voice had a soothing effect, and when he stopped,

the silence was broken only by the crackle of the flames. Afhash, angry and embittered just a few minutes ago, was looking mollified now. Inosa, initially inclined to be furious, was looking thoughtful: Raibhu's words had hinted at a side of the rambunctious, flirtatious, often clownish Afhash that she had not even imagined.

'I was lucky to have Grandfather, and later Shervaan the Elder,' she added, a little gruffly. 'If it hadn't been for them—and as for Vidyanjika Jijita, well...I find her fascinating, her words bring me so much hope, teach me so much. She was a remarkable woman.'

Afhash swallowed. For a moment, he looked torn, caught between the awkwardness of the situation, the still-raw hurt of that inferiority he had felt, and the essentially ebullient nature of his being. Afhash could not stay angry or brooding for long, though: he broke into a grin and said, 'Remarkable, like you?'

Inosa sighed. 'You're incorrigible,' she said, as she brushed off her dagger and replaced it in her pocket. The result of her work of the past half-hour was before them: a sturdy, well-shaped wooden spear with a sharp, dangerous-looking point. She placed it beside the rough bed she had made from leaves and dry moss, and drew her blanket over her as she lay down. 'I'm going to sleep. Goodnight, you two. Don't wander off anywhere.'

~

The morning air was clean and crisp. The sky was a greyish blue not yet completely lit up by the sun, which was only just beginning to rise, flooding the eastern skies with gold and orange streaks.

Inosa splashed her face with ice cold water from a spring, and rubbed the sleep out of her eyes. She spent a few more minutes in her ablutions, doing a thorough job of freshening up before she wiped her face on the hem of her tunic and stood up. The wooden spear she had made was lying beside her on the grass; she picked it up, hefted it, and then, smoothly and without a break, launched into an exercise routine. She dipped and lunged, she squatted and straightened. She whirled the spear around her head and brought it down. She threw it up into the air and caught it smartly by the shaft on its way down. She held it at a diagonal to the ground and leaped nimbly over it.

By the time she finished, fifteen minutes later, the sun was up and the sky had turned a beautiful pale blue. Inosa, panting with the exertion, took a deep breath and stood up from the half-squat that she had ended the routine with. She looked up.

Raibhu was standing opposite, watching her. He made no attempt to hide, or to disappear into the trees beyond. He just stood there, continuing to look at her.

'You've been standing here for quite a while, haven't you?' Inosa commented. 'Was I making a noise? Did that wake you?'

Raibhu shook his head. 'No. I just happened to come by, heading for the stream, when I saw you. Accidentally. You're pretty good.'

Inosa made a face. 'And you're pretty condescending.'

Raibhu shook his head emphatically. 'Absolutely not. I would not be so bold as to be condescending to *you*. You're a dangerous woman.'

Inosa raised an eyebrow. There was a defiant gleam in her eyes. 'You are making fun of me,' she said. 'Very well. Let's see who has a right to make fun of whom, okay? Let's have a challenge.'

'I wasn't making fun of you,' Raibhu protested. Inosa's expression remained as mulish as before, so he shrugged. 'Okay. Don't say I didn't warn you.' He rolled up his sleeves. 'Do you know how I got into the law office in the first place? Because I was such a good athlete. That was the main reason they took me on. And even now, I am their star athlete. Every year, when the annual autumn games take place in Dhaani, I win prizes for races, in swimming, and in boxing.' He grinned. 'Are you still sure you want to challenge me?'

Inosa hoisted her wooden spear on her shoulder, then took aim at a tall, very prominent pine tree that stood head and shoulders above the rest. One quick, sharp movement and the spear went flying to land thwack in the trunk of the tree. 'First one to pull out the spear wins!' Inosa yelled as she ran.

It was about two hundred metres to the tree, but the ground was by no means level. There were rocks, the stream at which Inosa had washed, and the gullies eroded into the banks of the stream when it was in spate. There were thick bushes, shrubs, scrubby grass and low-hanging tree branches that got in the way, scratching their faces and grabbing their clothes as Inosa and Raibhu ran towards the pine tree. They hurtled over some obstacles, went around others, pushed through still others. They ran, they climbed, they skidded down. They fell and got up again. They ran on, the pine tree growing nearer.

By the time they reached the tree, both Inosa and Raibhu were covered with dried leaves, streaks of mud, and cobwebs into which they had blundered. But both were also laughing, exhilarated and happy by the sheer thrill of the challenge. They reached the tree simultaneously, but it was Raibhu who leaped up a moment before Inosa did, and who—by virtue of being a few inches taller than her—was able to get his hands on the spear before she could. He grabbed it with a cry of joy and turned to Inosa. She was grinning back at him.

'Hah. That's all you two can manage? One little sprint, and you're panting like a bellows at a fire-pit.' Afhash emerged from the trees nearest their campsite. 'Let's even out the challenge,' he suggested. 'The two of you against me, all right? I promise you I'll trounce both of you. You too, Raibhu, law officer or not.'

Inosa shook her head. 'Not now,' she replied briskly. 'I would anyway have been coming to wake you up if you weren't already awake. Come along, let's get going.' And calmly taking her wooden spear from Raibhu, she led the way back towards their camp.

~

As the trio vanished into the woods, a clump of tall bushes near the stream parted. Very cautiously, Xindaar looked out. When he was certain, he stepped out, and behind him came a junior officer, a gawky young man who looked very much in awe of all that was around him—the woods, the suspicious quarry they were pursuing, Xindaar himself.

'A law officer, Master?' he asked Xindaar. 'And such a good athlete, too? But I didn't recognize him, Master.'

Xindaar gestured to him to keep his voice down. Then, just as silently, he gestured to the junior officer to follow him as he made his way through the trees, heading in the direction Inosa had led the two men.

~

It was late morning. The sun was bright, but little of its light filtered through the dense canopy of conifers that cloaked the mountains. Here and there, in clearings or in the occasional mountain meadow, there were wildflowers and grass, but otherwise, the trees dominated. As they walked along, Inosa would pause now and then, her sharp eyes having spotted something she could forage: wild mushrooms, morels, nuts, berries. She was quick at harvesting them, too: she barely even stopped to collect something and push it into an outer pocket of her travelling sack.

'We'll be coming to a village soon,' she said, buttoning down the pocket. The trail they had been following had been a barely-there thread of bare earth; it now joined a much-used path which descended in a series of loops. Within five minutes of Inosa's having announced the approach of a village, they had reached it: a typical Mandalan village of thatch-roofed wooden houses, each house surrounded by its patch of private land. According to the inclinations and needs of the occupants, this patch was put to different uses: some had made a kitchen garden here, growing purple pumpkins, trailing vines of white and blue beans, and tomato plants that stood as tall as trees against trellises. Others had planted fruit trees. Some had fenced off part of the yard and used it as a pen for yang-pra or for the short, long-haired cattle that were indigenous to the Sada Valley.

The smell of wood smoke, straw, and cooking hung in the air—and, drifting on the breeze as they entered the village, there came the buzz of several voices. People talking, discussing something in lowered voices. One voice, commanding and louder than the others, stood out. Raibhu, hearing it even before the three of them rounded the corner, paused, his eyebrows drawn together.

Inosa had not noticed that Raibhu had stopped; he quickly moved forward and tried to slow her down, but she had already turned the corner, and come up on the fringe of a crowd that thronged the village square.

'Remember, it is *you*,' the man standing at the front, atop a neatly-stacked pile of timber, was saying. 'You, here at the border, right across the river from Northern Mandala, who are the vanguard against infiltrators and spies. It is on you that the responsibility rests'—he made a sweeping dramatic gesture, pointing to each of his audience, seeming to address each one as an individual—'to be true Southerners. You must show the rest of the country what loyalty is all about.'

It was the Southern Army officer Raibhu and Afhash had encountered on the vaanik on their way to Sandha, the man who had been so suspicious of the two of them. Beside him, standing on the ground, were several of his colleagues, all of them armed, looking out over the small crowd of villagers. A little away from the soldiers stood a gaunt, thin-faced man, a green-and-brown patterned blanket thrown about his shoulders. Slung over one shoulder was a heavy leather pouch, the end of a celestial view-glass poking up from its half-shut mouth.

Inosa and Afhash, unaware and curious, had already

moved forward; Raibhu reached out to pull them back, to warn them—but it was too late. They had already been seen. In a crowd of people, all standing still, a few newcomers moving in the background immediately drew the attention of anybody standing facing the crowd—and especially if that person happened to be in the middle of inciting that crowd against possible foreign spies.

'What? What's the matter?' Inosa whispered as Raibhu backpedalled all three of them into the narrow lane through which they had come. Raibhu shook his head, motioning her to be silent, and gestured to his two companions to run, to follow him. Afhash, who had caught a glimpse of the officer, obeyed without demur. Inosa, recognizing the urgency in Raibhu's manner, complied without asking any more questions. They ran, cutting across village paths between orchards, a graveyard, a little field—and behind them, they could now hear shouts: 'That way! They've gone that way!' A dog was barking frantically somewhere, and the thud of boots on cobbled stone rang in the air.

The village doors were all locked or barred, their residents probably part of the crowd in the square. Raibhu, Inosa and Afhash went racing up a small path to a group of houses, and came up against a dead end. 'Not here, not here!' Raibhu said, whirling around and leading them down, racing and stumbling over the uneven path. Below, where the path forked, were more houses: all shut, all silent. There was no place to sneak in, no place where they could beg for sanctuary. They twisted and turned, searching for an escape route, a hidey-hole, anything that would keep them safe. Somewhere at the other end of the village, the sounds of pursuit still rang in the air.

Raibhu, his eyes alighting on a house that stood a little apart, turned towards it, gesturing to Inosa and Afhash to follow him. They raced, past a small patch of grass studded with wildflowers, past a little stream—and to the house Raibhu had seen. Whoever lived here had tried to put their little patch of surrounding land to maximum use. Fruit trees stood all along the outer fence, and from the foot of the trees till up to the doorstep of the house, orderly rows of vegetables grew. On each windowsill of the house, small wooden containers had been hung on horizontal poles, and in them grew an array of herbs and small plants. As if this wasn't all, a shed had been built on part of the land, by attaching a few wooden planks to one side of the roof and thus extending it a little beyond the cottage. Under this, fenced in by stacks of wood and bales of straw that lay heaped along one side, was a herd of yang-pra. The yang-pra, their rosy fleeces bobbing, milled about in the enclosure, baaing and bleating. Between the bulk of the house and the stacked wood and straw, the yang-pra pen was gloomy and dim; the pinkness of the yang-pras' fleeces looked almost luminescent in it.

It was for the dingy, barely discernible furthest corner of the yang-pra pen that Raibhu headed. He was about to vault over the fence surrounding the yang-pra when a movement off to one side caught his eye. Inosa, seeing his eyes widen, glanced the way he was looking. Afhash followed suit.

A little girl, about seven years old or so, was standing at the nearest window, gazing at them. She was still and silent as a statue; there was no knowing how long she had been there.

Raibhu paused. 'You two go on,' he whispered to Inosa

and Afhash. 'Go in and hide at the end among the yang-pra, I'll join you.' He gave them a gentle but firm nudge, and they vaulted over the fence to make their way through the herd of yang-pra. The animals, bleating nervously, scattered and tried to move away, but there was little place. With some jostling and shoving, Inosa and Afhash made it to the far end. It was dark here, and when they crouched, the herd of yang-pra shielded them from the sight of anybody outside the pen. Unless one knew someone was hiding behind the yang-pra, they would never guess. The yang-pra, too, calmed down after a few minutes, and seemed to accept the intruders as an unwelcome but necessary evil.

Raibhu reached the little girl, who by now had climbed out of the window and was standing outside. Her eyes, wide and grey in a thin but healthy, red-cheeked face, were unafraid, merely curious. As Inosa and Afhash watched from behind the shifting screen of woolly bodies, Raibhu bent and asked the child something. From the way he gestured, the questions woven by his hands, it was clear he was asking about her parents, her guardians. The girl shook her head, and waved her hand, pointing towards the mountains to the north. Whoever was supposed to be looking after her was gone, far away. Raibhu patted her shoulder and explained something, to which she listened attentively. Raibhu had put a hand in his pocket; he pulled out a tanka and offered it to the little girl. She seemed to refuse, but when Raibhu insisted, she accepted it. For a brief moment, her palm was upturned, the inside of her wrist visible. On it was tattooed a mark by now familiar to those who saw it. Inosa's eyes widened, and Raibhu looked momentarily intrigued.

It was a depiction of the constellation known as the Brihan Punj.

The little girl, the tanka clutched in her hand, ran off in the direction of the village square; Raibhu raced to the yang-pra pen and made his way through the herd of yang-pra to the end, where Inosa and Afhash crouched.

'Are you mad?' Afhash hissed. 'Why would you trust a complete stranger?'

'Shh,' Raibhu whispered back. 'If this works, we might get some respite.' He pulled his dagger out of his waistband, and seeing him, Inosa followed suit. Afhash, still looking uncertain and worried, also got out his dagger.

~

The officer who had been addressing the villagers motioned his men forward; they fanned out across the village. They scurried about, running along the lanes, checking each house, moving swiftly on as soon as they discovered a locked door, an empty yard. Their shouts rang out as they reported back, letting the others know of negative progress. The villagers, still grouped in anxious clusters in the village square, watched as the soldiers milled about, now disappearing into one lane, now emerging. The blanket-clad man, carrying the celestial view-glass, kept close on the heels of the officer, his alert gaze now here, now there. Now and then he would move forward, peering about to examine a small patch of crops more closely, or to say something to the officer.

The officer led his men up a slope, past a few houses—all of which were locked—and past the house with the improvised yang-pra pen. Two of the soldiers ran up the narrow path that led through the cramped kitchen garden and up to the front door. But a quick, cursory look around the house and the crowded yard, and they went back the way they had come with not even a glance towards the yang-pra. A few more seconds, and they were gone. Shouts of 'Nothing here, Master!' echoed in the still mountain air.

Raibhu swallowed. Afhash sat back, the tension releasing from him in a soft whoosh.

The officer was standing just short of the village square, arms akimbo, supervising the search operations. He was looking, eagle-eyed, at one of his men who had just climbed up a haystack, when a touch on his clothing made him look down. A little girl, all wide-eyed, red-cheeked innocence, was tugging on the cuff of his sleeve.

'Go away, child,' the officer said tersely. 'Go and play.'

The little girl looked a little scared, but she was not cowed by the soldier's dismissal.

'I know where they are,' she whispered.

'What? What do you mean?'

The little girl repeated, this time more urgently: 'I know where they are! The people you're looking for!'

The soldier was sceptical, as well he might be, given that his informant was so small. He was about to tell her to go, but the other man stopped him with a hand on his arm. His thin face was animated, his hand clenching, white-knuckled, around the celestial view-glass in its leather pouch as it hung from his shoulder.

'The Master will be here any moment now,' he said in an urgent whisper. 'Less than an hour ago, I received a messenger bhaagi from his birdmaster, with a note that the Master and his men will be here.' He glanced towards the little girl, who was standing patiently by. 'Don't ignore any lead you might get,' he added, before turning to the girl. 'Go on,' he said to her. 'Tell us what you saw.'

'Three men,' she said. 'They went past my home. And see,' she held out her hand, palm up, to show the tanka: 'See, this is what they gave me to keep quiet about it.'

The officer's eyes filled with amusement, though his companion looked grave. 'And you came along to tell us?' he said. 'Very well, where are they hidden?'

She shook her head. 'I don't know if they're hidden or not. They went that way,' she pointed to her right, to where the village lane petered out into a track that led up the mountainside.

The officer frowned. 'Are you sure? I've been standing within sight of this path, and I didn't see them go by.' He turned to his companion, seeking his opinion; the other man shook his head.

'Not from here,' the little girl replied blithely. 'From the other side. My home is there,' she pointed somewhere behind her, 'and there's a series of paths from there that connect to this track. They would have joined this path further up the mountain, behind that little group of trees.'

The officer, his frown still not gone, walked a little way up the path to confirm what the child had told him; the other man accompanied him. A few metres further up, the path curved behind a copse, just as the girl had described it. And a little beyond it, another path joined it. The two men, standing on tiptoe and seeing as far as they could, could see that this second path also joined to the village, curving around the homes on that side.

The officer hurried down, calling to his men as he did so. 'You get along home,' he told the girl. 'Well done.'

~

The little girl hurried into the yard and came in sight of the yang-pra pen, looking cautiously about. She was heading towards the wooden railing enclosing the herd when a hand fell on her shoulder. She whipped around, eyes wide and startled. The next moment, she relaxed and smiled shyly.

'I did what you told me,' she said. 'They've gone up the mountain.'

Raibhu smiled at her. 'I knew I could trust you. Thank you.' He was already gesturing to Inosa and Afhash, who—like Raibhu—had moved from the yang-pra pen into the shelter of a copse of fruit trees while the girl had been away. With a last look of gratitude towards the girl, and with Inosa giving her a quick pat on her cheek, the three of them ran off, through the gate and softly, soundlessly, into the woods.

~

At the other end of the village, further downhill, there was a sudden flurry of activity. Down the main track, which led up from the broader path down by the river, came a group of hill ponies. These were short, stocky ponies, standing half the height of the chestnut horses of the main Southern Mandalan areas. That was not the only difference; unlike the chestnuts, these horses were not all one colour; they were instead skewbald, a mix of white and chestnut.

They were ridden by men who seemed in a hurry to get to the village: hard-eyed, hard-bitten men, each with a dagger gleaming at his belt, some with slingshots dangling from their belts as well. At the forefront was their leader, a man who breathed menace from every pore. He was perhaps in his late fifties, broad-shouldered and muscular, and with a face that was ruggedly handsome yet sinister. This was a man who when he was younger, smooth-skinned and without the lines and folds of middle age, might have had the face of an angel but you would always wonder whether he was just any angel, or the angel of death himself. There was a hardness in his eyes: if you looked close, and if you were discerning, you might feel there was no heart behind those eyes, no conscience, no morality—and you would not be wrong.

He led his men, their ponies all at a gallop, up to the village and into it, right till the village square. Their entry was so noisy and so obviously intended to attract attention that the soldiers hurried down from the mountain trail on which they were just setting off. Their leader, cowering before the man who leaped off his pony, saluted and bowed, and then, for good measure, bowed again. The man beside him hastily flung off the tatty blanket he had draped around his shoulders, and moved forward.

'Master,' he breathed, his gaze fixed to the ground, his head bowed.

'Ah,' said the lead rider, flinging the reins aside and dismounting. 'Did you get my message, then?'

'Yes, Master. Not an hour back.'

'Good, good.' The man looked about him, his eyes sharp and unrelenting, taking in everything around him: the village, the soldiers, the mountains around. He turned to look at the man who had greeted him. 'You have done well,' he said. 'To have kept an eye on that woman so long and so well was not an easy task.' He drew in a deep breath. 'Go on now, get back to your post. I will need you to be beside your messenger bhaagis if my messages are to be sent on to the rest of my men.'

The other man, murmuring words of compliance and of subservience, straightened up, saluted, and moved off, picking up his blanket as he went.

The leader, his brief and uncharacteristic benevolence gone, turned to the soldier who stood before him.

'Well, then,' he said. 'What has been happening?'

~

Well above the village, screened by a dense thicket of bushes, Xindaar trained his celestial view-glass on three figures, each carrying a travelling sack, the one in front holding a long, spear-like stick, as they moved quickly up the mountain. 'What was that all about?' Xindaar murmured under his breath. He chewed his upper lip, puzzled. He was about to lower his view-glass when a flurry of movement in the village caught his attention. Quickly, Xindaar shifted his focus to that area and honed in on what was happening at the village Inosa and her two companions had left behind.

'A group of riders just arrived, Master,' whispered the junior officer with Xindaar.

'I know,' Xindaar said irritably. The next moment, his eyebrows snapped together and he muttered an oath.

'What happened, Master?'

For a moment, Xindaar paused. 'Here,' he said, handing the view-glass to the other man. 'Have a look and tell me who you think that is. I might be mistaken.'

The other man, his eyes full of curiosity, squinted down the view-glass at the scene in the village square. A gasp broke from him. 'It's Umur Naash,' he said. 'What's he doing here, in this godforsaken place?'

'I wonder,' Xindaar said, retrieving the view-glass. 'I wonder,' he repeated, and as he focused on the man named Umur Naash, there was on Xindaar's face a very disturbed expression.

Down at the village square, there was a brief but animated conversation between Umur Naash and the officer. They were too far, of course, for Xindaar to be able to hear anything, but he could guess, by the gesticulations that accompanied much of what the soldier said, what was going on. They had searched most of the village, the soldier was probably saying as he swept an arm about, indicating first the west, then the north and the east. And then—as the soldier's hand swept down, indicating the arrival of someone from a distant corner of the village—they had been given information. The people they were looking for had gone up that mountain, following that trail out of the village.

Umur Naash seemed to ask a question or two, to confirm what had been said. The soldier nodded vigorously, his face full of an earnest desire to please.

Umur Naash nodded and mounted his pony again. His men mounted up too, and a harsh bellow rang out, loud enough for even Xindaar to hear. The next moment, the group of riders had ridden off, single file, along the path and up the mountain trail.

Even before Umur Naash and his men had moved off, Xindaar had scrambled to his feet. 'I have to follow him to see what he's up to,' he whispered hurriedly to the junior officer. 'You go on, follow the other three. I'll catch up.'

'But how—'

'I have friends all around in these mountains,' Xindaar said. 'I'll find you, or them, at any rate.' Without another word, he went hurrying, making his way easily through the scattered trees and bushes across the mountainside, moving with the confidence of a man who knew these woods well. He cut across, not following any paths, in a trajectory that soon brought him to the mountain trail that Umur Naash was ascending. Xindaar looked up; the dust from the hooves of the ponies had not even settled yet.

He moved ahead fast, using bushes and trees to shield himself. It would not do to have Umur Naash suspect he was being followed.

~

'Afhash told me why you didn't want to face the soldier,' Inosa said, when they had finally slowed down a bit, now fairly certain that they weren't being followed. 'But do you think this is going to work? After all, if you've run, it can only convince him that there's reason for you to run. If he was only suspicious before, he will be certain now that there's something amiss.'

Raibhu nodded. 'True. But there's really no option, is there? If I wait around and risk him arresting me—even if only on suspicion—I'll be sunk. I don't want a repeat of what happened to my father.'

'Yes, that wouldn't do,' Inosa murmured. 'We should move on, even if you managed to send him off on a wild goose chase, it won't be for long. He'll realize soon enough that he's on the wrong trail, and he'll start searching for us again.' She paused, chewing on her lip as she thought. 'We'd better stay away from any villages or even other people. The deeper we go into the wilderness, the better it will be for us.' She suddenly held out a hand. 'Give me the map, please. Let me have another look at it.'

But when she had the map in her hand, Inosa did nothing more than give it a cursory look. 'And you're sure you don't know what this Aabra ka daabra thing refers to,' she said.

Raibhu shook his head. 'It's just the ditty that accompanied Father's favourite magic trick. That's all.'

'And there was nothing else?'

'What else would there be? It's all there in the map, isn't it, the route? Why?'

'If you want to get there without the soldiers getting hold of you first, you'll need to help me help you,' she said brusquely. 'So? Was there anything else? Did he say anything else about the route?'

Raibhu shook his head. 'There's the letter, but it didn't have anything to do with all of this. The only thing relevant was a bunch of instructions. That I had to get to this point and mix the mud from Father's and Mother's places of interment, and immerse them in the river. And of course that I had to go to Shervaan the Elder in Murki. That was all. The rest was all platitudes, last words from a father to a son.'

Inosa looked, narrow-eyed and speculative, at Raibhu for a few moments. Finally, she nodded. 'Let's go on, then.'

The pace Inosa set was bruising at first, taking them cross-country, leaving the trail behind. Raibhu and Afhash, only used to her taking them along a well-used trail till now, were taken aback by the confidence with which she moved forward, seeming to navigate her way just by occasional glances at peaks, boulders, and bends in the river down below. Now and then one of the men, worried by the unstopping way in which she took them ahead, would ask if she was sure of what she was doing. Every time Inosa would say, 'Trust me.' When Afhash asked her the question for the third time, she stopped and said, 'If you don't think I know what I'm doing, why don't you take over?' She stepped aside, gesturing to him to move forward and take the lead.

Afhash, red-faced, fell back again and said no more.

'Why did you trust the little girl in the village?' Inosa asked Raibhu sometime later, when they stopped at a little brook for a drink of water. 'The ploy worked, I suppose, since nobody's following us, but it could just as easily have gone wrong. She was a stranger, after all. What was to stop her running off with your tanka and never doing what you'd asked her to do?'

For a moment, Raibhu looked sheepish, as if too embarrassed to speak. Then, because Inosa was looking at him questioningly, he said, 'You will probably think me very superstitious if I tell you. Or very stupid. There was something tattooed on the girl's wrist.' He stopped, looked about briefly, as if searching for something, and finally reached out a hand towards Inosa's wooden spear. Taking it from her, he used its tip to draw something in the dust. It was a crude little drawing, but immediately recognizable. Six points arranged to form a bud.

'The Brihan Punj,' Inosa said. There was an odd intonation

in her voice: she was perhaps surprised, but one could not be sure of that.

'Yes,' Raibhu said. 'The constellation. Many years ago, when Father left me in Dhaani to keep me safe, I stayed with a friend of his. A very good man, and a brave one. He had once saved Father from the Emperor's men, and while I lived with him, he kept me safe.' He tapped the drawing in the dust with the end of the spear. 'He had exactly the same tattoo, on his wrist. *In exactly the same place, the same drawing?* I took that as an omen. I took it to mean the girl would help, just as Father's friend helped him, and me.'

Raibhu had been ready to be regarded with contempt by his two companions; he had steeled himself to be laughed at or scolded, or both. He was taken aback when Inosa, instead of saying anything, kept quiet and stared at the drawing. He was even more taken aback when Afhash said, 'I also know someone who has that tattoo. The exact same one.'

'What?' Raibhu said. 'Who?'

'The latest chief prison-keeper at Sandha Prison. He was the only one who ever believed Jaadum the Elder's assertion that he was innocent. He's a good man,' Afhash added, looking pensive. 'What does this mean, eh? A good prison-keeper. A good friend in Dhaani. A good girl in a village here. All people who help, two of them definitely people who risk their lives to help strangers. What does this tattoo mean?'

Raibhu shook his head wordlessly. Inosa said nothing, but there was a wary, thoughtful look in her eyes

'Do you know something we don't, Inosa?' he asked. 'Have you seen this tattoo before?'

For a moment, it looked as if Inosa was going to deny it;

but after a preliminary hesitation, she nodded. 'There were people around me, when I was a child, who bore it. My grandfather had the tattoo, so did a few others.'

'And? What does it signify?'

Inosa shrugged. 'Just that the one who bears the tattoo is committed to doing good, even at cost to themselves. Grandfather never told me exactly why it's this tattoo; why the Brihan Punj—but I always thought it was just a reminder. To be as radiant as the stars, as lofty as the heavens. To aspire to great heights, to rise above.'

Raibhu stared at the drawing he had made. 'Indeed,' he said, half to himself. 'Everyone I've met who has that tattoo has behaved with exemplary selflessness.' He continued to look, his expression thoughtful, before he rubbed out the drawing. 'Let's go,' he said, getting to his feet.

~

High up on the mountainside above the village, Umur Naash and his men rode their ponies slowly along a narrow, now nearly invisible trail. Umur Naash was no longer at the front of the group: the front place had been taken by a lithe, wiry man who walked along, bending down now and then to examine the ground, the grass, the bushes around. A guide, deputed to help the group catch up with those it was following. From the look of impatience on Umur Naash's face, the anger in his eyes and the way his knuckles tightened on the reins of his pony, it was obvious that the guide was not proving as competent as he had been expected to be.

Finally, when the man began to wander off the path, going off on short forays to the left and the right, Umur

Naash lost all semblance of patience. With a roar of anger, he jumped off his pony and went striding to the man. Behind him, all of Umur Naash's men also quickly dismounted. They did not move forward, but stood ready, poised to obey whatever command their master might give.

Right now, though, Umur Naash's attention was focused only on the guide, who had stopped, an expression of terror on his face as he whirled around to look at Umur Naash.

'What are you up to?' Umur Naash said, his voice low and silky and very dangerous.

The guide had gone pale with fright. He mumbled something inaudible.

'Speak up, you bastard.'

The guide swallowed. 'It's—the trail, Master. The trail is—well, it hasn't been used here. I think perhaps those people never came here.'

Umur Naash regarded the man thoughtfully. 'Do you mean to say you have led us all the way up from the village after nothing? Didn't you see the trail up till here from the village? Or did you just lead us up here because someone said they had seen them come up here?'

The man cringed. 'It's a well-used trail,' he said, his voice cracking under the strain. 'Till a point. The villagers probably use it to go up to the trees to fetch firewood or to graze their yang-pra—that's why,' he added hurriedly, as he saw his boss's mounting impatience—'that's why it seemed as if somebody had walked on this path recently. But this high up, the trail disappears.' He indicated the almost non-existent trail across the dust and grass. 'Nobody's been here for a long time, perhaps more than a week even.'

Even as the guide spoke, Umur Naash had been slowly and deliberately taking off the fine leather gloves he was wearing. One finger at a time, gently and caressingly, he slid off the gloves. Folded them and put them in his pocket. Then, as the guide finished, Umur Naash let fly at him. Again and again, with fists, with well-aimed kicks, and finally with the whip he had been using on his pony. The guide crumpled to the ground, trying to protect himself by curling up into a ball, but it was of little use. Umur Naash was merciless. He did not stop until the guide had gone utterly limp and still.

Then, throwing aside his whip and putting his gloves on once again, Umur Naash said in a brusque aside to one of his men, 'Pick him up and see if he's alive.'

The guide, his face and hands shredded and bleeding copiously, was hauled up by two of the men. The man whom Umur Naash had spoken to put a thumb and forefinger on the guide's inner wrist. He felt about a bit, then looked up. 'He's alive, Master. Just about.'

'Hmm. If he's just about alive, he's no use. Throw him over the cliff and let's go back to the village. Once we're there, find another guide.'

And with that, he remounted his pony. He turned the horse about and was gone, galloping downhill in the direction of the village. Behind him, the rest of his men mounted up and followed, all except for three. They were the ones who dragged the unconscious body of the battered guide to the edge of the mountain and flung him off it. Then they too went to their ponies, which had been tied to a convenient tree trunk, and rode down to the village.

~

The officer who had been addressing the crowd of villagers was an abject figure as he crouched before Umur Naash. 'I—I didn't do a thing, Master!' he wailed. He was on his knees, his face red with welts from Umur Naash's whip. He did not dare look up at Umur Naash; he kept his gaze firmly on Umur Naash's boots. But the end of Umur Naash's whip caught him under the chin and lifted it, forcing the man to look up.

'Of course you didn't, you bastard,' Umur Naash said conversationally. 'You didn't think. You simply listened to what a wily child told you, and you believed what she said. You sent me off on a wild goose chase.'

The soldier was blubbering, heedless of his humiliation in front of the entire village, in front of his own men. Umur Naash had that effect on even the bravest of men: he could reduce them to blithering, terrified creatures in mere moments.

'The girl,' Umur Naash said. 'Where is the girl?'

The soldier blinked. 'My men will find her, Master,' he stammered.

'Well, then. What are you waiting for? Send them to fetch her. Bring her to me.'

He stopped. 'Have you found a guide to replace the other one?' he asked, turning to his henchman.

The man blanched. 'Y—yes, Master,' he said, frantically looking left and right, searching among the villagers around him. His face suddenly cleared as he saw one of his men pushing through the crowd, holding by the sleeve a villager who had the rough and rugged look of an outdoorsman. 'Here he is,' he added, the relief on his face palpable.

'Take him with you when you go to fetch the girl,' Umur Naash said. 'Have him find out where those three really went, not where the girl said they went. Go.' He turned to look at the officer kneeling before him. 'Get up, you. If you want to stay alive, give me reason to not kill you. Go with them.' The man scrambled to his feet. Moments later, his men hurrying after him, he was gone, moving swiftly into the depths of the village.

The officer, his soldiers, and Umur Naash's man, along with the new guide, returned some time later. Umur Naash was standing, one foot tapping impatiently on the ground, but otherwise stock still. The officer's men were hustling the little girl along; she was crying, the tears coursing down her cheeks, her sobs the only sound to be heard even though the entire village had gathered there. As she came in sight, a woman called out from the anonymity of the crowd, 'Please! Please let her go, she's just a child!'

Umur Naash looked out over the crowd, searching for the voice, but when he could not zero in on any one person, he addressed all of them. 'Who are the parents of this child?' he asked. 'Come forward.'

Nobody emerged, but the newly-appointed guide volunteered to explain. 'Her parents died two years ago,' he said somewhat diffidently.

'Who looks after her, then? Who is responsible for her?' There was an ominous tone of menace in Umur Naash's voice and in his expression. The guide flinched.

'Well? I don't have all day,' Umur Naash said.

'She has an uncle and a cousin, Master.' It was the guide again, the strain showing in every line of his face. 'But they are woodsmen who have gone into the mountains to trap and hunt.' He looked helpless and scared as he finished: 'She has mostly been on her own these past few days.'

The calculating look on Umur Naash's face suggested he did not believe the guide. But all he said was, 'Ah. So if her relatives hardly care about her, they're unlikely to mourn her too much?' He took a couple of steps closer to the child, who was being held by two men. Seeing Umur Naash approach, she began screaming frantically and doubled her efforts to escape. It was all useless, of course, and Umur Naash watched her panic with a look of extreme pleasure.

'Little girl,' he said finally, bending down and stroking her cheek, 'There is nobody to look after you, is there? Nobody to teach you things, nobody to tell you what is right and what is wrong? Your uncle and your cousin would much rather go out hunting, yes?'

The little girl regarded him through eyes swimming with tears. When he gestured to her, prompting her to speak, she shook her head.

'So sad.' He patted her cheek, the sada stone ring on his finger glinting in the bright sunshine. In its depths, the pulse that mirrored Umur Naash's own heartbeat throbbed excitedly. The sun's rays caught the stone and shone for a moment, blood-red, on the girl's cheek. 'But no matter. I am there.' With a final pat, Umur Naash straightened up.

In the same instant, he swung his arm up and out, his fist smashing into the girl's jaw and sending her flying. As she landed, a small cloud of dust billowing up, her little body falling with a sickening crunch even as the echoes of her scream died into a series of whimpers, Umur Naash laughed.

He walked to her and began to kick her, his boots smashing into her body as he laughed. As the villagers around wept—and the braver ones begged him to stop—he continued to chortle to himself.

'Say thank you to me, you bitch,' Umur Naash said when he finally stopped. The little girl lay at his feet completely still, blood pooling around her and seeping into the earth. 'I have taught you things your people did not have the sense to tell you. It is wrong to lie. Wrong. Evil. Never lie.' He bent down and hooked a finger in the collar of the unconscious child's tunic, and twisted it. 'People who lie go straight to hell, understand?' He shook her, and her head bobbed on her neck as limply as a flower on a wilted stalk. Umur Naash stared into her face, at the mask of red that cloaked her features. Then, with a snort of disgust, he flung her away from him. Just as he was about to turn away, he noticed the girl's hand. Her arm was flung wide, the inside of the wrist clearly visible. Umur Naash noticed the tattoo on her skin, and frowned.

The next moment, though, he turned away to look at the guide. The man was staring at Umur Naash, his face pale with terror.

'So?' Umur Naash said. 'Did you find any signs of where those three people went, out of this village?'

The guide nodded. 'Near the house where we found the girl. She spends most of her time around there—three people had been there, and they went up the mountain.'

'Today?'

'Yes, Master. I followed the trail some way up. Perhaps a couple of hours have passed, but not much more.'

Umur Naash nodded. 'Lead the way, then.' He gestured

for his pony to be led up to him so that he could mount it. 'Have you been told what happened to the last guide?' he asked conversationally, just as he was about to put a foot in the stirrup. The guide nodded, his eyes wide with fright.

'Good,' Umur Naash said. 'It's good that you know.'

He swung himself up into the saddle. Then, with a blood-curdling shriek of mad fervour, imbued with all the thrill of the chase, he spurred his pony forward.

The hunt was on.

Chapter Eight

Year 5441 of the Emergence of Mandala

Umur Naash, his smooth, handsome young face expressionless, stands on a balcony of the Central Academy in Raffasi. It is a colonnaded building, double-storeyed, stretching for half a mile along the lake at the centre of the city. The columns of the building are shaped like the slender trunks of birches, with carved vines and leaves curled around each stone trunk. The tall arched windows of the façade are all stained glass, depicting scenes from nature: woodland, wildflowers, birds, leaves, animals. All the natural beauty of Mandala comes alive on this edifice.

... and in its grounds. On the space between the academy building and the lakeshore stretches a verdant garden. Surrounded by tall trees, its flower beds are a riot of colours, and a water channel runs between the building and the lake, the water rippling and gurgling down a stone-lined channel, its bed studded with multicoloured stones so that the water, flowing over the stones, looks almost like a rainbow turned to liquid.

But Umur Naash is not looking at the beauty of the water or the gardens before him. From his vantage point on the balcony, he can see straight down into a group of young people who are sitting in a circle beside the water channel and singing. Like Umur Naash, they are all obviously students of the academy, each of them wearing the multicoloured short over-tunic that symbolizes the diversity of the academy, its commitment to embracing all and sundry. One of these is the young woman whom Umur Naash is watching so intently.

She is exquisitely beautiful, with the perfect features of the quintessential Mandalan beauty. Umur Naash watches her with a ferocious intensity, as if devouring her with his eyes.

'Wah, wah! Wah, wah! So Umur Naash too is weak enough to fall in love!'

Umur Naash turns, a graceful languor in his movements, to look at the newcomer, a man of about Umur Naash's own age—perhaps about twenty years old—who grins cheekily at Umur Naash. While he is informal with Umur Naash, there is a stiff dignity on the latter's part which seems to suggest that Umur Naash holds this man in contempt, while the other man aspires to be on familiar terms with him. It is obvious, by looking at Umur Naash, to see why this should be so: the wealth and the taste that Umur Naash exudes is of an uncommon level. From the beautifully engraved zansal buckle at his belt, to the fine silver fur stole that is draped about his shoulders, it is clear that Umur Naash is very rich as well as very cultured.

'I shouldn't be surprised, though,' says Umur Naash's would-be friend, falling in step with him as they walk along the balcony. 'After all, with your love for beauty, it is to be expected that you would fall in love only with the most beautiful girl in the academy.'

Umur Naash walks on, his face impassive. They go down a staircase leading from the balcony to the garden, and then on to a path that rings the academy building. Ahead of them, the path converges with another, and they see a group of young women approaching. The woman Umur Naash has been admiring in the garden is one of them. Umur Naash pauses, as if thinking over what to say and do, and then he strides forward confidently.

The group of women stops. Some of them look uncertain, some are downright scared: they look ready to flee. The young woman whom Umur Naash is fascinated by flinches when he approaches. Umur Naash tries to say something to her, but she hurries away before he can get two words out. Umur Naash is left standing there, looking surprised and not a little annoyed.

This may be the first time he is approaching her, but it will not be the last. Again and again, on other days and in different situations, Umur Naash tries to speak to the woman. In the academy gardens, when she's sitting in the sunshine and reading a book. In the airy, window-lined dining hall of the academy, as she sits, eating and drinking with friends. In the library, with its vaulted ceilings and its floor-to-ceiling bookcases of dark, heavy humur wood, each case crowded with hundreds of leather-bound, gold-embossed books. Every time, the woman makes her escape, and Umur Naash is unable to express his love.

He is very persistent, though, and finally, one day, he is able to corner her in a corridor with no one else around.

'Yoksa,' he says, reaching out and holding her arm. 'Please, at least listen to what I have to say! Why do you avoid me so?'

Yoksa shakes her head. She has turned away from him; though she has stopped struggling to free her arm from his grip, she refuses to even look at him. Umur Naash looks at her, seeing the revulsion on her face, the way she leans away from him.

'What is it?' he asks, his voice low, not with passion but with something like disquiet. 'What is it, Yoksa? Why will you not even let me speak to you?'

'Let me go.' Yoksa's words come out strangled, as if it is a real effort for her to even say that.

'No.' Umur Naash's face is set. 'No. I will not let you go until you tell me why. Why do you avoid me?'

A moment of indecision, of internal struggle, and then Yoksa bursts out: 'Don't you know that I'm from the Sada Valley?'

Umur Naash is taken aback; so startled that he loosens his grip on her arm, and Yoksa quickly backs away, well out of range of him. But she does not leave yet, and Umur Naash, puzzled, asks, 'But why should your being from the Sada Valley make a difference?'

Yoksa pauses, as if scared to say anything. 'Tell me,' Umur Naash says. 'Tell me why.'

'How can you expect anyone from the Sada Valley to look on you with any sort of respect?' Yoksa retorts. Her face is contorted with contempt now. 'You are of the clan of Umur Tut Naash, you are of his blood!'

'But—' Umur Naash is utterly mystified now, unable to grasp Yoksa's meaning. 'Why? Why would you so hate Umur Tut Naash? What did he do? My ancestor was a great general, a powerful ruler! You should be grateful if his descendant should look on you with benevolence—'

He is not able to finish the sentence; Yoksa cuts him off midway with a harsh, bitter laugh. 'A great general! Hah! Say that to those who have been fed on the lies of the centuries since Umur Tut Naash invaded our land! Ask anyone from the Sada

Valley, and you will know what he really did.' Her anger has strengthened her; Yoksa turns away to leave, but as she goes, she looks over her shoulder and tells Umur Naash, 'Naash-Gar, if you want to know why a girl from the Sada Valley will always regard you with hatred, read the real history of Mandala, especially that of the Sada Valley. Not the one-sided view that passes for history.' Her eyes are full of contempt, and the way she emphasizes the honorific, 'Gar', it is clear that she wants to distance herself from Umur Naash.

'Yoksa-Gari,' Umur Naash murmurs, addressing her with equal formality, 'I am certain that whatever that history may be, it will not stop me from having you as my lady someday. You will be Naash-Gar's gari, mark my words. I will win you.'

But Yoksa has already turned away.

Umur Naash stands in the corridor, watching as she hurries away, out of sight.

~

They were walking so fast that even Inosa, used to the high altitude, was panting. Every now and then, whenever she would find a suitably high vantage point, she would shin up and take a quick peek at the trail behind them.

'I can't see anybody yet,' she said when Afhash looked at her questioningly. 'But they'll be following us. They can't be far behind; they would have realized soon enough that they had been misled.'

'Perhaps they aren't following?' Afhash said. 'I mean, all the soldier has to go on is a vague suspicion. And anybody would run from a soldier. It doesn't make us more suspicious just because we fled.'

'Fair enough,' Inosa conceded. As she had clambered down from the rock, she had slipped, and though Raibhu—quicker than Afhash—had leaped forward and managed to grab her before she fell—she had scraped the side of her arm in the process. Now she opened her leather water bottle, wet a handkerchief and tried to clean the wound, but Raibhu, seeing how difficult it was for her to do so one-handed, quietly took over the job. Without a word, he made her sit down while he took out from Inosa's travelling sack the little pouch of powdered calmroot stem she carried in it. As she had attended to him just the previous day, he now attended to her, while Inosa talked to Afhash.

'It would have been all right if we'd only run from them,' Inosa told Afhash. 'But sending them on a wild goose chase—that worsened matters, I think.' She flashed a glance at Raibhu, who looked abashed. 'Anyway, what's done is done.' She nodded to Raibhu, who had just finished bandaging her arm, and stood up. 'Let's try to put as much distance between ourselves and the soldiers.'

They had not gone very much further before the call of a bird rang out from somewhere in the surrounding mountains, the clear air carrying the sound far. Inosa froze in her tracks at the sound of it, and before her two companions could grasp what was happening, she had climbed up a tree and was looking about, her eyes searching the mountains around. When she came down, her face was strained, her eyes anxious.

'Listen,' she told Raibhu, catching him by the sleeve. 'We are definitely being followed. You two go up there,' she indicated a knoll some five hundred metres above where they were standing, 'and wait there for me. I'll go back and try to lay a false trail to put them off the scent.' She seemed to realize suddenly that she had caught hold of Raibhu's sleeve, and let go of it. Without another word, she turned and raced off downhill.

~

'Come on,' Raibhu said to Afhash. 'Let's go.'

Afhash had been quiet all this while, a simmering, seething quiet that had gone unnoticed in all the turmoil of the past several minutes. Now, as he and Raibhu walked to the knoll, he suddenly spoke up. 'She likes you, doesn't she? And you like her.'

'What?' Raibhu, caught off guard, was momentarily puzzled. Then he laughed, a self-conscious chuckle. 'Come on, Afhash, you're imagining things. Anybody would think you're jealous.'

'I am! Why shouldn't I be?' Afhash spat out, frustration brimming over in every syllable. 'Don't I have a right to like her too, to hope that she might like me? After all, she's not an elegant city girl like you would be familiar with. She's a village girl, a wild and free spirit. My sort of woman.' His voice softened, his eyes grew gentle. 'Have you seen how she walks? As if she knows where she's going, always. No diffidence there. No fear, no hesitation.'

Raibhu was regarding his friend quietly. He said nothing, but there was pain in his eyes, an empathy that did not necessarily translate into outright agreement. He had not intended it, but Afhash noticed it, and it made him bristle with indignation.

'You feel sorry for me,' Afhash said, glowering. 'You think I'm a fool to want her. Just because I'm illiterate—'

'I neither said nor thought anything of the kind,' Raibhu replied. They had reached the knoll, and he looked around. Right next to it was a dip in the ground, with bushes growing thick about its lip, forming a good shelter. He led the way into the shade of the bushes, and settled down in such a way that anyone coming up to the knoll was clearly visible to them, but they were screened by the bushes.

When he spoke next, Raibhu's voice was a whisper. 'Why not leave the decision to Inosa?' he said. 'It's her life, she will decide. What I want or what you want is immaterial if it's not also what Inosa wants.'

Afhash glared at him. 'That's easy for you to say. You can see how she feels. I can see it too. I saw the way the two of you were running and laughing this morning, when you competed to reach that spear of hers. And I saw how you bound her arm up, a little while ago. Or how you and Inosa talked about those philosophers—I've seen it all, and I know what it means!'

'Afhash—' Raibhu started to say, but Afhash was not listening.

'But if you love her so very much,' Afhash said, 'don't you want what's best for her? What will make her the happiest? Can't you see there's no future for her with you? Inosa can believe that one Mandala is the same as the other, and that Mandala is a matter of the heart, but the fact is that you're a Northerner and she's Southern, and our two lands are probably on the brink of war. A few days from now, and you'll be returning to Dhaani. You two will never see each other again.' He shook his head. 'No, Raibhu. It's no use. Why are you raising her hopes? Don't misunderstand me;

I'm not trying to tell you to give her up just because I want her for myself. I'm just pointing it out because I can see where this is going to end up. You can both be happy for a few days, and then you'll be separated forever. I don't want that to happen to two people I like.'

Raibhu stared at Afhash with an unhappy look on his face. When he said nothing, Afhash raised his eyebrows questioningly, urging Raibhu to reply. Raibhu, egged on, finally shook his head. 'There is no point talking about it,' he said quietly. 'I don't know how Inosa feels. Perhaps both you and I are reading much more into this than she intends. But I do know how I feel, and I know that what you say makes sense. It's completely logical. My heart, however, doesn't understand logic. I may tell myself to not like her because it's a love that will go nowhere, but my heart won't listen.'

Afhash looked bleakly at Raibhu before turning away. Neither of them spoke for several minutes. Then Afhash said, 'I wonder if Inosa's laying a false trail is going to be any use. Do you think it will work? If the soldier realized that the path the child had sent him on was the wrong one and he's taken the trouble of finding out where we really went, so that he's now following us—that means he's not going to give up easily.'

Raibhu nodded. 'I don't know why Inosa's even trying,' he agreed. 'We should focus on putting as much distance between them and us. And anyway, it's not as if we'll be forever trying to flee the soldiers. All we need to do is get to that spot Father marked on the map. Then, once I've put the mud from their graves into the river, we can go on to Raffasi. Or if the situation seems too precarious, maybe I can go back to Dhaani and you can go on to Raffasi? Make some enquiries, try to find out what really happened, whether there are any clues about who those people were, who killed Mother?'

Afhash was just about to say yes, he would, when Inosa arrived, running uphill. She was panting with the exertion of her sprint, and looked frazzled. 'Come on, let's go!' she gasped, not even pausing as she ran past. Raibhu and Afhash had scrambled to their feet as soon as they saw her, and they quickly fell into step behind her. Because the two of them were not as adept as her at running on these rugged mountain trails, Inosa was obliged to slow down. She toned her pace down to a brisk trot, and Raibhu, right behind her, asked, 'Why are they so adamant about following us? The soldiers can't be so idle that they have nothing better to do!'

Inosa huffed. 'You sent them off on a wild goose chase, that must have annoyed them. Anyway,' she added, 'they seem to be determined to get us. That bird call was no bird; it was a signal. They must have spread out on different trails; perhaps they aren't absolutely sure where we are...I hope so.'

At the next high point along the trail, she searched the trail behind them. 'I can't see any sign of them yet,' she said, climbing down from the boulder on to which she had climbed. 'Perhaps the false trail I laid has diverted them for the time being.

'Let's take a break,' she added. 'We need to stop, anyway, if we're to get to your destination without collapsing.'

The place Inosa chose for a break was not much further on, a secluded gully that was overgrown with bushes through much of its length. It was not easy to get into it—they had to burrow through the bushes, with Inosa crawling in right at the back while erasing the marks of their passage as carefully as she could—but once inside, they were unlikely to be spotted.

As soon as she had settled down, Inosa began undoing her travelling sack and pulling out things. Clean rags emerged, as did the pouch of powdered calmroot stem. She also took out dried fruit and some more of the triangular bread. 'Here,' she said, passing the food on to Raibhu and Afhash. 'You two start eating. Raibhu, you eat one-handed, I'll dress that wound on your other hand while you're eating.'

He tried to protest, but Inosa brushed aside his objections. 'Eat fast,' she said tersely. 'I'll eat once I'm done with this.' She took his hand in her own, and beyond her, Raibhu caught a look of sudden and intense anger on Afhash's face: a rage that threatened to spill over, until Afhash suddenly turned away and busied himself in tearing a bit of bread to pieces. His jaw was still clenched, and his face was pale. Raibhu glanced at Inosa, but she was oblivious; she had her back to Afhash, and had noticed nothing.

As she attended to Raibhu's hand, Inosa gave them quick, low-voiced instructions. 'Once you've finished eating, take off your shoes, massage your feet, lie down if you want. Get some rest. We'll only wait long enough for me to finish eating, then we'll go.'

'We aren't children, Inosa, and you aren't our mother,' Raibhu said. 'Why shouldn't you get some rest too? You've done more running about than we have.'

'And I'm more used to the mountains than either of you is.' She finished knotting a fresh handkerchief around Raibhu's hand. 'There. That's better. You're healing well.'

Raibhu was looking past her to Afhash. Afhash was noting the closeness between them: the calm proprietorial way in which Inosa had taken over, attending to Raibhu and telling him what to do, and the equally candid way in which the two of them spoke to each other. Afhash, Raibhu could see, did not like this matter-of-fact conversation between Inosa and Raibhu; he did not like that they had so soon discarded the mutual wariness of their meeting at Murki the previous day. Their very informality irked him.

Raibhu said gently, 'Inosa, it's all right, there's no need to be so worried. The soldiers may be suspicious enough to follow us, but how long will they do so? And if it seems that they're about to catch up, I'll make sure I draw them off. It's me they're suspicious of, it's me they would want to arrest, not the two of you. You and Afhash can slip away before they catch up—'

Inosa, indignation written all over her face, was about to retort but it was Afhash who interrupted Raibhu first. 'What do you think we are?!' he hissed. 'We'll leave you and run off, so you can get arrested on your own? You bastard, you have a low opinion of the two of us, don't you?'

Raibhu had begun shaking his head even as Afhash had begun speaking. 'No,' he replied, holding Afhash's shoulder, a grasp that Afhash tried to wriggle free from, he was so angry. 'No, that's not what I mean. I mean I can't get the two of you into trouble too, because of me. Much as I love—much as both of you mean to me, I can't have you arrested for my sake.'

'I don't care what you think,' Inosa said brusquely. 'The two of you have odd notions about loyalty and whatnot. My creed is simple. This: "No mortal being can know what lies beyond the veil. This life is all one can be sure of, one life in which to do good or to leave behind a legacy of pain and evil. All we can do is choose what we bequeath." Vidyanjika Jijita said that.' Inosa's anger had dissipated even as she quoted. Now, her voice softer and calmer, she added, 'The jijita meant that to imply that what we made of life depended upon us. But I take it further: I believe that if I choose to do something, I should do it well. I should put all my energies into it and do my very best, because that helps fulfil my own life.' She looked up, gazing deep into Raibhu's eyes, her own limpid and clear. 'Do you understand? I agreed to take you to the spot on your Father's map, and I will do that.'

She looked from Raibhu to Afhash and back again, a small but radiant smile on her face, which suddenly transformed Inosa from a strong-willed, indomitable young woman to a philosopher, the wisdom of many ages in her eyes. She looked, all at once, both kind and enlightened as well as determined, capable: a woman who knew what she had to do, and was going to do it, come what may.

'Shall we do that?' she asked. 'Shall we tell ourselves we have to take this to the end, no matter what it takes? We will not give up, we will try our hardest. We will not flee, and we will not think of telling others to flee.' Her gaze was resting on Raibhu again, and there was an intensity in it, as if these particular words were addressed more to him than to Afhash.

'Well?' she repeated, and after some hesitation, Raibhu and Afhash nodded.

'Good, let's go, then.'

~

They made good progress, and neither saw nor heard any more signs of pursuit. Raibhu, however, had begun to pay more attention to Inosa's behaviour, and he soon noticed the jitteriness that seemed to have caught hold of her. Every now and then, when she thought the men were not looking, she would surreptitiously glance back over the trail. Once, when they had to go single file to climb up a narrow track, she had to wait while Raibhu, followed by Afhash, went up; instead of waiting her turn, she utilized that time by climbing up a tree. Raibhu watched as her eyes, full of a dread he could not fathom, searched—for what? Raibhu said nothing, but he was beginning to worry.

When Inosa finally climbed up and joined him and Afhash, Raibhu said, 'Inosa, what's the matter? Are you still worried that we are being followed?'

Inosa did not say anything. She avoided Raibhu's eyes and shook her head in a non-committal way. Raibhu exchanged a glance with Afhash. The anger had melted away from Afhash's demeanour long before, and he raised his chin a little, wordlessly asking Raibhu what this was all about. Raibhu, in turn, mouthed back at him: You ask her. A passing of the baton, but also a way of including him. Of letting Afhash see that it was not as if Raibhu was trying to usurp Inosa and her worries all for himself.

Afhash looked a little surprised at Raibhu's urging him to talk to Inosa, but after a momentary hesitation, he spoke up. 'I can't see anyone, or any traces. Did you see something, Inosa?'

Inosa shook her head again, this time more emphatically. 'It's nothing,' she said gruffly. 'I'm just being cautious.'

'We shouldn't worry, eh,' Afhash said in a deliberately cheerful voice, as if he were forcing himself to be upbeat. 'You yourself said we should just go on, doing our best. And that whatever came our way, we'd tackle it. No point worrying. Right?'

Inosa looked at Afhash narrowly, and then turned her gaze to Raibhu, who said nothing. 'Right,' she said. 'Let's go on, then.'

But before she could move even a step forward, a sudden rumble filled the air, growing from a murmur to a roar within a matter of seconds. All three of them froze for a moment, but it was Inosa who flung them into the shelter of the rocks nearby, pushing Raibhu and Afhash ahead of her.

'What is it—' Raibhu began to say, but both Afhash and Inosa were looking terrified. That sound, frightening as it was, was not the steady thud-thud-thud of the war-carts on the move. It was not the sound of a landslide, or—Raibhu's eyes widened in sudden understanding as he looked up at the sky, just in time to see it appear. A fire ball, far away, but hurtling ever closer to the forested slopes of the mountains across the river. Inosa and Afhash had followed his lead, and all three of them watched as the fire ball collided with the ground, the impact causing reverberations, tremors and a huge cloud of dust that mushroomed up into the sky. Even as the sound of the impact died away, the frenzied tweeting and chirping and shrieking of hundreds of frightened birds filled the air.

Inosa was up on her feet immediately. 'It's only a fire ball,' she said, the relief in her voice palpable. 'I thought those soldiers were attacking us.' She glanced back at her two companions, still hunched in the lee of the rocks. 'Come on, let's go,' she said, and without waiting for them, she hefted her travelling sack on to her back and moved on.

Though Raibhu was the first to catch up with her, it was Afhash, huffing and puffing and staggering under the weight of his travelling sack, who spoke first. 'What do you mean, "it's only a fire ball", as if it were a field mouse or a bhaagi? Do you see fire balls crashing out of the sky every other day up here?'

'Of course not. I think it's probably been—let me see—' Inosa's eyebrows drew together as she thought it over. 'Probably about a year since the last one fell. So no, they aren't that frequent. But they are less dangerous than the people following us.'

'Less dangerous!' Afhash's voice emerged as a horrified squeak. 'A fire ball falls on you, you're incinerated before you even know it.'

Inosa, without breaking her stride, gave him a cheery grin. 'Exactly, you don't know it. But those—those soldiers,' she said, her voice and the smile wavering, 'they will make sure you know it when they catch up with you.' She nodded, in a decisive way. 'So let's pick up the pace. We cannot waste time chatting, all right? Come on.'

And this time, she raced ahead so fast that even Raibhu could not catch up for several minutes.

~

The sun was beginning to set when Inosa called a halt. 'Let's try to sleep early,' she said, leading them down a dried-up stream bed. 'That way, we can be up early and leave as soon as there's light enough to see by.' She was walking along, searching for a suitable place to camp, and soon chose a little clearing where the source of the erstwhile stream, a rivulet from snowmelt, had formed a little pool.

'Here,' she said, putting down her travelling sack. 'We'll camp here. Will you two be able to manage without a fire? If we only eat dried fruit and bread, and drink water, we should be fine.'

'Some calmroot infusion, at least?' Afhash pleaded. 'Surely that small a fire will not make a difference?' he looked around, and homed in on some fist-sized stones that lay in the stream bed. 'If I pile those up around a really tiny fire, and hem it in—well, no one will be able to see it. And I could put it out as soon as the water boils.'

He sounded so desperate that Inosa could not help but give in. 'Oh, all right,' she said with a quick grin, half-exasperated, half-amused. 'Light it now, so that at least the light that's still there in the sky will help subdue the light from the fire.'

Afhash was as good as his word: he nursed the fire, a tiny but bright little one, as if his entire life depended upon it. He built up an encircling wall of stones all around it, forming a rough stove, and he put the potful of water on top even before he had lit the fire. 'So that no flames can be seen from above,' he told Raibhu, who grinned and agreed that yes, it would be a disaster if a passing bhaagi saw the flame.

It was fiddly business, but the fire was finally lit, Afhash singeing his fingers in the process but doggedly carrying on. Raibhu and Inosa, meanwhile, had taken out some of the dried fruit, the nuts and bread Inosa had packed. By the time

Afhash had brewed calmroot infusion and put out the fire, they were ready to eat.

'What will you do once this is over, Afhash?' Raibhu said. 'You got out of prison only to come straight to Dhaani, but what will you do once I've gone?'

Afhash took the first sip of the infusion from his cup and breathed a sigh of deep contentment. 'Ah.' He pursed his lips, thinking over the question. 'What will I do? You mean before or after I become a great magician?

'Which reminds me,' he added, putting his cup aside and plunging a hand into his pocket. He withdrew the tanka and began flipping it. 'May as well get in some practice while I'm at it,' he added. 'So what we were talking of? What I'm going to do? Hmm...I don't know. Perhaps I need to go to school and at least learn to read and write, if I'm to even hope to have any ladies pay attention to me.' He grinned at Inosa, who made a face, playing along.

'And then, once I've mastered the art of magic and I've become all educated, I will be the most popular magician in all of Southern Mandala, and everybody will come from far and wide—'

Raibhu chuckled. 'You're incorrigible,' he said affectionately. 'I don't care what you do, but you must promise me one thing, all right? Please don't do anything that will land you in prison again.' There was so much earnestness in his tone that Afhash was taken aback. He nodded, in an embarrassed sort of way.

He did not say anything, though, and it was Inosa who spoke up. 'What about you,' she said, addressing Raibhu. 'What will you do once you're back in Dhaani?'

For just a moment, there was a look of misery and loss in Raibhu's eyes, as if he dreaded the thought of going back to Dhaani. It was a fleeting look, gone before anybody could have made note of it. 'If I haven't been suspended, I suppose I will rejoin the justice office.'

Inosa mulled over this before asking, 'And do the officers of the justice office get called upon to fight if Northern Mandala goes to war?' she asked.

'We might,' Raibhu conceded.

'Against Southern Mandala.'

'Against whichever country Northern Mandala fights.'

Inosa nodded. A few moments of thought, and then she said, 'It will not disturb you to fight people who were your own, till less than twenty years back? After all, you lived in Raffasi; this land isn't utterly alien to you.'

Raibhu frowned. 'What are you getting at, Inosa?'

She looked back at him, her face placid, non-threatening. 'I'm not trying to get at anything. I'm just trying to understand you and how you think, that's all.' Afhash, looking on, gave Inosa an annoyed glance, but neither did she notice it, nor did Raibhu.

'If you don't want to answer the question, don't,' Inosa said. 'It's not important.'

Raibhu shook his head. 'It's not that, it's just that I hadn't thought about it earlier.' He pondered over the question, fiddling with the handkerchief tied around his hand while he did so: smoothening its edge, straightening its folds. Finally, a small smile dawned on his face. 'You quoted Vidyanjika Jijita to us earlier today. Well, I'll quote Dayadhan Jijit to you now: "Precepts and platitudes are no more than guidelines.

Ultimately, it is your conscience that matters. Listen, always, to your conscience: that will be your best guide." That is my philosophy: to be true to myself. I follow my conscience. If I think someone is right, I will not hesitate to support and help that person. And vice versa, if I think someone is doing wrong—well, I will do everything I can to stop him. Or her... who they are doesn't matter.'

'You're being obtuse,' Inosa remarked. 'Or diplomatic, I don't know.' She chuckled, wagging her head as she did so.

'Neither. I'm being truthful. I don't tell myself that I have to behave in one defined way in every situation in which I find myself.' Raibhu's eyebrows drew together as he thought about his own idea of life, his own philosophy, and tried to articulate it. 'See. Let me put it this way. I'm a man, a Terrisan. A Northerner, even though I was born in what became Southern Mandala. A justice officer. Right? But that doesn't mean I think anybody else who's either of these—man, Terrisan, Northerner, justice officer—is automatically good. And I don't think anybody who isn't a man, a Terrisan, etcetera, is automatically bad. I take people at face value. I pay no heed to a man's, or a woman's, religion or nationality or—well, any of these other labels by which people tag themselves and others. To me, that is immaterial.' He paused. 'Does that make more sense?'

Before Inosa could react, Afhash said, in a voice of mock sadness, 'You poor sod. You poor, delusional sod. You are going to get into deep shit with this philosophy of yours, you realize that? I'm surprised you haven't been kicked out of the justice office by now, the Land Spirit alone knows how many criminals you've let off the hook simply because you thought they were basically good. Anyway, go back to

Dhaani. Hopefully, thanks to morons like you, we'll win any war that starts between our lands.' He was grinning as he said it, the bright cheerful grin robbing his words of harshness.

Inosa smiled too, and nodded. 'Afhash's right. With such a philosophy, isn't it difficult to be a justice officer? You would be better off turning a jijit and living out in the wilds. There would be fewer moral dilemmas to come up against.'

'Where's the fun in living away from all dilemmas and challenges?' Raibhu countered, his smile as bright as those on the faces of his two friends. 'Let me be. I like living like this. It tests me, but what is a philosophy which isn't tested?'

Inosa inclined her head, conceding the point. 'I pray, then, that the Spirits will be on your side and not try you more than you can bear,' she said quietly. There was a sincerity in her voice that made her words all the more poignant. Raibhu bowed his head but said nothing; Afhash merely looked impressed.

'And now,' said Inosa. 'I, at least, am going to go to sleep. I suggest you two do that too, so that we can all wake up before dawn and set off.' She glanced up at the eastern sky, where the Lesser Moon had just appeared above the silhouette of the forested slope. 'It's early yet,' she added, 'so we can still get a good bit of sleep.'

She had pulled out a blanket from her travelling sack even as she spoke. Now she quickly moved about, pulling dried grass and leaves into place to make a bed for herself. Within five minutes, bundled up in her blanket, she had lain down. Raibhu and Afhash followed her lead. The little camp fell silent.

~

The room was a small one, in a hut that stood on the edge of a hamlet overlooking the river. In the middle of the room stood a rough wooden table, in the centre of which stood a Southern Mandalan lantern, a three-sided glass pillar a foot high, with a little pyramid-shaped wick burning brightly at its centre. The golden light of the lantern shone on a crowd clustered around the table. An odd assortment of people had crowded into this space: there were wrinkled old faces, their eyes filled with the wisdom of a lifetime; there were apple-cheeked youngsters, barely in their teens, their eyes full of curiosity. There were others in between, of all ages from a pregnant young woman to a middle-aged man, sinewy and keen-eyed, who sat in one of the two chairs in the room.

It was to this man that Xindaar addressed himself.

'Please,' he said. 'Please believe me. What I tell you is the truth. I carry the proof of my trustworthiness, do I not?' He held out his hand to the man in front of him. Then he looked up, one by one, at the faces looking at him. Slowly, surely, all of them nodded.

'Well, then. Believe me. Umur Naash is an evil man. I have seen it with my own eyes. If you doubt me, send someone to that village to ask about the girl.'

He paused, as if waiting to see their reaction. It was a man, grey-eyed and lean-cheeked, who finally said, 'I will send one of my apprentices, right now. They will have their own village physician, of course, but there is no harm in offering help.' He looked for confirmation to the man who sat opposite Xindaar, and on seeing him nod, headed for the doorway of the hut, followed by the two teenagers who had been standing next to him.

'We believe you,' the man opposite Xindaar said. 'Tell us what we can do to help.'

The relief in Xindaar's eyes was palpable. 'Thank you,' he murmured. He hesitated, collecting his thoughts before he spoke again. 'I will need some able-bodied warriors,' he said, a little diffidently. 'Well, not warriors,' he amended, looking at the faces around him; these, he realized, would hardly be warriors. 'But people who can fight, who can go up against Umur Naash and his men.'

There was a chuckle from somewhere in the crowd surrounding him. Xindaar looked about, trying to see who it was who was so amused. But all around him he saw smiles. Small smiles, some of them no more than an amused glint in an eye or a slight upcurving of a mouth at its corners. When he looked back at the man seated opposite him, he was met with a big smile.

'You should know,' said the man, 'in each sizeable community—and ours is that, not all of us are here right now—there are always at least ten who are trained warriors. We have more than the requisite ten, and they will be at your service.'

Xindaar nodded, relieved. 'Thank you. And one last thing, if I may ask. Just one more favour. Can you get a message through to the law office at Murki? I brought not a single messenger bhaagi with me, so it will probably need someone to go all the way there.' He looked uncomfortable, aware that this was not a small thing he was asking.

But he was among friends, even if he had only just met them. 'Don't worry,' said the man facing him. 'We will use the network. From one village to another, the message will travel faster that way. I'll send someone right now till the next community. You write out your message, and it will be taken.'

He reached forward to squeeze Xindaar's hand, and the inside of his wrist was exposed briefly to view. It sported a tattoo which was the exact replica of the one on Xindaar's wrist.

It reminded Xindaar of something, of another hand moving forward to clasp his. His eyes lit up in sudden excitement. 'I think,' he said in a soft voice, 'there may be one other person we could ask for help. A trained warrior, too. Would you be able to send a message to him? He is not far from here.'

'Of course,' the man replied. He turned to one of the others in the room. 'Get paper and pen for our friend, please. And you, Maadhik, can you please inform Sanjovan that there will be messages to carry? He should be ready. Even if he needs to run through the night to deliver them.'

~

The Lesser Moon had reached its zenith some time back and was now beginning its descent. The Greater Moon, no longer the thin sliver it had been a couple of days earlier, but now resembling a flake of orange, shone down bright and luminous from its position of dominance in a star-studded sky.

Its light illuminated the three forms huddled around the remains of the fire Afhash had nursed in the centre of their camp. One of the blanket-wrapped forms stirred, then—slowly, so slowly that not a sound disturbed the silence of the night—it sat up.

Carefully, Inosa put aside her blanket. Just as carefully, she got to her feet and shifted her travelling sack into the space she had been occupying till a minute back. She pulled the blanket over the sack; the resultant shape would not have passed muster in better light, but anybody looking at it in the dappled moonlight here, under the trees, would be forgiven for thinking that someone was still sleeping under that blanket.

Silent as the moonlight itself, Inosa stepped around the sleeping forms of Raibhu and Afhash. They were fast asleep; she skirted round them, and without stopping, she headed away from their camp. She went in the direction they had come from earlier that day: retracing their steps, going down the same path. The brightness of the moonlight helped her, illuminating the way, and Inosa made good time.

The Lesser Moon was already hidden below the treeline and the Greater Moon had almost reached its zenith by the time Inosa saw the first signs of another camp ahead. This one was far larger than hers, and much less careful about keeping its presence hidden. From where she stood, on a ridge facing it, Inosa could see the glow of a large campfire that lit up the space around for several feet. She crouched, and keeping to the shadows, moved forward.

A few minutes later, and she was looking unhindered at the camp.

There were no tents, and the haphazard way in which men slept, some of them wrapped in blankets and lying on the ground while others sat with their backs against tree trunks and dozed as best as they could, suggested a group that had set off without any real planning having been done for night halts along the route. Her gaze wandered across the sturdy hill ponies tethered to the trees at one end of the clearing. Near them, at the point where the clearing opened out on to the trail, stood a man, alert and wide-eyed. The sentry. Even as Inosa watched, he moved off from where he was standing, and began pacing, eyes constantly darting to and fro, to and fro.

Inosa gave him a wide berth as she crept along, shielded by the trees, circling the camp. She came to a stop in the shadow of a large rock, at the far side of the clearing from where the sentry stood on duty. This was where the fire had been built, a big stonefire which was probably a testimony to Umur Naash's prosperity. An ordinary man out in the wild would have used wood to light a fire; Umur Naash paraded his wealth by carrying fire-stones and having his men light a stonefire. It roared and blazed, painting that side of the clearing many shades of yellow and orange.

It was surprising, given the heat of the fire, that one man should be sitting so close to it. He sat, head up and shoulders straight, no more than four feet from the fire. He was staring intently into the flames, so engrossed that it would seem there was something deeply interesting in the heart of the fire.

Inosa's eyebrows drew together. Curious, she moved closer, but still keeping within the shadow of the rock. Simultaneously, a stone fell over another in the stonefire, sending up a shower of sparks. The man's face lifted momentarily, and Inosa's eyes grew wide as she got a good look at him. Involuntarily, she stepped back, and barrelled into a strong, muscular body right behind her. She whirled, her hand going to the dagger at her belt, but the man behind her had already caught her, one steely arm winding about her waist and pulling her to him, the other reaching up to clap a hand across her mouth.

Chapter Nine

It was Raibhu. Inosa dropped her dagger to her side just as she was at the point of raising it to stab him. He was already pulling her away from the rock, back into the deep, sheltering shadows of the forest around them. Inosa offered no resistance, and when she gently tugged at his hand across her mouth, motioning to him to let her go, he obeyed.

'What's all this?' Raibhu asked Inosa when they were well out of earshot of anybody at the camp.

Instead of answering him, Inosa said, 'Let's move on, further away. Not here, we're too close.'

Raibhu went along with her, heading back towards their own camp, but when they could no longer even see the glow of the stonefire, he called a halt. 'Inosa. Tell me. What was that? Are those the men who've been following us? I didn't see the soldiers there, not a single one of them. So who are these people? Why do you think they're following us?'

Inosa looked discomfited. 'Let's go on,' she muttered. 'The sooner we finish what we have to do, the better it will be. Come on.'

She made to go on, but Raibhu stopped her, his hand on her arm. 'No. We're not moving from here until you tell me.

I saw the look on your face when you saw that man—who was he? Why does he frighten you so much?'

For a moment it seemed that Inosa would deny that she had been scared, that the very sight of that face, suddenly tilted up and with the firelight showing each feature in all its stark glory, had not made the sweat bead on her forehead. She had even been shaking her head in denial while Raibhu asked the question; but when he ended, when he waited for her reply, she stopped in her tracks and stared down at her feet.

'Tell me, Inosa. Trust me at least this much that you can say why you're so scared.'

Inosa finally heaved a sigh. 'It's—it's just that that man is a very evil one,' she said. 'He's a local warlord, and he's been terrorizing much of the Sada Valley for many years now. He's'—she shuddered visibly—'he's the devil incarnate.' She shook her head vehemently. 'Come on, please, we can't afford to stop. We have to get away!' She speeded up, and Raibhu kept pace with her.

'Why would this warlord want to follow us?' he asked. 'It makes no sense. We're just out on a simple, personal mission to fulfil Father's last wish. We have nothing that would be any use to anybody—why would anybody want to spend time and energy chasing us?'

Inosa said nothing. She just went on running as if her life depended upon it. It was difficult to run in the dark, with only the fitful light of the Greater Moon, as it shone between scudding clouds and the tall trees that cloaked the mountain. Both Inosa and Raibhu tripped and fell at times. They slowed down in places to a more cautious walk, and then, as soon as the ground looked more level and obstacle-free, they broke into a run.

And as soon as they could run without having to focus on not falling over, Raibhu tried to get an answer out of Inosa. 'For the love of the Spirits, tell me what's the matter!' he said, frustrated by her reticence. 'There's something you're not telling me. I have a right to know, because it impacts our travel. Have you done something that angered this warlord? Is he after you for revenge or something—'

'I'll tell you when we get to our camp,' Inosa said, vaulting over a fallen log. 'Let's just get back and get moving!'

Barely had she spoken the words than the night was split by a loud snarling. And mixed with that distinctly animal sound, the sound of human shouts: someone screaming, yelling in fear and rage.

'Afhash!' Raibhu gasped, and raced forward, pulling his dagger out. Behind him, Inosa too got out her dagger.

They burst into their camp together, to find that a great silver bear had invaded their space.

~

It was chaos. Afhash was darting around, picking up stones, sticks, whatever he could find that would serve as a missile. He would pick up a stone or a stick, and lob it at the hulking ghostly shape that was snuffling about among their travelling sacks. Very few of the projectiles Afhash sent its way hit the bear, and of those that did, even fewer seemed to have any effect on it. Every now and then the bear would raise its head and snarl at Afhash, who would immediately back off a bit and go back to shouting or trying to find more stones to throw at it. The bear seemed mostly oblivious of Afhash, paying as little attention to him as it would to a mouse scurrying across its path. It was a massive creature, after all, standing a good six feet tall at the shoulder when on its four legs. If it reared up on its hind legs, as it did occasionally, it loomed a terrifying ten feet high. With its shaggy silvery fur, its glowing red eyes and its mouth full of fangs, it was a frightening animal. But, as Raibhu and Inosa knew, the silver bear was less harmful than it looked; unless a bear was guarding its cubs, it could be driven off without too much difficulty.

Raibhu paused to break a thin branch from a sapling; in those few moments, Inosa raced past him, dagger raised and shrieking loudly to chase away the bear. Afhash, who had been too busy with the bear to even notice that reinforcements had arrived, whipped around. 'Inosa!' he shouted. 'No! Inosa, stay away!' And before Inosa could get within striking distance of the bear, Afhash had leaped at her, pushing her away, shielding her with his body, keeping her away from the bear. Inosa struggled with Afhash, pushing back and trying to break free, but she was no match for his greater weight and mass.

Behind them, Raibhu lunged towards the bear, dagger in one hand and the makeshift spear in the other. The animal was in no mood to stand its ground; in the usual way of silver bears, all it had wanted was the food which had attracted it in the first place. It backed away, and without Raibhu needing to even wound it, it turned tail and loped away.

With one massive heave, Inosa threw Afhash aside. 'What were you thinking of?' She shouted as she scrambled to her feet. 'You idiot! Instead of fighting me, you should've been fighting the bear! Can't you think?'

Afhash gave her an injured look. 'That's unfair, Inosa. I was just trying to protect you. You were trying to go at that creature with only a dagger, you would have been killed!'

'I know silver bears,' Inosa said icily, putting her dagger away and dusting herself down. 'They rarely attack humans, and that mostly when they're with cubs. This one came just to find a free meal, it would have been scared off easily enough.'

She glanced towards Raibhu. 'Are you all right?'

Raibhu nodded. 'Afhash?'

'Nothing wrong with me,' Afhash said, still looking upset at what he considered Inosa's uncalled for reprimand. 'But there would have been a lot wrong with Inosa. I saw that bear, it had such a wild, hungry look in its eyes. I swear, if I hadn't woken up and got out of its way, it would have eaten me up!'

'Don't be silly,' Inosa said. She was already looking through the ruins of their camp, examining their travelling sacks to see what damage the bear had done. 'Damn,' she muttered under her breath as she lifted the ragged remains of a bag which had contained dry fruit. The bear had ripped it to shreds. Most of the fruit had been eaten; the rest, whatever little that remained, had been trampled into the ground. The few pieces of now dry, stale bread had fared even worse: only a few crumbs remained, scattered here and there.

'It's all gone, isn't it?' Raibhu said in a low voice. He looked through his travelling sack, and was relieved to find that the smaller sack inside it—which he had brought from Dhaani—was untouched. Still Raibhu opened it and checked Jaadum's letter and map, and the containers that held the mud from the two sites of interment. Satisfied that they were all intact and undamaged, he closed the travelling sack.

'How much longer do we have to we travel?' he asked Inosa.

'A little more than a day,' Inosa replied. 'And then back, of course.' She sighed. 'I can forage as we go along, or if we need to, we'll hunt.' She looked about, towards the east. 'It's a long way from dawn yet, but we better move on.'

'Move on? What do you mean, move on?' Afhash was appalled, so shocked that he forgot the recent tongue-lashing he had received from Inosa. 'We're still a long way from dawn. And now that the bear's gone—'

It was Raibhu who answered him, cutting in before Afhash could rile up an already-annoyed Inosa even more. 'Someone's on our trail,' he told Afhash. 'Inosa went back to check on them, and I followed her to see. There's a large group of men, and Inosa says they're dangerous.'

Afhash frowned. 'Who? The soldiers?'

'No.' Raibhu glanced towards Inosa, but she was busy gathering up the travelling sacks, checking them and making sure that she had collected everything worth salvaging. 'Not the soldiers. Inosa says it's some local warlord. Someone who's been terrorizing the Sada Valley for many years now.'

Afhash looked puzzled. 'A warlord? Who? I may have been in prison for the past couple of years, but I know what's been happening. Who's this, Inosa?'

Inosa shook her head. 'You probably don't know of him. Come on, let's go.' She hitched her own travelling sack up onto her back.

'How wouldn't I know of him? Southern Mandala isn't huge, and if he's been making life so very miserable for people, I'd have known about him. Who's this?'

'I said let's go,' Inosa said, gritting her teeth. Raibhu, noticing her reaction, glanced pointedly at Afhash, silently begging him to back down and not irritate Inosa anymore; she was already upset enough. But Afhash was not paying any attention.

'I'll go, but only if you tell me first who this is,' he said stubbornly. 'Come on, Inosa. You expect us to get up in the middle of the night and start running; at least give me a good reason to do that. Why should I run because some local bandit happens to be in the vicinity? For all you know, he may not even know of our existence, and he may not be following us—'

This time it was Inosa who interrupted him, with a sudden snarl that sent Afhash back a step, it was so ferocious.

'You fool!' She snapped. 'It's Umur Naash! Have you heard that name? Yes, you have, haven't you? Well, Umur Naash is coming after us. Does that make you want to run?'

There was complete and utter silence for a moment. It was as if the world itself stood still, as if nature held its breath.

'No. Oh, no.'

Afhash drew in a deep, shuddering breath. 'The Land Spirit preserve us.' Snatching his travelling sack up from where it was lying at Inosa's feet, he turned to her, wild-eyed. 'Which way? Which way do we go?'

~

'You remember, when we were at that fairground, and we heard those men talking about the "Mighty Naash"?' panted Afhash, running along next to Raibhu. Inosa was a few paces ahead of them, using her familiarity with the terrain to choose the easiest path. 'I told you back then about him, a bit. That's Umur Naash. The Mighty Naash. He's—he's a monster, evil personified. Inosa is right. We can't be too far from him.'

Raibhu nodded. He had seen the terror in the faces of both his companions; even if he had never seen Umur Naash for himself, the reaction the man's name had elicited from Inosa and Afhash was enough to convince Raibhu that it would be safer to not fall prey to Umur Naash.

'But why is he after us?' Raibhu asked. 'We have nothing he could want.'

But Afhash had no answer to that. And Inosa was too far ahead and in too much of a hurry for him to stop her to ask questions.

A while later, now that the sun was well up and there was plenty of light, Inosa called a halt. 'We've been moving almost five hours without a break now,' she said. 'We'll collapse if we don't stop for a rest. Let's take a break, eat something, and then go on.' She had found a little rivulet, and beside this, she put down her travelling sack. 'We're out of food,' she added. 'I'll forage nearby. See if the two of you can find anything to eat. Don't go far; we can't afford to have anybody getting lost now. And get back soon. Be back within ten minutes, no more. If you can't find anything, don't go further, just come back.'

Ten minutes later, Raibhu returned to the spot Inosa had picked out for them. He had found a few bird's eggs as well as some berries, all of which he had brought along, wrapped in some grass and leaves. Afhash, to his surprise, was already back and was in the process of lighting a tiny fire. Beside him lay a dead bird. 'I'm good with an improvised catapult,' Afhash said, showing off a bit of twine wound around a forked stick. He grinned happily as the flames caught at the twigs he had built up into a pile. 'Here, you look after this fire. I'll get this bird ready to cook.'

Inosa, returning a couple of minutes later, brought with her more berries and some mushrooms. 'You're going to cook?' she hissed, seeing the little fire.

'Don't worry, there'll be no smoke,' Afhash soothed her. 'We're well under the trees, and the fire is small.'

'We'll be done quickly, don't worry,' Raibhu said. He rose to his feet. 'Come, sit down.'

Inosa sat down, handing over the results of her foraging, but she looked very distressed. 'We need to go on quickly,' she mumbled. 'We don't have the time to sit around cooking things.'

'We need time to rest,' Afhash said. He had already prepared the bird and wrapped it in leaves. With a sturdy stick, he dug under the fire and pushed the packet of leaves in, piling up burning wood around it. 'This will not take time. While we eat the rest of the things'—he took the mushrooms and the eggs, and quickly wrapped those up too in leaves, which he placed on top of the fire—'these will get cooked. By the time we're ready to move on, the bird will be done. We can eat it on the move. Now don't fret, and let's start with the fruit you two got.'

~

The guide was sitting on his haunches, examining the ground carefully. It was churned up, with torn leaves and grass, twigs, and scraps of food lying around. He peered more closely, then smiled a smile of satisfaction. 'Just as I said last night when we heard those screams,' he said. He was still gloating over his achievement and so he did not bother to look up. 'A silver bear attacked them. See,'—he indicated the bear's footprints in a patch of muddy ground—'that was where it finally turned and ran off. They are three, they must have scared it off easily enough.'

Umur Naash's whip came down suddenly and without warning on the man's back, sending him sprawling in the dirt he had been examining so closely just a moment before.

'I did not let you bring us here to give us a lecture on bears or show off for our benefit,' he snarled. 'Do you know where they have gone? If you do, take us there. If you don't—' he stopped, letting the statement hang menacingly in the air.

He waited long enough to see that the guide, cowering and begging for mercy, had got the message. Then he gestured to his men to get the man back on his feet. 'Get going,' he said. The guide, blood oozing from a dozen pinpricks from his fall among thorny bushes, scrambled up. Within moments, he had found the trail. 'Here,' he mumbled. And without even waiting to hear Umur Naash's acknowledgement, he ran, leading the way towards their quarry.

~

'I don't like this,' Inosa said, staring glumly ahead. They had just rounded a corner and the trail had brought them out of the forest and facing a slope which had caved in on one side. The site of the long-ago impact of a fire ball, it looked as if a giant fist had punched the mountainside, gouging out all vegetation, trees and plants and everything, along with the top soil it had held in place. All that remained in that concave crater-like slope was scree. Around the upper edge, some boulders stood, looking precarious, as if a nudge would be enough to topple them over the edge and send them hurtling down the slope.

The space was utterly devoid of shelter. Not one tree stood on this slope, not one bush: all there was was one boulder, about six feet across, approximately halfway down the slope. Other than that, the slope was stark, bare. Vulnerable.

'Can't we go another way?' Raibhu asked. His gaze wandered across the slope and beyond, to where the trees could again be seen.

'We would have to retrace our steps and go around this mountain from the back,' Inosa replied. 'That's too far. And we could run into Umur Naash and his men again.' She heaved a sigh and squared her shoulders. 'No, we'll have to do this. Let's just try to get across as quickly as we possibly can.'

Raibhu nodded. 'Let's be prepared to fight,' he said, as he pulled out his dagger. Afhash and Inosa followed suit, and Inosa got out her bow and arrows as well. She had been carrying her crude makeshift spear; she put it aside regretfully. 'I can't carry this and my bow at the same time,' she said. 'If either of you wants it, take it.' Before she had even finished speaking, Afhash had picked up the spear. 'All right,' he said. 'Ready.'

They exchanged glances, and at a signal from Raibhu, began running zigzag across the slope. They slipped on the scree, and the men, less sure-footed than Inosa, even fell a couple of times; but they took no notice of the resultant scrapes and bruises, and carried on. Halfway through, Raibhu turned to glance briefly in the direction from which they had come. The sun was shining down on the trees, and for a fraction of a second, it shone on something that was not wood or leaf or rock. Something metallic, something that gleamed.

'Down!' Raibhu cried. 'They're coming!'

The words had barely been uttered when a humur projectile whistled past them. It missed them, but the threat in that menacing sound was unmistakable.

The very next moment, all hell broke loose. Umur Naash's men burst out of the trees, firing humur projectiles and arrows, shouting as they came. Raibhu, as soon as he had seen the glint of sunlight reflecting off a humur projectile positioned in the slingshot, had led Inosa and Afhash straight for the sparse shelter offered by the single rock on the slope. They slid in behind this, a projectile ricocheting off the boulder and narrowly missing Raibhu as he plunged in after his two companions.

'This isn't going to hold them off for long,' Raibhu panted. 'We'll have to fight them off.'

'They have slingshots that launch humur projectiles,' Inosa said. 'But if we attack them all at once—I can use my arrows. What about stones, like when you,' she glanced at Afhash, 'tried to frighten off the bear?' Afhash nodded, and before either Raibhu or Inosa could add anything, he crouched and began gathering up all the small rocks he could find in the vicinity that could be used as missiles. Raibhu looked uphill, at the rocks that stood along the top of the slope, less than a hundred metres away.

'Listen,' said Raibhu. 'This is what I have in mind.'

The onslaught had continued throughout, Umur Naash's men now moving closer. They had realized that the rock protected the trio well from their projectiles, so they had put away their slingshots, saving their ammunition. As it was, it looked like an easy one-sided battle. A large gang, armed to the teeth, and that too with slingshots, against three who obviously didn't have a single weapon more deadly than a dagger between them. There was no doubt about how this was going to pan out. Umur Naash, standing far back under a pine tree and watching his men surge forward, smiled a small evil smile of satisfaction.

And then, suddenly, the tables were turned. Inosa and Afhash sprang out from behind the boulder, he throwing rocks at Umur Naash's men, and she shooting arrows. They moved about constantly, zigzagging, crouching, changing course, not letting themselves be sitting targets for Umur Naash's men.

Simultaneously, Raibhu had shot out from behind the boulder and gone racing uphill. He too zigzagged, and though a few projectiles came close to hitting him—one even spat up gravel almost at his feet, spewing dirt and dust in his face and blinding him briefly—he carried on. Below him on the slope, his friends battled Umur Naash's men, who had now come close enough for hand-to-hand combat. Inosa had nearly exhausted her arrows; she slung her bow back while she pulled out her dagger. Afhash had already got his dagger out and the spear borrowed from Inosa. He lunged forward, stabbing and slashing, followed closely by Inosa.

Uphill, Raibhu had reached the boulder he had been

heading for. It was an unusual rock, balanced precariously atop another, much smaller rock. This was what had attracted Raibhu to it in the first place, and now he put his plan into action. Leaning into the bigger rock with his side, he pushed.

And pushed again. The rock had looked deceptively easy to topple, but it was heavier and more firmly seated on the smaller rock. Raibhu did not expend unnecessary energy on it; as soon as he realized he would not be able to shift the boulder on his own, he cast a quick glance around him. Just a couple of feet away was a rock a little bigger than a human head. Raibhu looked back towards where Inosa and Afhash were fighting Umur Naash's men; he was half-hidden from them by the bulk of the boulder. A couple of Umur Naash's men were headed uphill, and Raibhu threw a few well-aimed rocks at them, knocking one out completely so that he went rolling down the slope, and briefly stunning the other. Then Raibhu whirled about, picked up the rock, and scurried back into the shelter of the boulder. It took him another few seconds to wedge the small rock under the boulder.

Inosa and Afhash slashed and stabbed, drawing blood, felling Umur Naash's men, dodging daggers and flying kicks as best as they could. They were fighting bravely, but they were horribly outnumbered. From the triumphant look on Umur Naash's face as he watched his men swarm ahead, it was obvious that he too knew he was within inches of victory. That victory was inevitable.

And then there came a thudding sound, a vague rumble. Raibhu, using the little rock as a lever, had managed to dislodge the large boulder. It teetered for a few moments, swaying dangerously, looking as if it may fall any which way, possibly even back on Raibhu. But he had moved out of the way, and even before the boulder finally toppled over and went rolling down the slope, he had fled, racing across the slope to the far end, heading for the shelter of the trees. On the slope below, Inosa and Afhash, anticipating the rock fall, had been better prepared for it than had been Umur Naash's men. While Umur Naash's men were caught unawares, Inosa and Afhash broke loose and ran, heading away from them. They raced towards the trees where Raibhu, higher up the slope, was also headed.

Umur Naash's men turned and ran back towards where Umur Naash had been standing. He was shouting, screaming at them. 'Follow them! Don't let them get away!'—but nobody was listening. For once, the terror that Umur Naash aroused was negated by the roar of the rock as it tumbled down the slope, loosening other rocks and more gravel as it sped downhill, until there was a huge cloud of dust and gravel hanging over the slope. At the bottom, where the mountainside crater curved up into a lip, the boulder came to a shuddering stop.

~

A little above where Umur Naash stood, a face pale with fright stared out. It was a junior law officer of Southern Mandala, the man Xindaar had deputed to keep following Inosa and her companions. He had watched as Inosa and Afhash, one minute fighting Umur Naash's men, had suddenly turned and fled, their figures obliterated the next minute by the rocks, the gravel and the dust. When the boulder had gone its way and the dust had settled enough for the opposite slope to be somewhat visible again, the officer peered closely through his celestial view-glass once again. But he could see nothing there.

A sudden flood of shouts and angry curses rang through the air, drawing the officer's attention. He shifted his focus to where Umur Naash had emerged from the trees and was facing his men who had retreated from the gravel-covered slope so ignominiously. 'You bastards! How dare you turn tail and come running back here?' he shouted. 'Go! Go and find them. Find them now, and bring them back. If you come back to me without those three, I will kill each one of you with my own hands! Understand? Understand, you sons of bitches?!' He whipped around, turning to the guide, who had been standing with him all this while and had not participated in the melee. 'What are you standing here for? Go!'

The officer watched as the line of Umur Naash's men, led by the guide, went cautiously back the way they had come, across the scree-covered slope. They walked slowly and carefully, casting fearful glances uphill every now and then, as if expecting another boulder to come tumbling down towards them. But there was silence, and the dust had settled by the time they climbed up the lip of the crater and disappeared into the forest beyond it.

The officer peered down at Umur Naash. The warlord had seated himself on a rock to wait. Beside him stood three men, all armed and ready. Three others ranged about, walking back and forth, guarding their master's back and looking for signs of the returning group. Minutes passed by. The sun climbed in the sky. The birds, which had flown away in fright when the boulder had crashed downhill, returned, chirping and settling back.

Silence reigned. An uneasy and tense silence.

~

Raibhu, running downhill, and Inosa and Afhash, racing across the slope, met in the shadow of the trees. Their paths converged, but they did not stop. Inosa surged ahead, rushing deep into the forest and away from the narrow, hardly-there trail which led through it. 'Quick,' she said, over her shoulder. 'Quick, quick!' Raibhu and Afhash scrambled after her.

It was only when they had run several minutes and there was no sign of pursuit that Inosa stopped long enough to ask, 'Are you two well? All right?' Her glance settled on Afhash, whose left sleeve had a big rip through it, a rip through which blood had spread. 'I'll attend to that,' Inosa said, shrugging off her travelling sack and hurrying to pull out rags and dried herbs. 'Anything else? Are you fine otherwise? You, Raibhu?'

She was already tying up Afhash's arm when Raibhu said, 'Inosa. You have to tell us why Umur Naash is following us. It can't be because Afhash ran away from his sada stone mines years ago'—he saw the puzzlement on Inosa's face—and added, 'I'll tell you later. I don't even know Umur Naash. And if it's you he's after, why? What did you do, Inosa? Why is he hell-bent on capturing us, or killing us?'

Inosa did not answer him at once. She peered into the pouch in which she had been carrying the powdered calmroot stem, and then upturned it. A little dust floated out, but that was it. 'Damn,' she muttered under her breath. 'Damn, damn. We've used up more than I'd thought we'd need.'

She stood up, and looked Raibhu in the eye. 'I didn't do anything,' she said brusquely. 'And we don't have the time to talk just now; his men will catch up with us. Let's go.' She paused, noting the dazed look on Afhash's face and the curiosity coupled with suspicion in Raibhu's. 'Please,' she said quietly. 'Please listen to me. Let's go and immerse the mud you're carrying in the river, and once that's done, I'll tell you. All right?'

Raibhu looked for a moment as if he was going to dig in his heels; but he finally nodded. 'All right,' he said.

'And,' he added, 'let's make sure we don't leave a trail for them to follow. Or at least as scattered a trail as we can manage. It'll mean taking a detour, but I suppose you'll be able to keep us on track despite that?'

Inosa agreed. 'If we're careful, it won't take us too far out of the way. As it is,' she admitted, 'I have been leading both of you on a somewhat convoluted route, not exactly what's shown on the map. The route on the map is a very straightforward one, just the type Umur Naash's men would be familiar with.' She picked up her travelling sack. 'Let's go.'

This time Raibhu and Inosa led the way in tandem, Inosa pointing the approximate direction in which they were to head, and Raibhu deciding the route they would take over the next hundred metres or so. He made them all take off their shoes and socks and stuff them into their travelling sacks, for a start. Then he led the way, stepping carefully on rocks, leaping from one to the other. Once, when they reached a stream that rippled merrily along on a pebbled bed, Raibhu insisted on walking in it as far as it would lead them on their way. 'Nobody will be able to see tracks in the stream bed,' he said, wading in.

It was tough going but Raibhu, looking back occasionally, was satisfied that if they were leaving a trail, it was a very faint one, not one easily discernible to even the average woodsman.

Looking back, he could also see that Afhash, who was walking behind Raibhu and Inosa, was having trouble keeping up. His arm was obviously more painful than he was letting on, and he had perhaps sustained other injuries that he had chosen not to tell his companions about. He was looking pale, and when he thought nobody was watching, he allowed his expression to relax into the tiredness and pain he was feeling.

'Go on,' Raibhu told Inosa in an undertone. 'Lead the way. If you think we're going too far off-course, get out of the stream, but do it only where there are rocks or gravel, okay?'

'Where are you going?' Inosa asked, immediately suspicious.

'Nowhere. Just falling back. I'll walk with Afhash.' And before she could say anything, he had slowed down and turned, walking back a few steps to meet Afhash. Inosa, her expression softening momentarily, turned and then carried on.

'What's the matter?' Afhash asked. Raibhu, looking at him close up, saw the pain in his eyes, and the anxiety that clouded them.

'Nothing,' he replied. 'Give me your travelling sack.'

'Why?' Suddenly defensive, Afhash tightened his grip on his travelling sack. 'What do you want?'

'You're hurt, you fool.' Raibhu gently but firmly loosened his friend's grip on the sack. 'I don't want you collapsing on the way.' Afhash still didn't let the sack go. 'Did you get injured somewhere else too?' Raibhu asked, still holding on to the travelling sack. The two of them were still walking, Afhash moving in a somewhat ungainly fashion that was not merely a result of the fact that he was wading through ankle-deep water.

'It's nothing.'

'I don't believe you, but let it be. Just do me one favour, Afhash. Let me help you, please? You insisted on coming with me on this trip, now I insist that you let me help you.'

Afhash hesitated, pain battling with self-respect. Then pain capitulated; he surrendered the travelling sack to Raibhu.

~

Umur Naash stood with one foot resting on a fallen log. One hand, its sada stone ring glinting brightly in the sunshine, rested on his thigh, its forefinger tapping impatiently in a staccato that conveyed some of the anger of the man himself. The other hand held a custom-made weapon: a slingshot and a dagger combined. The slingshot was crafted from the darkest, strongest humur wood, and built into its handle was a knife blade that could be flicked in and out easily.

From where he stood, Umur Naash could see around well: he was on a height, the ground sloping away on three sides, offering him an almost perfect view of the mountain meadow before him and the stretches of forest on either side. Of course, the forest was too dense for Umur Naash to be able to see much of what lay below the canopy of the trees, but that was what his men were for. They were swarming through the woods, crisscrossing it, searching desperately for some sign of the route their quarry had taken.

They had made no progress so far. It was showing in the increasingly frantic scurrying of the men, and in the increasing frustration of the man who stood above, watching them. The finger drumming on this thigh stopped suddenly. With a wild scream of rage, he lifted his slingshot with one hand, and with the other pulled humur projectiles from the leather pouch at his belt. One after the other, with the unerring speed and accuracy that comes of long practice, he fitted projectiles into the slingshot and let them fly at the men who milled around there below him. One, two, three. A thin scream rose up in the air, followed by sharp cries of pain and fear as three men fell, and the others scurried for shelter, their panic overshadowing everything else.

Umur Naash fitted another projectile into his slingshot, but this time, instead of letting it fly, he shouted, 'You bastards! For every five minutes you don't bring me any news, I'm going to get rid of one of you worthless idiots! Get to it now! Find them!'

A couple of minutes passed before Umur Naash put his slingshot down. His men had all vanished; he could no longer even catch the occasional glimpse of one of them under the trees.

'Master...?' The single word was so low as to be barely audible. Umur Naash whipped around, the slingshot poised for action again.

The man who had come up behind him was a minion, a terrified youngster barely out of his teens. 'My name is Sengaar, Master,' he said diffidently. He had backed off a couple of steps when Umur Naash's murderous gaze met his own, but it seemed he was made of sterner stuff than most of his comrades.

Instead of speaking, Sengaar stretched out a trembling hand. In it he held three arrows.

'What's this?' Umur Naash snapped. Despite himself, despite his fury, he seemed to be impressed by the young man's temerity: it took guts to come anywhere near the wrath of Umur Naash. One never knew when that wrath would explode.

Sengaar's voice shook when he spoke, but he said all he had to say without stopping. 'It's from that slope where we fought them, Master. The youngest of them, the girlish one, he was firing arrows. I picked these up after they left. I thought, if we could go and borrow a couple of dogs from a nearby village, the arrows could be used—'

Umur Naash's eyebrow had lifted when he had heard whose the arrows were. As he listened to Sengaar, his eyes narrowed in speculation, as if his brain was racing ahead, seeking for itself how those arrows could be put to use. Even before the man finished speaking, Umur Naash broke in impatiently. 'Yes, yes. Go, then! Go, quick. Take two of those fellows down there with you. The three of you go to three different villages, and see if you can get hunters with dogs. Quick!'

He watched as Sengaar loped off downhill into the forest, calling to his colleagues as he went.

'Not much longer,' Umur Naash murmured to himself. 'Just a little while.'

~

Inosa turned around to look at Raibhu and Afhash. They were about ten steps behind her, and Afhash was looking more in pain than before. Raibhu was not only shouldering Afhash's travelling sack, he was also helping his friend along. Inosa stepped out of the stream onto a flattish rock. Leaving her travelling sack on the rock, she went scampering uphill, leaping nimbly from one rock to the other until she had reached a point from where she could look out over the slope beyond.

By the time she came back, the way she had gone up, Afhash and Raibhu had reached the rock on which her travelling sack lay. Raibhu had seated Afhash on the rock, and was undoing the bandage on his arm. It was sodden with blood. Inosa winced when she saw it.

'He needs more than just bandages,' Inosa said as she searched through her travelling sack for a clean rag to replace the blood-soaked one. She found two, one of which she rolled up into a pad to press over the wound. While Raibhu helped her tie the other rag around Afhash's arm, Inosa told him what she had in mind. 'He needs medicine, he'll get worse if this wound gets infected.'

'Then?'

'I went up and had a look,' Inosa said, tilting her chin to indicate the hill she had ascended just a few minutes before. 'There are plants and other things I can use. I saw birch trees, their bark is excellent for healing wounds. And I saw yarrow, that helps too. Even if I gather enough of those to make an infusion and a poultice, it should help. Maybe some calmroot, too...let's see.'

'I'll come with you,' Raibhu said. 'It'll get done faster. Afhash,' he looked around quickly, and saw a few bushes not far from where they sat. 'That clump of bushes will shelter you while we're gone, right? You'll be safe there.' Afhash was too weak to offer more than a token protest, and Raibhu caught him under the arms and helped him to the bushes in question. Inosa picked up their travelling sacks and placed them under the bushes. 'Keep your dagger out,' she instructed Afhash. 'All right? And if you see or hear anything, call. Or whistle, whatever. We won't be far; it's just a short distance away.'

As they set off, Inosa said to Raibhu, 'I'll show you how to strip the bark from the birches. That's easy, and it'll get done soon. I'll see if I can find yarrow or calmroot; if I can, well and good. Otherwise, the birch bark will have to do.' She looked back down at the clump of bushes where they had left Afhash; he could not be seen from where they climbed uphill. 'As soon as you've gathered enough birch bark—I'll tell you how much you'll need—go back to him.'

'I won't leave you alone, Inosa. You could be in danger.'

Inosa looked taken aback, but she shook her head. They were almost at the top of the slope now. 'Afhash is injured, he may not be able to defend himself if he's attacked. I can take care of myself. The damsel will shout if she's in distress,' she added, her face lighting up with a rare grin. She pulled herself up one last lot of rocks. 'Here we are. Come on.'

~

Sengaar stood at a crossroads along the main trail. A low whistle, echoing in the woods, made him look to his left, suddenly alert. An older man emerged, waving to the boy, who waved back.

'You didn't find a hunting dog, either, eh, Sengaar?' the

older man said when he reached his younger colleague. They hesitated, standing together on the ridge, wondering what to do. Their third companion, Murfan, was still gone.

It was Sengaar who spoke this time. 'We can't go back empty-handed,' he said flatly. 'He'll kill us.'

'Let's go on. There might be another village. This way? What do you think? You didn't go in this direction, did you? And Murfan, I know; he went that way.' They looked simultaneously in the direction indicated, and in unison too they nodded. 'Let's go this way.' They set off along the track, which wound its way high above a stream and then past a grove of birch trees.

Sengaar, who was walking in front, suddenly froze. He turned to his companion with a finger raised to his lips, indicating silence. Sure that the message was understood, he pointed downhill, towards the birch trees. Two people were moving about there. Or at least two. One was easily seen; it was the 'girlish' youth Umur Naash had been told about. Inosa moved about on the fringes of the grove, bending down and gathering calmroot and yarrow. She moved systematically and quickly, gathering leaves from some plants, uprooting a few of the others. Beyond her, Raibhu could be seen moving among the white-trunked birches: the trees provided a screen for him, offering only occasional and fleeting glimpses.

Sengaar dropped to a crouch behind a bush; his colleague followed suit. On both faces was extreme joy. 'They're here!' whispered Sengaar. 'Did you see all three of them? I definitely saw at least two.'

'I don't know,' the other admitted. 'Two, definitely. The third, I don't know. But where would he be? They stuck together, he'd be close by. Or dead.'

'Look, now that we know where they are, should we go back and report? If Murfan manages to get a dog, we can bring it here at once. Even if they're gone by then, we'll have a trail to follow.'

The other nodded. 'Okay.'

Still crouching, the two of them moved back the way they had come. When they were well away from the grove of birches and were no longer in danger of being seen, they straightened up.

Below, Afhash, alerted by the soft sound of padding feet on the trail above the stream, turned his head. Completely unaware of his presence, the two men walked surreptitiously along, hurrying to wherever they were going. Afhash frowned, and tightened his grip on his dagger, preparing to defend himself.

But he went unnoticed. The men moved away, disappearing into the woods. Afhash leaned back, the breath whooshing out of him in relief. He was too busy congratulating himself on a lucky escape to see that the track the men followed formed a loop higher up the slope. From there, they could have a more panoramic view of what was happening below.

Afhash was well hidden by the bushes where he lay, but Inosa and Raibhu were not so lucky.

~

Inosa had come upon a few bushes of Mandalan feverberries, a proven remedy used to eradicate infections and bring down fevers. The small orange-coloured fruit were sparse on the bush—it had probably all been nibbled away by birds, deer and the like—but Inosa was not bothered with that. She pulled out her dagger and quickly cut off some twigs, leaves and all. The thorns of the bush made it difficult to grasp the twigs, and since she was only carrying a small pouch for the herbs she had hoped to collect, she would not be able to fit these in. Inosa hurriedly pulled out a large handkerchief from her tunic pocket, and bending down, she spread it on the ground.

She was piling the prickly twigs of the Mandalan feverberries onto the cloth when a shadow fell across it.

Startled, Inosa looked up, her eyes widening with fear and dismay as she did so.

Two men, one middle-aged and the other a beardless adolescent, stood in front of her, looking down speculatively at what she was doing.

'Zangar, my child,' said the older man, turning briefly to the youngster beside him. 'Do you see what I see? Those are feverberries, are they not?'

The boy named Zangar nodded, eyes wide as he stared at Inosa.

'And where someone is gathering feverberries, there will be someone who is in dire need of healing,' said the older man, turning back to regard Inosa with interest. 'And, you look perfectly healthy to me.'

Chapter Ten

Year 5441 of the Emergence of Mandala

Twin shadows fall across the table, blocking the light from the single window through which the fading light of the setting sun streams in.

Umur Naash, sitting at the table, looks up, blinking as he does so. He looks haggard and gaunt, a far cry from the suave and debonair young man who, three days earlier, had met Yoksa in the academy. He is unshaven and dishevelled, and amidst the piles of books that surround him lie the remains of various half-eaten meals and cups of calmroot infusion. He is at home, and it is obvious, from the appearance of the room, that Umur Naash's aesthetic sense is reflected in his surroundings. Fine paintings hang on the walls; one window, which looks out onto a view of distant mountains beyond a brilliant blue lake, has been skilfully framed so that it appears, to a swift glance, as if it were a painting rather than a window. Delicate carpets of silk woven with zansal thread line the floor, and the cushions on the divan and chairs are embroidered with manodium thread and studded with tiny chips of mother-of-pearl. This is the house of a cultured man, but also a very wealthy man.

'What is it?' Umur Naash snaps, glaring at the two men.

They are his classmates, one of them the man who had stumbled upon Umur Naash watching Yoksa in the lakeside garden.

'You've been missing from the academy these past three days, Umur Naash my friend,' one of them replies. 'We've been worried about you. All we knew was that you'd borrowed a load of books from the academy's library, and that was all.'

Umur Naash straightens, stretches, and then gets to his feet, rubbing his eyes as he does so. 'I'm all right,' he says. 'I've been reading about the history of my family.'

'In books?' His friends look surprised. 'Ah,' one of them adds as he remembers. 'Of course, yours is a very illustrious family, isn't it?'

Umur Naash regards him with contempt but says nothing. He looks out of the window at the beauty of the sunset outside. He shakes his head, and a strange expression dawns on his face: a combination of anticipation, longing, and loathing.

The next day, Umur Naash is back in the academy. He paces impatiently about outside one of the large lecture halls with their many rows of plain wooden benches. When the lecture finishes and the students come pouring out of the lecture hall, Umur Naash moves forward to intercept Yoksa. He approaches her with respect, his face dignified and even sombre as he says, 'Yoksa-Gari? May I speak to you, please? It's important.' He sees her eyes widen, and she tries to move away, to catch up with her friends. 'Please,' Umur Naash adds in a low voice. 'It's not about what was so distasteful to you, I won't trouble you with that again. This is about what you told me about.'

Yoksa, despite her fear and suspicion, allows her curiosity to get the better of her.

'I read the real history of my clan,' Umur Naash says,

when he is alone with her. They are in the lecture room. It is an oval-shaped room, its tall pillars stretching up into a high vaulted ceiling, its windows looking out onto a copse of trees right outside. The room is empty, as is the corridor outside. The acoustics of this chamber are designed for even a normal speaking voice to carry to the farthest corner of the room; Umur Naash speaks in a barely audible whisper, but it can be heard clearly all across the room.

'I read about Umur Tut Naash's plundering of the Sada Valley,' says Umur Naash. 'And how his rule was opposed by the people of the Sada Valley.' He pauses, chews his lip, and turns to look at her. 'But so what? Umur Tut Naash was still a great general, a powerful man who wasn't afraid to put the weak and the stupid in their place—'

'He was a tyrant!' Yoksa cries out, too furious and indignant to hold it in. 'A greedy, rapacious tyrant!'

'So be it. He was also a very wealthy, cultured, and ambitious man. As I am. Any woman would feel herself honoured to be given the opportunity to be wife to such a man. Any woman should consider it a privilege to have me by her side.'

Yoksa is staring at him, her eyes wide with disbelief now. 'You must be mad,' she breathes. 'Stark raving mad. I despise your clan, all the people of the Sada Valley do! And I despise you. Do you not understand, Umur Naash? I hate you. I would not marry you if you were the last man on earth!'

In two strides, Umur Naash reaches her. His hands move, tightening around her throat before Yoksa even realizes what is happening. She struggles to free herself, to somehow ward him off, but Umur Naash is too strong for her. Inexorably, his grip tightens, Yoksa's eyes start bulging and she's gasping for breath.

Umur Naash's anger has morphed into a deadly, menacing rage; his mouth widens in a slow, satisfied smile as he sees his victim's life blur into death.

'So all the people of the Sada Valley despise my family, do they?' he murmurs, his mouth so close to Yoksa's ear that anybody would think he was whispering sweet nothings into it. 'Well, here is where I start repaying the favour. I will give your people something more to remember me by. I vow that all this beauty and this wealth that your beloved Sada Valley prides itself upon'—each word is now spat out, full of rage—'I will lay waste to it. Every ounce of beauty I will suck out of the Sada Valley.'

Yoksa goes limp, and Umur Naash lets her lifeless body drop to the ground. He takes out a handkerchief from his trouser pocket to dust his hands, and a beautifully ornamented dagger in an embroidered leather sheath, also in the pocket, drops out accidentally. Umur Naash bends to pick it up from the floor, and something occurs to him. With a malicious smile and a gleam in his eye, he sits down on his haunches beside Yoksa's corpse, and slides the dagger out of its sheath.

Sometime later, a watchman goes down the corridor, turning off lights, checking that the windows are all closed, and locking the lecture rooms. It is he who finds Yoksa's body lying at the back of the lecture room, half-hidden by the wooden benches around it. Her face has been cut up, carefully sliced and mutilated till not a sign remains of the beauty that she had once possessed.

~

Of the two men who had come upon Inosa, it was the older one who addressed her. 'One of your friends is hurt,' he said. It was not a question, but a statement. He pointed to Inosa's wrist as he spoke, and she, involuntarily glancing in the direction his finger indicated, saw that the cuff of her sleeve was stained with Afhash's blood. Inosa's grip tightened on her dagger. 'No,' she mumbled. She glanced from the man who spoke to the other, a youth perhaps no more than fifteen years old, his eyes bright with curiosity, and yet with a definite touch of apprehension in them.

'Someone is definitely wounded,' the man insisted. His grey eyes had a fine mesh of crow's feet at the corners, and Inosa saw that there were laugh lines, too, bracketing his mouth. A man whom she could easily have imagined smiling and kind. Even now, she realized with a sudden start of hope, he was not accusatory or belligerent; he was merely stating a fact. 'And,' he continued, 'you seem to have some idea of what to do about it. That's why you're collecting this. And this,' he indicated her pouch, out of which spilled some calmroot and more herbs. 'All good for healing wounds.'

'What's going on?'

Raibhu had stepped out of the grove of birch trees, dagger at the ready. He had used a scarf to tie the lengths of birch bark together and slung the bundle from one shoulder.

The older man looked at him with interest. 'You're all well, except for that bound-up hand,' he remarked. 'And since you seem to use it without any difficulty, it's probably not so very bad, either. Then your other friend must be injured? If you've had to leave him behind to gather bark and medicinal plants, he must be in a bad way.'

Raibhu's eyes had narrowed in suspicion. The man noticed it, and smiled. 'We are from the village nearby,' he said, indicating a mountain not far from where they stood. 'The old crater is visible from our village. We saw what happened.'

Inosa had stood up too by now, and was standing beside Raibhu.

'Those men are not from around here,' the man said. There was bitterness in his tone and something between resentment and pain in his eyes. 'We are peaceable folk, we do not wage war. Not between ourselves and not against strangers. Not unless we are forced to defend ourselves.' He paused. 'Those were outsiders.' He raised a hand to hitch up the satchel that hung from one shoulder, and in that moment, the inside of his wrist was visible. On it was a tattoo which by now had become familiar to Raibhu. His eyes widened in sudden recognition.

'I'm a village physician,' the man said. 'And this is my apprentice, Zangar. After you escaped into the woods, we tried to follow you because we found a blood trail part of the way. I hoped we could be of some help. Will you take us to your friend? While the herbs you've collected are good, it will take you time to prepare poultices and so on. I can begin the work of healing before that.'

Raibhu and Inosa exchanged a glance, and because Inosa still did not look convinced, Raibhu leaned forward, gesturing to the physician to hold out his hand. 'Look here,' he told Inosa, turning up the man's wrist to reveal the tattoo on it. Inosa saw it, and, after a momentary hesitation, she nodded. 'All right. Let's go.'

A few minutes later, the physician was kneeling beside Afhash, hard at work. He was fast and efficient, his fingers moving assuredly as he cleaned, wiped, applied a poultice, bandaged—and simultaneously kept an eye on the apprentice who had got out a little pot from the satchel, filled it with water, and set it over a tiny fire he had built in the lee of the bushes. Into it the physician had emptied some dried herbs from a pouch, which the apprentice watched over, stirring occasionally.

'You better get out of the way of the people who did this to you,' the physician advised as he cleaned his hands after attending to Afhash's wounds. 'They are in the vicinity, we came across signs of them while we were looking for you. And if we found you, there's no reason why they shouldn't, either.' He wiped his hands and stood up. 'Umur Naash is the devil incarnate. You don't want to run into him again.'

'You know who he is?' Raibhu asked.

'Of course. Who doesn't know Umur Naash in the Sada Valley?' The man glanced into the pot the apprentice was managing, and murmured: 'A couple of minutes more.' Then he looked up and said to Raibhu, 'I suppose you aren't from these parts? Take it from me; what you experienced back there with Umur Naash and his men, when your friend was injured: that was just a fraction of what he's capable of. Stay away from Umur Naash. He is more brutal than you can imagine.'

For a while, Raibhu just gazed at the physician's quiet, gentle face and his capable hands. Then he asked, 'You know him, but you still came to our help? Wouldn't that endanger you?'

The physician placed a hand on his apprentice's shoulder. 'That's it. Take it off the flame.' He turned to Raibhu and asked, 'Do you have a vessel of some sort? A pot, tumbler, something I can pour this into?'

Inosa rummaged about in her travelling sack and unearthed the pot they had been using to brew their calmroot infusion. The apprentice poured the infusion into it, threw some earth over the remains of the fire, and stood up. The physician nodded and said, 'Well done, Zangar. Go on, child, I will catch up with you.'

The apprentice raced off, obviously relieved to be leaving this potentially dangerous patient and his companions. The physician smiled understandingly and raised his hand, showing the tattoo on his wrist to Raibhu. 'You recognized this,' he said quietly. 'And it made you trust me. Isn't that enough?'

And with that enigmatic statement, he too left.

Unseen by them all, three men watched from further up the hill. Murfan, the third of the men Umur Naash had sent out to find hunting dogs, had caught up with Sengaar and the third man, and he too was empty-handed. They remained still and silent until the physician had left; then they too went their way, hurrying back to where their master awaited them.

~

'If you didn't find a dog, you shouldn't have returned,' Umur Naash said in a silken voice that was menacing because it was so smooth. 'Or didn't you know that?'

The three men in front of him squirmed. But of the three, Sengaar looked less discomfited than the others. And it was on him whom Umur Naash vented his ire.

'You were very certain that you would be able to find a dog and find them,' he murmured. 'What happened, then?'

'We didn't find a single dog in the villages, Master,' agreed Sengaar. 'But we found our quarry, or where they were last. And we saw someone else, someone who could help us find them again, if need be. A physician and his apprentice, from a village nearby.'

Umur Naash's eyes brightened momentarily; the next instant, though, he hooded them, as if wary of letting his men see his enthusiasm. 'All right,' he said finally. 'Let's see whether you're telling the truth.'

~

Inosa was swirling the still-steaming infusion in the pot and blowing on it to cool it. The figure of the physician could still be seen, climbing the slope beyond.

'It should be cool enough to drink now,' Inosa said, holding out the pot to Afhash. 'Drink up, and let's go. If the physician could find us, Umur Naash's men certainly will.'

Five minutes later, they were again moving. Inosa had taken Afhash's travelling sack besides her own, and had told Raibhu, 'You need your strength to help Afhash. It's better if he doesn't strain himself too much.'

She was still careful about not leaving any traces, taking them over rocks and on gravel. Occasionally she would let Raibhu take Afhash further on while Inosa herself took a detour and laid out a clearly marked trail which led nowhere. 'Perhaps it'll send them on a wild goose chase for a while,' she said, panting as she rejoined them. 'Every minute counts.'

It was late in the afternoon when Inosa called a halt at a point where a massive old tree had fallen over and wedged itself in between a cluster of boulders, forming a series of small caves and hidey-holes. 'This would be a good place to settle down and rest for a while,' she said. 'We need to eat and rest if we're to be strong enough to keep going.'

'How far are we from the point on the map?' Raibhu asked.

'Not far—can you hear the sound of the river? You can, can't you? Which is also why I chose this place. I was thinking you could sit here and mix the contents of the two containers without being disturbed. Then, quickly, get out and go and immerse the lot when we're sure the coast is clear. We can leave immediately after that.'

Raibhu nodded. 'All right.' He helped Afhash in under the shelter provided by the tree and rocks, going deep in where they would be well hidden from sight. Inosa crept in after them, pulling in the travelling sacks. 'You sit here with Afhash,' she told Raibhu. 'Get him comfortable. I'll go out, obliterate the signs of our coming here, and bring back something to eat.'

It was only much later that Raibhu got around to opening the two containers he had packed in the small travelling sack he had brought into Southern Mandala from Dhaani. They had waited for Inosa to return; in the meantime, Raibhu had insisted that Afhash lie down and sleep. When Inosa returned, bringing with her some berries and nuts, they ate. After all of that was out of the way, Raibhu got out the travelling sack.

He first took out the container with the mud from where his mother had been interred. For a few moments, his hands lingered on the faded but still colourful old embroidered scarf in which the urn was wrapped; Inosa, watching him, saw the sheen of moisture cloud his eyes briefly before he undid the knot on the scarf and opened it, revealing the finely engraved manodium vessel inside. Raibhu hesitated, before saying half to himself, 'Let's get the mud from where Father was interred, too. I'll mix them in as soon as I open this.' He got out the much plainer but larger container in which he had put in a handful of earth from the memorial stone in the sacred ground at Sandha Prison.

Then, carefully, he unscrewed the lid off the manodium vessel.

Its open mouth was covered over with a piece of folded paper. And underneath the paper, the vessel was full of plain grey ashes. There was not a pinch of earth there, just ashes. On top of the ashes was a small pouch made of leather.

Raibhu stared, blinking in bewilderment at what he saw before him.

~

The village that Xindaar had visited at night looked quite different during the day. Instead of a lot of people crowding into one small hut, there were very few to be seen in the fields and yards around. Some small children were playing in one yard, while their mothers worked in the kitchens of their adjoining homes. Across a set of small terraced fields just below the village, the only space on the mountain where there was room for fields, five or six men were at work.

Everybody came to a sudden standstill when Umur Naash, leading his band of men, came thundering into the village, their belligerent shouts ringing in the air. The women ran out of their kitchens in a panic, hurrying to scoop up their offspring and whisk them away to safety. The men in the fields stopped, sickles and hoes and other tools still in their hands.

One very old man, sitting on a low stone bench outside a home, was the one the leader of the newcomers chose to accost.

'You!' shouted Umur Naash, spittle flying. 'Where does the village physician live?'

The old man flinched. Though he did not cower at Umur Naash's feet, he was not brave enough—or foolhardy enough—to stand up to Umur Naash. With a trembling finger, he pointed towards a small hut a little further along the dirt track. He did not have to say a word: the group of men strode off, following Umur Naash, immediately. The next moment, Umur Naash was banging hard on the door of the physician's house.

It was the physician who opened it. His face wore a resigned, stoic look. This man had known, even before he opened the door, what he was in for. He did not flee, he did not fight back; he allowed himself to be pushed back violently until he hit the wall behind him. Umur Naash, with a stranglehold on the man's neck, shouted into his face: 'Where did they go? Where did they go after you tied up his arm?'

The side of the physician's head had hit the corner of a shelf; a blood vessel in his temple exploded and blood began flowing down his cheek. He ignored it and simply said, 'I don't know.'

The light coming in through the doorway had been blocked by Umur Naash's men crowding into the room;

but in the meagre light from the single window, they all saw that there was another person there; the physician's teenaged apprentice, huddled into a ball, was trying unsuccessfully to hide under the bed.

Without Umur Naash's having to say a word, a couple of his men dived in under the bed and pulled the boy out. He was gibbering and crying, begging to be allowed to go. 'I don't know anything, Master, I don't know, I don't—' Umur Naash slapped him hard, and then punched him in the stomach for good measure.

'We don't know,' the physician interjected. 'When we left, they were still where I had bandaged his arm. If your men saw that, they know where it was. Zangar and I left. They must have moved away later.'

The man had raised his hand to wipe away the blood flowing from his wounded temple. His tunic sleeve had fallen back, and the tattoo on his wrist was clearly visible. For just a moment, and then he turned his hand and the tattoo was hidden. Quick as a flash, Umur Naash caught his wrist and wrenched it around so that he could examine it more closely. Sudden recognition dawned as he looked at that stylized image of the Brihan Punj. He had seen it before, after all, on the small wrist of the little girl who had sent them on a wild-goose chase just the other day.

'What's this?' Umur Naash asked the physician. 'What does this tattoo mean? Why do some of you people have it?'

The physician said nothing. The blood continued to flow down his cheek and dripped off the edge of his jaw, onto the shoulder of his tunic.

'I will ask you only one more time,' Umur Naash said

quietly. 'What. Is. This. Tattoo. What. Does. It. Mean.' Each word was bitten off, slamming shut in that menacing way of Umur Naash's.

The physician still maintained a stoic silence, and the sight of him, all bloodied and shaken up but still showing no fear, seemed to madden Umur Naash even more. With a sudden howl of rage, Umur Naash flung himself at the man. He used his fists, his boots and his knee, and was reaching to pull out his whip when the apprentice tore himself free of his captors. He flung himself at Umur Naash's feet, blubbering and begging for mercy.

'Please, Master,' he wept. 'Please don't beat my teacher. Please. I'll tell you, just let him be. Please!'

'Zangar—' the physician cried out in dismay, but Umur Naash cut him short with a blow that knocked him unconscious.

'All right,' Umur Naash said to the apprentice. 'Speak.'

~

Slowly, as if he still could not believe what he was seeing, Raibhu picked up the small leather pouch that sat atop the ashes. Something golden gleamed under it, half-hidden by the ashes. He picked it up, and brushed off the ashes. It was a manodium pendant, dangling from a chain of fine blue zansal. The pendant's shape, two crescent moons, one small and one large, clasped together, was immediately recognizable.

'It's a wedding pendant,' Inosa said softly. 'The symbol of marriage, the two moons coming together for all eternity.'

Raibhu nodded 'This was Mother's,' he said softly. 'Look,' and he turned the wedding pendant over to show them that its other side was as intricately engraved as its front was: on its back were depicted tiny stars surrounding a mountain. The sky and the land, the symbols, respectively, of the Nabhang and the Terrisan.

'Father gave this to Mother when they got married,' Raibhu explained. 'She cherished it deeply.' A thought came to him, and he said the next words slowly, as if realizing the significance of them even as he spoke. 'She often said that she would not be parted from it even in death.' His eyes widened, he glanced again at the vessel full of ashes.

'By the Spirits,' he whispered, his voice full of awe.

'Raibhu,' Afhash said sympathetically, reaching out a hand to touch his friend on the arm. It was a gentle touch, meant to comfort, and Raibhu caught Afhash's arm, turning to him in a sudden burst of emotion. 'Afhash,' he murmured. 'Afhash, these are Mother's ashes.'

Afhash stared, taken aback. 'Are you sure? I mean—how can you be sure?'

'You were the one who told me that Father always kept this vessel safely, and that he wouldn't let it out of his sight. He even gave very specific instructions in that letter about bringing it here. Why would he send a vessel full of ashes, with Mother's wedding pendant on top, calling it the mud from the site of her interment, if it wasn't anything to do with her? Even the scarf around this,' he touched the old scarf briefly, 'is hers.' He took a deep breath, steadying himself.

'It's just the sort of thing Father would have done. Mother died, and he honoured the religion she had been born into by consigning her body to the flames so that her spirit could rise into the sky, rather than be taken into the embrace of the land. He wanted her to return to Nabhang in her death.

'I don't understand,' he said, the next moment. 'Father said Mother died that night. But how could he have had her consigned to the flames in that short a while? And why would he, anyway? Why would he hurry to perform her last rites? He knew I would have wanted to be there, too.' He shook his head, at a loss.

The silence was broken by Inosa, who had been quiet all this while. 'Do you want to see what's inside that leather pouch on top of the ashes?' she said.

Inside the leather pouch, folded carefully, was a piece of thick paper. This, like the second page of Jaadum's letter, was a map. Drawn meticulously in Jaadum's own hand, and with the Aabra ka daabra ditty scrawled prominently across the top of it, it depicted part of the stretch of the Sada River.

Raibhu, after having looked at it, passed it on to Inosa. 'You're better at this than I am,' he said. 'What do you think? Is this a replica of that other map? Was Father providing a backup map, in case we lost that one?'

Inosa examined the map. 'Some of it is the same,' she said. 'But there's more. Look, this part—from Murki till here—this is the same. But from here onwards, it's different.' Her finger travelled along a line, and stopped. 'Look,' she said in a voice suddenly very low.

Raibhu looked. '*Asi's site of interment*,' he read.

He turned a startled gaze on Inosa. 'There's a mistake here. How can that be? If Mother's body was consigned to the flames, how can there be a site of interment?'

'And see where it is,' Inosa murmured. When Raibhu

opened his mouth to ask what was noteworthy about that, she shook her head, her cheeks flushing as she stammered out a quick retraction. 'No, no. I didn't mean that; I was thinking of something else.' She studied the map with greater intensity, but Raibhu could see that it was just a diversionary tactic: Inosa was trying to cover up a slip. He watched her as she looked at the map. Afhash, having looked once at the map, had lain down again so that he could continue to rest and get his strength back. He did not, however, intend to lie back and be silent.

'Perhaps Jaadum the Elder got Asi the Elder's body consigned to the flames at that spot,' he volunteered, 'and so he liked to think of that spot as where she was interred.'

'That spot is even more remote than this is,' Raibhu countered. 'Where, deep in the wilderness, would he have found a Nabhang priest to perform the rituals for her? And even if he built a pyre and consigned her to the flames by himself, why? Why did he do that?' As he spoke, Raibhu had reached into his travelling sack and retrieved Jaadum's letter from it. He now opened it, spreading out both the letter as well as the map. The map he moved to place next to the one he had unearthed from the container of ashes.

'Look,' he said. 'These are sheets of the same paper. They're new and fresh. Father wrote these out and made the maps perhaps just days before I arrived in Sandha. Shortly before he died.' He traced a finger around the spot marked *Asi's site of interment*. 'He knew what he was doing, I'm convinced of it. There was a good reason why he sent me here. But why, I don't know. Why did he write Aabra ka daabra on both these maps? What did he really want to tell me?' He pursed his lips, thinking his way through the mysteries that had suddenly been thrown up by this new discovery.

'And,' he added, 'if Mother was consigned to the flames and her ashes are here in this vessel, what is buried in Asi's site of interment?'

A silence, tense and charged with suspense, fell over the three of them. Somewhere above them, on the slope nearby, a pair of squirrels fought, chittering angrily and creating a ruckus as they raced about.

'I think I know something about that,' Inosa said quietly. 'Something that will change life as we know it.'

'Our life?' said Afhash. 'It will change our lives? What do you mean?'

Inosa shook her head. 'Not just our lives, not just us three.' She turned her gaze to the map, the letter, and the two vessels that sat there in front of them. 'No. It will change the life of our entire land.'

She looked up, her gaze going from Raibhu to Afhash and back again, her eyes full of wonder as well as dread. 'It is a treasure,' she said in a voice so low that they had to strain to hear her. 'A treasure, the likes of which will amaze the world. And change it.'

Raibhu blinked. Afhash and he exchanged a look of scepticism, but when they looked back at Inosa, her expression was one of such unreal wonder, that it transferred some of its awe to them too. The three of them stared at the letter, two of them wondering what lay ahead, the third readying to tell them what she knew.

~

Across the mountains, far away but drawing inexorably closer to where Raibhu, Inosa and Afhash sheltered, came a small band of fierce men. At their head rode Umur Naash, the bloodlust hot in his eyes. A few paces ahead, just enough to be in the lead, rode Sengaar, and seated on the saddle behind him was the ashen-faced apprentice they had dragged from the village: he was showing them the way, pointing them to where their prey had fled.

And further back, deeper into the mountains, Xindaar spoke urgently to those he trusted, trying to garner support, trying to persuade. A vague dread filled him; it was not as if he knew exactly what or why he should be prepared, but the need to be prepared could not be denied.

~

From somewhere far in the distance came the call of a night-bhaagi, a low, echoing hoot that hung in the air, chilling and eerie. A moment, and it was answered by another hoot, and then the harsh cackling-barking sounds of a pack of Mandalan fire wolves, searching for prey deep in the mountains. Like another predator, merciless as the wolves, but not—unlike them, who hunted only when they were hungry, and to satisfy their hunger—a rapacious monster, his thirst for blood insatiable.

'A treasure?' Raibhu repeated. 'What do you mean? What is a treasure? Don't talk in riddles, please; I'm confused enough as it is.'

'You, Raibhu,' Inosa said, 'have been wondering all these years what happened to your mother, isn't it? How she died, who killed her.' She paused, her lips pursed, her gaze suddenly turned inward, as if she needed to think what she could say, what she could not. Finally, making up her mind, Inosa looked at her companions.

'Your mother died defending an ancient treasure,' she said, her voice soft but with each syllable clear and sharp. 'It's a treasure of great antiquity; Mandala owes its origin to it—and it's an object of immense power. The legendary Emperor Tanit Mahabeyan was given the treasure in the course of its history. It has been in the hands of the greatest in Mandala's history, and the very worst. Umur Naash's ancestor, the tyrant Umur Tut Naash, got his hands on it, and might have destroyed Mandala had it not been for'—she hesitated.

'Had it not been for whom? Who stopped him?'

'The custodian of the treasure,' Inosa finished. 'The treasure is so powerful, it has had to be guarded with a custodian's life all these many millennia. Lives have been lost in the process, but the treasure has been kept safe.'

Outside, now not too far, they heard the crazed barking of the fire wolves, interspersed with the terrified screams of some animal, a deer perhaps, that they had brought down.

'Umur Naash has been in pursuit of that treasure these past twenty years and more,' Inosa said. 'His greed for it brought him to our doorstep, and my Grandfather paid for it with his life. So too did Asi the Elder. Years later, Shervaan the Elder. Your father,' she said, looking into Raibhu's face, 'has I think lived and died with his entire being centred on keeping the treasure safe.'

She turned her head, to look towards the space where they had entered this hideaway for the night. 'Umur Naash is evil made flesh,' she whispered, her voice trembling. 'He feels no pity, no pain, nothing. He will stop at nothing to get his hands on the treasure.'

Raibhu shook his head, puzzled. 'None of this is making any sense, Inosa,' he said. 'Where is the treasure? What can it do? And how can *we* stop Umur Naash?'

'I think it's time I told you all I know about the treasure,' Inosa said. 'The story began long ago, when Mandala was a land submerged under the waters.'

Chapter Eleven

'The story goes that many millennia ago, what is now Mandala was a huge lake,' said Inosa, having first taken a sip from the small leather water bottle beside her. 'Some huge demons, full of malice for the people of Mandala, had flooded the land until nothing remained above water except the highest peaks. The few people who managed to flee the water and escape to these high peaks were starving, ill, and despondent. Finally, unable to bear it any longer, they went to the sage Mahamandalam Jijit and begged him to come to their aid. Mahamandalam Jijit killed the demons, drained the lake, and thus freed Mandala from its watery fetters.' Inosa saw the boredom on the faces of her two listeners and lifted a hand, silencing the imminent protests. 'Yes, I know you know all of this, since this is the common legend about Mandala's origins. But there's more, so bear with me.

'That is not the correct version of the story. The truth is, Mahamandalam Jijit was not alone. He was one of the six great jijits of Mandala, you know; and when the beleaguered people of the flooded land went to ask for help, they didn't go just to Mahamandalam Jijit, they went to the six jijits, who were gathered together.'

~

A small group of people, bedraggled and harried-looking, their faces drawn and their eyes bloodshot, trudge wearily up a mountain. They help each other up until finally they reach near the summit. Here, beside a crystalline stream tumbling down from a glacier, is a large cave. In the sky above the cave whirls a cloud of unearthly beauty: it is opalescent, every swirl and every curve a different shade of pink or gold or mauve or green. The climbers, though stumbling with exhaustion, haggard and thin with long days of not eating or sleeping, look up at the cloud and smile as if in relief. This, their faces seem to say, is hope: a cloud that is all silver lining.

At the mouth of the cave, sitting with his legs folded neatly under him, sits a clean-shaven, bald-headed man, his scalp decorated with swirling tattoos of clouds, mountains and streams, signifying the greatest of the mystics, the people who are above devotion to any one Spirit, but who worship all of them, and whom the Spirits themselves venerate.

The little delegation of people comes to a standstill in front of the jijit, all of them bowing before him. The leader, a grey-haired man, comes forward, hands joined, pleading for help. Tears flow down his cheeks as he falls at the feet of the jijit. The jijit looks at the man with pity in his eyes, and then looks across the land stretching all across at the foot of the mountain and beyond. It is almost completely submerged in water: a few peaks jut out above the watery expanse, but that is all.

The jijit puts a hand on the old man's shoulder, patting him, offering sympathy and consolation. He gets to his feet, and enters the cave behind him. Shortly after, he emerges, and with him come five other jijits, three women and two men. Like the jijit who sits at the mouth of the cave, they too are clad in undecorated robes of coarse cotton, and their shaven scalps bear the tattoos his does. The people kneel and pay obeisance to the jijits, who raise their hands in blessing.

~

'The six jijits were very powerful; their long and intense meditation had given them a vast amount of power which combined to drain away the water from the land,' said Inosa.

~

Mandala, pristine and beautiful, basks in the sunlight. The water remains in lakes, little streams and rivers like the Chansar, the Sada, and the Naham, in its abode of the eternal snows, but the rest is all good, arable land. Looking down from the mountain, one can see people hard at work on the land: building homes, planting trees, tilling fields.

On the mountain, the group of people who had first approached the jijit for help has come again. This time they have come bearing tokens of their gratitude: baskets of fruit, garlands of flowers, and sacks of grain. The sages accept these gifts graciously, but when the group is about to retreat, the jijit whom the people had first approached comes forward, holding in his arms a flattish hexagonal box.

~

'The six jijits loved Mandala so much, and they felt so deeply for the people of the land, that they decided to leave them a lasting gift, a treasure that they could use. The treasure was a means of reviving and focussing the energies that the six jijits had used to drain the water away from the land,' Inosa continued. Raibhu and Afhash were by now wearing twin expressions of incredulity, but they said nothing.

'There were three parts to the treasure, two tangible and one not,' continued Inosa. 'One was the box itself in which the treasure was stored; the other was the key. The third, the intangible element, was the mantra which the jijits taught the people. The person who was to use the treasure would have to recite the mantra while inserting the key in its slot on the lid of the treasure box. The mantra had to be correctly recited, the key had to be correctly inserted. Moreover, the treasure had the power in it to accept only those whom it deemed powerful enough to use the treasure to its full potential.'

~

The six jijits watch on as the old man who is the leader of the group reverentially takes the treasure box in his hands. He places it on a flat rock and kneels over it, holding the ornate, star-shaped manodium key in his hands. As he lowers the key into the star-shaped slot on the lid of the box, he recites the mantra. He turns the key, pushing it deep into the slot. Simultaneously, a thin, needle-like projection emerges from the centre of the slot, pushing up through a minute hole in the centre of the key. The needle pierces the palm of the man holding the key, making his blood well up and trickle down, seeping through a fine filigree in the lid, down...down into the treasure. A sudden flare lights up the inside of the treasure box, and the aura spreads, lighting up the outside too, where the wide-eyed people look on in wonder.

~

'That first man to hold the treasure was a lucky one,' said Inosa, 'because the treasure accepted him. Over the many centuries that followed, there were many others who held the key and pushed it down into the lid of the treasure, but their blood was not acceptable to the treasure; though they did everything right, were word-perfect with the mantra and held the key correctly, they were denied access to the treasure.'

Her voice was so sure, her narration of the tale so mesmerizing that despite their scepticism, both Raibhu and Afhash were now staring at Inosa intently. If nothing else, her story was an engrossing one.

'Naturally,' she said, 'if the treasure was so powerful that it could be expected to survive for many centuries, the people had to think of some way to ensure that the knowledge needed to access it would not be lost. So their scribes documented it, writing down the story of the origin of the treasure, and how it was to be used. This precious document, along with the treasure, was safely stored away in one of the most sacred shrines of Mandala.

'It would have remained secure had not a terrible fate struck Mandala twelve hundred years after the Emergence of Mandala. Or,' she smiled briefly, her dimples twinkling with amusement, 'Twelve hundred years as per the Emperor Tanit Mahabeyan. You do know, don't you, that this calendar of ours is thanks to him? Nobody really knows when Mandala emerged from the lake; when Tanit Mahabeyan ascended the throne four hundred and fifty years ago, he arbitrarily declared that the emergence of Mandala would be counted from five thousand years before the coronation of Tanit Mahabeyan.' She shook her head, as if bemused by the vagaries of egoistic rulers. 'Anyhow. In the year 1200 after the Emergence of Mandala, Vandaav the Tyrannical came to power as the Emperor of Mandala.'

Raibhu suddenly began to look even more attentive, as if the mention of Vandaav the Tyrannical had made him sit up and take notice. 'The Mandalan chronicles talk of Vandaav,' he remarked. 'They say he led his armies into raids all across Mandala, looting his own people.'

Inosa nodded. 'He was a ruthless man who craved power and wealth above all else. It was because of Vandaav that the treasure underwent a change in the way it was safeguarded.'

~

Year 1215 of the Emergence of Mandala

Mayhem. Mounted warriors, brandishing spears, maces, and swords, uttering blood-curdling war cries, swoop down on a settlement. Clouds of dust rise from under the clattering hooves of the horses as they bear down on the local people. Men and women run, screaming, trying to protect their children from the deadly horde that is attacking them. Swords gleam, arrows fly. Heads and limbs are lopped off, blood runs in the streets. Gloating troops, their arms full of precious metals and gems, sacks of grain and fruit, pour out of buildings which are set aflame as soon as the plunderers are out of them.

A Nabhang shrine, its spire soaring up into the sky, becomes the target for a large troop of galloping horsemen. They swoop in on it, breaking down the silvered gates of the shrine and riding their horses into it. Inside the shrine, they go crashing through the halls, breaking the skylights that line the ceiling, pulling down the silken drapes along the walls, and gouging out the pieces of lunarstone that decorate the interiors of the building. Their swords dripping blood, they crowd into the central prayer chamber of the shrine, open to the skies and with the Sky Altar at one end. In front of the Sky Altar stands the high priest, surrounded by acolytes, some of them weeping or cowering, the others stony-faced, stoic.

There is a thunderous clip-clop, and a huge, night-black rishya, its nostrils flaring and its single horn polished as bright as silver, comes galloping into the chamber. The man mounted on the rishya dismounts and moves forward, the soldiers making way for him, bowing as he walks past them towards the Sky Altar.

He is a larger-than-life figure, broad-shouldered and tall. An aura of power emanates from him, one that makes the soldiers around him fall silent and come to a standstill. For a moment, he stands, arms akimbo, looking up at the Sky Altar before him. Then he snatches a heavy mace from the nearest soldier and swings it at the Sky Altar, unmindful of the priest and the acolyte in front of it. Instinctively, they scatter, and the man swings the mace again, this time striking the Sky Altar with it. For a few moments after the impact, the tall, vertical slabs of white marble look as if they might keep standing. But then, with an increasingly louder sound of crumbling, they begin to shiver. Vandaav, the mace held over his shoulder, stands back out of the path of danger, watching with satisfaction. Behind him, his soldiers, less stolid and less brave, turn tail and flee the prayer chamber.

Vandaav is therefore the only one around when the echoing roar has died away and the dust has settled somewhat. It is then that Vandaav notices that there is something in the gloomy depths of the wrecked Sky Altar. Behind the shattered stone slabs, half-covered by dust and fragments of stone, something gleams. Curious, he steps forward. Brushing away the dust and debris covering it, he looks down at the treasure box.

~

'Vandaav's discovery of the treasure was disastrous for Mandala,' Inosa said. 'He was able to channel its power to plunder and pillage Mandala even more. It is said that by using the treasure, he was able to lead his armies so deep into Mandala that they were gone for several months, returning with much more wealth than Vandaav had already acquired.'

'Wait,' said Raibhu. 'How was he able to channel its power? What does the treasure do? Can it'—he gestured, trying to settle on an option, a possibility—'oh, I don't know. Can it move mountains? Can it create armies of warriors? Or what? What does the treasure do?'

'I don't know,' Inosa mumbled, looking shamefaced, as if she thought Raibhu would blame her for her ignorance. 'Nobody knows. It isn't written anywhere, and it wasn't passed down.' She waved a hand, dismissing the question and its half-answer simultaneously. 'Listen. Listen first.'

'Just one question,' Raibhu pleaded. 'Just one, and then I'll be quiet.' He saw the impatience in Inosa's expression, and because she did not expressly tell him to keep his questions for later, he barrelled on. 'Vandaav was evil, then how could he have used the treasure? Didn't the treasure stop him?'

'The treasure does not—*did* not—block someone from using it only because the person's intentions were bad or evil,'

Inosa said hurriedly. 'I told you, don't interrupt me. Your questions can wait. There is a lot I need to tell you.'

Raibhu nodded, chastened. 'Go on.'

'While Vandaav was alive, there was no going up against him; it was impossible. He was ruthless, and to oppose him in any way was suicidal. Some did try, but they all failed; every single one was executed brutally.' She took another sip of water from her water bottle. 'When Vandaav died, in 1236EM, the entire land breathed a sigh of relief. Vandaav's son, who had grown up under the shadow of his much more ruthless and charismatic father, just did not have the wherewithal to continue the legacy of the tyrant. The chronicles record a rumour that Vandaav gave his son the treasure and told him to activate it, but the treasure would not respond to the younger man's efforts. It sensed his inability, his worthlessness. Vandaav was furious; perhaps he deemed it an insult to himself—and he had his son imprisoned for that.

'Anyhow, after Vandaav's death, his son refused the throne; he was too broken in mind and spirit, anyway, to rule. A gentler ruler, a more placid man, was nominated by the councils to be Emperor. He, and the councils, decided that the devastation Vandaav had wrought was so terrible that Mandala could not risk a repeat. They could not have the treasure fall into the hands of evil men again.'

As she spoke, telling of what happened to the treasure in the wake of Vandaav's rape of Mandala, her audience could almost imagine it happening. The sorrowing people, shaken and bereaved, each mourning the loss of homes, families, possessions, peace of mind. The councils and wise people sifting through the debris, retrieving the treasure that

Vandaav had thrown aside after having exploited it to fulfil his own ambitions and satisfy his own craving for wealth.

The rebuilding of the land, the gradual recovery. And the elders congregating to confer, to decide on a course of action that would ensure, as far as possible, that the treasure did not fall prey to evil again. Long debates ensued, many viewpoints were suggested and argued as the elders met in council. Finally, it was decided: a custodian would be appointed to safeguard the treasure. It would be the custodian's duty to protect the treasure and to ensure that, as far as it was possible, only those with good intentions could access the treasure.

~

The elders, Aaboneer and Nabhang and Terrisan, come together against a backdrop of the newly repaired Nabhang Shrine. They walk in, their multihued robes flapping about in the wind, and go deep into a secluded chamber within the temple. Here, within an enclosed space, shielded from curious eyes, the leader of the elders takes out the treasure box. He turns, and ceremonially holding it high, walks to where a man, clear-eyed and muscular, kneels down and accepts the treasure box. He raises it to his forehead, offering it his respect.

This is a man who has proven himself, again and again, to put his land and its people, their goodwill and their welfare, first. When a huge fireball wiped out a valley and ravaged dozens of villages, this man was at the forefront, rescuing people and taking them to safety. When the Sada burst its banks and flooded the Valley, he nearly drowned while trying to save people marooned on water-logged islands and among the marshes, but he was soon back again, working to help, regardless of his own safety. All his time, his strength, and his admittedly meagre wealth go towards helping others. He is brave, indefatigable, and true to the spirit of selflessness that is embodied in the treasure.

He has been carefully chosen. He has been watched, every action and every public utterance minutely observed. Much thought and the collective minds of the greatest men and women of the age have gone into making this selection. This man holds now, in hands proven to be capable, the possible fate of Mandala, its security and welfare.

~

Furthermore, the custodian was charged with appointing a successor. It was his or her duty to find somebody suitable: somebody both committed to preserving the ethos of Mandala, as well as able to guard the treasure. The moral stature of the successor and his or her physical ability were both essential factors. Where a custodian found undoubted moral worth in a candidate but was sceptical of the candidate's physical abilities to guard the treasure, it was the custodian's duty to spend, if necessary, months or years training the candidate.

Raibhu froze, his eyes widening. Images flashed through his mind. Inosa's grandfather and Shervaan, standing opposite Jaadum in the clearing in the woods. Long, rigorous days of training, with Jaadum mirroring every move of the two older men. Kicks, punches, throws. Lethal jabs and graceful, almost dancer-like jumps and leaps. And the sack, with its contents so precious that Grandfather took it along wherever he went, and kept a close watch on it. The sack, for the sake of which little Inosa had injured Raibhu.

He turned to Inosa, bursting with questions, but she shook her head gently, cutting him off even before he could speak.

'The elders felt that they had made a mistake in not taking greater care to conceal the treasure,' she continued. Even if Vandaav was gone, what guarantee was there that nobody would come, following in his footsteps, looking for the treasure? Others, as ruthless and as vicious as him, may be attracted, drawn by the fabled and now proven limitless power of the treasure. It was important to not just guard the treasure, but to suppress the stories of it. It would be best if the treasure, till now so revered that it was placed at the feet of one of our supreme Spirits, be not even talked about.

So an edict was sent out to all corners of Mandala: the treasure was now no more to be mentioned. From all literature, from all traditional songs and folklore, from all religious rituals—from every means by which words are passed on from one generation to the next—all mention of the treasure was expunged. Magistrates, elders, priests and others in authority were tasked with punishing, whether by warning or by more drastic measures, those who spoke of the treasure.

Generations passed. Slowly, the treasure passed out of memory. Eventually, only the custodian—whoever he or she might be at a point in time—knew of it, of its legend and how it was to be used.

'Then, less than four hundred years after Vandaav the Tyrannical,' said Inosa, 'there came to the throne of Mandala its eighth Emperor. Tanit Mahabeyan, the disciple of the Venerable Dayadhan Jijit.'

Afhash broke into a grin. 'Even I have heard of Tanit Mahabeyan and Dayadhan Jijit!' he said, gleefully.

Inosa ignored him. 'Tanit Mahabeyan was such a good ruler and so obviously concerned about the welfare of the people of Mandala, that the custodian of the treasure deemed him worthy of the treasure. He decided that if one person could be depended upon to use the treasure for the greatest good, it was Tanit Mahabeyan.'

~

Dhaani: Emperor Tanit Mahabeyan's Private Chamber Year 5025 of the Emergence of Mandala

The Emperor Tanit Mahabeyan looks narrowly at the battle-scarred man who has just offered up a greasy, dirty, sack-wrapped package to him.

'Much is not as it seems?' Tanit Mahabeyan asks, echoing the man's words. The man's quiet, level voice seems to have mollified the Emperor somewhat; his indignation has gone, but the scepticism is still there, the fear that he is being made the butt of some joke.

'That,' says the man, indicating the package, 'is not what it appears, Your Majesty.' He bows his head. 'I have held it in my custody, safeguarded it with my life, these past eleven years, Your Majesty. In all those years, since it has come into my possession, I have watched you. I have attended your court, I have listened to you speak. I have seen how your people work: your officers, your ministers, the soldiers in your armies. I have worked alongside the farmers in their fields and the craftsmen in their workshops. The general populace and the privileged,

the people close to you and the ones far away, who only know of you through the laws you pass, the policies you implement: it is from these that I have learnt the most about you.' He sits straighter, his shoulders squared as he looked into the Emperor's face. His own face, with that livid scar slashing across it, is set, serene as a statue's.

'You, Your Majesty, are the man who deserves to command this,' he says. 'The treasure of the six jijits is now yours. I hand it over to you, trusting in your ability to use it for the greatest good.'

Tanit Mahabeyan's expression has changed from scepticism to curiosity, a realization that this is no joke, that this mysterious gift from an equally mysterious visitor is beyond its plebeian wrapping. With a tremor in his hand, he carefully lifts up one corner of the filthy sacking. There is a gleam, a sudden glow from whatever lies beneath. A promise of something great.

~

'With the help of the treasure, Tanit Mahabeyan was able to introduce new crafts to Mandala, initiate reforms in agriculture and the economy, reduce taxation, and start a scheme to provide employment to the poor,' Inosa said.

'And of course nobody knows how the treasure helped him do that,' Raibhu remarked.

Inosa nodded. 'All that is written in the chronicles is that after he had been handed the treasure and had presumably used it, Tanit Mahabeyan was not to be seen in court for two months. He disappeared, and nobody knew where he had gone.' Inosa shook her head. 'The same sort of thing happened to Vandaav the Tyrannical, though in Vandaav's case, he disappeared twice. The first time, he vanished for a day, all by himself. Then he returned, and within a few hours, he disappeared again—this time with most of his army. Men and horses and all. They were gone for three days, and when they emerged out of the woods, they were bloodstained, but loaded down with valuables. The villagers and forest dwellers who watched them surreptitiously whispered that they had gone deep into the woods and found a grand treasure.'

'Is that what the treasure does, then?' Afhash interrupted, breathless and excited. 'It opens up a huge hoard of precious stones?'

Inosa shook her head. 'I told you, I don't know. But it can't have been that, because Tanit Mahabeyan did not bring back any of that from when he disappeared along with the treasure. He came back empty-handed, but he brought with him grand ideas, schemes which helped him change the face of Mandala.'

Raibhu was chewing on his lip as he listened to Inosa. 'It's very odd,' he murmured, when she had finished. 'Two different men, and two completely different outcomes of using the treasure. So can the treasure do different things for different people?'

Inosa shrugged. There was silence for a few moments as they pondered over it. Afhash was the first one to break the silence when he said, 'Perhaps the treasure grants your greatest wish, it gives you whatever you want the most.' Even as he spoke, he was thinking ahead, and his voice rose with excitement as he hurried on. 'Look, isn't it plausible that what Vandaav wanted the most was wealth? He must have wished for all the riches his army could carry, and the treasure granted the wish.'

'How do you account for the bloodstained soldiers, then?' Inosa said, shaking her head in denial of Afhash's theory. 'If the treasure could produce all that wealth out of nowhere, there would not have been such ominous signs of violence.'

'Whose was the blood, by the way?' Raibhu asked. 'Do the chronicles say whom Vandaav victimized?'

'It was never discovered. Perhaps they were wilderness dwellers, people who lived too deep in the forests to be known to those who inhabited the larger cities and towns.'

Raibhu looked unconvinced. 'Forest dwellers, and possessing such valuables? I doubt it.'

'You're right,' Inosa said after a moment. 'It doesn't sound likely. And if one assumes that Tanit Mahabeyan's greatest wish was to find ways to improve Mandala, then his disappearing into the wilderness with the treasure for two months too seems a little strange. Did he meet some jijit in the forests, someone who imparted great wisdom and knowledge to the Emperor?'

'Maybe,' said Afhash, again whipping himself up into a fervour, 'maybe the treasure really does conjure up a jijit! Who knows, the six jijits of the legend, themselves? That works, doesn't it? They could give Vandaav all the wealth he wanted, and they could give the Emperor all the wisdom he wanted—'

'I doubt if the jijits would have catered to the likes of Vandaav,' Inosa said drily. She sighed. 'I don't know, as I said. And I suppose we never will know until...' her voice trailed off. 'Let's get back to the story. About Tanit Mahabeyan. His son, like Vandaav's, was not a patch on the father. Vandaav's son was not as tyrannical and ambitious as his father had been; Tanit Mahabeyan's son was nowhere near as wise as his father was. Tanit Mahabeyan perhaps feared the consequences should the treasure be handed over to the callow young prince. So, instead of passing it on to his heir, he preferred to give it back to the custodian who had offered him the treasure in the first place.

'When he returned the treasure, the Emperor said that it had struck him that the treasure could still be misused. No matter how dedicated and capable the custodian, no matter how closely guarded the secret of the treasure, it was still vulnerable. By way of thanks for having been allowed to use the treasure, Tanit Mahabeyan suggested that he initiate an exercise in building stronger safeguards around the treasure.

'So he sent for the wisest people in the land. From far and wide came men and women who brought with them much knowledge, long experience, and wisdom. Among these people who came in response to Tanit Mahabeyan's summons were a couple of people who looked somewhat exotic.'

~

Emperor Tanit Mahabeyan's Palace, Dhaani
Year 5033 of the Emergence of Mandala

A large, circular chamber deep in the palace of Tanit Mahabeyan. The chamber has a domed ceiling and a shallow bowl-shaped pool in the centre of the floor. Right above this pool is a sky light from the rim of which hang zansal wires, some as thin as a human hair, others thicker than a finger. The zansal wires act as an Aeolian harp, catching the winds and thrumming in tune with them. The water into which they flow swirls and eddies in response to the music of the wires. The edge of the pool has been daubed with sands of different shades of silver and gold. Every time the waters lap them, the sands gleam briefly like stardust underwater.

Heavily armed soldiers stand outside, guarding the massive doors of the chamber, but they are the only servants or servitors of any kind to be seen. Inside the chamber, there are the Emperor, the custodian, and about fifteen other people.

Among them are a couple of Aaboneer priests in long blueish-silvery robes that recall the many hues of water; a Nabhang priestess, her robe edged with stars punched out of zansal; an ascetic with ash smeared on his body and his skin turned leathery and dark through long years of meditation in the wilderness; a Terrisan priest with his robes many shades of beige and tan and brown; and several people whose religion is not apparent. All of them are seated on the same level as the Emperor, sitting in a circle around the central pool. Above them, quietly circling the chamber, hovers a fluffy white golbol, purifying the air as it moves.

There is a knock at the door, and Tanit Mahabeyan goes to see who asks for permission to enter.

'Your guests, Your Majesty,' says his chamberlain, who stands outside. Tanit Mahabeyan welcomes two people, a man and a woman. Both have an odd appearance of timelessness: their eyes look old and wise, but their complexions are clear and unwrinkled, their bodies supple and their hair without a strand of grey in them. Instead of the long coats, leggings and turbans worn by Tanit Mahabeyan and the others, these two wear strikingly different clothing: short tunics, dhotis, and cloaks. The embroidery and weaves of their clothes are far more evolved and intricate than that worn by even the Emperor himself.

Tanit Mahabeyan bows to these newcomers and welcomes them in. 'These are my guests,' he tells the small group gathered in the chamber. 'They, I think, can provide us invaluable help in this endeavour of ours.'

~

The people whom Tanit Mahabeyan had gathered together worked on protecting the treasure. For a week, they were ensconced in that chamber, hard at work. Each night, they emerged from the chamber only to go to their respective rooms in the palace, to rest briefly and to eat before they were back.

At the end of that week, some of these people left, going with the blessings and good wishes of the Emperor and the others who stayed behind in the chamber, still hard at work. Those who departed did not, however, wash their hands of the work they had been entrusted. No; they went on important missions, travelling to the furthest corners of Mandala.

~

Somewhere in Mandala
Year 5033 of the Emergence of Mandala

A path leads through a dense forest of cedars, the forest floor dark and cool, an air of deep tranquillity all around. Along the path walk two figures, moving steadily onwards to their destination, which lies in a clearing deep in the heart of the cedar forest. This clearing is an ancient crater formed by one of the many fireballs that strike Mandala. There are many craters across Mandala, but there is something special about this one: the fireball that collided with the ground here perhaps contained some minerals that reacted with the local soil and the rock. In that moment of fire and intense heat, it painted this crater in magical silver and crystal. The entire crater looks as if its walls and floor had been studded with diamonds and embroidered with silver by a seamstress without equal.

Right in the middle of the silvery crater stands a small Nabhang shrine, its walls crafted from very plain white stone, as if to emphasize the grandeur all around. A single spire, needle sharp, soars up into the sky, pointing to the stars to which the ethereal beauty here owes its existence.

The two visitors, emissaries from Tanit Mahabeyan, are met by the priest of the shrine, who comes forward with folded hands. He leads them inside the shrine, and from deep within the small but beautiful Sky Altar, he retrieves something.

With great reverence, he lifts up an object in his two cupped palms: the object glows so brightly that it's impossible to tell what it is, what form or shape. The priest hands it over to the emissaries who have come all the way from Tanit Mahabeyan in Dhaani; the object is accepted with as much reverence.

In another part of Mandala, another of the wise people whom the Emperor had sent out. He arrives at an old Terrisan sanctuary high up in the mountains, where eternal snows cloak the mountains and the valleys between them are desert, stark and colourful in soil and rock in a thousand shades of purple and grey, orange and ochre and green. The only person at the temple is an old caretaker, who talks to the emissary quietly while grinding a piece of bright green stone into fine powder. After a while, the caretaker takes his staff in hand and indicates to the emissary that he is to follow him. Together they climb up, high, to where the sun shines down on snowy fields and the mouth of a large cave. The emissary follows the caretaker down into the cave, which leads deep into the womb of the ground, where caverns and grottoes form a honeycomb of wild and unbelievable beauty.

When the emissary emerges along with the caretaker some time later, he is carrying something wrapped in birch bark.

~

When the wise people were all back together in Tanit Mahabeyan's palace in Dhaani, they convened once again and worked long and hard on the treasure, strengthening it, consolidating it, reformulating the mantra that protected it. When they were done, when the treasure was handed back into the safekeeping of the custodian, it was better protected, safer.

'For several centuries,' Inosa said, 'The treasure stayed safe. After Tanit Mahabeyan and the people he had gathered to strengthen the treasure had all died, the only living person who knew about the treasure at any point in time was the custodian. Only the custodian knew where it was and how it was to be used; he or she was also the only one who knew where the document about the treasure was kept, a secret so obscure that not even those who guarded the document knew quite what it was, or what its significance. Almost three hundred years after the reign of Tanit Mahabeyan, the treasure and its legend were being passed on, by word of mouth, from one custodian to the next.' She paused and took a deep breath. 'Until 5270EM, when a new tyrant arose in Mandala. Umur Tut Naash.'

Raibhu and Afhash spoke simultaneously, their voices amplifying the incredulity both felt. 'Umur Naash!'

Inosa had known what effect she would have. She gave a small, triumphant smile. 'Not this one. An ancestor of his, from what we were able to gather. Which is probably why this Umur Naash is after us.' She saw the sudden gleam of heightened interest in Raibhu's eyes, and hurried to add, 'Let me finish. There's not much now.

'Umur Tut Naash had been a famous general, and had won many campaigns in his time. It seems success went to his head; by the time he was about forty years old, he had won so many victories that he decided he would be the most suitable man to rule Mandala. So he strode into the middle of a public audience at the court of the Emperor and held a sword to the Emperor's throat. Perhaps his audacity was what won him the day; perhaps the Emperor was too weak-willed to make even a token protest. Umur Tut Naash did not ascend the throne formally; but everybody in Mandala knew, from then on, whose policies were implemented, who was the one who made the laws that governed the land.'

'I've never heard of him,' Afhash said frankly. Raibhu nodded, as if agreeing, but then clarified, 'I've only heard of him vaguely. I don't think the chronicles of Mandala say much about him.'

'They don't,' Inosa conceded. 'Because it was a shameful period for Mandala. One man had bribed and intimidated all the top ministers of the land, and had gathered around him such a formidable force that he could terrorise all of Mandala without being opposed by *anyone*. After Umur Tut Naash finally died, the people of Mandala could not wait to erase even the memory of him from the books.

'But,' she added, 'while he was alive, he was a terror. All of Mandala feared him as they had feared no one before him, since Vandaav at least.'

~

Somewhere in the Mandalan countryside
Year 5278 of the Emergence of Mandala

A cold, rainy day in Mandala. It is grey and drizzling, but the troop of horsemen galloping down the road chasing a few bedraggled peasants does not seem to mind the rain. The man at the head of the group has a full beard and sharp, piercing eyes. This is a face Mandala may forget over the next few years, when Umur Tut Naash is dead and gone, but it is a face that the Sada Valley, at least, will remember in the form of this ruthless man's even more ruthless descendant.

Umur Tut Naash and his men chase the ragged group of men through the fields and then pursue the remaining survivor uphill. This man takes shelter in an ancient Aaboneer temple, small and forgotten, which sits in a willow grove beside a dry streambed. Umur Tut Naash kills the man and orders his men to destroy the temple. He stands aside, walking about in the willow grove, admiring the beauty of the mountains that rise in the far distance, while his man set about battering the little temple with their heavy maces and spears.

Shortly after, one of the men comes to Umur Tut Naash, carrying something they've found amidst the debris of the temple. It's a document, an old one handwritten on birch bark paper. Umur Tut Naash looks at it with disdain, and then, as he begins reading, he becomes more engrossed...

~

'That's what we're assuming happened. It's possible there was a long-forgotten copy of the document left behind in the temple,' said Inosa. 'Umur Tut Naash must have been intrigued enough to set out to find out all he could about the treasure. Of course, with the sort of resources he could command, it was just a matter of time before he was able to find it.'

~

Mandala
Year 5279 of the Emergence of Mandala

The thundering of horses' hooves, followed by men shouting. Somewhere in the moonless night, someone bangs on a door, yelling for it to be opened. When there is no response, repeated thuds indicate that the door is being attacked. It finally falls open with a crash, and the men outside are illuminated by the torches they hold up. They hesitate for just a moment, to get their bearings in the pitch dark of the hut they're entering. In that moment, there comes barrelling out of the dark a single man. He holds a sword in one hand and a dagger in the other, and strapped across his back is a flat box wrapped in a sack. He fights, kicking and lunging, using sword and dagger at the same time. It looks as if he will succeed; he kills or injures all the men crowding around the door—but no, even as he breaks free from them and tries to run, reinforcements arrive. They have been waiting close by, and at the head of them is Umur Tut Naash.

The custodian tries to put up a fight, but he is badly outnumbered. The treasure in its sack is taken forcibly from him, and he is thrashed to within an inch of his life. Umur

Tut Naash and his men leave, Naash racing ahead to get the treasure into the safe secrecy of his own rooms.

But the man he's left for dead is not dead, after all. The custodian, though badly wounded, hauls himself up once his attackers have gone. Bleeding and broken, he somehow manages to get onto the horse of one of the men he's killed, and rides off towards the nearest settlement. He goes to a dear friend, who is aghast to see the custodian's condition. While the custodian is ushered into the house and is attended to, the friend sends word to others. Soon, a group of people have gathered, all of them armed and determined-looking, ready to help the custodian.

~

The custodian had friends. Not a single one knew about the existence of the treasure, but they knew that their friend was a special man, and they were aware that he had been given a special responsibility. When he appealed to them, they came readily, even though none of them knew what they were really helping in. Led by the custodian, they went stealthily to Umur Tut Naash's palace and stormed it, using the element of surprise to overpower Naash's guards and gain access to the innermost chambers of the palace, where Umur Tut Naash was even then in the process of trying to activate the treasure.

~

In the middle of the night. A single lamp illuminates the sumptuous chamber in which Umur Tut Naash stands. Heavy silk drapes embroidered with manodium thread hang at the windows, thick carpets line the floor, and the furniture, made of dark and heavy humur wood, is intricately carved and polished to a gloss. A golbol circles near the ceiling, and the bed along one wall is covered with a heavy quilt made of some thick golden fur. On it rest several oblong bolsters and round cushions, all richly embroidered.

On a round table sits the treasure box. Umur Tut Naash, his eyes closed, holds the key of the treasure poised over the slot in the lid of the treasure box. He lowers the key, fits it in and begins turning the key, all the while intoning the mantra...

When, suddenly, there is a furore outside. Umur Tut Naash snaps out of the trance-like state he had almost entered into. But before he can do anything, the heavy wooden door to his chamber bursts open. Umur Tut Naash's soldiers are trying to ward off the intruders, but they are being pushed back. Someone outside starts shouting for reinforcements; meanwhile, the custodian and his friends enter. Umur Tut Naash tries to keep a hold on the treasure and fight back at the same time, and the treasure box goes flying and falls down amid the bolsters and cushions on the bed nearby.

Both Umur Tut Naash and the custodian simultaneously leap for the treasure. Some of the custodian's friends are fighting at the door, keeping Umur Tut Naash's men at bay; the others try to restrain Umur Tut Naash himself, at least until the custodian is able to gather up the treasure box and its key. The lid of the box has come loose, but the custodian quickly slaps it back in place. Then, sliding it into its sack, he makes his escape, his friends fighting, helping to cover his retreat all the way. Umur Tut Naash is left screaming with rage and vowing vengeance.

What nobody, not the custodian, not even Umur Tut

Naash himself, knows is that the loose lid of the treasure box has caused something to slip out of the box. Something small enough to fit within a man's fist. Something that glows faintly as it slips down between the thick mattress and the side of the heavy, humurwood bedstead. For a moment or two, a faint glow marks the narrow space into which it's slipped, but then all is darkness again. Outside the room, in the corridor, Umur Tut Naash is shouting, cursing, baying for the blood of the custodian who has stolen a march over him.

~

'The custodian knew that Umur Tut Naash would leave no stone unturned to find him, so he left Dhaani that very night, not even returning to his own home before he fled. Nobody, not even the people who had accompanied him on that raid of Umur Tut Naash's palace, knew where he had gone.' Inosa sat back. 'He disappeared, and it was only when Umur Tut Naash had died that he returned to Dhaani. Custodians came and went, the treasure stayed safe. And then, about fifty years or so ago, my Grandfather was appointed the custodian.'

Raibhu sat up with a smile of triumph. 'I knew it,' he said. 'And he was training my Father to be the next custodian? What about Shervaan the Elder?'

'Shervaan the Elder was like Grandfather's brother; they had no secrets from each other. I don't think any custodian ever had so devoted a friend and supporter as Shervaan the Elder was to my Grandfather,' Inosa replied. Her eyes had softened at the memory of the two old men. 'Grandfather had seen Jaadum the Elder often, in protest gatherings and public forums against Emperor Dhanjog Mahabeyan, during magic shows, and elsewhere. He was very impressed, and finally took the plunge and asked Jaadum the Elder. He accepted, so Grandfather and Shervaan the Elder began his training.'

Raibhu nodded. 'That's where we met.' He grinned at Inosa, for the moment forgetting Afhash. Inosa smiled back, but there was urgency in her expression: her story was not over.

'Grandfather had tried to activate the treasure,' Inosa said, 'when he was younger. He told me, years later, that he had been so certain that it would work for him, that when it didn't, he felt humiliated. Chastised, as if he had been scolded for presuming that he was on the same level as Tanit Mahabeyan.' A small smile flitted across her face, gone almost before it had been seen. 'It made him go and search out the document to re-examine it once again, just to check that what he was doing was all correct. Whether the mantra was correct, whether he was inserting the key correctly.'

'And?'

'And it still didn't work. Grandfather was humble enough to admit that he wasn't the one meant to wield the treasure. He couldn't even tell whether there would be anyone in his lifetime who may be able to do it; but it was time to hand over the charge to another custodian.'

'Why did he never offer the custodianship of the treasure to Shervaan the Elder?' asked Raibhu.

Inosa shook her head. 'Shervaan the Elder had told Grandfather long ago that while he was happy to help Grandfather guard the treasure, he did not want the final responsibility to be his. And anyway, Shervaan the Elder was the same age as Grandfather; the next custodian would ideally be someone much younger, who could guard the treasure for the next few decades.' She smiled a little ruefully. 'I wanted to be the custodian, and I was very upset when Grandfather said no. He said I was too young, but I was convinced he didn't give it to me because I was a girl.'

'But you certainly took it upon yourself to guard it anyway,' Raibhu said. 'And how very conscientious you were!'

Inosa's smile turned embarrassed. 'I'm sorry for having injured you. Really, I am.' She paused, gathering her thoughts. 'But I have to tell you one last thing, about the treasure. About when it was last seen.' Raibhu nodded, and Afhash, following his lead, also nodded to Inosa to continue.

'It happened one night eighteen years ago,' Inosa said, with a meaningful glance at Raibhu. She saw his eyes widen, and she inclined her head, wordlessly telling him to be patient for a little longer. 'That was the night Grandfather and Jaadum the Elder had chosen for the treasure to be ritually handed over to Jaadum the Elder. Grandfather had told me that it was a sacred ritual, and that little children should not be there to see it, but I had made up my mind to watch.'

~

Year 5457 of the Emergence of Mandala
Inosa's Home in Murki

It is shortly after sundown. Even as the last lingering traces of pink and gold in the sky melt away into the darkness, little Inosa watches from a copse of trees near her home in Murki.

Jaadum and Asi have just arrived at her home; from where Inosa sits, she can see Grandfather and Shervaan receive them at the door. When the couple have gone indoors with the two older men, Inosa slips out from behind the tree trunk where she's been hidden, and scoots over to the house. At the back of the house, abutting it, is a makeshift shed which is used to store firewood and other odds and ends. Inosa clambers over the piles of firewood, to the wooden wall separating the shed from the room beyond. There are knotholes in the wall, one low enough for Inosa to be able to huddle down and peer through. She settles there, watching what's happening inside.

Jaadum, Asi and Shervaan look on as Grandfather puts the sack containing the treasure box on the rough wooden table in the centre of the small room that makes up the bulk of the hut. Grandfather's voice is a murmur as he offers the sack containing the treasure to Jaadum. Jaadum opens it, takes out the treasure box and then opens the lid, to have a look at the contents. When Jaadum puts the lid back on the box, Grandfather indicates that he should now use the key. Jaadum looks a little awestruck, solemn because of the gravity of this ritual: he takes the star-shaped key and inserts it in the slot on the lid of the treasure box, speaking the mantra as he does so. The needle pierces his palm, Jaadum's blood flows through the slot and into the treasure box. Nothing happens.

Grandfather nods, as if this was to be expected. Jaadum inclines his head, and placing both hands on the treasure box, murmurs some words. His voice is too low for little Inosa to hear, and just then, too, there is a disturbance: she hears the sound of galloping horses, men shouting. Inosa scrambles up, terror-struck. As she races out of the shed and runs into the shelter of the trees nearby, a group of riders arrives at the front door of Grandfather's house. Grandfather and Shervaan are already alert, their daggers at the ready, facing the door. Jaadum hurries to put the treasure safely back in the sack; at the same time, he is trying to push Asi behind him, so that he can protect her.

Despite their readiness, they are not prepared for what comes: the door jamb is shot off with a hail of humur projectiles, and a massive kick sends the door flying in, falling flat and raising a cloud of dust. Umur Naash looms, tall and strikingly handsome, in the doorway. For just a moment, he looks longingly towards the sack Jaadum has just pushed the treasure into. Then he's charging ahead, and Grandfather, Shervaan, and Jaadum meet him and his men halfway. A fierce fight breaks out, and though her husband keeps trying to push her out of harm's way, Asi refuses to back down. She grabs whatever improvised weapon she can lay her hands on, and strikes out at the attackers. Asi is more fervent than she is skilled as a fighter; she is quickly struck down. One of Umur Naash's men, slashing left and right with his dagger, wounds Asi badly. She collapses, blood pouring out of her stomach and chest. Jaadum, distressed at the sight of his wounded wife, loses focus for a moment and is also wounded, though only superficially.

Umur Naash and his men are too many and too well-armed, and even Grandfather realizes that. As he continues to fight, he says to Jaadum over his shoulder, 'Go! Take Asi and what has been entrusted to you! If we escape, I'll come to meet you. Three days from now. Monday morning, nine o'clock. At the riverbank at Jurwad. All right?'

Shervaan, standing next to Grandfather, nods, urging

Jaadum on; the next moment, he is swinging his stick, catching one of Umur Naash's men in the midriff.

Jaadum slings the sack containing the treasure onto his back, and smashes open a window, because to try to get out of the door, the way all blocked by Umur Naash and his men, would be impossible. Grandfather and Shervaan are fighting with renewed vigour in their attempt to cover Jaadum's departure, but even as Jaadum and Asi are leaving, Grandfather is stabbed; Jaadum halts momentarily, dismayed; but Shervaan the Elder shouts at him to carry on.

Jaadum manages to get Asi out through the window, and climbs out himself. Already, Umur Naash, having seen Jaadum escape through the window, is ordering his men to leave the house and go around to the back. Jaadum, trying to support his dying wife and keep a hold on the treasure, looks frantically about him for some means of escape.

A little hand tugs at his sleeve, and he looks down. It is Inosa, her eyes full of fear as her gaze darts towards the room beyond, from which the sounds of a ferocious fight can be heard. But scared though she is, little Inosa is brave enough to have ventured out of her hiding place to come to the aid of Jaadum and the dying Asi.

'Come,' Inosa says. Already, they can hear Umur Naash's men come pouring out of the house. Quickly, Inosa leads Jaadum around to the back of the house, and from there into the copse beyond. She moves swiftly, very sure of where she's going, even in the dark. Jaadum follows, knowing well enough that he needs help, even if it's offered by a little girl.

Asi slips and falls. 'Go,' she murmurs to Jaadum. 'I will only hold you up. Go, my love.' Jaadum, tears streaming down his face, refuses. He realizes Asi can barely even stand now, so he lifts her up in his arms. 'Go on, Inosa,' he says stoically.

It is heavy going, and they can hear the sounds of pursuit, but Inosa is so adept at this that soon Umur Naash's men fall behind: they are hopelessly lost in the dark of the woods at night.

'You should go back, Inosa,' Jaadum says. 'Your Grandfather will be worried about you.' Even as he says it, Jaadum remembers that Umur Naash and his men had seriously injured Inosa's Grandfather; perhaps, by now, Shervaan too has been wounded. 'Go, but watch the house carefully before you go in, all right? Those men may still be around.'

'I'm fine,' Inosa says stubbornly, lower lip jutting out and arms folded across her chest. 'I can't go and just leave you and Asi the Elder like this.'

'Please, my child. I will be all right. My wife will be fine. I needed your help back then, and if you had not come, I don't know what would have happened to us.' Jaadum pats Inosa's head with a hand reddened with Asi's blood. 'Go, child. You need to go back. Thank you for your help. May the Spirits keep you safe and give you a long life.' The hand pauses, as if in blessing. When Inosa looks up, there are tears in Jaadum's eyes.

~

Tears glistened in Inosa's eyes. 'I refused to just leave them there in the middle of the forest,' she said. 'They would be completely lost, and Asi the Elder was dying. Even I could see that.' Her voice was thick with emotion. 'So I insisted on taking them a little further. There was a cave further on, overlooking the river and high up on the mountain. Remote enough for them to be safe there for a while. I gathered some herbs and tried to ensure that Asi the Elder would at least be in less pain—but she was almost gone, and finally Jaadum the Elder insisted I go.'

She stopped, too overcome to go on. Tears were coursing down her cheeks, and she swiped at them in a half-annoyed way, as if angry at this weakness.

'Thank you, Inosa,' Raibhu said quietly. 'You were kind to my parents when they needed it. Even though you were a child. Thank you; I don't know if Mother was able to say it to you, but I do, on her behalf.'

Inosa nodded by way of acknowledgement. She was still looking embarrassed, and it took a few moments more before she was composed enough to say, 'I hurried home. In taking your parents to safety, I'd ended up taking them quite far, so it took me several hours to get back home. When I got there, Umur Naash and his men were gone, and Grandfather had died. Shervaan the Elder was there, injured but not too badly. He told me that the men had all run off in pursuit of us, and when Shervaan the Elder was trying to attend to Grandfather, he discovered that the key of the treasure had fallen under the table. Maybe it had slipped out of the sack, maybe Jaadum the Elder had overlooked it in his hurry to pack everything away. We kept it safely, and Shervaan the Elder said he would go to Jurwad on Monday morning to meet Jaadum the Elder.'

She drew in a deep breath. 'That was what happened. I think Asi the Elder died in that cave.'

Chapter Twelve

Afhash looked stunned. He had been shaking his head in disbelief for the past several minutes; now he burst out, 'Inosa, are you sure? You were a child, how would you have known all this? I'm not saying you're lying'—he had seen the indignation in her expression, and hurried to make amends—'but do you seriously believe all this could have happened? It must have been a dream,' he added, patting her hand in a commiserating way.

'Don't be daft,' Raibhu said before Inosa could lash out at Afhash. 'Can't you see, it fits in? It all fits in. All those men descended on our home late that night, waiting for Father. And Father, when I met him, had been in a fight: he was bruised and wounded in places. And he told me that Mother had been killed. I knew already that he and Mother had gone somewhere, on an important mission; I had just assumed that it was part of their campaign against Emperor Dhanjog Mahabeyan. But I'd seen Inosa's Grandfather and Shervaan the Elder training Father, in that quiet little clearing in the woods beyond Murki. Many times...' his eyes narrowed as he remembered other episodes, other details. 'And how about where Father was arrested? You yourself told me that Father was arrested at Jurwad shortly after North and

South Mandala had split. With what Inosa's told us, we have definite proof that Father was supposed to be at Jurwad to meet Inosa's Grandfather.'

'Shervaan the Elder went to Jurwad on that day, and I went along with him. We thought we'd be able to hand over the key to Jaadum the Elder and make sure he was fine,' Inosa volunteered. 'But Jaadum the Elder never came. We waited all day long, until it was dark.'

'He'd already been arrested on suspicion of being a spy,' Raibhu said, nodding.

Afhash nodded, suitably chastened. 'But then,' he said, 'where is the treasure? Jaadum the Elder had it with him when he left Inosa's home; did he bring it to your home in Raffasi when he came to fetch you? Did he take it along when he took you to Dhaani?'

Raibhu shook his head. 'No. He had nothing on him when he came home. And when we left home, the only thing we had was that sack which contained our disguises. There was nothing else in it. I know; I carried it most of the way, and Father never even bothered to look at it after we'd bundled our old clothing into it.'

'And he didn't have anything of the sort in prison,' Afhash added. 'The only thing dear to him that he kept in his cell was that urn'—he indicated the little vessel that contained Asi's ashes. 'It wasn't as if he carried that around with him everywhere, either.'

'That isn't the treasure,' Inosa said. She hesitated, as if unsure about continuing.

'Go on, Inosa,' Raibhu said, after a moment. 'You have an idea, don't you?'

Inosa closed her eyes, debating within herself. 'I don't know,' she whispered, her eyes still closed. 'Maybe I'm completely wrong.'

'Tell us, anyway.'

There was silence. Outside the secluded shelter offered by the tree trunk and rocks, they could hear birds: the musical songs of the little nectar-suckers, the maddened banging against a tree trunk of a tree-borer searching for worms, the heavy tread of a ground-bhaagi making its way through the undergrowth. Dawn was nearly here, the birds and the other creatures of the woods were already up and about.

'Sometime between when I left him at the cave and when he came to you, Jaadum the Elder left the treasure somewhere,' Inosa said to Raibhu.

'The sensible thing to do, surely? He must have guessed that Umur Naash wouldn't give up so easily. If Umur Naash knew where to attack, and knew that the treasure was important, it wasn't too much to expect that he'd also have found out where we lived. After his men lost you three in the woods, it would have been the most obvious thing for them to come to our home in Raffasi and camp out there, waiting for Father to come home.'

'Yes. Jaadum the Elder knew it was unsafe to take the treasure home. If I had been in his place, I would have buried the treasure in the woods, and come back for it later, once I was sure Umur Naash wasn't following me anymore.'

'In the woods?' Afhash burst out. 'The woods are huge! How would anybody know exactly where, under which tree, which rock, what?'

Inosa pointed to the map, which still lay spread out beside Raibhu. 'That. You would draw a map for it.'

Afhash stared at her, bewildered. Raibhu, however, was quicker to catch on. 'You mean', he said, 'that "Asi's site of interment"—that's actually—' he let the sentence trail off, his eyes widening as he realized the implications of the conclusion he had reached.

Inosa nodded. 'That place marked "Asi's site of interment" is the cave where I left them that night. If Jaadum the Elder cremated your mother that night, then what would be buried in her site of interment, since she couldn't possibly have had a site of interment?'

The three of them looked at each other, eyes full of wonder. That a mythical treasure which harboured untold but mysterious power, that had shaped Mandala's history, could be within reach was a fact both tantalizing as well as frightening.

'By all the Spirits,' Raibhu whispered, in an awed voice. 'It's so near.'

'Yes,' Inosa said. 'I think so, yes. But.' She stopped, letting that word hang in the air.

'But,' Raibhu echoed her. 'Umur Naash has not given up. And he will not, I think, not until he has the treasure in his hands.'

Inosa nodded. 'Your family and mine died fulfilling their duty as custodians. Nobody else out there has a responsibility towards the safeguarding of the treasure. It's up to us. You and I, Raibhu: we can decide now whether or not we will take it upon ourselves to protect it from Umur Naash.'

'And me,' Afhash butted in. 'Don't leave me out of this. I will be right there with you if you're going to get yourselves into trouble.'

Outside, from a distance came the low trilling call of a bird. Others joined in, filling the air with their song.

'The sun is coming up,' Inosa said, peering out from between the twigs she had positioned at the mouth of their hideaway to camouflage it. 'We had best be moving out. I have a feeling Umur Naash will not be too far behind us, and the more distance we can put between us, the better it will be.' She glanced back at the two men. 'Shall we go?'

'Who would have thought,' said Afhash, as he crawled out behind Raibhu and stood up, dusting himself off, 'that we'd find ourselves in such an adventure?' He stretched, hoisted his travelling sack on his shoulder, and added, 'What an adventure it's been, eh.'

'I have a feeling it's only just beginning,' Raibhu replied.

They hurried to catch up with Inosa, who was already striding ahead.

'Did you hear what this fellow said?' Afhash said when they had caught up with her. 'That this adventure is only just beginning. Idiot.' He looked over his shoulder and grinned at Raibhu. 'All that's happened so far, Umur Naash and the silver bear and this incredible treasure: isn't that adventure enough for you? What, when the treasure is in your hands, you'll squint at it and say that it's no treasure?' He nudged Raibhu in the ribs.

Though Raibhu smiled affectionately back at his friend, there lingered in his eyes a thoughtfulness that made Afhash raise his eyebrows in question. 'What? What're you thinking? That you'll run away with the treasure as soon as we get it?'

Raibhu could not help a laugh. 'Of course not, you moron. No. I was thinking'—he drew in a deep breath, steadying himself in a moment of emotion—'I was thinking that there could be no greater treasure than what I already have, you know. Friends, people who care about me.' He glanced at Afhash and at Inosa, who had slowed down and was smiling at him. 'That's enough treasure for me, to be secure in this. In you two.'

For a moment, all three of them stopped, standing on a little knoll, the first golden rays of the morning sun washing over them. A moment, and then Afhash broke the spell. 'Come along, you two,' he said. 'We're getting late.'

Epilogue

Within an hour of them having set out from their night's hideaway, clouds had begun to gather higher up along the mountainside. As they ascended, the clouds grew denser and heavier, until—a mere three hours past dawn—it began to rain. At first, there were scattered raindrops, a light drizzle that would hinder none but the most fastidious. Swiftly, though, the rain turned torrential, and Inosa called a halt, ducking into a cave she knew of.

'This area is dotted with caves,' she said, wringing out the edge of her tunic and pulling a rag from her travelling sack to wipe herself down with while the two men tried to dry themselves as best as they could. 'The cave where I led your parents that day isn't too far, perhaps only a couple of hours if we don't take any detours.'

'And if this rain lets up,' Raibhu remarked, peering out through the screen of bushes and creepers that hid the mouth of the cave, making it well-nigh impossible to spot from the outside—unless one happened to be like Inosa, born and bred to these woods.

'It doesn't look as if it's going to stop in a hurry,' Inosa agreed. 'But in a way, it's probably good. The rain will have washed out our tracks; it will make it that much more difficult for Umur Naash's men to pick up the trail again.'

'Also, if it's holding us up, it'll hold him up too,' Afhash added. 'Why don't we make ourselves comfortable and have a bite to eat and drink, eh?'

It was only much later, when they were warm and as well-fed as they could be in the circumstances, that Raibhu said, 'I cannot help but wonder what it is the treasure does. It's such a mystery.'

Inosa, whittling a bunch of twigs into makeshift arrows, gave a brief smile. 'That was what Grandfather was most curious about. He said he only wanted the treasure to let him in, to let him wield it, to find out what it was capable of doing. He insisted he wasn't greedy; just dying of curiosity.'

'But it refused him. Like it refused my father.'

'The treasure isn't all that bright then,' Afhash remarked, 'if it couldn't recognize the worth of Jaadum the Elder. Not,' he was quick to add, turning to Inosa, 'that I mean to say that your grandfather was in any way deficient, but Jaadum the Elder I knew personally. He was the finest man I ever knew.' He realized that this too might be misconstrued by Inosa, and with an embarrassed shrug, he said, 'If your grandfather considered Jaadum the Elder worthy of being the custodian, isn't that proof enough?'

'Yes. But neither Grandfather nor Jaadum the Elder were accepted by the treasure,' Inosa said. 'No matter how good or how capable.'

They were still arguing over it when Raibhu, having gone into a reverie, suddenly spoke up. 'I wonder if there was something wrong in the way they were accessing the treasure.

Were they saying the mantra right? Was the treasure box broken? Was something wrong?' He looked intently at Inosa. 'Do you know?'

Inosa shook her head, puzzled. 'Why should anything be wrong? Grandfather would have known it, and he would have told Shervaan the Elder. They had no secrets, not even from me.'

'Which means you know the mantra too?'

'Of course I do. Do you want it?' She paused only long enough to see Raibhu's eager nod of assent, and then she recited:

> Meet the blue where snow and water ice where beckons
> Away distressed fear the refuge their washed find
> Guidance way the shown and seek are the mighty
> Blood of heavens where before a bow the sacrifice
> Lives land land below in the forever spring
> And portends joy peace and a rainbow
> The Mandala there strength the lies of spirit
> Glowing summoned bright forth shining.'

Raibhu blinked.

'What? But—but that's utter gibberish!' he said. 'How can that possibly be the mantra?'

~

On a little knoll overlooking the frothing waters of the river that ran at the base of the mountains, a ceremony was being performed. It was obvious that this knoll was often used for rituals of this kind: on it was built a flat platform of stone, smoothened and delicately carved around its edges. At one end of the platform stood three objects: a small basket full of good clay; a two-handled terracotta jar full of water; and a tall, fragile harp-like instrument threaded through with very fine strings of zansal, that hummed in the light breeze. Earth, water and air: the three elements, the three representatives of the Spirits.

All distinctly Mandalan.

But the six people who stood on the stone platform were dressed in a way not familiar to Mandalans: dhotis, fitted tunics and cloaks clothed the men, and the women wore long tunics with skirts. The three adolescents who formed part of the group wore simple, unadorned clothing, only a thin edge of embroidery decorating their cloaks. Of the older people—one woman and two men—it was the woman who was dressed in the most functional way, a sturdy leather apron tied about her waist, over a rough tunic and skirt that had both seen better days. The men, in contrast to her, were flamboyantly attired, their clothes lavishly embellished in patterns far more evolved and intricate than any known in Mandala.

If one watched carefully, it became apparent that the men were conducting the ritual currently in progress. The taller one of them, a handsome middle-aged man, his eyes gentle and wise, was speaking. 'You step into our society today, as full-fledged members of our world,' he said, facing the three young people, two girls and a boy, all between sixteen and eighteen years of age. 'While this brings with it more freedom, it also brings greater responsibilities. And this, this particular step which all three of you have decided to take, is added responsibility. You may still step back from it, and no one will hold it against you. But if you will persevere, you will be expected to never flinch, to never step back.' He paused, and looked pointedly towards the three before him.

'Yes, O Keeper of Secrets,' said the three in unison.

The man smiled. 'Very well, then. We can begin. Althima?' He turned to the woman, who nodded and sat down cross-legged, placing before her a large leather pouch. From this she pulled out and arranged neatly a few objects: a bunch of thin needles, made of bone or ivory, tied loosely together with thread; a stoppered vial of glass, filled with black ink; a clean napkin; and a small bundle of fresh golbol wool, known for its purifying properties. She looked up. 'Come, then,' she said, addressing the three young people. 'Who will go first?'

One of the two girls stepped forward, and at Althima's indication, seated herself beside the woman.

Althima worked quickly but surely, choosing a needle from the bundle before her, dipping it in the vial of ink, and positioning it over the inside of the girl's wrist. Both women glanced up simultaneously at the Keeper of Secrets, and Althima said, 'I am ready.'

The Keeper of Secrets nodded. 'Repeat after me,' he said to the girl. 'For good always.'

'For good always,' said the girl, as Althima pricked her skin with the needle.

'Without fear and without bias, without care for oneself,' continued the Keeper of Secrets. 'For peace, for goodwill. For the land that is ours. For our Mandala.'

Each phrase was dutifully intoned by the girl. By the time she had finished, Althima had finished too. She laid aside the needle and picking up the napkin, gently mopped up the blood that had appeared on the girl's wrist. Then, having bound it up with the golbol cotton, she smiled reassuringly at the girl. 'There you go,' she murmured. 'It will heal within a few hours.'

The sun, shining out of a clear blue sky, shone on Althima's wrist as she continued her work, tattooing the wrists of the other two young people. On the inside of it, tiny but startlingly beautiful and precise, was a representation of the Brihan Punj constellation, each of its six stars represented by a minute star.

The same tattoo appeared on the wrists of the Keeper of Secrets as well as the other man who stood beside him, witnessing the ritual. And now, as Althima did her part of the ceremony, it was being imprinted, for life, on the wrists of the young people present.

~

'Naash-Gar. Master.'

Umur Naash, sitting in the tent that had been erected for him at a little distance from where his men were encamped, scowled at the interruption. He looked down at the leather-bound journal he had been reading, and as if committing something to memory, he murmured under his breath with his eyes closed. When he reopened his eyes, it was to glare at the man sitting in front of him, kneeling before Umur Naash.

It was Afhash. Dirty and bedraggled, in stark contrast to Umur Naash, who despite having been on the trail as long as Afhash and his companions, looked as elegant as ever. Unflappable, and in complete control of the situation.

'If you think you can fool me,' said Umur Naash, 'you are

an even greater fool than I had imagined.' He waited for that to sink in, before adding, 'you know that my men surround us on all sides. They have searched you below before bringing you in here, so it is unlikely that you have any weapons on you, but let me warn you—'

'If I had come to harm you, Naash-Gar,' said Afhash, heedless of the fury he might invite at this interruption, 'I would have slunk in. I would not have requested it.' He shook his head. 'I know you, Master. Who doesn't know you, in the Sada Valley? But I know you better than most, because I have seen you up close even when I was a child. I know just what you are capable of, and I see no reason to continue to endanger myself by standing in your path.'

Umur Naash frowned, annoyed but intrigued in spite of himself.

'Raibhu and Inosa might have reason to resent you,' Afhash said. 'Oh, I know; they've told me everything about you, and about the treasure. Perhaps,' he added in a conspiratorial whisper, 'Inosa has actually told me more about the treasure than even you know.'

Involuntarily, Umur Naash's gaze went to the leather-bound journal he had been looking at.

'Your ancestor's memoirs, I take it,' said Afhash. 'Yes, I suppose, given that he had the treasure for a brief while in his hands, he knew more about it than the average Mandalan. Far more. But Inosa's grandfather was the custodian; there was nothing about the treasure he didn't know.'

Umur Naash was tiring of Afhash's long-windedness. 'Say what you have to say,' he growled. 'I don't have time for this nonsense.'

Though he continued to kneel on the ground in front of Umur Naash, Afhash lifted his chin to look up at the warlord. 'I have come to offer you a chance at the treasure,' he said, his voice clear and firm. 'Raibhu and Inosa have been discussing it, and they have unearthed aspects about it you cannot even begin to guess at.'

The confidence he had brought with him had turned the edge into arrogance, and it drew from Umur Naash a snarl and a swing of the whip that lay beside him. Afhash did not flinch; he waited until Umur Naash had settled back onto the camp stool on which he was seated.

'The treasure is mine,' Umur Naash said, his voice rasping and harsh, his chest heaving with the fury that had built up in him. 'Do you understand? Mine. My ancestor lost it, but I will have it back. And I will wield it. It cannot deny me.' He let out a sudden bark of laughter. 'Tell that to your friends. No matter what they think, no matter what they do, the treasure will come to me. It will obey me.'

'It won't.'

Afhash's words hung in the air, ominous even though they sounded so ludicrous.

'Those two have figured out something you don't know yet,' Afhash said. 'And without that knowledge, the treasure's going to be useless to you.

'I have come to offer my services,' he finished. 'I will help you get the treasure.'

Umur Naash gazed narrowly at the young man in front of him, but he could see no duplicity in that gaunt, earnest face. Afhash, jealous and stricken by a sense of inferiority, had been driven to betrayal.

NEXT IN THE MANDALA PURANA SERIES

THE TURN: TREASURES OF MANDALA

What is the secret that was handed to Tanit Mahabeyan all those centuries ago? What power can it unleash, what wonders and what horrors is it capable of? Is there a treasure that lies behind it, and why does Umur Naash pursue it with such a single-minded obsession that he will slaughter and destroy to get his hands on it? If there is a treasure, where is it now, and what do Raibhu, Afhash and Inosa face if they must come between it and Umur Naash?

Look out for the sequel to *The Pledge* where the adventures of Raibhu, Afhash and Inosa come to an unexpected and heart-stopping conclusion.

Acknowledgements

From Madhulika

This book owes itself to Amit Bolakani, whose original idea it was to have a trio on a dangerous and mysterious mission across a wild and beautiful land. He, and Kannan Iyer, are due my gratitude for having allowed me to be a part of this project—in many ways as exciting and full of ups and downs, twists and turns as the adventure of Raibhu, Inosa and Afhash.

To Kannan I owe special thanks: this was the first time I wrote a full-length book in collaboration with anyone else, and Kannan was a superb collaborator. His insight, creativity, and attention to detail contributed immensely to *The Pledge*. Kannan, I must also thank you for never taking the easy way out, never deciding that we could be lazy: those years of slogging, those countless phone calls to discuss each plot point and how we could make it work: exemplary.

Special thanks to my husband, Tarun, who this time round wasn't just a beta reader, but also more. As an avid reader of fantasy fiction, Tarun was my sounding board umpteen times during this project. Thank you, and for the support and love, without which I can never write.

From Kannan

I thank Amit Bolakani for his unquestioning trust in me and Madhulika, even as the novel took huge and significant deviations from his original idea. He graciously and generously allowed us to raise his baby, the way we saw fit.

I have never written a book, leave alone a collaborative one and that too with an accomplished writer like Madhulika. Not surprisingly, I had my fingers crossed when the writing began. But what a rich collaborative journey it has been!

Madhulika's openness to relentlessly examine and re-examine every aspect, whether a 'small' word or a 'big' plot point, was nothing short of extraordinary. For one who has authored so many original books, it must not have been easy to let another voice so deep into her creative process. I greatly appreciate the class, absolute integrity and passion with which Madhulika did this. I will forever cherish the hundreds of intense hours of brainstorming with her. Thank you, Madhulika.

I couldn't have written this book without the unquestioning and total love and support of my wife Preetha. I don't how she did it, because I must have been an insufferable companion during the long months of obsessive writing.

I would like to dedicate this book to my parents Subbalakshmi and Rajagopalan (late) and to my in-laws Sudha (late) and Varadarajan.

From Madhulika and Kannan

Thanks, too, are due to Renuka Chatterjee and Ravi Singh at Speaking Tiger, who thought this book worthy of publication.

Renuka Chatterjee also saw it through from inception to finish, and as always, made the book that much better. Aruna Ghose, ever-patient editor, without whose sharp and wise insights this book would have been much rougher. Maithili Doshi, who designed the striking cover and Tanu Dogra, book publicist *sans pareil.* What would we do without all of you?